Julie Corbin is Scottish and grew up just outside Edinburgh. She has lived in East Sussex for the last twenty-five years and raised he close to the Ashdown Forest. S and combines running the m boarding school with writing n

She speaks at writing events, book groups and libraries, and runs writing workshops for beginners and more experienced writers.

Visit Julie's website at www.juliecorbin.com and follow her on Twitter @Julie_Corbin

Whispers
of a
Scandal

JULIE CORBIN

HODDER

First published in Great Britain in 2021 by Hodder & Stoughton
An Hachette UK company

1

Copyright Julie Corbin 2021

A CIP catalogue record for this title is available from the British Library

Paperback ISBN 978 1 529 37121 5
eBook ISBN 978 1 529 37119 2

Typeset in Plantin Light by Palimpsest Book Production Limited,
Falkirk, Stirlingshire

Printed and bound in Great Britain by Clays Ltd, Elcograf S.p.A.

Hodder & Stoughton policy is to use papers that are natural, renewable
and recyclable products and made from wood grown in sustainable forests.
The logging and manufacturing processes are expected to conform to the
environmental regulations of the country of origin.

Hodder & Stoughton Ltd
Carmelite House
50 Victoria Embankment
London EC4Y 0DZ

www.hodder.co.uk

For my book group friends, Jackie, Annie, Angie and Audrey, who remind me how much I love reading.

Prologue

There is no going back in life. No way to return to what was before, to wind back the clock, choose to walk right instead of left.

So we live with what happens. We make adjustments and we endure.

It began with the notes, and it ended with a funeral.

And afterwards I asked myself, how could I not have known?

Chapter One

NINA

The first crack of thunder sends the crows up into the air. They circle above the treetops, feathers gleaming, beaks gaping as they screech at the sky. Within seconds, the rain starts pelting down. I shiver, pull my coat in closer, and hurry into the school grounds, shielding my head with my arm and running the last hundred metres to the classroom block, stopping just inside the main entrance to take a breath and check my phone.

Nothing.

I've texted Robin three times over the course of the day and he's yet to reply. He was operating on the victim of a car crash overnight and he's yet to come home. He hasn't seen the latest note that was in Lily's bag when she got back from school yesterday. I want to forewarn him so that his first sight of the message isn't in front of a class full of parents.

I write a fourth text:

Robin, I'm really hoping we can talk before the parents' evening begins. Are you still coming? There's been another note. It's shocking, and it mentions you in particular.

My finger hovers over my usual *xx* but I resist, press send and glance up. Cars are arriving in front of the building, a reminder that tonight's ordeal will be starting soon. I'm not ready to face any of the other parents and turn around quickly to make a beeline for the loos.

'Nina.'

'Jeez!' I jump as Maxine Mayfair steps out of the shadows. 'You gave me a fright!' *Has she been standing behind me all this time?*

She looks me up and down, literally, from head to foot as if assessing how on trend I am. 'I'm loving your mac.' She reaches across to feel the material, her fingers brushing over the lapel. She is our celebrity parent, an Instagram influencer; lifestyle and beauty are her specialities. 'It's a quality brand,' she adds before meeting my eyes.

I know this is my cue to start a conversation about fashion but I'm not interested in labels. I shop for comfort and practicality.

Her head tilts to one side. 'You look washed out.'

'I've been better.'

She frowns. 'I'm so sorry about what's been happening to Lily.'

'I'm hoping that after tonight we'll know who's been targeting her,' I say, watching for a change in Maxine's expression. When there's any bullying or bad behaviour in Lily's class, Maxine's son Max is usually caught up in it. I wait for her to acknowledge this but she doesn't.

'You know, I'm not . . .' She trails off. 'You're usually so well groomed.' Her hand reaches out again, this time to rub the ends of my hair between her fingers and thumb. 'There are some great products that can help with split ends.'

Bel would say, *Tell someone who cares, Max-ine,* her Glaswegian accent sounding both melodic and mildly threatening. Rachel would widen her eyes and play along, *Are there? Do you have any samples?*

Right now I'm too tired for anything but a vague smile before I move past her to duck into the children's toilets. There are no mirrors above the miniature sinks so I rummage in my handbag for my compact and hold it up in front of my face. Okay, so Maxine has a point. My curly hair is a split-end tangle that needs a cut and condition. My face is ghostly pale, prominent cheekbones and dark eyes making me look as if I'm suffering from an ongoing trauma. Anxiety does that to me: drains me of all colour and light. These last few weeks have taken their toll, and while I can just about cope with my own troubles, seeing Lily upset has led to sleepless nights and a nagging feeling of helplessness.

I balance the mirror on the windowsill and pull my hair up into a high ponytail before applying some blusher and lip gloss. I've spent the whole day worrying about Lily and how the notes are affecting her self-esteem. There have been three so far. The first one came a week ago, and although disturbing, it was easy enough to ignore. The second, a few days later, made it clear that ignoring the first one was wishful thinking and that's when I approached Lily's teacher, Angela Fleming. I remember the look of shock on her face as she read them. 'What on earth?' she asked, wide eyes meeting mine. 'This is *completely* unacceptable.' She shook her head against the words on the page. 'I'll call a parents' meeting. We'll soon get to the bottom of it.'

And now with the third note, I sense that whoever is writing them is just warming up. Why my daughter is being picked on, why this person has it in for my family, I have no clue, but I know that we're right to try to stop the abuse now before it gets any worse.

The Year Five classroom is on the first floor of the 1960s brick building. I climb the stone staircase worn by years of running feet, holding on to the wooden banister that has long lost its sheen, chips and penknife carvings breaking up the smoothness. I stop at the tall windows halfway up to peer out into the rain, searching the car park for Robin's car, a white Porsche, so even in weather like this it's easy to spot.

It isn't there.

Inside the classroom, desks are pushed back and the chairs are arranged in a horseshoe, three rows deep, facing the front. Mrs Fleming greets me at the door. She is small and round and has decades of experience. She has every child and every parent's measure and isn't afraid to take charge.

'This weather! Hopefully it won't keep people away.'

'I think it'll pass,' I say, trying to smile.

'Are you all right?' Her brow is creased. 'I know this must be hard for you.' She strokes my upper arm. 'Lily is such a sweetheart, and whoever's doing this will be caught, and they will be punished, Nina. Make no mistake.' She lowers her voice. 'Temporary exclusion or worse.' Her eyes reinforce this promise before they flick beyond me towards more parents who are coming into the room. 'Let's talk at the end.'

She squeezes my hand before moving away, and I'm left standing alone for one long second before Bel comes up behind me and slips her arm through mine. 'Hello, gorgeous. Let's bag ourselves a seat.'

This time I do smile. 'Gorgeous I'm not. But thank you anyway.' We walk in step towards the centre of the horseshoe. 'I bumped into Maxine on the way in. Never a good thing.'

'She of the alliterative name and the superior sneer,' Bel says. 'What did she say to you?'

'My hair's a mess and I look tired.'

'Charming,' Bel says, reflexively touching her own hair which is bottle-blonde, short and neat, a pixie cut framing her heart-shaped face. 'I wouldn't be surprised if it's her son who's sending the notes.'

'I've been thinking the same and – oh!' I suddenly remember. 'It wasn't my turn to book the table, was it?'

'Rachel's done it.' She nods towards Rachel who is standing in front of a display board. 'We've got the corner table in The Hare.'

'Brilliant – thank you.' I turn to sit down. The seat is lower than my brain registers and I drop suddenly, my feet coming up off the floor in front of me.

'Not been drinking already have you?' Rachel's husband Bryn is grinning down at me. He's a big bear of a man with hands like shovels and eyes that are kinder than Mother Teresa's.

'Not yet.' I smile, for a moment forgetting the reason we're all here, until I catch sight of two mothers whispering and glancing at me. 'I could do with one, though.'

'This is all a bit shit, isn't it?' he says, his expression twisting with sympathy.

'It is.' I sigh. 'I'm really hoping it can be sorted before Lily starts refusing to come to school.'

'We're here for you,' Bryn says, touching my shoulder. 'Anything you need. Just say the word.'

'Thank you.' His kindness triggers a lump in my throat and I blink several times to hold off the tears.

'Quick! Eyes left.' Bel brings a welcome distraction as she takes the seat beside me and nudges me to follow her gaze to the doorway. Maxine is coming into the room. She lets her powder blue, leather jacket slide seductively off her shoulders, gently shaking her head from side to side so that her hair rises and falls in a wave of auburn gloss that's begging to be stroked. Her pearl pink sweatshirt has gold cursive script across the front: *Influencer* and underneath this *AMA*.

Two of the dads hover close by. 'Their tongues are literally hanging out,' Bel says.

'She is beautiful though,' I say, wishing I didn't feel the need to always play fair. She has never been anything other than indifferent towards me and, more to the point, her son is a bully. And if he is writing the notes then he's causing no end of upset for my daughter. I should be loading on the criticisms not the compliments.

'Is she beautiful?' Bel scrunches up her nose. 'She knows how to apply make-up, but if you examine her bone structure, it's not great.' She looks round at me. 'She'd kill for your cheekbones.'

'Hardly!' I laugh. Having just seen myself in the mirror, I doubt she covets any part of me except for my mac. 'What does AMA stand for?'

'Ask me anything. It's an online thing. Usually with people at the top of their game like Barack Obama or Margaret Atwood. Not the wannabes.'

'Ask her anything?' I repeat, stifling another laugh with my hand. 'Open season for the dads!'

'It's just giving them an excuse to stare at her tits,' Bel says. A text sounds and she pulls out her mobile. 'Miro's train's almost at the station. He'll be here soon.'

I take a breath. 'I'm not sure Robin's going to make it.'

'What?' Bel's expression says it all.

'He had an emergency surgery overnight and hasn't been home since. He must be caught up with that . . . I think.'

'You think or you know?' Her eyebrows are raised.

'He's not been answering his texts,' I admit.

Bel shakes her head. 'He doesn't half pick his times to be a dick,' she says quietly.

Before I have the chance to reply, Rachel collapses into the seat to the other side of me. 'Hello, lovelies!' She's carrying her coat and two bags, which she dumps on the floor in front of her. 'What have I missed?'

'Maxine's working the room and Robin isn't coming,' Bel says.

'Oh.' Rachel's blue eyes widen but she's always ready to give Robin the benefit of the doubt. 'I suppose that's the problem with being a surgeon. You can't always get home on time.' She takes my hand. 'Well, we're here for you, Nina. Aren't we, Bel?'

'Yup.'

She leans in, and our shoulders knock together like we're teammates. Rachel does the same and I feel held, bookended by their support. To hell with Robin and his silences. I need to stop hoping for the impossible. My two best friends will help get Lily and me through this.

Parents start choosing seats around us, and I smile, say 'hello', but find most are reluctant to even meet my eye, never mind return a greeting. I feel the smile freeze on my face and Bel whispers into my ear, 'Don't let it bother you. You know what this class can be like.'

I do know what this class can be like. We're only three weeks into the autumn term but we've been mixing for some time, not just at parents' evenings, but children's birthday parties and parent socials, to say nothing of bumping into each other in the village shops or doctors' surgery. Most of the children have been together since nursery, and almost all of the parents and children have been in my garden when I've offered it up for fundraising events. At least half of the parents have strongly held views and I've overheard many a spirited argument, whether it's decisions around what new equipment to add to the playground or how to treat head lice. Still,

I'm not sure why most of them are avoiding my eye now. I don't take sides and I haven't pointed my finger at any child, not even Max. Or not yet, at least.

Mrs Fleming closes the door and walks to the front. 'If I could have your attention, please.'

The mood quickly shifts from casual to focused as the chatting stops and all eyes face the front. Almost all of the seats are taken now; every child has either one or two parents present. My heart begins to beat faster. I hold my hands together on my lap and take a deep breath.

'So, thank you everyone for coming along this evening,' Mrs Fleming says. 'Unfortunately, as many of you may already know, we have a situation that is very concerning.' She pauses. 'Someone has been slipping malicious notes into Lily Myers' school bag.' She glances across at me. 'Not surprisingly, this has been extremely upsetting for Nina and Robin, and most especially for Lily.'

She pauses again and one of the dads asks, 'Can you be sure it's a child in this class who's writing the notes?'

'No, and having discussed it with both the headmaster and our local youth police officer, we don't want to make assumptions at this stage. It could be one of the children in this class but, equally, it could be another member of our school community. There will be a whole-school assembly on Friday when we'll talk about bullying generally, but in the meantime, we feel it's best to fill you in on what's been happening so that you can talk to your children.'

'What do the notes say?' another dad asks.

'I have them here.' Mrs Fleming lifts some papers off her desk. 'Nina has given me permission to show them to you.' She catches my eye to check I haven't changed my mind, and I nod my assent. 'Two were left last week and the third came today.' She clears her throat. 'I should warn you that they are graphic.'

Rachel takes my hand. She and Bel have seen the notes. We pored over them together, trying to recognise the writing (we couldn't), and trying to imagine why on earth a child was doing this to Lily. Bel even smelled the paper to see whether there were any clues there. There were none – the paper smelled of Lily's favourite lunch: tuna and cucumber sandwiches.

My jaw tenses as Mrs Fleming walks across to the projector. I've been dreading this moment. I know that the notes are going to be even more shocking, magnified several times and projected onto the whiteboard. And I'm right. As soon as the first note appears the mood in the room sharpens. Backs straighten and several parents let out small gasps of shock. The first note says:

This class has secrets all the parents tell lies

The writing is simplistic, letters crudely formed with black marker pen. The second note is more direct:

Your mum is a hore

This makes me shrink inside. I feel embarrassed, ashamed even, like this is some secret I've been keeping and now everyone knows about it.

'The third note came today,' Mrs Fleming says as she places it on the projector.

Your dad is not a hero doctor he is a kunt

I try to breathe into the silence, but the air is caught in my throat. I turn to look at Rachel who has a single tear

11

running down her cheek. 'So awful to think that someone is writing such terrible things to Lily,' she says quietly.

'Does Robin know about the last note?' Bel whispers into my other ear.

I shake my head. 'I texted him, but . . .' I shrug and stare straight ahead. I wish Robin had replied. I wish he'd made the effort to come this evening. But he didn't, and there's really nothing more I can say.

Chapter Two

At first none of the other parents speak. There's a shuffling of feet and bodies, murmurs between couples and then: 'Why are we only hearing about this now?' one of the mothers asks. 'Surely we should have been told after the first message?'

Mrs Fleming glances across at me and I shift in my seat before saying, 'When Lily showed Robin and I the first note, we hoped it might be a one-off, not worth making a fuss about. After the second one, I came to school and spoke to Mrs Fleming. We agreed that something needed to be done. The third one only arrived today after we'd already set up the meeting.'

'Is Lily okay?' Amira, our local GP and mother of four boys, asks. 'This must be so upsetting for her.'

'She is upset,' I acknowledge, touched by Amira's thoughtfulness. 'She doesn't understand why it's happening.' I glance sideways, genuinely expecting Robin to be next to me, for him to have materialised in the time between Mrs Fleming opening the meeting and now. *How can he not be here? Why doesn't he care enough to show up?* 'Obviously,' I add. 'Like all of us, we want to protect our children from everything that hurts them so . . . it's difficult.'

'Does Lily have any idea who might be writing them?' Amira asks. 'I mean, it's hard to tell from the writing but children share secrets, don't they? My boys haven't said anything but—'

'It's unlikely to be a boy,' a dad butts in. 'Surely this is more of a girls thing?'

'A jealous friend?' someone at the back says. 'Children can be devious.'

'We're not ruling out anyone at this point,' Mrs Fleming says. 'Child or adult.'

'Surely not an adult?' a voice to my left calls out.

Mrs Fleming's expression is resigned. 'As I said, the youth officer feels it's too early to narrow it down.'

'Whoever's writing them can't spell, and doesn't much like punctuation,' one of the dads observes. 'Would that narrow it down?'

'An adult could be deliberately misspelling the words,' Amira says.

'And generally speaking children don't see swear words written down so they're more likely to spell them phonetically,' Mrs Fleming says. 'As for punctuation, it's left off text messages and so on. Most children won't use it unless writing formally.'

The door opens and Bel's husband, Miro, walks in. He is over six feet tall and has an obvious physicality and warmth. He smiles around the horseshoe, his eyes coming to rest on the teacher. 'I'm sorry I'm late, Angela. Trains were slow this evening.'

'No problem, Miro.' She smiles a welcome. 'We're not long started.'

Bel pats the empty seat she saved next to her and Miro takes off his suit jacket before sitting down.

'I don't want to be contentious in any way,' a dad called Jeremy begins, 'but we all know that this class has

14

had its fair share of bullying, and maybe we should be questioning those children who have been guilty of picking on others in the past.'

There is a heartbeat of calm, several pairs of eyes flicking towards Maxine whose face gives nothing away, before a mother who's fairly new to the class leans forward, and says lightly, 'I think you're taking a very simplistic view, Jeremy. Children are complex. They often express their needs obliquely.'

'I've no idea what that means,' he replies flatly. 'For me it's simple. Some of the kids have form so let's ask those kids first.'

'Form?' It's the same mother. 'Do you really think that's a fair adjective to use to describe a child?' Her tone is placatory with a side order of patronising. 'Wouldn't it be better for us to address the underlying issue?' She points to the screen. 'There are layers of fear and anger at play here.'

'As usual we drown in psychobabble.' He folds his arms and eyeballs her. 'Isn't there a vaccine for that?'

'There's no need for rudeness, Jeremy,' another mum joins in. 'We're all entitled to an opinion.'

'Could we just stick to the point?' prompts a dad sitting close to the door. He makes a show of looking at his watch. 'I need to be home in an hour.'

One comment follows another and I gradually tune out. I was hoping for better but knew that, in all likelihood, the meeting would quickly lose focus. From the corner of my eye, I watch Miro and Bel lean in to each other. Bel whispers something into his ear. He links his fingers through hers and bends his head to kiss the back of her hand before their eyes meet again and she smiles.

The moment is over within a few seconds but it speaks of them as a couple. They are the gold standard for a

15

happy marriage. I felt this the moment I met them. They could have been good at projecting marital harmony without actually living it, but after spending multiple weekends in their company and having holidayed together twice, I know that their symbiosis is real. They have a togetherness about them that is natural, unforced. I have long ago given up wishing for the same, and witnessing this moment makes me feel lonelier than ever. I have my two best friends either side of me but they both have loving husbands to support them. I am a lesser part of their lives than they are of mine.

I stare down at my feet and breathe deeply. I can't cry. I *won't* cry. Not here.

'. . . we have moved away from a discussion that is helpful,' Mrs Fleming is saying loudly.

'I'm just—' a persistent Jeremy continues.

'Please, Mr Parker!' She punches a flat hand towards him. 'Let's end the meeting on a constructive note. We can, as a community, reach agreement.' She pauses, pinning down the warring parents with stern eyes, leaving them in no doubt about who's in charge. 'I have taken advice from our local youth officer, Jennie Jackson, and we have agreed the following approach.' She ticks off each point on her fingers. 'One, you will go home and speak to your children. You'll help them to understand how serious this is and encourage them to tell you if they know anything. Two, if your child does tell you something, no matter how small the detail, you will report that back to me. Three, this is not a subject for gossip or conjecture and any information passed on to me will be kept in confidence.'

'So the culprit's name won't be shared with the class?' Jeremy pipes up again.

'I didn't say that,' Mrs Fleming replies tersely.

'The children need to see that someone who does wrong is punished. Surely that's a good life lesson? I mean . . .' He trails off under the scrutiny of her disapproval, shaking his head as he stares at the wall.

'If another note arrives, Jennie will come to school and meet with the class. For now, let's stay focused.'

She turns away and gradually people stand up and head for the door, an undercurrent of mumbling and discontent marring their exit.

'Another friendly parents' evening,' Bel says, taking my hand and pulling me to my feet. 'You did really well, hon.'

'I wish,' I say under my breath, glancing at Rachel who is caught up in a conversation with the mum behind us.

'I arrived just in time for daggers drawn.' Miro bends to kiss my cheek. 'Did Robin not make it?'

'Don't go there,' Bel says, rolling her eyes.

Miro's expression is sympathetic. 'If ever you want to set Bel on him, Nina, I'll happily lend her out to you.'

'Robin was held up in a surgery,' I blurt out, smiling widely, feeling foolish but propelled by the need to defend Robin in front of any stray parents who might be listening in. And, right now, defending Robin feels like defending myself. I don't want to be a victim. And I don't want Lily to be a victim. I know how destructive sliding into a negative mindset can be. I've been there and done that and I'll do everything in my power to prevent it happening again.

'Fair dues,' Miro replies. 'He didn't get that MBE for nothing.' He circles an arm around his wife's waist. 'You three off for your debrief?'

'We are,' Bel says, giving me a reassuring smile. 'This could be happening to any of our girls and we need to stick together.'

'Too right,' Miro says.

'Well done, lovely.' Rachel has finished talking and comes to join us. She hugs me tightly, her bags knocking against my hip. 'You're so brave. I'd be in bits. Literally. It's so sinister.' She stares at the bags she's carrying as if she suddenly doesn't know who they belong to. 'There's no way I'm taking these to the pub.' She walks off to give them to Bryn who's talking motorbikes with the resident biker dad.

'Vera's been handing in some lovely work this term,' Mrs Fleming tells Bel and Miro. 'We've been studying the rainforest and it's really taken hold of her imagination.' She points to a display board over by the window. 'Her latest piece is on the wall there.'

They go off to have a look and Mrs Fleming pulls me in close. 'How do you think that went?'

'I think it's good that everyone knows now,' I say, then wince as I hear 'whore' whispered just behind me. I whirl round to see who has said it but faces are turned away from me. It might have been Jeremy – he's close by – but I'm not sure it was even a man's voice.

'The trouble with this class is that it always degenerates into argy-bargy,' Mrs Fleming says. Clearly she didn't hear the whisper. 'In all my years of teaching I've never had a group of parents quite like it.'

'Still, I think everyone got the message,' I say. My lips are trembling and I try to pull them into a smile. 'Fingers crossed one of the children will tell their parents who's doing it and we can move on.'

'I'm sorry Robin couldn't make it,' she says, her expression regretful. 'Greg saw him at the clinic last week. He's been given the all clear.' She smiles, her relief palpable. 'We know how lucky he's been to have such an accomplished surgeon.'

I listen to her sing Robin's praises for close to a minute, nodding in all the right places, even managing a genuine smile, until another parent comes over to speak to her and I say my goodbyes. I head for the stairs, see Rachel and Bel at the bottom and run down to meet them, 'whore' still ringing in my ears.

Chapter Three

The Hare is heaving, not a seat to spare, except for our reserved space in the corner. We weave through the crowd and sit down at the oval wooden table, three small candles and a vase of meadow flowers in the centre to welcome us. I'm on the edge of my nerves and hope that neither Bel nor Rachel will launch straight into their thoughts on the evening. My stomach is turning over; I'm not sure I'll be able to eat anything.

The waitress comes across with the menus and Rachel places a hand on her arm. 'Would you mind getting me a pint of cranberry juice before we order, please?' she asks. 'I'm desperate.' The waitress smiles and goes up to the bar.

'You've been having too much sex again,' Bel says, half-joking.

'I wish,' Rachel replies, and then she makes a face. 'Actually, I don't wish. I know it's not fashionable but once a week is enough for me, and it's hardly worth it when most times I end up with cystitis. I'm permanently on antibiotics. My gut bacteria's shot – and why don't women talk about it?' She pauses to throw up her arms and look to us for answers. 'I can't be the only one.' She frowns. 'It's just as well Bryn's sex drive matches mine otherwise he'd be off shagging some other woman.'

Rachel spots something in Bel's facial expression that I don't, because she adds, 'Don't judge. We can't all be like you two. It's obvious you and Miro are all over each other. And as for you.' She throws me a huffy look. 'With a face and a figure like yours, I'm sure you're beating Robin off with a stick.'

I say nothing. My nerves are settling but I'm not ready to talk yet.

'Here you go.' The waitress plonks a tall glass in front of Rachel and she makes a grab for it, drinking at least a third in the time it takes for the waitress to ask for our order. Bel and I plump for our usual – a stir-fry of prawns and noodles with a glass of Prosecco. Rachel does what she always does. The menu hasn't changed in five years but still she pores over it as if she expects to discover something new. I love her optimism.

'The day you order a vegan burger,' Bel says to her, 'is the day I'll stop being your friend.'

'I'll have a . . . I think . . .' She taps the tabletop with her nails. 'I'd like . . .' She takes a mouthful of juice. 'I'm in two minds . . .' She lays the menu to one side. 'I'll have haddock and chips, please. And a G and T.' Her usual.

The waitress repeats our order back to us then goes behind the bar. Bel drums her hands on the table and says, 'So that was a shitshow.'

'What's wrong with the parents in our class?' Rachel asks, frowning. 'Any excuse for an argument.'

'I know.' I lean my elbows on the table and support my chin with my hands. 'Let's just be ourselves for a bit. Can we talk about something else?'

They both agree and we chat about everything and

nothing: drama club, the improved school lunches, the rogue piano teacher, fundraising to extend the climbing frame, the latest series of *The Crown*. We each have our own opinions, our own likes and dislikes, but somehow we always manage to meet in the middle.

The waitress brings our drinks, and fifteen minutes later, our plates are in front of us. There is a full minute of concentrated eating before Bel glances at me cautiously and asks, 'Should we go back to the notes?'

I nod. Good food, good company; I feel stronger now.

'This class has secrets.' Bel twists strands of noodles around the tines of her fork. 'Why would a child write that?'

I swallow a mouthful before saying, 'Because they've been earwigging their parents' conversations?'

'Yes, but, what child? What parents? What secret?'

'It could be anyone,' I say. 'That's the problem. We all have secrets.'

'I don't have secrets,' Rachel says. She pushes her bowl of chips into the centre of the table. 'Help me with these otherwise I'll eat them all.'

'I bet you do have secrets,' Bel says.

'I don't have secrets,' she says again, her blue eyes wide with honesty.

'You might not call it a secret,' Bel says. 'But it's something you keep hidden.'

'I don't. I really—' She stops. Her face flushes, a rising tide of red that begins at her throat and ends at her hairline.

'What?' Bel holds her fork midway between mouth and plate. 'Go on.'

'It's nothing.' She shakes her head.

'It doesn't look like nothing,' Bel persists.

Rachel raises her glass to her lips and turns her head

23

slightly to the side as she drinks. I catch the watery glint of tears in her eyes. I glance at Bel and give a small shake of my head.

'So what about you then, Nina?' Bel asks.

'I think we should keep trying to work out who's writing the notes,' I reply, refusing to put myself under her spotlight. 'Language like that isn't on children's programming so that must mean either there's no parental control on their internet settings—' I reach for one of Rachel's chips and dunk it in the small dish of tomato ketchup '—or this is a child who hears their parents swearing at each other. But is that credible? Who calls a woman a whore?'

'Maybe husband Max calls Maxine that when he's had enough of her flirting with other men,' Rachel says. She's recovered from Bel's probing and is tucking in to her fish. Unbelievably Maxine's husband is also called Max. They are a self-styled brand of Maxes.

'And child Max is listening in?' I say.

'I guess child Max seems like the main suspect,' Rachel says. 'But I'm not convinced. I know he's often verbally abusive and there was that time when he lashed out at Carys.'

'I remember that,' I say. Of our three girls, Carys is the most confident and Max's personality is similar. In Year Four, they were bickering about who should take the lead in a game they were playing, and there was some name-calling from both sides. It ended up with Max pushing Carys on the stairs, spraining her wrist.

'And Maxine defended him,' Bel adds. 'Her angelic boy.'

Rachel shrugs. 'I'm under no illusions. Carys can be a right little madam. I don't think she was blameless. And, to be fair, I've got to know another side of Max

24

and he's not all bad.' Rachel is a teaching assistant in Year Three, not our class, but she sees the children around the school and hears the chat in the staffroom. 'The notes are something else.' She winces. 'They're calculated and devious. I asked Carys if she thought it could be him and she said no, he's not as bad as adults think.'

'Vera told me the same,' Bel says.

'Lily too.' I chew on a prawn, thinking. 'I guess we have to believe our girls. If they're sure that what you see is what you get with Max then chances are they're right. In fact, I think that's true of all the boys. They seem straightforward. They're more likely to shout something mean in the playground than go to all the bother of writing notes and waiting for the right moment to put them in Lily's bag.'

We discuss the other seven girls in the class. Rachel doesn't share confidential information from staff meetings but it's common knowledge that none of the other girls have ever been flagged up for poor behaviour and they don't fit the bill for something so spiteful as writing and sending the notes. That said, beyond the odd play date and birthday party, none of us have spent much time with them. Lily, Carys and Vera have been firm friends since they met in nursery and they are a happy trio, always choosing to spend time with each other, rarely falling out.

'They are a mini us,' Rachel says. 'We've really lucked out with their friendship.' She's smiling, her expression sincere. It's one of the things I like about her; she wears her feelings on her face.

The waitress returns to remove our plates and leave us with the dessert menus. 'Don't let me have any pudding.' Rachel pulls her hands in towards her chest as if afraid they will move of their own accord, snatch hold of the menu and order for her. And then she'll be eating profiteroles before she knows it. 'I'm on the five/two diet and I've already broken it with the batter on the fish.' She sighs. 'It was delicious though.'

'That's what counts,' I say. 'We have to let ourselves off the hook some of the time.'

'I'm always letting myself off the hook.' She pulls at the waistband on her trousers and sighs. She gives herself a hard time over the extra weight she carries. She doesn't need to. But I get it; we all have those things we beat ourselves up about. I certainly have things I'd like to change about my life.

'I wish we could do more to help Lily,' Bel says. 'What can we do, Nina? Is there anything?'

'You're both such a support to me. And the girls support each other. I couldn't ask for more, I really couldn't. Well . . .' My mouth turns down. 'I could ask for more. I could ask for this not to be happening in the first place, and I could ask for Robin to take more of an interest but hey ho.' I knock back the last of my Prosecco. 'I'd better get going. I said to Harry I'd be back by ten-thirty.'

'My turn to pay,' Bel says.

While she's up at the bar, Rachel turns to me, her expression cloudy. 'Thanks for stopping Bel from pushing me on the secrets thing.'

'She's like a dog with a bone sometimes,' I say, intrigued as to what Rachel's secret might be. The tears in her eyes were instant, from her having the thought to almost crying, as if a raw nerve had been exposed. She always appears so open, transparent even. The idea of her hiding something, especially from Bel and I, feels totally out of character.

'She's a lot braver than me.'

'She's a lot braver than all of us!' I kiss her cheek. 'You are the warmest, kindest person I know, Rachel Davies. Do not sell yourself short.'

Once we're paid up, I leave Rachel and Bel to walk together – their houses are in the same direction – and begin the walk back home.

It's been raining again and the road is slick with water. Trees grow along either side, their roots drilling under the pavements to erupt in lumps and bumps, puddles collecting in the hollows.

The road is narrow, quiet, off the beaten track, and for most of the way there are no street lamps. There have been complaints on the Facebook community page about the dark patches but nothing has been done about them yet.

I'm able to use my phone torch so I'm not usually bothered by the lack of light but all this talk of secrets has made me jumpy. My mind loops back to the class meeting, when I felt as if I was losing my grip, sliding once more into loneliness and depression, and I shudder at the thought of going back there again.

I quicken my step, sense a shadow lurking just outside my line of vision and turn swiftly to check but there's nothing – no one – there. I listen for the sound of footsteps, imagine I can hear a held breath, but if there is such a sound then it's drowned out by the pulsing in my ears.

'Calm down,' I tell myself, but my body doesn't hear me and I start to run, torch aimed down at my feet so that I don't trip up. When I spy the pool of light from my front porch, still thirty metres in the distance, I gulp in wet air and some of the tension slides off my shoulders. But even as my hand reaches for the door handle, I can't shake the feeling of eyes watching me, focused on my back, homing in on a target.

Chapter Four

I close the front door firmly behind me and take a moment to catch my breath before going into the large kitchen cum family room. Harry, my sixteen-year-old stepson from Robin's first marriage, is on one sofa; Robin is on the other. I'm surprised to see my husband. I was so keen to get indoors that I didn't notice his car in the driveway. I immediately wonder how long he's been here.

'Hello!' I smile at them both, and hug Harry who has stood up to greet me, before I bend to kiss Robin's cheek.

'You're cold!' he says, recoiling.

'It's one of those damp evenings,' I say, my tone light. 'You been back long?'

'Just got here. Harry had the girls tucked up in bed and asleep when I arrived.'

Harry grins at us both. His hair hangs over one eye, his head tilted to one side. He is shy and sometimes awkward, but totally adored by both the girls and myself for his sense of fun and endless patience. Just having him around completes our family in a way that I'm forever grateful for.

'Were they good?' I ask him.

'Yeah.' His grin widens. 'After their homework, they did some drawings for you. They're on the kitchen table.'

'Thank you, love.' I slip two twenty-pound notes into his hand. 'You're a godsend.'

'He doesn't need to be paid!' Robin jumps to his feet. 'Do you, Harry?' He lands a playful punch in the shallow of Harry's shoulder making him stumble back a step. 'He's family.'

Harry recovers quickly and rises to the challenge, holds up his fists, bouncing from one foot to the other and from side to side, ready to spar with his dad. Robin plays along for a few seconds then wishes him a good night and wanders off towards the kitchen. I follow Harry to the front door. 'Was Lily okay?'

'Yeah, she was a bit sad but not too bad.' He slides his feet into trainers. 'Did any of the parents know who was writing the notes?'

'No. We're no further forward, really.' I open the door for him. 'And you know Lily. She takes everything to heart so I'm not sure where we'll be if another note turns up in her bag.'

'Yeah.' His expression is serious. 'School can be hard on kids. It's a shame it's Lily who's being picked on. I don't think Poppy would care as much.'

'Tell me about it!' I say, my eyes wide. 'She's tough, that one.'

'She keeps going on about getting a dog?'

I nod. 'She knows I'll give in eventually.'

'My mum says hi, by the way. She wanted me to ask if you could lend her a big pot for the weekend. She's having some people round.'

'Sure. I'll take one with me when I go to the meeting tomorrow.' Harry's mum Aimee runs various initiatives, including the Community Fridge and a women's workshop that is for women who want to 'fully realise their potential'. It wasn't my choice to join but Rachel was keen so Bel and I agreed to go along too.

I hug Harry again as he goes through the door. 'Text me when you arrive home!' I call after him.

'Will do.' He jogs off and I close the door behind him. I know some people find my friendship with Aimee unusual – ex-wife and current wife don't normally form a bond – but she'd been separated from Robin for years when I first met her. Their marriage was 'a mistake' she told me. Two people trying to do the right thing because there was a baby on the way.

Robin hadn't told me much about Aimee or about Ashdown village, except that she was his ex and the village was a great place to grow up in. Set in the Ashdown Forest, it's equidistant from the hubbub of London and the coastal city of Brighton. Robin has memories of an idyllic childhood, building camps in the woods and finding frogspawn in the streams that meander through the trees. When we moved here, Aimee smoothed the path for me, and Harry's infrequent visits became weekly, then daily. Now we're at the point where he doesn't even ask if his dad will be home because he comes to spend time with the girls and me.

I turn the key in the lock and take a second to think about what I'm going to say to Robin before joining him in the kitchen. He has a bottle of lager in his hand and is staring through the window into the pitch-black garden. I'm annoyed about him not coming to the parents' evening but I'm also tired and not in the mood for an argument. 'Too much cloud cover for a moon tonight,' I say, standing next to him, our shoulders briefly touching before he repositions his feet.

'You want one?' He tilts the lager in my direction and

I nod. He goes over to the fridge and takes another bottle out, uses the edge of the work surface to pop the metal cap off the top. He's been doing this since we moved in almost six years ago, and now the work surface has small marks running along the length of it. I mentioned it once and he accused me of trying to tame him. The conversation began light-heartedly enough but spiralled into a full-blown argument about how much I supposedly restricted his enjoyment.

So now I say nothing. I've learned to choose my battles.

He passes me the bottle. 'How was the parents' evening?'

I don't tell him. Instead I say, 'Did you get my texts?'

He shrugs. 'My phone was out of charge.'

'That's strange.' I frown. 'It looked like they were delivered.'

'Did it?' He's unconcerned. 'I had a long surgery. A partial lung transplant.'

'Was it successful?'

'It was.' He smiles at me. 'Touch and go at one point but we got there in the end.'

My heart is beating faster. So this is the way it's to be. No *How's Lily? How are you? I'm so sorry I couldn't make it.* I put the bottle down on the counter then walk in front of him so that my back is to the window. We are the same height, our legs, torsos and heads level with each other. But where I am olive-skinned and dark-haired, he is pale-skinned with sandy blond hair. 'The texts were to tell you about the third note,' I say, my hands tightening into fists. 'I didn't want you turning up without knowing what it said.'

'Oh?'

He looks directly at me for the first time since I've

come home. His eyes are a deep, warm violet and, even now, as angry as I feel, I am drawn to them.

I blink to break the spell and take a breath before saying, 'Your dad is not a hero doctor. He is a cunt.' I don't swear as a rule but this moment is an exception and I say the c word with relish, enjoying the punch of the harsh syllable as it hits the air and registers on his face. There is a small tightening around his mouth and his eyes darken before they break away from mine. 'What do you think, Robin?' I ask, my tone light.

'I don't think anything!' He's rattled. His head shakes from side to side. 'You can't look for logic in these notes.' He lifts his chin before drinking from the bottle and I watch his Adam's apple bulge with each swallow. 'It's just some kid who's picking on Lily because he knows he'll get a reaction.'

'You're not bothered?'

'Why should I be? Lily might have mentioned my MBE. It could have sounded like bragging and the kid is jealous.'

'So, there hasn't been a complaining patient at your door?'

'Calling me a cunt?' His eyes widen. 'Sometimes patients swear but it's never personal. And it's certainly not directed at me!' He takes another swig of lager before saying, 'The second note said you were a whore. Has anyone at your company ever called you that?'

I consider that for a second. 'Well . . . like any boss I've heard the odd muttering behind my back but not—'

He laughs before I can finish. 'If that's the environment you work in, perhaps you should think about changing career.'

When he makes statements like this I wonder whether he's challenging me or if he genuinely doesn't join the dots of our life. Not that it matters. Once again I remind myself that I pick my battles. So I don't say it's the money I earn that allows us to live in a house like this. Or that the Porsche he drives – and loves – was something he could never have afforded to buy for himself – it was a fortieth birthday present from me. Robin was given an MBE in the Queen's Honours list. He is a pioneering surgeon and he deserves all the accolades he gets for that. But our society doesn't financially reward doctors nearly half as well as it rewards the likes of me – a company lawyer, specialising in high-value mergers and acquisitions. I earn four times that of an NHS consultant. And no, that isn't fair.

And then there's the child support. Robin married Aimee then followed their divorce with a long-term relationship with Letitia, also a surgeon. I have three stepchildren – Harry, and twelve-year-old identical twin boys, Rory and Craig, who live in Glasgow with Letitia. She has since remarried, and we rarely see the twins, but the child support is substantial. Don't get me wrong, I don't begrudge his children the money. I knew about them when we married and was perfectly prepared to see the lion's share of Robin's salary head in their direction. I earn more than enough to support the four of us but sometimes, when Robin comes over all superior as if my job is lesser than his – he likes to say I'm a slave to capitalism – it rankles.

As Jane, my business partner told me, 'We are enablers, Nina. We make our spouses' dreams possible. Robin never has to do private work or worry about child support because you provide the means for him to shine at his career and maintain a high standard of living. And my husband can piss tens of thousands up against the wall with his tropical fish store.'

There are days when I would trade Robin puffing out his chest over his MBE for a simple tropical fish store. But I've made my bed; it's the lying in it that I can no longer stomach.

'Why do we have so much yoghurt?' he asks. He's rummaging around in the fridge, moving jars and containers, and bags of vegetables, slamming them down on the shelves. 'And condiments. We could open a bloody shop.'

I move across to stand beside him. 'What are you looking for?'

'I'm low on insulin.'

Robin is a Type 1 diabetic, and despite the fact that he's a doctor, he's not particularly good at looking after his own health. He wears a sensor on his upper arm that monitors his blood sugar levels and gives a twenty-minute warning before his levels sink too low. This is linked to a phone app that alerts the wearer to the problem. Robin shares these details with me because he knows I'll keep an eye on the readings for him. He also expects me to order his insulin but I've been so hurt and angry with him these past few weeks that I haven't done it.

It's time he took responsibility for himself.

I point to the box on the top shelf. 'That's all we have.'

'I'll have to get some from the pharmacy then.' He closes the fridge door and glares at me. 'So, did the witches' coven work out who's writing the notes?' He likes to call us that; he thinks it's funny.

'There's no obvious culprit,' I say. 'But Mrs Fleming—'

He doesn't let me finish. 'Her husband Gary was at the clinic last week. He's—'

'His name's Greg,' I interrupt loudly. 'She told me already. More to the point, she's spoken to the police about the notes.'

His mouth turns down. 'Is that really necessary?'

'Yes!' I say, wondering why he doesn't get how much this is affecting Lily. 'It's better if they stop, isn't it?'

He stretches out his neck, dropping his head to one side and then the other. 'I think we should ignore them.'

'What?' My expression is scathing. 'That would work if they were coming to you or me but they're upsetting Lily.'

'Well, maybe we should help her not to care.' I go to speak and he holds up a hand. 'Hear me out, Nina. Lily lacks resilience. This is an opportunity for a life lesson, and the way we present this to her is important.'

'Robin, almost any child would be upset. I don't think Lily is unusual.'

'She needs a shift in perspective. If we indulge her anxiety, she'll see herself as a victim.' He speaks confidently as if he is an expert.

'She's nine,' I remind him flatly. 'I get what you're saying but I've not indulged her anxiety. Far from it.'

'We should talk to her tomorrow after school,' he says. 'I'll see whether I can get her to understand that, in the grand scheme of things, this is nothing!' He throws out his arms. 'A miniature molehill on the landscape of life.' He takes a last drink of his lager and opens the bifold doors into the back garden.

'Where are you going?'

'To the sauna!' he calls back, walking away from me.

'At this time?' He doesn't reply. 'I'd like to lock the door.'

'Leave it open!' he shouts. 'I won't be long.'

The bifolds don't have a key and can only be secured with bolts from the inside. As a village we're practically crime-free but years of living in London have taken their toll. I close it behind him, resisting the urge to snap the bolts into place.

The sauna is part of a Scandinavian-style cabin at the bottom of the garden. It's tucked beneath an overhanging willow, and offers a beautiful view over sloping fields and the distant reservoir. Inside, there are three separate areas: a living room with wood burner, kitchenette and a sofa bed for guests; a study; and a fully functioning sauna with shower and toilet. When we bought the house, I thought we would rarely use the cabin but I grew to enjoy having a sauna after exercise. And on summer evenings, Bel, Rachel and I sit on the verandah and watch the sunset.

Two or three days a week I work from home, and the cabin has become my space. The internet connection is good and it's far enough away from the house for me to feel I'm in shouting distance if the children are off school. Robin has only been using the sauna for the past couple of months. And I know why. I've been itching all evening to get hold of my laptop and my eyes search around the room for it just as a text sounds. I pull my phone from my pocket and see it's from Harry.

Got home safely. Cheers for the money.
Harry xx

That reminds me about the girls' drawings and I spot them on the kitchen table. Poppy has drawn the huge face of a furry brown dog, a lurid pink tongue hanging out of one side of its mouth. Lily has drawn our family. I'm holding both the girls' hands, and a super-skinny Harry is holding Lily's other hand, her blonde hair a stark bright yellow. Poppy is dark-haired, like me, and seems to be balancing on one leg. Robin is standing slightly apart. He has a medal pinned to his chest.

I hear a sound behind me and turn quickly. Lily is

standing there, staring straight ahead, her eyes unseeing. She's wearing a white nightie with small flowers embroidered at the neckline that she loves but is several sizes too big and swamps her, making her look slight and vulnerable. She's been sleepwalking on and off for about six months, but since the notes started it's become every night. She usually finds her way either into my bed or downstairs. Once I even found her pulling at the front door.

I take her shoulders and gently turn her around towards the stairs. Sometimes I can steer her all the way back to her bed without her waking up but tonight that doesn't work and she gives a sudden shudder before her eyes squint against the light. 'You're awake, sweetheart,' I say, stroking wisps of hair away from her face. 'You've had a little wander again.'

She rubs her eyes and stares down at her bare feet, toes tucked under as if gripping the wooden floor. 'I came downstairs?'

'You did. But that's okay. We can soon have you back in bed.'

I watch her eyes begin to focus and then she frowns as she remembers where I was going this evening. 'What happened at the parents' meeting?'

'Well.' I go down onto one knee in front of her so that I can look up into her face. 'Mrs Fleming showed the parents the notes and everyone agreed they would ask their children whether they knew who might be writing them.' She gives a slight nod. 'We also agreed that people only write mean things like that when they're jealous or upset about something in their own lives,' I add, not sure we did actually agree on that but I'm searching for something that sounds reassuring.

Her head jerks up. 'But the notes could be true.'

'Of course they're not true!' I pull her in for a hug

but she resists, her body unyielding. 'Is that what you're worried about?' She sighs and rubs at her eyes again. 'How could nasty words like that be true?' I ask.

Her teeth gnaw at her bottom lip. 'Where's Daddy?'

'He's just gone down to the sauna.'

'Why?'

'To relax, I think.'

'Can I sleep in your bed tonight?'

'Of course you can.' She cleaves to me then, her arms and legs circling my body. 'Let's get you back upstairs.'

She's small for a nine-year-old but still my knees almost buckle when I get to the top of the stairs. The bed is a super king with more than enough space for three bodies but I'm expecting Robin to sleep elsewhere. He's never liked the girls coming into our room, no matter what nightmares they might have had. Lily's sleepwalking is no good reason either. He believes in strict demarcation lines and I've accommodated that by settling Lily or Poppy back in their own beds more often than not.

But lately, whether Lily's in beside me or not, Robin has been sleeping in the spare room. And if, in the morning, I ask him why he didn't come to bed, he'll tell me he didn't want to disturb me.

'Daddy suggested we have a chat tomorrow after school,' I tell Lily as she slides under the covers.

'What about?'

'About the notes,' I say, my tone upbeat. I plump the pillow behind her head, the released air blowing her hair out so that she almost smiles. 'It's a good idea, isn't it?'

'Did he go to the parents' meeting with you?'

'He wasn't able to make it.'

'So you went all by yourself?' Another worried frown creases her forehead. 'Were you lonely?'

'No, I wasn't lonely,' I lie. 'Rachel sat one side of me and Bel sat on the other so I was with my friends.'

I fetch her two favourite teddies from her bedroom and place them either side of her. 'Just like Vera and Carys,' I say as she snuggles down with them. 'Your best friends.'

'Are you coming to bed now?' she asks.

'In a minute. I'm going to check on Poppy and tidy up downstairs.'

'Three kisses,' she says.

I stretch across the bed and place a kiss on either cheek and one on her forehead. 'One for love, two for respect, three for charity.' I introduced the idea of three kisses that stood for all things good because Poppy is strong-willed and hates to share with her sister. Lily is always willing to give away her last penny, and while she's taken the idea of charity doubly to heart, Poppy ignores it completely.

'If I give all my pocket money to Children in Need,' Lily asks, 'do you think the notes will stop?'

I reassure her that she is the most generous girl I know, that all the money she raised from baking with Carys and Vera has gone to children who need help, and that if anyone is keeping score—

'God?'

'God . . .' I acknowledge. I'm neither a believer nor a non-believer but I strive for balance. 'And Mother Nature because she has given us so much beauty. And in my experience, what you give to the world, the world gives back to you.' I pause. 'Maybe not immediately but over time.'

She closes her eyes then, and I start to retreat. I leave the hall light on and push open the door to Poppy's bedroom. The light shines on her face, long lashes dipping down onto her flushed cheeks. Bel calls her

Cherub because she is angelic to look at, but behind the pretty face is a fiery, determined six-year-old. I bend down to kiss her cheeks and forehead three times too then go downstairs.

I find my laptop on a side table in the living room and place it in front of me on the kitchen island. Two months ago, I bought some software from a small electronic shop off the Euston Road that I pass on my walk from the tube station. I'd looked inside several times but didn't go in until it was empty of customers. I opened the door and sidled up to the desk, saying quickly, 'I need to track someone. Do you know where I can get the tech?'

'Sure.' The assistant smiled at me, completely unfazed. 'I've got everything you need.'

I bought a tracker for the Porsche and stuck it to the car's underbelly in less time than it takes to boil a kettle. I installed an app that mirrors Robin's phone with mine so that I can read his texts and emails. And last week I hid a voice-activated recorder in the main room in the cabin.

I'm doing this because Robin's having an affair and, this time, I'm approaching his behaviour in a clinical, hard-hearted way. I'm not crying. I'm not trying to talk him round, drawing his attention to the family he'll lose, begging him to go to couples therapy with me – again – because we've been down this road before. I'm taking control, and if that means using spyware then so be it.

I log onto a program hidden in a file marked 'household accounts' and see that the software in the cabin is activated. He's on his mobile. I listen to the conversation he's having. I can't hear the woman's voice but I can hear everything he says. Purple prose, my grandma would have called it.

Listening in to his secret life makes me sick to my stomach – twice I've been too upset to continue and have rushed to the loo to retch over the sink. It's punishing but necessary because I can't weaken. And I know myself – I weaken. I crumble. I give in. I imagine my girls in tears and decide that, for the good of the whole family, I should stick with the status quo, uncomfortable as it is, and pretend I don't know what he's up to. But I did that before and look where it got me?

I check the tracker and find that just after the parents' evening, the Porsche was parked three miles from here in Jubilee Road, nowhere near a hospital, never mind an operating theatre. The address rings a bell, a loud bell, and I quickly check the class parents' address list. One of our parents lives in Jubilee Road, I'm sure of it, and when I scroll down to the name, I'm not surprised to see who it is.

Maxine.

Maxine lives in Jubilee Road.

My hands shake as I close the laptop and climb the stairs to bed.

Chapter Five

BEL

I first saw Nina at pick-up time on a Friday. She was standing with her back to me talking to another nursery mum, dark curly hair in a loose knot at her neck, wearing fitted jeans and a white silk shirt that was tucked in at one side, the other side floating outwards like a cloud in the breeze. Vera had told me there was a new girl in her class. *Her name is Lily and she has a baby sister called Poppy. And she's really nice, Mummy.* I wasn't expecting to make a new friend but when Nina turned around and smiled at me, I felt an uptick in my heart.

'Hi, I'm Nina.' She held out her hand and I took it, her fingers long and slim in my smaller, rougher palm. 'Our girls seem to have come up with a plan.'

I told Miro about her that evening. 'She's so lovely! So friendly and kind! She's a breath of fresh air! You would never guess she's some sort of high-end lawyer. Rachel really likes her too.' This was me talking. Me, who never, but *never*, gushes about anyone. 'We've been invited to their place for a barbecue on Sunday.'

'You sound like you're in love,' he said laughing. 'Can this woman really be so perfect?'

Yes, she can. Almost six years on and she is the best friend I have. Rachel too, of course. But whereas Rachel is water, I am earth or fire. If it's just the two of us, she can drown me with her fears and I scare her with my heat. Nina is all air. She has an effortless grace that lifts all three of us, keeps Rachel's head above water, my fist out of the flames.

It sounds fanciful, and I'm not prone to romance or fairy tale – it doesn't fit with the Bel I am most of the time – but Nina is the only person I've ever met who illuminates a part of me that no one else even imagines is there. She makes me funnier, wiser, kinder. She is one of life's blessings.

'How was the pub?' Miro asks me when I reach home after my evening in The Hare with Rachel and Nina. He's lounging on the sofa watching a *Top Gear* rerun.

'Food was good.' I throw myself down beside him. 'And I think we managed to cheer Nina up. She seemed really down when we first arrived.' I kiss him. He tastes of lager and his usual peanuts, which he consumes by the bagful.

'No wonder,' he says. 'And Robin not even bothering to show.'

'He's such an arrogant git,' I say, snuggling into Miro's shoulder. 'I really don't know what she sees in him.' I think back to her expression when we first arrived in the pub. She looked so sad, so beaten. It really isn't like her, and while I know she's worried about Lily, I get the feeling there's something more behind it.

'I know what that means,' Miro says.

'What?' I look at his face and his eyes gesture towards my lap. I'm holding his left hand tightly while I twirl his wedding ring round his finger. I do this whenever I'm scared that I've hurt someone's feelings, made a misstep, said the wrong thing.

'I know. Yeah.' I sigh. 'I think I might have been too pushy with Rachel. I didn't mean to. You know what I'm like.'

'What did you say?' he asks his tone resigned.

'We were talking about secrets, because that's mentioned in the first note, and she suddenly looked . . . I dunno, stricken.'

'Stricken?' he queries.

'Yeah, like she'd just remembered something and was horrified.'

'I thought you three already knew each other's secrets?'

'So did I! And Rachel always seems like such an open book. She got quite upset. Looked like she was going to start crying.' I pause to think. 'It's all fine now, though. We chatted on the way home. I was my best self.'

He hauls himself up – quite literally, I can tell he's been sat there for hours – and pulls me up after him. 'Time for bed.' His hands stray down to the tops of my thighs and he lifts me up, my legs automatically wrapping around him. He's a foot taller than me and it means he can carry me around as if I weigh nothing and it makes me feel giddy, like a teenager on a roller coaster.

We end up in bed, like we always do. Rachel was right – we have a lot of sex. I'm not bragging. It just happens, most nights, nine times out of ten. We never talk about it. We've never sat down like some couples do and discussed what we like, want, crave, or any of the details of our desire. For me, it's all instinct and the animal takes over. Miro smells right to me. When I'm within three feet of him, I feel my insides perk up, like a sleeping lion that catches a delicious scent on the breeze. Then my brain shifts gear and starts to edge me towards getting naked with him.

When we've finished – on top of the duvet, door

45

closed in case Vera wakes up – we go through the evening rituals: the teeth cleaning, locking the doors, checking Vera hasn't kicked her covers off, and then we lie back, both heads on one pillow and I say, 'How would you feel if the notes were going to Vera?'

'I wouldn't like it but I don't think I'd be too upset. Vera would be able to handle it.'

'You would at least show up, though? You'd support me and Vera through it?'

'Of course.'

'When Nina and Robin moved to the village it was meant to be a fresh start,' I say slowly. 'He had an affair when Poppy was a baby.'

'Did he?' Miro turns to face me. I can just about make out his features through the darkness. 'You've never told me that.'

'Nina told me and Rachel when we were away for that spa weekend.' My voice drops to a whisper. 'We've never spoken about it again so don't say anything.'

'Gotcha.' He pulls me in close.

'He's such a flirt at work.' I sigh. 'Our paths don't cross every day but whenever they do, I get the feeling he's eyeing up the young nurses.'

'Bel!' Miro laughs. 'I can't believe that!'

'He does! You must have noticed he's one of those men who looks at women to assess their shagging potential.'

He thinks about this. 'Maybe. I suppose. I haven't spent much time in his company lately.'

'I hope he's not having another affair.'

'That's quite a conclusion to jump to,' Miro says.

'I know, but . . .' I trail off. I'm tired now. It's been a long day. My eyelids close, my thoughts drift and I fall asleep, my head on Miro's shoulder.

★　　★　　★

When Miro's in bed beside me I'm a deep, relaxed sleeper and the next thing I know it's the morning and he's pulling the covers off the bed.

'Wakey, wakey.'

I open one eye and reach out my hand to take hold of the mug of coffee he's brought for me, prop myself up on two pillows and blow on the drink before sipping it slowly. Miro goes into the bathroom next door and Vera joins him. This is their morning routine. She sits on the edge of the bath, holding his towel, while he shaves. I expect her to mention the parents' meeting but she doesn't. She talks about how many times she scored when they played netball yesterday and how she can't wait for secondary school because then they'll be in proper teams and will play against other schools.

'Mum and I saw your drawing pinned up on the classroom wall last night,' Miro says.

'On the display board?' she asks. 'The picture of the sloth?'

'Not as lazy as you think.'

'That was the title of the poem.' I can hear the smile in her voice. 'Because everyone thinks sloths are really slow and hopeless but they're not.'

She tells her dad about the research she's been doing and I listen in, smiling along with them. Vera always has a different take on things. Her piece was one of a dozen, all with a drawing of a rainforest animal, describing what it is and how it lives. Her grinning sloth was clinging to a thick tree branch, her poem wrapped around him like a word hug.

I'm almost finished my coffee when Miro pops his head around the door. 'I'm leaving for the station, Bel.'

'Okay.' I swing my legs round onto the floor. 'I'm up.'

The rhythm of our week is set, if not quite in stone

then in jelly. I mostly work on Mondays, Tuesdays and Wednesdays and that means Vera has wraparound care those days: breakfast club and a choice of after-school activities. She never complains because Lily also attends those days. Rachel runs a couple of the after-school clubs so Carys joins the girls then too.

I have a quick shower and get dressed in my usual practical clothes: chinos, flat shoes and a crisp, cotton blouse. (I like ironing.) I rarely wear make-up. My granny always called me her 'wee pixie' and I've stayed that way. I'm a Scottish Mia Farrow without the acting career or all those children.

When I come downstairs, Vera is waiting for me at the front door. She's drawing hearts on the small black-board pinned to the wall where I write shopping lists and things not to forget.

'Morning, poppet.' I kiss the top of her head. 'You ready for school?' She doesn't reply. She's busy shading in the hearts. 'One minute,' I say. I grab my bag and keys from the living room and come back to the front door. 'Do you have your lunch box?'

'Daddy gave it to me.' She finishes the final heart and puts the chalk on the ledge. 'Did you find out who's writing the notes?'

'No, but Mrs Fleming asked the parents to speak to their children.' I open the front door and she follows me out onto the step. 'Hopefully we'll find out that way.'

She looks up at me, her expression thoughtful. 'Mrs Fleming will find out because she finds everything out.'

'I'm sure you're right.' We walk to the car, Vera taking the long way round so that she can check on the vege-table beds that she's been working on with Miro. 'It must be very upsetting for Lily,' I call across to her. 'Do you talk about it, the three of you?'

'No, because it makes Lily sad,' she calls back.

'No wonder,' I say. 'All looking well with the beetroot?'

'More little shoots are coming up,' she says, her tone bright. 'Daddy said they would.'

We climb into the car and I start the engine. The journey to school takes less than two minutes and when we get there Vera gives me a quick kiss on the cheek and then I watch her walk to the main door where one of the teachers is welcoming the children inside. Her gait leans slightly to one side so that every fourth or fifth step she makes a limp-shuffle movement to try to straighten up.

I was pleased to hear her talk about netball this morning. She's always been keen on sport and doesn't allow her disability to get her down. She was born at twenty-six weeks and spent her first three months in an incubator. We were told she had been starved of oxygen and would only walk with support and would most probably never be toilet trained. I still have a detailed memory of the moment we were told this, Vera only six months old, both doctor and nurse suitably sombre, their faces alternating sympathy and watchfulness.

'But she's not going to die?' I said at once and Miro gripped my hand so tightly that I shook him off.

No, no, she wasn't going to die. She would be compromised, that's all.

I smiled at them both, at Miro who had tears running down his face, at my baby girl swaddled to the nines in a soft tartan blanket my granny had knitted. 'She'll walk,' I said. 'I know she will.'

They were sceptical, these medics and Miro and my family and my friends and everyone I knew. They wanted me to manage my expectations. I get that. But if there's a fight to be had, I'm on the front line with my wits

49

about me and a spear in my hand. I wasn't doing it to prove people wrong – I didn't and don't care about that. I was doing it for Vera. There are close to eight billion people on the planet and I gave birth to one of them. How could I not fight for her right to walk and talk and benefit from a normal childhood?

I listen to Barack Obama's autobiography as I drive to work, inspired by the dignity and intelligence of the man. I'm a white woman, living in the south east of England, a hospital pharmacist, specialising in cancer treatment. My life couldn't be more different from his but, in the ways that matter, I aspire to have his wisdom and equanimity.

Of course as soon as I think this I'm tested. Robin is standing in the car park talking to a paramedic. I know his reputation as a doctor is unimpeachable. But as a man? I've never warmed to him. I've always found him distant and a bit superior, as if spending time with the rank and file bores him. Nina deserves a way better husband than this, someone who will support her and the girls instead of constantly ducking out to be here or there or anywhere else but at home.

My attention stays on him until he's inside the building. If he is having an affair then it's statistically likely to be someone from work. I might just start keeping an eye on him.

From a distance.

There's no harm in that. I'm sure even Obama would agree with me there.

Chapter Six

During my lunch break, I buy a pregnancy test. My period is over two weeks late and I don't sense that it's on the way. I pee on the stick and then sit in the cubicle waiting. I keep my eyes shut until I've counted down the seconds and then I stare at the stick quickly, as if taking it by surprise – my gaze urgent and sudden – will influence the result.

It doesn't.

The test is negative.

I sigh, let my head slump forward.

Miro will be disappointed. I'm disappointed too but somehow my disappointment doesn't really count because I know his need is greater than mine. All these years when he wanted another child and I resisted. And now, with my fortieth birthday on the horizon, it's looking as if it's too late.

I won't tell him yet.

As soon as I'm outside the loo, I call him to say hello. We do this most lunchtimes to hear each other's voices, anchor ourselves to one another like two ships on the high seas. We never talk for long, just enough for a quick check-in.

'How's it going?' I say.

'Nina was on the train this morning.'

'Did you sit beside her?'

'We waved. She was up in first class, doing work on her laptop.'

'Did she look okay?'

'Fine. We walked through Victoria Station together. We didn't talk about school. You know she's selling her company?'

'She told me, yeah.' My hand shakes as I remember the negative test. I should tell him. Now. 'What do you fancy for tea?'

'You've got your women's workshop haven't you?'

'Oh, no. Yes.' I sigh. 'I forgot about that.' It's the group run by Aimee. Not my favourite but I made a promise to Rachel, and Nina did too, so I have to go. I can't let my friends down. 'I'll make it before I leave.'

'I'm having sushi for lunch,' he says. 'Chicken?'

'I'll do your mum's sweet and sour recipe.' *To make up for not being pregnant.*

'Yes!' He gives a whoop; it's his favourite. 'I'll look forward to that.'

'Love you.'

'Love you too.'

I go back into work and almost immediately begin to chair a meeting focusing on one of the drug trials we're hoping to run, a treatment for a rare sarcoma that is showing promising results in Belgium and Germany. The trial will have to be approved by NICE or else the funds raised privately. Neither will be easy so we spend time during the meeting making sure our stats and supporting research is sound. When we have a break, I tell my colleagues I'm going for a walk. 'To get my steps up,' I say, pointing to the Fitbit on my wrist. And that's half of the reason. The other half is that I want to keep my eye on Robin, but when I go up to High Dependency Unit, on the pretext of checking out one of their drug regimens, he's nowhere to be seen.

It's just before five o'clock when I'm back at school to collect Vera. I'm a few minutes early so I wait for her inside the building close to where her design technology club is held. There are a couple of other mums waiting too. I smile at them both and they half-smile back. Neither of them speak to me because a couple of years ago we had an argument about vaccinations. I normally try to steer clear of this topic, but that day, I couldn't help myself. When I was eight, we lost my brother to meningitis. Had he been alive today, he would have been vaccinated and he would have lived. Nina turned up just as my blood began to boil and I accused one of the mums of wilfully endangering her child's life. The sight of Nina's face when she heard me say this brought me to my senses and I immediately apologised.

Afterwards Nina reminded me that everyone is entitled to their own opinion and to make their own choices. And when I'm with her I believe that. But then when I'm back in the hospital and am reminded of how paper-thin the membrane between life and death can be, I grow angry again because the loss of a child is devastating and my brother's death changed my life forever. Before he died I was a happy-go-lucky child, outgoing and full of giggles. After his death, I buried my head in books, became aloof and distant as I couldn't bear to witness my mum fall apart. She lost all of her confidence and smiles. She grew weepy, insubstantial, fragile as a raindrop on a leaf, always about to fall to the ground or evaporate.

If my brother hadn't died, perhaps my mum would have stayed away from the drink and my character would have naturally drifted towards a more benign, smiley version of me. But, as it is, I don't have to dig very deep to find my fire.

Vera comes out of the classroom last because she burnt her finger on the glue gun again and had to run it under cold water. She shows it to me and I agree it will have blistered by morning.

'Did Lily not stay for design tech?' I ask her when we're in the car.

'No.' She hesitates before adding, 'Because there was another note.'

'What? How come?' I glance round at her. 'What did it say?'

'I don't know because she didn't notice until three o'clock and then she was crying because Max got the blame and Mrs Fleming called Nina and she wasn't there because she was in London so Harry came instead because he has no lessons on a Wednesday afternoon.' She takes a breath. 'Did you bring something to eat?'

'That's awful. Geez! Poor Lily.' I shake my head. 'So is it Max who's been writing the notes?'

'I'm so hungry!'

'We'll be home in less than a minute!'

'I'm counting down.' She begins a loud count from sixty backwards and reaches nineteen as we pull up in front of our house. 'Can I have crisps?'

'How about a banana?'

'Mini cheddars?'

The negotiations go back and forth until we agree on a handful of peanuts. 'Dinner will be ready in less than twenty minutes,' I tell her. 'So don't start playing any online games.'

I quickly call Nina's mobile but it goes straight to voicemail so I begin preparing one meal for Vera and another for Miro. Vera is a picky eater – always has been – so despite all my parenting instincts, I often take the line of least resistance and give her exactly what I know she'll eat: plain pasta quills, carrot batons, a tablespoon of sweetcorn and another of grated cheese, each portion in separate piles on the plate.

When her pasta's ready, I sit down opposite her with a bowl of grapes and a cup of tea. 'Is that all you're having?' she asks me, as if she is the mum.

'I had a big lunch.' I'm still thinking about the bombshell she dropped when I collected her. 'So another note, huh?'

She gives me a tired look. 'I don't want to talk about it, Mummy.' She carefully squeezes ketchup onto the plate between the pasta and the carrots before adding, 'It makes me sad.'

'Okay. I'm sorry.' I take her hand and kiss it. 'What would you like to talk about?'

'Erm . . .' She stares up at the ceiling before saying, 'My name!'

'Well.' I smile. This is a conversation we often have. She loves to be reminded of how her name connects with the wider family. 'As you know, your dad has four sisters but none of them were called after their mum, so when you came along, Daddy said you had to be Vera, after his mum, your *babunia*.'

'No one else in the whole school is called Vera.' She dips a carrot baton into the tomato sauce and uses it as a pencil to write the letters of her name around the edge of the plate before biting off the end. 'So people always know it's me.'

'And do you like that?' I ask.

'Carys says that if I meet a boy called Aloe then we'll be aloe vera and we'll be joined forever like you and Dad.'

I laugh. 'I'm not sure Aloe is a boy's name but you never know.'

'It could be his nickname.' She sits back in her seat and smiles at me. 'Tell me again about you and Dad.'

I tell her again, about how we met as gap students on a ski season in Méribel. A friend instantly sandwiched our names together and henceforth we were known as Mirobel, invited everywhere as a couple. Meant to be. Joined at the hip. From hello, nice to meet you, to boyfriend and girlfriend in less than twenty-four hours. We were in neighbouring chalets where we cooked and cleaned for the guests and stole a couple of hours in the afternoon to ski together. We were both from Glasgow. His family were Polish and mine were Irish so we were both raised as Catholics. We attended different schools but still, how had we never met? How had we gone through the whole of our teens without being drawn together when the magnetism between us was so strong?

'And is aloe vera a place in France?' Vera asks.

'No, it's a plant,' I tell her, reaching across with a piece of kitchen roll to wipe sauce off her cheek. 'A healing plant, very good for the skin and for digestion.' I turn to look at the clock on the wall. 'Eleri's looking after you until Daddy gets home. She'll be here in a wee while.' Eleri is Rachel's eldest daughter, my go-to babysitter.

'Eleri's going out with Harry,' Vera says, her eyes following the swirls of sauce on her plate.

'Harry who?' I ask.

'Harry!' She widens her eyes. 'Lily's half-brother.'

'Of course!' I nod. 'I've met him at Nina's. He seems like a very nice lad.'

'We saw them kissing.' She grins. 'Me and Lily and Carys.'

'You were spying on them?'

'Not *spying*.' Vera pushes her plate away. 'We just saw them round the corner and then we hid. They didn't know we were watching.'

'That makes it all right then, does it? The three amigos out gathering intel.'

'Daddy says it's good to pay attention to what's going on around you.'

'He's right. It is.' I stand up and take the dishes over to the sink.

'Is Carys coming too?'

'Not on a school night, poppet.'

'Why not?' She sits back in her seat, her bottom lip jutting out. Every other Friday Miro and I go out on a date night and Carys always comes with her sister. 'We could have done our homework together.'

'I'm sorry, Vera, but she can come at the weekend.'

'Lily too?'

'Of course.'

She gets down from her chair and takes a second to steady herself before crossing over to the door. 'Is it because of the notes?' she asks. 'Is that why you're going out again?'

I pause stacking the dishwasher to give her my full attention. 'It's our women's group, remember?'

'Where you discuss your feelings?'

'Kind of.' I roll my eyes. 'I don't find that sort of thing easy so mostly I stay quiet.'

'Good luck with that.' Her cheeks dimple and she leaves the room, calling back, 'You like yourself better when you don't argue with people!'

'You sound like your dad!' I shout, smiling to myself. Thankfully, I'm more likely to fall asleep at the group than I am to pick a fight with anyone. I go upstairs to change and come back down to find a missed call from Nina and a text saying:

Another note in the school bag. We need to talk. See you at 6.45 xx

I'm about to call her again when the bell goes and the door opens. 'It's only me!' Eleri comes inside. She is sweet sixteen, hard working and glass half-full. She has sailed through her teenage years and Rachel and Bryn are rightly proud of her.

'Hi, love.' I give her a hug. 'Did you have time to eat something?' I ask her.

'I did, thanks, Bel.' She slides her shoes off in the hallway. 'I had dinner at home so I'm fine.'

'Miro will be back in an hour and a half tops.'

She nods. 'After Vera's done her homework I thought we might walk over the fields to Lily's house, if that's okay with you?'

'Rain is forecast so you might get caught in it,' I reply. And then I remember. 'Is Harry babysitting?' I glance at my feet, trying not to make it obvious that I know.

Eleri stares back shyly. 'Who told you?'

'You know what nine-year-old girls are like.' I tilt my head. 'They thrive on gossip.'

'We're just friends, really. Well.' She smiles to herself. 'Maybe a bit more than that but please don't tell my mum! I'm planning for Harry to meet them at the weekend. It'll be a surprise.'

'I'm sure they'll be delighted. I know Nina and the girls love him.' I lean on the banister and tip my head to one side to call upstairs, 'Vera! Eleri is here!' She appears almost at once, clattering down the stairs, magazine in her hand, page open for her to show Eleri an article.

I leave them to it and get back into the car. The women's group meets in the community hall in the neighbouring village, and I live the furthest away so I collect Rachel and Nina en route. Rachel is ready on the step when I pull up in front of her house.

'That was a bit of a rush!' She collapses onto the back seat. 'Carys wanted me to help her with her homework. Luckily Bryn came to the rescue because I can't concentrate after six in the evening.' She pulls at the seatbelt and locks it in place. 'Did Eleri arrive okay?'

'Yeah. She's so reliable.' I indicate right and drive along the lane leading to Nina's. 'Vera loves having her to babysit.'

'She's saving up her money to travel after her A levels. I think she might have a secret boyfriend but we're yet to be introduced.'

It's on the tip of my tongue to tell her it's Harry but I manage not to. It's not my news to share.

Nina is also waiting outside and when I stop beside her, she immediately climbs into the front seat. 'Are you okay?' I ask at once. 'What does the latest note say?'

'There was another note?' Rachel leans forward. 'When? Today?'

'Let's not talk about it yet,' Nina says, her tone weary. 'I've had an hour of comforting an upset Lily, no Robin despite the fact he'd promised to be home in time to talk to her, and Poppy winding me up about a dog.' She briefly closes her eyes, her head dropping back against the headrest. 'And breathe,' she says, sighing on the out breath. Then she turns to me and smiles. 'So what else is new?'

'Miro's in for a disappointment,' I blurt out. 'My period's late but I did a pregnancy test and it was negative.'

'Oh, I'm sorry.' I feel the comfort of Rachel's hand on my shoulder. 'I know how much you both want this.'

'I'm pushing forty! Time is running out!' I give a short laugh. 'I shouldn't think my eggs are up to much. I imagine them limping along the fallopian tube, short-sighted, gammy-legged.'

'Maybe that's where you're going wrong,' Nina says, her hand touching my knee.

'I should be visualising a happy, healthy egg, bouncing along like a rubber ball?'

'There's probably a visualisation that lies between those two extremes,' she says and I laugh, glance across at her. I expect her to be smiling but she isn't, the look on her face is one I can't quite place – somewhere between unease and pity.

It makes me shrink inside.

Chapter Seven

I'm not a joiner. I'm in a book group at work – a serious one, all about the words, not the wine because the reading bug has kept me gripped since childhood – but apart from that I don't function well in groups. I start to feel uncomfortable and invariably say the wrong thing at the wrong time. Still, Harry's mum Aimee is lovely, and we joined this group for Rachel not for me. She lost her mum suddenly a couple of years ago and she has struggled to cope. The group has really worked for her and, in truth, I often feel a genuine sense of wellbeing afterwards. And it should take my mind off the negative pregnancy test. Maybe Nina is right and I need to think positively instead of assuming the worst.

The meetings always follow the same structure: quiet meditation for the first ten minutes, then Aimee introduces a topic of discussion for fifty minutes, followed by tea and cake and more relaxed chat for a further thirty.

Aimee is petite, red-haired and kind-eyed. She wears leggings and tight crop tops as if she's ever ready for a yoga class. She covers up with long, colourful cashmere cardigans that must have once cost a fortune but are now drooping at the edges. Despite this, or maybe because of it, she manages to look stylish, her hoop earrings and tumble of hair finishing the look.

As soon as we arrive she gives Nina a warm hug. 'Here's the pot you asked for,' Nina says passing her a bag. 'I've got an even bigger one at home if you need it.'

'Thank you so much.' Aimee glances down into the bag. 'This is perfect.' She leans back to regard Nina in much the way a mother scrutinises her child's every feature. 'You look pale, Nina. Is everything okay?'

I don't hear Nina's reply because it's drowned out by the sound of other women arriving. I've always admired the way Nina and Aimee get along, putting Harry first and being there for each other. Nina is one of those people who can rise above circumstances that would floor most of us.

As creatures of habit we sit where we always do, Rachel, Nina and I making a beeline for the spot in the circle that's closest to the window. It's only twenty-four hours since the parents' meeting and I'm keen to find out what the latest note says but as I reach across to ask Nina, Aimee begins.

'We have a new member joining us this week,' she says, indicating a point halfway round the circle. My eyes follow and widen, not quite believing what they see. It's Maxine Mayfair. I hadn't even noticed her. She's less glamorous than she usually is. She's wearing grey clothes, no make-up and is blending into the chair as if she is of no account.

'Welcome, Maxine,' several women murmur.

I glance sideways at Nina. If Maxine's son has been writing the notes then this might be difficult for Nina but, as ever, she appears serene.

'Let's begin by acknowledging where we are within

62

ourselves,' Aimee says. 'Whatever worries or negativity we are holding on to, be it in our thoughts, in our hearts or in our bodies, this is the time to let go.' Her voice is light and encouraging. I automatically close my eyes, hands lying loose on my lap. 'Become aware of your breath.' She pauses while we do this. 'Breathe in through your nose . . . hold for the count of three . . . and then breathe out through your mouth.'

I do exactly this and feel a sense of wellbeing permeate through me. If you'd told me a few years ago that I'd be sitting in a circle with a dozen other women, breathing in and out to the beat of my own inner drum, I'd have laughed at you. But now I'm hooked.

Ten minutes pass and the feeling in the room – or is it just in me? – has subtly changed. The air seems to have expanded somehow to accommodate a more relaxed feel.

'So.' Aimee's smile includes each and every one of us. 'After last week's session on childhood patterns, it feels like a natural progression to talk about what it means to know ourselves.' She gives us some stats on mental health and how this can feed into our relationships, especially parenting. 'Children show us our blind spots, don't they? They help us to reflect on our own bias and limitations but it's worth remembering that they also show us where we shine.'

'My children have challenged me a lot over the years,' one woman remarks. 'At times a bit too much.' She gives a wry laugh. 'But I'm not sure where I'd be without them.'

'Since I've become a grandmother, I've grown closer to my mothering instinct again,' another woman says. 'I'm much better this time round, not just because I can hand them back but because I feel wiser.' She gives a surprised smile as she says this, as if it's only just occurred to her.

'I'd love to know myself better,' Maxine says. 'But I guess I'm just tired.'

I'm surprised to hear her speak and I stare across at her, waiting for what will come next.

'I'm tired of everything, really,' she says, as if someone has just asked her to elaborate. 'Of husbands and kids, work and mortgages, and loan payments, and having to get up every morning and put on my make-up, and not eat what I want to eat and . . .' She trails off, then glances round the circle, taking in each of our faces before adding, 'Thank you for letting me join your group. I'm sorry if this isn't the right thing to say. I don't want to be negative.'

Several voices reassure her that being honest is what we're about, and then Aimee adds, 'Remember this is a safe space, Maxine. Where we hold each other's truths with respect.'

'Okay.' She nods, pleased to be given permission. 'My son is in trouble at school and I'm not sure how to make it better.'

I glance sideways at Nina and notice that although she is lounging back on the chair, her posture seemingly relaxed, her hands are clasped tightly on her lap.

'I feel that he's being picked on,' Maxine continues. 'Unfairly marked out as a troublemaker when he's anything but.'

'That's very worrying,' a woman called Sarah remarks. 'Who's marking him out?'

'The teacher,' Maxine says. 'She has it in for him.'

Nina shifts in her seat. I have the feeling she's going to walk out but she doesn't. She lifts her bag onto her lap and starts to rummage through it. The sound is disruptive and Aimee glances across at her, her expression questioning. I have an urgent sense that everything is about to go pear-shaped. I can't bear the thought of Nina breaking down in front of these women so I blurt out the first thing that comes into my head. 'I think it was Edith Wharton,' I state loudly, 'who said all people are great estates and we can only know that aspect of a person that butts up against us.'

'Interesting.' Aimee nods and then frowns. She looks at Maxine then back to me as if trying to work out how my statement ties in with what Maxine has just shared. 'So, Bel, you're saying that we can never really know anyone?'

'We can know aspects of a person. We can predict how a person might behave based on our past experience but we can't be sure. I mean—' I speak directly to Aimee '—I know you as a facilitator for this group. I don't know you as a work colleague, a daughter or mother or sexual partner. I know what I see here but I don't know any more than that. The rest I make up. I fill in the blanks.'

Silence. A few people are nodding but most are baffled. I don't blame them. I'm rambling on because I'm experiencing a slow, creeping anxiety. 'People are complex,' I finish lamely and glance at Nina. Her bag is back on the floor and her arms are crossed.

'I think Bel has a point.' Nina comes to my rescue. 'We all make up our minds about each other. And we need to be careful of that. But conversely, I think that if someone consistently shows you who they are then you need to stop giving them the benefit of the doubt and listen.'

Is she talking to Maxine? Does Nina mean that she needs to stop making excuses for her son?

'Could you expand on that?' Aimee says. She looks as unsure as I feel.

'Well, there's someone in my life who consistently lets me down and instead of me admitting this, I have pretended, made excuses, acted as if it will all be okay just because I want it to be.'

I get it, then. It must be Robin she's talking about.

Aimee's nodding. 'Does this chime with anyone?'

Several women say it does and they begin to tell us about their lives, about the people who have let them down and what they have learned from that. I try to relax again, to regain the ease I felt after the ten-minute meditation. Except that Maxine is sitting in this circle and I feel in my bones that she has more to say. Maybe she simply wants to share her disappointment with Mrs Fleming, or garner sympathy for Max, but I doubt it. I feel like she's here to challenge Nina.

'I'm not sure I'm brave enough to see my daughter objectively,' one woman is saying. We know from previous meetings that her daughter has a drug problem. 'Because if I face the facts, then I'll have to do something about it, be tougher on her, and that will be hard.'

'We all live with compromise,' Nina says. 'It just depends where we draw the line.'

I'm watching Maxine as Nina says this and when she opens her mouth to comment, I say loudly, 'Do I dare disturb the universe?' Several faces stare at me blankly. 'T.S. Eliot. I love his poetry.' I sense Nina's eyes on the side of my head. 'I completed an Open University degree a couple of years ago,' I add. 'English literature.' Nina reaches across and touches my hand. The look on her face tells me that I needn't worry. She's got this.

'To get back to my son,' Maxine says loudly. 'He's been accused of bullying, and I think it's unfair. I mean, don't get me wrong, I'm not saying he's perfect! But I don't think it was him.' Maxine stares in our direction, eyes fixing on Nina. 'Hiding behind notes. It's just not his style.'

Aimee is becoming increasingly concerned by the looks that are passing between Maxine and Nina. I watch as the penny drops and she frowns. 'Sorry, Maxine, but if you have something specific to discuss with another member of the group then this forum is not the best space for that.'

'It's okay,' Nina says, her tone light. 'What did you want to say, Maxine?'

'Well, just that Mrs Fleming's got it wrong! Max is a naughty boy sometimes, we know that but, in this case, I think he's being picked on.' Her voice wavers. 'I think Lily's a lovely little girl and I'm really sorry this is happening but I can't stand by and allow my son to be the scapegoat.'

I glance at Nina who has returned to being an oasis of calm, her face relaxed, her eyes sympathetic. Rachel, on the other hand, looks as if she's holding her breath. Her eyes meet mine and open wider as if to say, *What the fuck is going on?*

Aimee is waiting for Nina to speak but Maxine adds, 'This last note, for example, why would Max write something like that?'

Nina stares down at her feet and once more I'm curious about what this fourth note says.

'What is this about?' one of the women asks. 'Can you share with the group?'

'We four have children in the same year,' Nina says, pointing to Maxine and then Rachel and I. She goes on to explain about the notes and the parent-teacher meeting. 'It's become a big deal. I wish it hadn't but my daughter is struggling to cope and so I had to involve Mrs Fleming, her class teacher.'

'So what do the notes say?' someone else asks.

'That the class has secrets,' Nina replies, and then she sighs as if she's had enough of the whole thing.

'And the rest,' Maxine adds sharply. Her voice is really loud now. 'Today there was one about dead babies.' There's a collective gasp when she says this. 'My son wouldn't write anything like that. I know he wouldn't.'

'Dead babies?' I mouth at Rachel and she shrugs.

Nina glances at Aimee before saying, 'Perhaps we *should* take this conversation elsewhere, Maxine?'

'Why?' she snaps. 'So your friends don't hear? I thought this meeting was about honesty?'

'Okay.' Aimee swivels towards her. 'I can see that you're upset, Maxine.' Her expression is sympathetic, her tone firm. 'But this is neither the time nor the place.'

'I'm sorry.' Maxine shrinks back as if stung, pulling her legs underneath the chair, her arms into her body. 'I'm sorry, everyone.' Her chin is down so when she looks across at Nina, it's up through her lashes, a Princess Diana-like glance of shy apology. 'I'm sorry, Nina.'

'I understand you're upset. I feel the same way,' Nina tells her flatly. 'But I don't want to discuss it any further.'

'I suggest we move on.' Aimee's tone is brisk now. She gives a small clap of her hands. 'I wonder whether any of you had a chance to read the article I mentioned last time?'

The article was called 'Rethinking Ageing' and was all about staying socially and intellectually engaged. It's an easier topic and everyone has their own experience to share. Everyone except the mothers of Year Five children. The four of us don't add to the discussion but sit quietly instead, glancing at each other every now and then. Finally it's time for tea and cake and I breathe a sigh of relief.

'Should we just make a break for it now?' I suggest to Nina and Rachel.

'The pub?' Rachel says, her expression brightening.

'I think we should stay,' Nina says, her eyes steely. 'I'm going to have a word with Maxine.' She turns to survey the room, spotting her in the far corner. 'Wish me luck.'

'Nina.' I stop her with a hand on her arm. 'What was that about dead babies?'

A shadow passes across her face. 'I think it's better if we wait until after the meeting. You could all come back to mine?'

Rachel and I both nod our agreement and then we get swept into a conversation with Aimee and a couple of others. Every now and then my eyes are drawn to Nina and Maxine. Maxine's arms are folded and she's moving from one foot to another, barely speaking. Nina's body language is forever Nina – calm, open, inclusive. She's doing more of the talking.

After ten minutes they both go outside and I see them through the window. Nina is holding her phone out between them. It looks like she has it on speaker because every now and then Maxine leans forward, arms still folded, to talk into the handset. Immediately after the call, Maxine drives off and Nina comes back inside, her expression giving nothing away.

Chapter Eight

NINA

'That was intense,' Rachel says as soon as we reach the car.

'I mean, what the hell? Why did Aimee let Maxine into the group?' Bel says.

'She didn't know about the history,' Rachel says. 'She can't be blamed for that.'

'I suppose.' Bel looks round at me. I'm in the back this time. 'Are you okay, Nina?'

I nod. 'Let's just get back to mine and have a drink.'

I don't speak at all on the journey home. The drive back to the village is along narrow country lanes where trees grow either side and meet in the middle, barely above the roof of the car. It's murky, eerie and suffocating, until we turn a bend and drive out of the valley, climbing higher and higher towards the ridge.

Bel has to do an emergency stop as four young stags cross the road in front of us. They move casually, staring at us with interest, antlers proud, dark eyes large and unblinking. 'Almost two hundred and seventy-six,' Bel says under her breath, referring to the number of collisions so far this year, the sign regularly updated by the conservators of the forest. We see the sign every time we drive to the supermarket. Lily is always upset at the thought of another deer dying; Poppy more inclined to think about the people in the car. It's their territory, Lily will say. Not ours.

Bel drives along the ridge at the top of the forest where the vista is far-reaching, north towards London and south towards the Downs and beyond that, France. The sun is setting in a spectacular show of colour: pink, gold and red melding into hot fire and earthy, rich orange. I feel so lucky to live here, surrounded by nature in all her glory.

Robin isn't home yet, just as I thought, despite the fact that he'd agreed to chat to Lily tonight. How can he be so good with his patients and yet so careless with his own children? I thank Harry for watching the girls and see him out the door, then go into the kitchen where Bel has poured three glasses of wine from a bottle I had chilling in the fridge. 'So, tell us,' she says. 'What did Maxine have to say for herself?'

I take a greedy mouthful of wine and sit up on a stool opposite my two friends, wishing this could all just go away, that we could go back to the everyday minutiae of our lives. 'She's upset because Mrs Fleming caught Max with his hand in Lily's bag, and there was another note inside. Lily hadn't seen it so Mrs Fleming thought he must have been putting it in there.'

'So it was him,' Rachel says, her tone hushed with shock.

'Maxine says not.' I take another gulp of wine. 'We called Mrs Fleming when we were outside. I asked her not to speak to the youth officer about it yet. She's agreed for now.'

'You don't look convinced,' Bel says. 'You don't think it was him?'

'I don't know what to think! Lily was really upset this

evening. She's sure it can't be him. She seemed more upset about Max being accused than another note turning up.'

'What does it say?' Rachel asks.

I hesitate, glance at Bel who looks as eager as Rachel to find out what's been written.

I bring the note out of my back pocket and pass it across the breakfast bar to them. The room is still as they read the scrawl.

Your mums best friend killed a baby and her husband doesn't know

'Eh?' Rachel frowns across at me. 'What's that supposed to mean?'

I don't speak. I'm waiting for Bel's reaction. She has a sixth sense, always has. She knows when I'm down, when I'm covering up or just plain fed up. And she knows when there's trouble ahead. I'm sure that both times she spoke at the meeting this evening were because she was anxious. She knew a shock was coming; she just didn't know the how and why of it.

Now she does.

Bel hands the paper back to me, not meeting my eye. Her lips are pale and trembling. Her eyes fill with tears. I reach across to her but she pulls back, both hands in fists.

'I don't understand,' Rachel says, her head swivelling quickly as she looks at Bel and then me and back to Bel again. 'What am I missing?'

'It's about me,' Bel says quietly.

'You haven't killed a baby!' Rachel says, her tone astonished. 'That's ridiculous!'

'Rachel.' I hold her hand across the breakfast bar. 'We

need . . .' I can't finish the sentence because I'm anxious that this thing – spite, cruelty, bullying; I don't know what to call it – is running away from us. 'We need to take a breath.'

'But . . .' Her eyes are wide. 'What's going on?'

'Apart from you two, nobody else knows that I had an abortion,' Bel says, her tone low.

Rachel gasps. 'That can't be what it means!' Her eyes squint as if she's staring into the sun. 'Nina?'

'I think Bel's right,' I say softly.

'I'm one of Nina's best friends. Everyone knows that.' Bel's voice is so quiet that Rachel and I lean in to hear her better. 'I told you both about the abortion a few years ago when we were at the spa. I have *never* told anyone except the two of you.' Her eyes are narrowed when she stares up at us. 'Who did you tell?'

'Bel, don't.' I move to the other side of the breakfast bar and place myself between her and Rachel whose face has flushed, a rash of red spreading from her neck to her cheeks.

'You know I tell Bryn everything.' Rachel's indrawn breath is a gulp of tears. 'But he would never say anything. He just wouldn't! He's not a gossip. You know that!'

Bel scrapes her stool across the tiled floor, the sound so sharp and scratchy that it sends a shiver down my spine. The door to the downstairs loo slams shut behind her.

'Nina, abortion isn't baby killing!' Rachel whispers, grabbing my arm. 'It's perfectly legal. And she was only eight weeks pregnant.'

'Some people call it killing though, don't they?' I say, wondering why Rachel doesn't get it.

'Anti-abortion groups and—' she searches for the right reference '—other people . . . with very strong views on when life begins. They're extreme though, aren't they?'

'Bel and Miro are Catholics. You know how involved they are with the church.'

'I forget she's religious.' Rachel's eyes drift as she thinks about this. 'It's not something she talks about.'

'At the spa, she told us how much she regretted having the abortion.' I bite my lip. 'This will bring back all the pain and the guilt.'

Rachel takes a shaky breath. 'What can we do to help her?'

'Listen to her. Try to understand.' I smile. 'All the things you're good at.'

'Am I?' She blinks away tears. 'Is it okay that I told Bryn? She didn't ask us not to, did she?'

'Not explicitly.' I give Rachel a hug and she holds on to me, not letting go until we hear the bathroom door open.

Bel comes back into the kitchen. Her expression is stormy, her short hair sticking up as if she's been pulling at it. 'If Miro finds out about the abortion he'll leave me.' Her teeth are chattering. She grabs for her wine but when she begins to drink, her teeth bite down on the glass and a chunk breaks off. Within seconds she has blood on her lips and when she coughs, blood splatters onto her raised hand.

Rachel and I both step forward to help her. Rachel takes the wine glass out of her hand and I lead her to the sink. I turn the tap on and she spits the broken piece into the sink, red blood turning pink when it mixes with the water. She washes her hands then scoops cold water into her mouth, swirling and spitting until the blood flow lessens.

'I think you might have cut your tongue,' I say, handing her a pad of tissues. 'Are you sure there's no glass embedded in it?'

'I'm fine.' She walks past me and stands at the window, the tissues wedged between her steepled fingers that she balances beneath her chin. Her eyes close and she rocks back and forward, her lips moving in what I assume is a silent prayer. Since I read the note, my mind has been racing ahead to who could have known about the abortion. I didn't tell Robin – I didn't tell anyone – and I'm sorry that Rachel told Bryn. He's not vindictive but, like any of us, he might have let it slip without meaning to.

Rachel takes the broken glass from the sink and matches it with the wine glass. 'There's a tiny piece missing,' she says quietly.

Bel ignores her. She also ignores the slow trickle of blood travelling down her chin onto the white tissue, staining it red. Rachel gathers some more tissues and moves towards Bel to give them to her but at the last second she hesitates. She glances at me for help and I place a hand under Bel's elbow before saying gently, 'This is horrible for you, hon. I'm so sorry.'

Bel doesn't respond and Rachel's voice is shaky when she says, 'I don't understand why we're being targeted like this!'

Bel's eyes snap towards her. 'You're not being targeted, Rachel.'

'But I might be next.'

'Why? How? What are you hiding? Oh, I remember.' She taps her head, eyes wide, feigning a light-bulb moment. 'You have a secret.'

Rachel's eyes immediately fill with tears. 'It's not . . . I haven't . . .'

'It's not? You haven't?' Bel's voice is growing louder, mocking Rachel. 'It's not worth sharing? You haven't even told Bryn? Yet five minutes ago you said you tell Bryn everything.'

'I haven't told Bryn because—' She stops on a sob.

'Because what, Rachel? Because *what*?'

Her tone is vindictive and it makes me wince. 'Bel.' I try to grab her attention by pulling her elbow but she shrugs me off. 'Please! Enough now,' I say.

'I tell you something *deeply* personal, *in* confidence, and *that's* what you share with him.' Bel's finger stabs the air close to Rachel's face, and then she impatiently rubs the blood off her chin. 'Not anything about yourself. Never that!'

'You can't make this my fault!'

'At the spa day, Nina told us about Robin's affair and I told you about the abortion. But you didn't share anything, Rachel!' She's shouting now. 'So what *is* your big secret, the one that even Bryn doesn't know?'

Rachel can't speak. She has turned her back on us, her shoulders heaving as she cries into a tissue. I take a tight hold of Bel and turn her towards me, forcing her to look at me. 'Rachel didn't do this. She isn't writing the notes,' I state loudly. 'And there is no sense in her telling us what she wants to keep private.'

'Solidarity? Isn't that why women share their feelings? To deepen an existing friendship?' Bel shouts. 'She's just a fucking spectator!'

'Stop it, Bel!' She recoils at my raised voice, falling back a couple of steps so that she bumps her arm on the windowpane. She stands rubbing her elbow and I wait a second until her eyes meet mine again. 'Bryn won't have told anyone. He probably forgot about it seconds later,' I say quietly, mentally crossing my fingers that I'm right about this. 'He's a man's man. You know he is.'

She pulls away from me then and walks across to the sink to rinse out her mouth again. Rachel has stopped crying but her face is still turned away from the room. They are polar opposites and this isn't the first time I've had to tell one of them what the other one thinks or feels. And while I accept it's my role to do that, I want to fast-forward to a point where emotions have calmed and we can remember to have each other's backs.

For what feels like ages, the three of us stand apart. Rachel is beside the glass door that concertinas open on summer days, kitchen and garden becoming seamlessly joined. But for now there is only darkness through the glass – a dense, liquid black devoid of even a glimmer of light.

Bel remains by the sink, patting at her lip, staring at the wall of teal-coloured tiles that are the staple of modern, newly fitted kitchens everywhere. And I am standing at the opposite wall, behind the family sofa where Poppy hides her toys – all sizes of dolls, Lego models, and small china animals that belonged to me when I was a girl. If ever I suggest we give some away she is able to name and claim every last one.

I try to work out how many hours we've all been together in here, celebrating children's parties, baking for summer fetes and Christmas fairs, impromptu dance sessions with the girls or just sitting on the sofas catching up with each other's lives.

We're better than this. That's what I'm thinking when at last we all look up. Rachel's expression is pleading and Bel's is challenging. It's Bel who speaks first. 'So what about you then, Nina?' she asks, her voice silky smooth. 'One of the notes said you're a whore. Are you?'

I don't like her tone. She wants to offload some of the hurt she's feeling. She's already made Rachel cry and now she wants me weeping as well. *We need to stick together.* That's what I want to tell her but she's in no

78

mood to hear this and I'm not about to join her in her misery, so I say softly, 'No more than you're a baby killer.'

She winces at this, and then her head drops onto her chest. I don't want to rub it in – I just want her to stop with the accusations – and now that she's quiet, I immediately give ground. 'But I am keeping a secret.' Her eyes snap up to meet mine and Rachel takes a step closer. 'What I told you both at the spa was part one and now there's a part two.'

'Tell us,' Bel says, her eyes bright, hungry for a distraction from her own story. Rachel too is looking at me as if she can't wait for the reveal. My mouth tightens. *What's happening to us?*

We're supposed to be friends.

Chapter Nine

'So tell us,' Bel repeats, moving across the room towards me. 'What's part two?'

I don't answer her immediately. 'Come and sit down, Rachel,' I say quietly. At the sound of my voice she comes across to the sofa and sits down on the edge of it, as far away from Bel as she can get.

'So tell us, Nina,' Bel says for the third time, her insistence beginning to irritate me.

'Well . . . as you know, the last time Robin had an affair, he gas-lighted me, told me I was neurotic, denied everything, and to this day, I would have thought he was telling the truth had it not been for me catching him at it.' I shudder. 'Literally, coming home from work early and finding them on the sofa in the family room.'

'In flagrante,' Bel says. 'What a tosser.'

'Yup.' I shake my head against the details, images that rise up in front of me like ghosts, shagging, naked, moaning ghosts. I'd laugh if it wasn't still so shocking. 'You know that expression, fool me once shame on you?' They both nod. 'Well, I wasn't going to be fooled twice, so—' I stop talking and listen. 'Hang on.'

The living area is a double-height space with a galleried landing above the staircase that leads to the bedrooms. A four-feet-high wall runs along the length of the gallery, and behind that open space, a vantage point to look down into the living room below. On occasion the girls have hidden up there, listening in to conversations, until suddenly one of them – usually Poppy – peeps up above the parapet to make a comment. Both girls are sound sleepers (until they're not) so I decide to check on them before saying any more.

I take the carpeted stairs two at a time and look along the gallery. No small girls, just several island clusters of abandoned toys. I check their bedrooms and find them both fast asleep, Lily under mounds of teddies, Poppy spread out like a starfish. Before I go back down, I peer through the landing window out into the driveway. Still no sign of the Porsche.

When I come into the living room, I'm relieved to hear Bel saying, 'I'm sorry, Rae. I know it's not your fault. I shouldn't have gone off on one.'

'And I shouldn't have told Bryn,' she acknowledges. 'What you told us was for our ears only.' They reach across the sofa to take hands. 'But honestly, Bel, he really won't have told anyone.'

I sit down again and they both stare at me expectantly. 'As I was saying, Robin and his affair.' I raise my eyebrows. 'Well, now he's at it again but I'm one step ahead of him.'

'What?' Rachel is shocked. '*Again?* How could he? *Why?*'

'How are you ahead of him?' Bel asks, leaning forward.

'I placed a tracker on the Porsche and I've cloned his phone so that all the messages and emails he gets, are copied to my mobile.'

'Wow!' Bel falls back in the seat, her expression admiring. 'Respect, Nina.'

I incline my head. 'This time I won't be hysterical or sobbing. I'll present him with the facts and the divorce papers. I have them ready.' I shiver and pull the blanket off the back of the sofa and around my shoulders. I'm making it sound so simple, so led by my head, as if my heart has taken leave of absence and is letting me get on with it, instead of lying broken beneath his feet.

'Oh, Nina,' Rachel says, her eyes bright with tears. 'I'm so sorry it's come to this. You must be devastated.'

'It's not easy.' I blink against the gathering storm in my own eyes. 'But there are worse things.'

'Too right,' Bel says. 'You're strong. You can do this.'

'I can do it.' I try to smile. 'My worry is the girls. Although Robin isn't around that much, he is their dad, and they'll be really upset.' I pull the blanket in tighter. 'Lily's got enough going on as it is.'

'We'll help however we can,' Rachel says. 'The notes will stop. At some point. They will.'

'Thank you. I know I can rely on you both.' Even as I say this I'm not entirely sure I can rely on them and I wonder at the wisdom of telling them about the divorce papers. What if one of them were to warn Robin? Tell him about the spyware?

But why would they?

It's for the girls, I remind myself. *They need strong friendships if their parents are about to divorce.*

'There's lots of advice online on how to approach telling children about divorce,' Bel says.

I nod. 'All I can hope is that Robin will prioritise us doing it well.' I pick away at the blanket, pulling a blue thread hard until it snaps. 'He's one for making promises but not following through.'

'That's so unfair,' Rachel says quietly. She shakes her head. 'I had no idea life was this difficult for you.' She comes to sit beside me and pulls me in for a hug. I let my head drop down onto her shoulder and when she lets me go she kisses my cheek and whispers, 'You can do this, Nina. I know you can.'

'So during the parents' evening,' Bel asks. She's wearing her thinking face. 'When he said he had a late surgery—'

'He was nowhere even close to the hospital.' I give a short laugh. 'The tracker doesn't lie.'

'What a bastard,' Bel says softly.

'He's so convincing, I think he even convinces himself and ends up believing his own lies.'

'All the best liars do that,' Rachel says.

'Any idea who the woman is?' Bel asks. 'I could put some feelers out at the hospital, see whether a name comes up, find reasons to go up to the High Dependency Unit.' She hesitates. 'I went up there the other day because I had a feeling something was going on.'

'How?' I ask, wondering where this is coming from.

'Just . . . you didn't seem yourself at the pub last night. Even with the notes.'

I stare up at the ceiling where a toy monkey hangs on the light fitting, thrown from the gallery by Poppy. I know Bel is blessed with a certain intuition but still I find this unnerving because she did it without telling me first.

'I have your best interests at heart, Nina,' she says, reaching for my hand.

I look at Bel and then Rachel and see two women who share so many aspects of my life. Our children are in and out of each other's houses as if each one is their own home. We are intertwined, like clematis or ivy that have grown side by side, shoots spreading and wrapping round each other, sharing water and light. To disentangle us now would mean cutting us off at the roots.

'I hear Robin's side of his phone calls,' I say. 'He calls her M.' I try to laugh. 'And I can't help but think it's Maxine.'

'Really?' Rachel's hand goes up to her mouth. 'Oh my God.'

'Why?' Bel is leaning forward again.

'Last night his car was parked on Jubilee Road. Maxine lives there.'

'But she was at the parents' evening.'

I nod. 'That's true, but he arrived at her house about the same time as we got to the pub.' I look at Bel. 'You're right about me being upset last night. Most of it was about the notes, and feeling embarrassed, ashamed even.' They both go to speak but I shake my head. 'I know. It's not logical to feel shame but I do because who wants to be called a whore? Have it projected up onto a whiteboard for all to see? And at the back of my mind, I suspected Robin was off with his woman.'

'Jesus.' Rachel sits back, her eyes wide with sympathy.

'And that's why I won't be coming to any meeting where the parents are shown the latest note,' Bel says quietly. She stands up and goes across to the kitchen island, returning at once with three fresh glasses and the rest of the bottle. 'So the tracker gives you timings and everything?' she asks, pouring wine for us all.

'It does. It's a gift for the spouse who's being cheated on.'

'Fuck.' She shakes her head. 'I hate that you're having to go through this, Nina, but I'm really glad you're getting the jump on him.'

'There are lots of people whose names begin with M, though, aren't there?' Rachel's question is tentative. 'I mean, it's not that I don't want to believe you, but—'

'You're right. And that's exactly why I need to talk it through.'

'What else makes you think it's her?' Bel asks.

'You know she jogs along the public footpath over the hedge at the bottom of our garden? Well, at least three times during the summer she stopped to talk to Robin. I saw them from the cabin.'

'Was she was doing her look-at-my-tits dance?' Bel says.

'She was. She was all giggles and touching his arm and hanging on his every word.'

'You're so great. You're my hero,' Bel says in a breathy voice.

'It certainly looked that way. And the woman Robin had an affair with the first time was physically very similar to Maxine. A parent in Lily's nursery back in Putney, flirty and . . .'

'Brainless? Superficial?' Bel says.

'She was a bitch,' I say with more than a hint of venom. 'A real piece of work. She turned up at my door after I'd caught them at it and he'd told her it was over. She went on about how much they loved each other, gave me details of their multiple meetings.' I shudder as I tell them about the day she told me they'd had sex in my bed. I'd taken the girls to my parents' for the weekend and they spent that time shagging each other all over my house.

'That's too much,' Rachel says, her face twisting with revulsion.

'And once she even followed me to work, crashed a client meeting. I had to call security.'

'She became a stalker?' Bel asks.

'In the end, I threatened her with the police. Meanwhile Robin told me he was sorry, that it was all a mistake, that he'd tried to reason with her and now I could see how manipulative she was.'

'The innocent man,' Bel remarks. 'She made him do it. It really wasn't his fault.'

'Exactly.' I sigh, try to banish the whole experience on a long breath out. 'Anyway, I'm not a complete pushover. I forced him to accept responsibility and then we had weeks of counselling. It was a few months later that we found this house and we moved down here.' I throw the blanket to one side and jump up. 'Let me get some snacks. I'm starving all of a sudden.'

We spend the next half hour eating cheese and biscuits and working our way through another bottle. Rachel has already let Bryn know she'll be late and at ten-thirty Bel is out in the hallway doing the same with Miro. 'I'll leave the car here,' I hear her tell him. 'Bryn says he'll pick us up.'

'Maxine's husband works away a lot,' Rachel says as I pour her some more wine. 'Or so she says in her Instagram posts.'

'You should drive over there.' Bel comes back into the room. 'You can drop the girls with me or Rachel and see exactly where he goes.'

'I've been thinking about doing that,' I tell them. Bel is keen for me to confront the woman, whether it's Maxine or someone else, while Rachel advises me to bide my time. There's no easy answer and when we've exhausted the subject I steer us back to the latest note, because even when I'm talking about Robin, the problem of the notes looms large in my mind. It feels more urgent, and easier to solve, somehow. 'We need to work out how someone could have found out about the abortion, Bel. If we find the answer to that then we'll know who's writing the notes.'

Bel's face falls as she remembers what's been written about her. Her eyes fill again and she snatches at her wine glass, drinks several mouthfuls then tops it up again, her hand shaking.

'Could someone have been listening at the spa?' Rachel asks gently.

'No!' Bel snaps back, the shake of her head letting Rachel know just how stupid she thinks the suggestion is. 'We were two hundred miles from here, in the hot tub outside the chalet. The nearest accommodation was about thirty metres away.'

'Sorry, I thought . . .' Rachel's lip trembles and I catch her eye, give her what I hope is a supportive smile.

'Is it possible that someone saw your doctor's notes?' I ask Bel. 'Could it be that?'

Bel blows out a breath as she considers this. 'The anti-vaxxers have it in for me but none of them work in the GP surgery. They're too anti-establishment for that.'

'Well, there's Amira,' Rachel says. 'But she's our doctor! She's taken an oath. It can't be her.'

'Maxine and her are friends, though, aren't they?' I say.

'I'm not so sure,' Rachel says. 'Max often plays with Amira's boys but I don't know whether that makes them friends.'

'Let's presume it is Max who's writing the notes,' I say. 'Suppose that Maxine is having an affair with Robin, and Amira did discuss Bel's medical history then . . .' I trail off, not sure where I'm going with this.

'I just don't buy that,' Rachel says. 'If Maxine's having an affair with Robin then she's hardly going to discredit him by calling him a 'C U Next Tuesday.'

'Yes, but it would be Max who's writing them, not

her! If he knows what his mum's up to and doesn't like it, he might want to put a stop to it,' Bel says. 'By discrediting Robin.'

'Maybe. But that doesn't explain the last note, and I still don't think that Amira would break patient confidentiality,' Rachel replies. 'She would risk losing her job.'

We all think on this for a moment before Bel kicks off her shoes and draws her legs up underneath her. 'It doesn't matter who wrote the note.' Her tone is flat. 'And it doesn't matter how they found out. It's true, isn't it?'

'It does matter,' I say, watching despondency settle on Bel's shoulders. 'Because it's more specific than the other notes and it's a lie.'

'It's not a lie. Abortion is a mortal sin,' she tells us, her mouth tight. 'Miro and I should be parents to two children. And the irony is that here I am trying for another baby. We've had three rounds of IVF. We'll end up bankrupt. And it serves me right.' She stands up and then immediately sits back down again. 'What matters is whether or not I tell Miro now before the next note names and shames me.'

'Don't tell him,' Rachel and I say at the same time. 'Never,' Rachel adds. 'If you're sure he won't forgive you—'

'He will *never* forgive me.'

'Then you can't risk destroying your marriage! I mean, you've suffered, for God's sake. You've taken the punishment. There's no virtue in honesty. Not with something like this.' She stands up and begins to pace. 'This is about being an adult, Bel. Not saying what comes into your head because you think it will ease your conscience. Be clear – it won't! Think about how much it would affect your lives. If Miro feels betrayed and leaves for a while, or for good, then it would impact on Vera. Think about her. If you can't keep quiet for yourself then keep quiet for your daughter.'

It's a long speech for Rachel and she delivers it with passion. I can't help but think it's more about herself than it is about Bel. It makes me wonder what secret she's holding back on and whether, somehow, we might find out in the next note.

Chapter Ten

A few minutes after midnight, Bryn turns up in his van, cheerful as ever. 'You've had a good night then, you three?' he says, the Welsh lilt in his voice making me smile.

Rachel gives him a hug and climbs into the front. I grab Bel and whisper, 'Don't do anything rash. It *will* be okay.'

'Sure it will,' she says, resignation in her tone.

I wave them away and go back inside, checking my mobile before bed. I haven't looked at it since we got back from Aimee's group and I see that at nine-twenty, Robin sent a text.

Long surgery. My patient will need some intervention overnight. Will catch some shut-eye here while I can. Kiss the girls for me.

All so plausible. So very, very plausible. The MBE-award-winning surgeon who pioneered a new surgical technique and makes himself available to his patients, twenty-four seven. The NHS relies on men and women like this, those who are willing to put job before family.

I don't reply. I go straight to my laptop to see where his car is parked. In Jubilee Road. Again. He must be well and truly smitten to be so indiscreet. Jubilee Road is an upmarket housing development, but still, the Porsche will stand out like a cat amongst dogs; it's hardly your regular car.

Somehow I sleep, my dreams fuzzy and fearful, people I know and love flitting on and off the stage, a random blur of scenarios: the three of us at the spa, sharing secrets, only Rachel staying quiet, white tape across her mouth; Lily sleepwalking her way into the Porsche, hiding in the back watching Robin kissing a woman with Maxine's face; Poppy finding a stray dog and bringing it home, then me coming across it in my room, its teeth ripping through the divorce papers. Each scenario makes a twisted sort of sense that leaves me feeling anxious and headachy.

The girls are always up at six and I'm woken by the sound of giggling and then shrieking – Poppy winding her sister up as usual. I make them scrambled eggs on toast for breakfast and sit down opposite them with a couple of painkillers and my first coffee of the day.

'Where's Daddy?' Lily asks.

'He's left for work already.' The lie is automatic. One day soon I'll be able to stop doing this.

'He's always going out early and coming home late,' Poppy says squirming on her stool. *You have ants in your pants*, my dad would say to me at that age and I'd laugh, squirm even more. He is the king of joie de vivre, my dad. Daughters are supposed to be attracted to men with qualities like their dads, aren't they? So what possessed me to choose such an absent father for my children? The fact that Robin had three sons he barely saw by two different women was surely an in-your-face clue that he wasn't a family man. But there I was, taken in by his charm and intelligence, convinced he was a man with strong values. More fool me.

'Maybe Daddy's a vampire,' Poppy adds.

'A vampire would do the opposite,' Lily says. 'They only go out at night.'

'Is he coming home tonight?' Poppy asks. 'Because he promised we would talk about getting a puppy.'

'He has an important job,' Lily says, fulfilling her role as sensible big sister. 'That's why he's late so much.'

'I know *that*,' Poppy says. 'But we are his *children!*' My thoughts exactly. I almost smile. 'It's really rid-ic-u-lous,' she adds, sounding out all four syllables. Ridiculous is one of her new words and she likes to say it a lot.

Within minutes Lily has finished everything on her plate while Poppy's eggs have yet to be touched. She has her fork in her mouth and is knocking it against her teeth. The noise multiplies the pain in my head.

'Poppy!' I say sharply. 'Are you going to eat your eggs?'

'They're really, really *horrible.*' She pushes the plate away from her. 'Really the worst thing I've *ever* tasted.' She shudders and sticks out her tongue. 'Ridiculous.'

'You're not going to be sick are you?' I ask, poised to grab her and hang her over the sink.

'She's faking it,' Lily says.

Poppy lets out a howl –'I'm not a faker!' – and throws her fork at her sister who ducks so that it flies over her head and lands on the floor, skidding to a halt under the table.

I scoop Poppy off the stool – 'You are *not* to throw things, Poppy!' – and set her down on the worktop. 'My head is sore and I have a lot to do today so please let's get through breakfast without any arguments.'

Poppy folds her arms and drops her head. Lily slides off her stool to come round and give me a hug. 'Sorry, Mummy. And sorry, Poppy. You're not a faker.'

Poppy's head jerks up towards her sister. 'Can I have your pink sharpie?' she asks, seizing the moment.

'Yes,' Lily replies. 'But don't take it to school.' She tightens her arms around my waist. 'You're not going to London today are you?'

'No. I'm working from home.' I kiss the top of her head. She looks tired, thin and pale. I place the back of my hand on her forehead. She's neither hot nor cold. I don't think she's ill as much as run-down. And it can't help that her sleep is often disturbed. Robin says there's nothing that can be done about her sleepwalking but I make a mental note to look into it.

Poppy is lying flat across the breakfast bar, reaching into the bread bin. 'Would you like me to make you some fresh toast, Poppy?' I don't like her going to school without any breakfast but sometimes that means I have to go along with her antics and that can be galling.

'With chocolate spread?' She sits up again, rubbing her hands together.

'You can't have chocolate spread,' Lily says at once. 'It's not the weekend.'

'She's right, Poppy,' I say. 'How about banana?'

'It's yuck.'

'Jam, then?'

Her bottom lip juts out. 'You're getting the pink sharpie,' Lily reminds her, her voice light and persuasive.

Poppy sighs and slides across the worktop, knocking into the fruit bowl before slithering back onto her stool.

'And then straight upstairs to get dressed,' I say, putting two slices of bread into the toaster.

'What will happen to Max?' Lily is frowning up at me. 'Because he's got the blame but it wasn't him who wrote the notes.'

I stop looking for jam and give her my full attention.

'How do you know that, darling?' When we spoke about this yesterday, before I went to women's group, she was crying quietly, too upset to speak. Now she seems calm and I hope that means she will be able to explain to me why she's so sure he's innocent.

'Because he told me.'

'He might be lying,' Poppy pipes up.

'He doesn't lie!' Lily shouts, stamping her foot at the same time, something she never does.

'Okay, okay.' I give Poppy a warning glance and smile down at Lily. 'I spoke to his mum last night, and we called Mrs Fleming. We agreed that if there are no more notes then we won't need to do anything else.' I say this knowing that, in all likelihood, there will be another note but we'll cross that bridge when we come to it.

'That's good.' She takes a deep breath and smiles her lovely, sweet, little girl smile that makes my heart lift. 'Thank heavens.' This is something my dad says all the time and the echo of him in her voice warms my heart.

'But, darling, if it's not Max then we still need to find out who—'

'I don't care,' she says abruptly. 'I don't want to talk about it anymore.'

'I understand.' I stroke her hair and she gives me another quick hug before going across to the sink. And then a thought occurs to me. 'If another note should end up in your bag—' she gives me a weary look '—and I *really* hope it doesn't, but if it does, how about you don't read it, don't say anything to Mrs Fleming and just bring it straight home for me to deal with?'

She frowns. 'Why?'

'Because it's less of a fuss,' Poppy says. She has been listening attentively all this time, waiting for the right moment to add her tuppence worth.

'That's right.' I kneel down in front of Lily. 'Then you don't have to be upset by what it says and no one gets into trouble.'

She thinks for a minute, staring off into the middle distance. 'But you'll have to read it.'

'I can handle it.'

She considers this, her lips pulled in as if to stop herself speaking. 'Okay,' she says at last. 'I'll do that.'

I feel the load on my mind lighten a little. I'll be able to let Bel know at drop-off time and then, if there is a naming and shaming in the next note, the whole class won't find out. Children won't be going back to their parents saying Vera's mum killed a baby. Because it's one thing being called names, as Robin and I have, but quite another when Bel's medical confidentiality has been breached. I mentally keep my fingers crossed that she hasn't already told Miro and blown her life apart.

The toast jumps up and I push it back down again because it isn't well enough done. *Robin can get the toaster when we divorce.* That's the thought that pops into my head, surprising me so much that I feel my eyes widening. I can't imagine ever fighting over who gets what. He can have more than his share – the house, a fair financial settlement, all of the furniture inside and outside our home. What he can't have is my kids. That is my uncrossable line. I am willing to share custody, of course – he is their father. But the main carer will continue to be me. No ifs, no buts.

'If we had a dog our heating bills would be lower and we wouldn't need as many jumpers because dogs are always hot,' Poppy announces. I was wondering when we would get back to dogs. This has been going on for three weeks now. Every break in conversation punctuated with a reason to get a puppy.

'Their core temperature is higher than ours,' Lily says. 'Harry told me that.' She's tipped Poppy's eggs into the compost bin and is stacking the plates in the dishwasher.

'And we wouldn't need to put the alarm on because the dog will bark at a robber.'

'We don't have an alarm,' Lily says.

'And you never get fat if you have a dog because you have to walk it.'

'I hear you, Poppy.' I go across to the sitting area and gather up last night's glasses and the empty plates from the coffee table. Both the girls follow me.

'Who was here?' Lily asks.

'Bel and Rachel.' Poppy has climbed onto the sofa and is walking along the back of it. Since she saw Olympic gymnasts on TV she likes to pretend the sofa back is a balance beam. As I watch them both – Poppy counting her steps, lifting and pointing her toes, and Lily gathering together a spilt packet of hair ties, it occurs to me that a puppy isn't such a bad idea. A dog's loyalty and sense of fun adds to the family, and with Robin and I soon to be split between homes, a dog would help absorb some of the girls' anxiety. 'I tell you what, Poppy. Why don't you research dog breeds to see which one would best suit us?'

She turns to look at me and wobbles, arms out, one leg bending. 'I'm only six!' She jumps high, legs and arms flailing for maximum drama, and lands on the cushions. 'I can't do everything! That's ridiculous!'

'Really, Mummy?' Lily says, her face lit up. 'We can get a dog?'

I nod. 'As long as we're in agreement about looking after it, then yes!'

'I never thought we would!' She does a happy twirl and grabs her sister's hand. 'We'll research the breeds together, Poppy. Let's make a plan while we get dressed.'

They're halfway up the stairs when Poppy comes running back into the kitchen. 'You can eat your toast on the way to school,' I say.

'But I have something to tell you,' she loud-whispers, grinning up at me, all missing front teeth and dimples. 'Max is Lily's boyfriend.' She puts her fingers to her lips. 'But don't tell her you know.'

Walking the girls to school is one of my most precious times of day, second only to the bedtime story. This morning they skip along either side of me, holding my hands, reciting the pros and cons of different breeds of dog. They always get along much better in the open air. There's never any squabbling, just a friendly, cooperative harmony. The school is only two hundred metres away and by the time we arrive they've yet to pinpoint a breed but they're sure they want a dog with proper fur and long legs. 'So he can run as fast as the wind!' Poppy says.

Drop-off time is mostly done at speed, children jumping out of cars, some reluctant, others happily throwing bags on backs before they run towards the classroom blocks. Some children wait in the playground directly in front of the school gym until their friends arrive. Lily and Poppy kiss me goodbye and run across to claim two of the swings, dropping their bags at the entrance to the play area. Watching this makes me wonder whether the bully has to be a child from Year Five. Anyone could slip a note into Lily's bag, lying as it is at the edge of the playground. Parents I know and ones I don't, children that Lily interacts with in the playground but I would be hard pressed to recognise, even the school janitor – everyone is potentially a suspect. I make a mental note to speak to Mrs Fleming about it.

To my left is the car park where Maxine's car has just

pulled up. I watch her as she climbs out. She is wearing tight jeans and a colourful crop top, showing off her midriff, her hair set in waves across her shoulders. Max runs to join the girls in the playground and I watch Lily's face light up when she sees him. He stops in front of her to tell her a story, acting the part, walking like a chicken and then miming an explosion. She's very quickly in fits of the giggles. It makes me laugh too.

Poppy was right, then. No wonder Lily was upset yesterday evening. And I see why she believes him. It's hard to imagine that a boy who likes her this much would have the guile to be so duplicitous. He is natural and unguarded with her. And yet for years I've considered him to be the class bully. I'm not sure how that sits with me now. There was the incident with Carys, and a couple of other situations that Max seemed to orchestrate. But then, there are two sides to every story, and maybe he's one of those kids who ends up in the wrong place at the wrong time.

'They get on well, don't they?'

Maxine is by my side. She smells of expensive perfume: jasmine and rose and a musky tone that makes me think of sex. More specifically – Robin and her having sex. I feel my face tighten and when I glance round at her I'm unsmiling.

'That was another reason I was so sure he wasn't writing the notes,' she continues. 'He's been asking for weeks if Lily could come for a play date.' She is in full make-up. She should be going to the Oscars, not dropping her children at school. 'What do you think?'

'I'd need to ask her,' I say.

'Of course.' She licks her plump lower lip. 'I'm sorry about last night. I hope you don't feel that I came to the meeting to get at you.'

'Why else would you have come?' I ask frankly, letting her know that I'm not about to be taken in by her.

'To join in with the group.' Her face is so heavily made-up – sculpted cheekbones, false eyelashes, full lips forming an exaggerated pout – that it's difficult to tell whether she's being sincere. With this much make-up on, her face has lost its ability to form a unique expression. 'Often I feel quite isolated,' she adds.

'I thought you had a million followers on Instagram,' I say lightly.

'Yes, but that's my job.'

'You weren't wearing make-up last night. Is that because we were all women?' She moves back a step when I say this. I know I'm being bitchy but I can't help myself. I have a strong sense of déjà vu. Kimberley, the woman with whom Robin had his first affair, did this to me too. Came over all friendly in the playground. Invited the girls to play. Suggested we go out for the evening together. The deceit of it amazes me still.

'I don't wear make-up when I go somewhere as myself, my naked self. Without all this.' She uses her right index finger to point inward, sweeping the length of her body with a flourish. She's wearing a bra that pushes her breasts up into two large, firm domes. A bit much for a school playground?

'It's a very particular look,' I say.

'*Love Island* meets *Housewives of Beverly Hills*.' She smiles and then sighs. 'That's what my husband says.'

'Sounds like he doesn't approve?'

'He wants me to make money. This is what I can do.' Another wave of the hand. 'We can't all be high-flyers.'

'And is your husband away at the moment? I notice he wasn't at the parents' evening.'

'He's a structural engineer for large builds. He's in

Egypt just now.' She sighs. 'He comes home every other weekend but Max could do with him around more.' She pauses. I think she's waiting for me to sympathise but all I see when I look at her is a woman I don't understand. Or is it that she's simply looking for a father figure for Max? Someone who's around more? Because if so, then she's barking up the wrong tree with Robin. 'Talking of husbands, you must be so proud of Robin. How did you and the girls enjoy your trip to the palace?'

I laugh at this. If she is shagging him then she's as bold and brazen as a . . . And, just like that, with the word in my mind, I remember. I *have* been called a whore before. By Robin. Bile rises into my throat and I feel the urge to retch.

'Are you okay?' Maxine takes hold of my elbow. 'Your face has gone grey.'

'I'm fine.' My hand is covering my mouth while I wait until the nausea recedes. 'I just felt a bit sick all of a sudden.'

'That happens to me if I don't have any breakfast.'

'Nina!' Bel calls out to me from across the playground. I wave back and start to walk towards her, briefly looking over my shoulder to say, 'Bye, Maxine.'

'You'll let me know about a play date?' Her voice is hopeful.

'Sure,' I say, although I have no intention of doing so. I join Bel at the edge of the playground. The children have been asked to line up and the teacher on duty is giving them their instructions. Stragglers are still exiting cars and running to join their lines, the younger ones adding on at the end, the older year groups using elbows and smiles to squeeze into their places in alphabetical order between their classmates. I can see Poppy holding her best friend's hand, and Lily further away, deep in conversation with Vera, their expressions intense, as if they're discussing something serious.

'I've got such a hangover,' Bel says, but I can tell by the stoop of her shoulders that it's not just the wine. The weight of last night's revelation is dragging at her. 'How much did I drink?'

'A bottle. At least.' I hug her tight. 'How are you doing? You didn't say anything to Miro, did you?'

'No, I didn't tell him. He was asleep when I got home, then up early, so—' she bites her lip '—I'm still deciding what to do next.'

'Nothing! Do nothing.'

'That's difficult for me.' She scratches her head. 'So, are you and Maxine getting chummy?'

'Hardly.' I'm not going to be drawn on that now. 'Listen. I spoke to Lily and she's promised that if another note appears in her bag she won't read it, or tell Mrs Fleming. She'll bring it home for me to deal with.'

'Okay.' She brightens slightly. 'That saves Vera finding out what it says.'

'Exactly. And by not giving whoever is doing this the attention that a parents' evening and police involvement bring, maybe they'll stop.'

She nods. 'It's possible, I suppose.'

'This could all blow over, Bel. Really. There's no sense in pre-empting what might never happen.'

'I hope you're right, Nina,' she says quietly. 'I really do.'

Chapter Eleven

I walk back home the long way round, striding out in my trainers, breathing deeply, visualising the bare skin on my arms absorbing the sun's energy. The landscape is varied: scrubland giving way to clumps of trees, trees giving way to streams and small ponds. Part of the walk borders open land where cows graze, and then, midway, there is a length of a hundred metres or so where the canopy blocks out the light. It's damp and dingy, not a place to linger. The girls always race through this section, often shrieking, as they scare each other with stories of tree spirits who tempt children deep into the forest and goblins who lie in wait – long, gnarled fingers just inches from their running feet.

I want to enjoy the fresh air, to avoid thinking and simply feel, but as soon as the trees bear down on me, my mind darkens along with the landscape, and I'm reminded again – Robin called me a whore last year. I walked right into it. In my defence, I was trying to improve our sex life, not have him reject me. Even now, the memory floods me with shame and regret.

We had counselling after the affair, when we promised each other that we would always make time to talk, to have date nights, to ensure we didn't drift apart. But there we were, not having made love for a month. I'd tried talking to him, explained that I felt we needed to make more time for intimacy. He told me that I'd been listening to too much *Woman's Hour* and that it would happen organically, when it needed to. I made advances when we were in bed – and was rebuffed.

Two months down the line and I found myself jealous of Bel who seemed to have such an uncomplicated sex life. I would normally talk to my two friends about all my worries but this was too close to home so I discussed it with Jane, my business partner. She is a straight-talking no-bullshit lawyer who tackles most problems with a keen intellect and a spreadsheet. 'You need to inject some spice,' she'd told me. 'Men are visual creatures. Buy some new underwear. Or, even better, an outfit. There must be some role-play that would dial him up. Be confident. Blow his brains out.' She'd looked up at me with a raised eyebrow. 'A bump of coke would help too.'

I passed on the coke but spent almost two hours in the John Lewis on Oxford Street. Shopping really isn't my bag. Jane and I have a personal shopper who brings a selection of outfits to the office for us for professional wear, and for everything else, I shop online. But I was making an effort, for my marriage, and it felt good to do that. An assistant at one of the beauty counters taught me how to use make-up differently – she gave me smooth skin with a youthful glow, smoky eyes, a pout to die for. All the stuff that sells attraction. Upstairs in the lingerie department, I bought a red silk combo that seemed hugely insubstantial for the money but when I tried it on, it fitted like a second skin, skimming my curves with a sexy shiver. I looked incredible – me, but not me – Nina 2.0. If a robotics expert remodelled me as the perfect sexual version of myself, this is how I would have looked.

But then I thought about what Jane had said and decided that the new underwear was sexy but relatively tame. Maybe role-play was the way to go? I knew Robin had a thing for Catwoman. I remembered when we first met he'd said that she was his fantasy date. I looked online and found an outfit: a full-body, ultra-shine PVC cat suit with a split crotch. It even had a whip.

When it arrived, I hid it at the back of the wardrobe until the following Saturday when the girls were on sleepovers. Robin and I went out for a run together and when we got back to the house I hoped he might join me in the shower and then I'd be able to forgo the risk I was taking. Because it really did feel like a risk. I was about to dress up in a PVC one-piece and crack the whip at him. What could go wrong?

Everything, as it turned out.

Robin was sitting on the decking outside the cabin. The sun was just setting and the air was sweet with the scent of roses. I swallowed a shot of vodka then sashayed down to join him wearing the provocative get-up: killer heels, full-body suit, zip low over the bust, a model's pout. I even walked differently, the sexy upgraded version of me was able to swing her hips. When I reached the decking, I cracked the whip, standing at an angle so that he couldn't yet see the split crotch. I expected him to reach for me. My smile was real, my excitement genuine until I saw the expression on his face.

'What on earth?' He looked . . . confused, then disgusted, and finally amused. 'What's got into you?'

'I've been shopping. Do you like?' I did what I thought was a feline Catwoman move, a slinky elongated twist. 'I thought we could have some fun this evening.'

'This is you making an effort?'

'Yes, but.' I pulled my legs together. 'That's good, isn't it?'

His expression said not. 'It's contrived.'

'What man doesn't want his wife to be sexier?' I asked him, trying to inject a jokey tone.

'You're an objectively beautiful woman, Nina, no doubt about it. But you're not a sexy one. That isn't your strength.'

'Jesus!' I almost laughed. 'Kick me while I'm down, why don't you?'

'It's about knowing who you are! You're a lawyer. You're diligent, organised, intelligent.' He stood up, clearly unable to be close to me. 'That's where you're most comfortable.' He walked away from me, up towards the house, shouting behind him, 'Look at yourself in the mirror! You look like a whore!'

I reeled back against the cabin and, from the corner of my eye, caught the flash of brown hair, the glint of sunshine on sunglasses. Someone was walking along the path less than five metres away, definitely within earshot. At the time I thought it might have been Rachel because she often walked that way when she was going to the farm shop, but she never mentioned it and so neither did I.

Shame engulfed me in a wave of red-hot, flaming misery. I should have made sure he'd had a drink, waited until it was darker, lit candles. But in truth, it wouldn't have made any difference. My husband didn't fancy me. Not even in an any-port-in-a-storm kind of a way. I couldn't get my head around it. I was hurt, humiliated and desperately sad. I walked back up to the house, unable to lift my face from its view of the ground. I expected to find Robin inside the house but his car was gone. I squashed the cat suit deep into the bin and, although it was barely eight o'clock, I went to bed where I remained dry-eyed and wide awake until morning. The evening I hoped we might have had was further from my reach than ever.

When I told Jane – not all of it, not the put-downs, not the phrases that really stung – she said to me, 'Fuck! He's a control freak. I did wonder the few times I've met him.' She pursed her lips. 'It's because you did it by yourself. He's the lord and master type. He's intimidated by you! Everything has to be his idea.' She shook her head. 'But honestly, Nina, I'd consider dumping him. He sounds like a right prick.'

If I had been watching my life as a movie I would have looked at this woman – me – and felt sorry for her. I would have found her a bit too try-hard. Maybe a touch desperate, embarrassing, pathetic even.

And the man? I would have said he was cruel and unfeeling, devoid of empathy. He clearly didn't love her. Nobody who loved their partner would treat them that way.

I should have ended it then but I wanted to make it work for the sake of the girls. I soldiered on as if there were greener pastures over the hill. There weren't.

The writing was on the wall, had been for years, but I stubbornly refused to read it.

I'm working in the cabin today and once I've got in and had a cup of coffee, I grab my laptop and mobile and walk to the bottom of the garden. Robin was down here last night again so I'm expecting to have to tidy up first, but when I open the door the space is neat and clean. There are no mugs or glasses lying about, no dirty plates, no towels left lying on the bench in the sauna. And there's a different smell about the place, a sandal-wood-like essential oil that I wouldn't normally use. Twice a year Robin will spend an enormous amount of money on his clothes and toiletries. But essential oils for the sauna? He's never done that before.

I stand still for a moment and feel the hairs rise on the back of my neck. The cabin really is far too tidy. That along with the unusual scent makes me think he's brought his woman here. Would he? Would he really do that? Is he that careless? He could bring her round the side of the house and I would be none the wiser. But if it's Maxine, then who's looking after Max?

The voice-activated recording device that disguises itself as a phone charger is plugged in just above the skirting board. I didn't listen last night because I thought it would be more of the same – Robin talking to 'M' on the phone, letting her know how much he wants to have her on top of him. I can do without hearing any more of that but I won't be able to settle down to work unless I listen now. So, I do. I log onto my laptop and open up the file. I spend a couple of minutes hearing snippets of the recording. As before, although I strain my ears, I can't make out enough of the woman's voice to determine whether it's Maxine or not. All I can hear is Robin's persuasive tones as they talk about where they would like to holiday together.

I close the file, my jaw tight, anger flaming in my chest. *I need to hold my nerve. I'm getting divorced. I will get through this.*

My main work focus is completing the paperwork to sell the company Jane and I set up twelve years ago. We met at university and ended up as colleagues, working as in-house lawyers for one of the major banks. We identified a gap in the market to provide a mergers and acquisitions service and, although it's been tough, we've made a success of it. Financial contract law is both complex and nuanced and we became the go-to consultancy.

But now I'm weary of the responsibility. We have over twenty lawyers and forty support staff working for us, and this weighs heavily on me: their mortgages, their children to feed, expectations to fulfil. They have placed their trust in Jane and I to attract business and I don't take that trust lightly. After the sale, I'll remain on the board of directors and keep their interests front and centre while the new owner's injection of cash and contacts will make day-to-day business much easier.

I'm hoping it will be the best of both worlds. Jane wants to cut loose and live on a beach somewhere in Greece or Thailand, give her husband the opportunity to pursue his love of all things fish, in the natural environment where they belong. And I want to work fewer hours, spend more time with my girls, see more of my parents and brother, learn yoga, improve my Spanish, walk more and sleep more.

At lunchtime I go up to the house and am surprised to find Robin in the kitchen. 'Why aren't you at work?' he asks me.

'I always work from home on a Thursday,' I remind him. 'Why are you here?'

'I was due some time off,' he says. He's shovelling food into his mouth. I can tell from the packaging that he bought it from our local deli.

'The girls will be glad to see you here when they get home.'

'I won't be here at home time. I need to go into work later.' He reads while he eats, a research paper one of his peers has written. Twice he snorts and declares, 'This really does lack academic rigour.' I heat up some soup and sit at the opposite end of the kitchen island.

Sexual attraction is a strange beast. We were so in love, once. It was an all-consuming passion that I was utterly convinced would last. I wasn't a headstrong, optimistic, naïve eighteen-year-old. I was a grown woman on the wrong side of thirty who believed I'd found my soul mate. But now when I look at him, I see beyond the physical attraction, beyond my blind spot. I see him for who he is: an arrogant man who lies with ease, someone I once loved but now feel very little for.

'I'd like us to have a chat after you've eaten,' I tell him. *Because what am I waiting for?* The divorce papers are drawn up, the girls are at school and I've spent the morning in the cabin where I know in my gut that he has brought his latest woman. *In our garden? His children asleep in the house?* That and the memory of him calling me a whore is enough to tip me into a conviction that there is no time like the present.

He glances up from the paper. 'Why is that?'

'I have some solicitor's documents I'd like to discuss with you.'

'Your business sale?' He raises the fork to his mouth. 'I wondered when you were going to run the figures past me. It's important we get the best deal.'

I've never taken Robin's business advice, just as he has never asked me how to dissect a lung. Is he really this full of himself? Or is this just men and women? He automatically assumes that where money and strategy are concerned his advice is worth seeking.

'I'll gather everything together,' I say. 'I thought we could meet in the snug.'

'Why the snug?'

The kitchen island is strewn with packaging that Robin

has left there and I point to the dining table, covered in children's books and pens, paper and craft materials. 'I don't have time to clear up.' The snug is a small room at the front of the house. We tend to use it in the winter, light the wood burner, and with the curtains closed it becomes a cosy, family space. I pour a glass of water and say, 'I'll see you there in a minute?'

'Sure.' He doesn't look up. 'I have to go out soon but I can spare you half an hour or so.'

I collect two slim folders from my bedside drawer and go to the snug. I could have thrown the packaging in the bin and wiped down the kitchen island but I want to meet him in here because I can control the space. I arrange two upright chairs opposite each other with the card table in between, and sit on the seat facing the door to wait for him. Facing the door is always a tactical advantage. I know plenty of lawyers who will never sit with their back to the door in a restaurant. Better to see what's coming their way.

I wait five minutes and then he arrives. 'I'm not sure why the *BMJ* even published that paper.' He sits down and lays his hand on the folder closest to him on the table. I have an identical one in front of me.

'Before you start reading, Robin. I want you to know that this is not an ambush,' I say, in my best business-like voice. 'I – and I'm sure you feel the same – want what's best for our girls and also for your sons.'

He stares at me. 'You're giving the money from your company to the children? Is it a tax move?'

'This isn't about my company.'

There's a flicker, then. A flash of apprehension crosses his face and is quickly replaced by a tight, closed-off look. He opens the folder and reads. By now, I know every word of the document so I don't look at my copy – I

111

watch him. I see the anger build in the set of his jaw and the rigidity in his shoulders. Every now and then, he snorts and then his eyes flash up to mine with an aggression that is palpable.

Five minutes go by and, at the end of it he pushes the folder away and sits back with his arms folded. 'What's brought this on?'

'I'd like a divorce.'

'Why?' He inclines his head, the innocent man having to endure the vagaries of a woman's emotions.

'I'm unhappy. Our relationship is over, Robin. We both know it.'

'Nina.' He gives a short laugh. 'You think I'm going to agree to this? You think that there is any chance I'm going to allow you to be primary caregiver to our girls?'

I already am.

He leans in towards me. 'I know you, Nina. You don't have the strength to carry this through. You don't have the strength and you don't have a good enough reason.' He says all this in an entirely equitable tone. There are more ways to use anger than shouts and threats, and Robin has always been particularly good at belittling and destabilising me.

'I suggest you engage a solicitor,' I say. 'I will pay the fees. I'm hoping that we can put the girls at the centre of our decision-making, which is why I'm suggesting shared custody.'

'If the girls are at the centre of our decision-making, then we don't get divorced.' He sits back, waving his hands as if it's a done deal. 'They love having me here. You know they do.'

'And you'll still be in their lives. When you're ready, we can sit down together and talk to them. I intend to go part-time and am happy to fit around your schedule.

We can take into account what evenings you're able to leave work to be with them. We can share weeknights and weekends. The amount of contact you have with them will, in fact, increase.' I have practised all this in my head and when I hear it out loud I think it sounds fair.

Robin doesn't. His mouth hardens because he doesn't want to organise his life around the girls. He wants them to be there when he feels like giving them attention. He tells me that I'm selfish and manipulative, cold in fact. Icy. 'You think you're a wonderful mother? Lily is an emotional wreck and Poppy is a brat.' His tone is surprisingly soft, gentle almost. 'I see the way other parents look at you. You're out of your depth.' He tries to reach for my hand but I pull it back onto my lap. 'Sweetheart, you won't cope on your own.'

I'm already on my own. This is Robin trying to manipulate me, to make me feel as if I'm not good enough. It's his usual tactic and I'm not falling for it.

He opens the divorce petition at the second page and reads, 'The Petitioner is willing to be generous, and to this end will not require the Respondent to declare personal assets.' He shakes his head, laughing. 'You think I'm an idiot? I know this is so that you won't have to share the profit from the sale of your business.'

Half of it can be yours. That's up to your solicitor to negotiate.

He continues to rant and cajole, and it triggers a memory – one of the discussions we had during therapy. 'Adultery only exists in the shadows,' the therapist told us. 'The secret nature of adultery provides the erotic charge. Unfortunately, some adults become addicted to that charge.'

He's clearly hooked on his new woman so you'd think

he'd want a way out. You'd think he would be glad to have the decision made for him. Not only is the divorce package generous but I'm going to pay costs.

But no. He doesn't want a way out because he doesn't want out. He wants me to continue in a marriage that's becoming increasingly toxic. But as he said to me after the first affair, 'Isn't disappointment preferable to loneliness? I know I've let you down but I can improve. I know I can be a better man.'

He can't. And I am both disappointed and lonely. You don't have to be alone to be lonely.

'Tell me what's brought this on?' he says.

I don't reply. A senior Queen's Counsel once told me that knowing when to keep quiet is a skill that will win you cases and make you rich because silences are often more important than what is said. Let them do the talking. Hand them a rope, watch them shape it into a noose and let them hang themselves.

I don't want Robin to metaphorically hang himself. I want him to accept that our marriage is over so that we can move on.

I let him rant and only tune back in when he starts to shout: 'This is completely irrational! So I'm home late a few times a month – I'm a surgeon, Nina! I don't push papers around all day. I don't have the luxury of working from home. I bring you flowers, I—'

'Just stop, Robin, please,' I say. I'm not about to share the fact that I've been spying on him but I think it's time to move the conversation on. 'I know you're having an affair. I recognise the signs.'

'Nina!' His head is shaking – small, jerky movements. 'My darling, you are sadly mistaken.'

'I won't be fooled by you again,' I say, without emotion. 'Last time, you had me believing I was losing my mind.

Even when I started on antidepressants and jumped at the sight of my own shadow, you weren't truthful with me.' I give a short laugh. 'If it was the nineteenth century I expect you would have had me incarcerated in a draughty asylum on a hill.' I sit back, wishing I'd bitten my tongue sooner. This will only give him something to grasp hold of. And he does.

'I see what this is about.' He nods slowly, the wise man. 'You've not been able to let go of what happened when we lived in London.' His worried frown tells me that this is particularly troubling. 'I truly thought we had moved beyond that.'

The first time I met Robin's mum, she told me that Robin's dad had had at least four affairs that she knew of, and most probably several other one-night stands. I remember having three thoughts in quick succession: that she deserved better, that I could barely imagine how hurt and lonely she must have been, and that there was no way I could tolerate the same from Robin.

'I didn't have a career,' she told me. 'It was easy for him to treat me the way he did. I know I could have left him but he would have made my life extremely difficult, kept Robin away from me and kept me short of money.' She grabbed my sleeve and said fiercely, '*Never* let Robin do that to you, Nina. Hold on to your career. Be smart.'

I reassured her that it would never happen because Robin wasn't like that! His father was a dinosaur, a patriarch. Robin was modern. He believed in equality and respect. Back then, I was in love. Back then I believed in him. I never imagined for one moment that he would cheat on me.

But, as it turned out, his mother knew him best. Like father like son.

'. . . whatever help you need,' he is saying. 'I promise

to support you. I'm sure I'll be able to swing a bit more time off. My registrar will step up.'

'Please engage a solicitor,' I say. 'Our marriage is over, and despite the fact that you're shagging around, I'm petitioning for a no-fault divorce. I don't want our lives dragged through the courts.' I pause to take a breath. 'And I don't expect you do either.'

'I want to save this marriage, Nina.' His smile is almost sincere. 'Let's try therapy again.'

'We've done that already and we made an agreement. A set of promises, in front of the therapist, which we both signed.' I open his folder and find his copy at the back. I point to the second promise: I will not engage in extramarital sex. 'This promise has been broken.'

'Really, Nina?' He leans in towards me. 'This paranoia is an ongoing issue for you and one for which I have suggested you seek help.' A weary tone now. 'But you don't. You persist in misreading the situation.'

I'm tempted to wipe the smirk off his face by telling him about the spyware, but it's enough to know that I am on solid ground, and allowing him to talk is a sobering reminder that he can lie more convincingly than anyone I've ever met. 'I'm going back to work,' I say, standing up. 'Please engage a solicitor and forward me the details.' I walk away from him then, and he follows me as far as the bifold doors.

'It's not happening, Nina!' he calls after me. 'I'll fight you all the way!'

Chapter Twelve

BEL

I watch Nina walk home from morning drop-off, admiring her self-control. If I was her, I'd pin Maxine down and ask her outright about Robin, force the truth out from her puffy pout, crack the veneer of her painted face.

I'm not in the best of moods, and, as usual, I'm prepared to come out swinging. I'm scared shitless that Miro will find out what I did. I woke up this morning thinking that of course it matters who wrote the notes! Why did I tell Nina and Rachel that it didn't? Someone wants to terrify and expose me, and I need to find out who it is.

I walk along to Nina's to collect my car from last night then drive home and do a frenetic hour of housework, all the while trying to ignore the fire in my belly. I planned to wait until this afternoon, to go to the GP surgery when it's quieter, but the feeling inside me is too urgent and I'm propelled through the front door and along the road.

The sign-in console for appointments isn't working so the queue for the receptionists is longer than normal. There are seven people ahead of me, and two receptionists on duty. I should leave. It makes sense to leave now, and to return when they're quieter but I can't do that. I'm here and I'm looking for answers.

When I get to the front of the queue, I give the receptionist a stiff smile and say, 'I'd like to speak to the practice manager, please.'

'Mr Bellamy. Can I tell him what it's about?'

'I'd rather speak directly to him.'

'Your name?'

'Annabel Novak.'

'Let me see if he's busy.' She gives an audible sigh and presses a button on the phone, turning away from me when the call is answered so that I can't hear what she's saying. When she places the receiver back onto the cradle, she looks up at me and says, 'I'm sorry, Mrs Novak, but he's busy at the moment. He suggests you make an appointment for the next week or so.'

'I need to speak to him now.'

'As you can see we have a really busy morning surgery.' She points beyond me to where every seat and some of the standing room is taken. Most people are looking at their phones but several are staring at me with interest.

'Yes, you are busy,' I say. 'But I wouldn't be here if it wasn't really important.'

She sighs again, gives me a death stare and stands up. I watch her walk deliberately slowly around the corner to where the offices are. The remaining receptionist is busy chasing up test results and the people in the queue are becoming fidgety.

'She's taking her time with you, isn't she?' an older man wearing a wax jacket and leaning heavily on a walking stick calls out to me. I shrug, give him my what-can-you-do face.

Over a minute ticks by before she returns. 'Mr Bellamy says it's really important that you give me some idea as to what your request is pertaining to.' She says this loudly, enunciating every syllable of every word as if English is my second language.

'The thing is, *Tracy*—' I read her name badge '—my reason for seeing Mr Bellamy is *private*.' I pause to let that sink in. 'What's more, I'd like to request—' I point to the sign on the wall that says as much '—that my enquiry be dealt with away from the front desk.'

She stares at me stubbornly. My fists tighten. 'I'm going to wait over there.' I point to a free spot in the corner. 'I'm not leaving until I see him.' I walk across, lean my back against the wall and fold my arms. Tracy holds my eyes for several seconds, her mouth a sneer of disapproval.

A small child is playing on the carpet close to my feet. He's lying on his side, head resting on one arm while his free hand runs a flaming red fire engine backward and forward in front of his eyes. He's captivated by the turning of the wheels, his mouth making broom-broom noises to match the engine's progress. *I could have had a little boy.* I clear my throat and tighten my folded arms. I can't let my mind go there. It hurts too much.

'Bell!' I look up and see Amira. 'What brings you here?'

'I was hoping to speak to Mr Bellamy.'

'Maybe I can help?' She smiles. 'Do you want to come along to my room?'

'I don't want to take up your time if you have patients to see.'

'It's not one of my working days. I'm catching up with paperwork so I'd be grateful of the interruption.' I glance across at Tracy who is watching us talk. 'Tracy will buzz me if Dan becomes available,' Amira says.

And then I get it. 'Did she ask you to speak to me?' I say to Amira as I follow her along the corridor.

'Yes.' She opens the door to her room and ushers me in ahead of her. 'But don't take it personally. Dan has the accountant in and every minute costs.' She sits down and crosses her ankles. 'You're not forgetting about the quiz night tomorrow?'

'No,' I reply automatically. With my head so full of worry, it had actually slipped my mind. 'We're looking forward to it.'

'Great!' She gives a small gleeful clap. 'I think it'll be a fun evening, and if it's anything like last year, your team will be walking off with the prize.'

Amira puts us all to shame. She has her job as a GP, four little boys and somehow manages to find time to organise fundraising for class projects. For the last four years, we've made up a table with Rachel and Bryn, Nina and Robin, although last year Harry came instead of Robin who was attending a surgical conference in Berlin. Harry enjoyed himself so much that he's signed up to be Nina's partner this year too.

'So.' Amira arranges her hands on her lap. 'What can we do for you today?'

I hesitate. I'm not sure I want to unburden myself to Amira but if I do get to speak to Dan Bellamy, she'll find out anyway. And there is the slim chance that she could be the one who leaked my medical details to Maxine. Slim but possible. 'Can I speak to you confidentially?' I ask.

'Of course.' She regards me with her listening face. It's something all good doctors and nurses can do. The listening face lets you know that you have their full, undivided attention. 'You are my patient.'

I take a breath. 'The notes that are being slipped into Lily Myers' bag, there was another one yesterday and it mentioned medical details that no one knows apart

120

from me, Nina and Rachel who haven't told anyone. Apart from Bryn. Rachel told Bryn.' She's nodding me on. 'My point being, is there any way that my medical details could have been leaked?'

'You suspect the leak came from here?' She's astounded.

'That's right.'

'No, Bel. It's not possible.' She gives an emphatic shake of her head. 'Absolutely not.'

'It is possible,' I insist. 'It might not be probable, but it is possible. My whole medical history is held within these walls and there are a lot of people who have access to those details.'

'Every single person who works here signs up to a confidentiality protocol. Doctors and nurses access notes for treatment purposes—'

'What about support staff?'

'They access notes too sometimes, for example, to let patients know about test results and the like, but they—'

'I know all about confidentiality protocols and GDPR. I'm a senior hospital pharmacist; we have to follow strict procedures.'The fire in my belly is growing ever warmer. 'Nevertheless, I know that these protocols can be, and are, broken.'

'Bel.' Her expression is pained. She seems genuinely blindsided by my request as if the very idea of a breach in confidentiality is something totally beyond the pale. 'I can only assure you that what you're saying is irregular and highly unlikely.'

'But possible,' I insist again. 'So is there any way you can check?'

'Well . . .' She has a think. 'I can speak to our IT support and see whether he can find out who has recently accessed your notes.'

'It might not have been recent,' I tell her, because I really have no idea. 'The person could have been sitting on this information for some time.'

She stops holding my eye and looks round the room. 'I'll speak to IT Support and let them know how important your enquiry is. In the meantime, would you like to lodge a formal complaint? We have a process for this.'

'No. I'd just like to know who's been looking at my notes.'

She scratches above her eyebrow. 'Okay, Bel. We can do that.'

'Thank you.' I go to stand up but she stops me with a question.

'What exactly is worrying you, Bel?' she asks. 'Can you tell me what the note said?'

In the natural world fire never transforms into water but in the core of me, at that moment, it happens and I feel an almost overwhelming urge to cry. I take a tissue from my pocket and blow my nose loudly, drumming my feet on the floor and humming. These three simultaneous actions always stop me crying. I'm not embarrassed to cry in front of Amira – she'll have seen far worse – but crying doesn't help because it becomes the focus. I won't be able to talk or think clearly and Amira will help stem the tearful tide and then send me off home with a promise of an appointment the next day.

I walk around in a circle, sit back down again and say, 'It's about my husband not finding out that I had an abortion.'

'Ah.' She purses her lips. 'I see.'

'We're practising Catholics, but more than that, we tell each other everything. He's my best friend, my life partner. I mean—' I throw out my arms '—we have a great marriage! We're a really close couple.'

She nods. 'I've seen you together.'

'But when his dad was dying and he was away a fair bit, I took a decision, a *monumental* decision, without telling him. And, the thing is, I can't even understand why I did it. I remember the feelings I had at the time. I can name them all, but I can also discount them all. And yet, that isn't what I did then. *Then*, I decided abortion was the answer. *Me*.' I press my fist into my chest. 'It was an awful thing to do and I've regretted it ever since.'

'I understand you're worried—'

'Amira, it's a bit more than a *worry*.' I'm trying hard not to raise my voice. 'I'm scared stiff Miro will find out. Last night I lay awake staring at the ceiling, seeing my whole life fall apart before my eyes.'

She asks me exactly what the note said and I tell her. 'That doesn't sound conclusive to me,' she says.

'Well, it does to me.' I'm quiet now. I've said all I can say, laid myself bare and now I'm exhausted.

'How is your IVF going?' she asks.

'I'm not pregnant.' I stand up. 'Anyway, thank you for your time. I'll let you get back to your paperwork.'

'Bel.' She stops me at the door. 'Don't let this get on top of you.'

'I won't,' I say, knowing that's exactly what's happening. I arrived at the doctors' surgery a woman on a mission, ready to tackle whoever had leaked my information. And I'm no further forward. I don't think Amira was involved but I don't know that for sure.

I leave the practice feeling defeated.

It was all so much better in my head.

Chapter Thirteen

I spend time outside, pulling weeds from the borders, tidying the greenhouse and then taking some homegrown potatoes to one of my elderly neighbours. Before I collect Vera from school, I visit the church. We're a small parish and the inside is less decorative than most Catholic churches, but I find the simplicity helps me to focus. I stay on my knees for thirty minutes, finding peace in the rhythm of the prayer and the quality of the silence.

When I arrive at school for pick-up time, Vera and her friends are playing on the climbing frame. It's a beautiful early October day and parents are lingering to chat. Several of the mums glance at me then look away, some give me a half-smile and one a tentative, 'Hi'.

Maxine is at the centre of a circle of women; they're all hanging on her every word. One of them looks across at Nina as she arrives in the playground as if she is the topic of conversation. I approach the circle and when I'm a few feet away a mum I know by sight but have never spoken to sees me approach, then pulls on Maxine's sleeve and she immediately stops talking.

'Hi, everyone!' I say. 'How's it going?'

'Fine!' Maxine smiles, blinking her long lashes several times. 'I was just talking about the quiz night tomorrow.'

'Ah, were you? I thought you were talking about the notes,' I say. Two of the mothers stare at their feet. 'Any idea who might be writing them?'

'None at all,' Maxine says, eyes bright as she blinks some more. 'Lily's a close friend of Max's so he's *very* concerned. The poor love could barely sleep last night.'

Close friend, my arse. I leave them to their sotto voce gossiping and head over to Nina who's holding Lily's bag tightly to her chest. I feel my stomach lurch. I'm afraid to ask her whether there have been any more notes but I don't have to, because as soon as she sees me she says, 'Nothing in Lily's bag today.'

'Phew!' I let my shoulders drop. 'That's something, I suppose.'

'We've only got tomorrow to get through and then it's the weekend.'

Rachel comes out of the building, shooing small children ahead of her. They surround her with their questions and their triumphs, one little boy calling out, 'Look at me, Mrs Davies! I'm at the top of the slide.'

'Well done, Arthur.' She stops to watch him. 'Legs straight on the way down!' When he reaches the bottom, she claps and cheers then walks swiftly towards us. 'There was a staff meeting this morning and the notes were on the agenda,' she says breathlessly. 'Angela said that although she caught Max with his hand in Lily's bag, she's not completely sure that it's him.' She looks guilty as she says this. 'We're all bound by confidentiality but obviously, I couldn't not tell you two.'

Nina frowns at this. 'I have to agree with her,' she says. 'I watched him with Lily at drop-off this morning and they get on really well. According to Poppy, he's her boyfriend.'

'Some children lie really easily, though,' I say, then I

glance back towards the gossiping huddle. 'For that matter, so do some adults.' Both my friends give me a tired look. 'Sorry. I'm not at my most cheerful. By the way—' I remind them about the quiz night tomorrow. 'Is there a rota to help with the set-up?'

'We're not on it,' Rachel says. 'I checked this morning.'

'I was talking to Amira earlier. She mentioned our win last year.' I smile at the memory.

'It was Harry's music knowledge that got us over the finishing line,' Rachel says. 'He's coming with you again, Nina, isn't he?'

She nods and turns to me. 'When did you see Amira?' she asks.

'I went to the surgery. She is my doctor!' Their faces tell me they're waiting for the rest. 'Okay, so I couldn't help it. I wasn't going to go but I had to find out whether it was possible and—' I shrug. 'It's as I thought: every Tom, Dick or Harriet can look at the notes. They promise confidentiality but . . .' I trail off. 'Who knows?'

'Changing the subject,' Rachel says, her tone light. 'Did your period start?'

'No.' I stare her cheerfulness down. There's nothing Rachel likes more than a newborn and now she's got me in her sights. 'It should be here by now but maybe I'm going into an early menopause.'

'Or maybe you're pregnant, you silly mare!' Rachel says undaunted. 'You should take another test. You can have false negatives but not false positives. Don't drink too much and ideally it should be the first urine of the day.'

'Yes, Mum,' I say. My hand drops down to my stomach, pressing hard against my trousers. If my period was coming I'd be bloated and this would hurt. And it doesn't hurt, but still, I daren't hope.

'Bel, imagine.' Rachel hugs me. 'You could be pregnant! And that will make all of this fade away.'

I smile at her. 'You really are an optimist, Rachel.'

'Promise me you'll take another test.'

'I'll do it when I'm at work.' I glance at Nina whose eyes are fixed on the ground. I can see her thoughts are elsewhere. 'You okay, hon?'

She folds her arms protectively. 'I asked Robin for a divorce today.'

'Oh God.' Rachel's hand shoots up to her mouth. 'How did he take it?'

'Not well.' She bites her lip. 'He didn't shout or anything but he did his usual thing of putting me down, trying to undermine my confidence in myself.'

'What a bastard,' I say.

'He's not going to make it easy, that's for sure.'

'Mummy!'

We all glance across at Poppy whose tights are caught in the buckle of her friend's shoe. They are rolling on the ground giggling as they try to separate themselves.

'Stay still!' Nina calls out to her, walking across to disentangle them. 'Try not to tear your tights!'

'I had no idea Robin was that bad,' Rachel whispers to me.

'Me neither. But that's Nina all over. She doesn't complain. She's kept it all to herself.'

Rachel's eyes fill up. 'I just feel so sorry for her,' she says.

'Me too. It's really shit.' Vera has stopped playing on the slide and is standing close by chatting to a boy in the year above. 'Vera! Are you ready to go?'

She nods her assent, and while she fetches her bag, I say goodbye to Rachel and then to Nina who has managed to separate the girls and is pushing the pulled threads in

Poppy's tights through the small hole so that they don't unravel further. 'Did you see us, Aunty Bel?' Poppy asks me. 'We were joined like twins! It was ridiculous!'

'I did see you, Cherub.' I muss her hair and she leans into my hand. She is a mini version of her mum, all dark eyes and wide smile. I use my thumb and pinkie finger as a pretend phone, holding my hand up to my ear as I signal to Nina. 'Call me if you need me,' I mouth at her. She nods and Vera comes running towards me, her school bag rattling on her back where she has multiple key rings dangling from the zip. I'm still worried about her gait, which is even more 'sideways' pronounced than normal but it turns out Miro is already on the case because when I get home and open the front door he is standing there.

'Surprise!' he says. Vera runs at him and he lifts her up into the air. 'I know it's a school night but there wasn't much going on at work so I thought I'd come home early and take my two favourite girls out for a drive.'

I smile and kiss his cheek. There's really no resisting him.

'Yay!' Vera says, hugging him tighter. 'Can we stop for pizza?'

'Or fish and chips on the beach?' he suggests.

I know what he has in mind. We enjoy going down to the coast to walk along the path on top of the cliffs at Beachy Head. Miro invented a game that incorporates all of the exercises Vera needs to strengthen her leg. He makes it fun – we all hop on one leg for ten steps then we change legs and hop for another ten. We jog for a hundred steps then we stop to do ten star jumps. We repeat this several times until one of us spots an 'escape' – the mast of a ship or the white and red striped lighthouse that hugs the rocks below or a walker with two dogs – and then the spotter can order the other players to choose a forfeit. Miro calls the game the Novak Olympics and Vera loves to take part.

We all climb into the car, Vera in the front so that she can chat to her dad. 'You don't mind if we talk in Polish, do you, love?' Miro asks me.

'Of course not.' I reach forward and squeeze Vera's shoulder. 'I love that you can speak Polish.'

I rest my head against the headrest and close my eyes, listening to the sound of their voices, the intonation familiar but the meaning lost on me. I know a few words – *cora* means daughter and *matka* means mum – and I wish I'd put more effort into learning more but every time I tried to learn, something came along to redirect my attention, and as everyone in Miro's family speaks English, there was never any real urgency.

My parents-in-law, Jan and Vera Novak, moved the family to Glasgow in the late eighties. Miro, at the tail end of four sisters, was only eight. Vera worked at the university and Jan, who had been a ski instructor, began work as a bus driver. They thought it would be an ideal opportunity for their children to learn English. They planned to stay one year at most, but one year became two and then three until they stopped pining for the mountains because it was as if they had always lived in Glasgow.

By the time I met Miro, his parents' marriage was coming to an amicable end and Jan had returned to Zakopane, where the Tatra Mountains crouched on his doorstep. The air was fresh, and crisp snow reflected the sunlight; the food was familiar and the lifestyle more akin to his rhythms. Before our Vera was born, Miro and I spent happy holidays with him on the mountains, hiking in the summer, skiing in the winter.

'Look, Mummy, it's the sea!' Vera calls out and I open my eyes to see the steel-grey water rise and roll towards the land.

Miro parks the car in our familiar spot and I brace myself for the wind that more often than not steals the breath from my body but today there's a cool, gentle breeze.

We set off on our Olympic journey, all managing several repetitions of hopping, jogging and star jumps before Vera starts looking for an escape. We're not in position to see the lighthouse and there is a haze over the water that obscures any ships. A sole person walks towards us with one playful spaniel and Vera's face falls. She's tired after a full day at school. Before I can say anything, Miro lifts her up, tosses her over his shoulder and begins a brisk walk along the path, whistling a marching song from his childhood. Vera is laughing as she pummels his back. 'Put me down, Daddy!'

He pretends not to hear her until we have climbed a soft incline then he drops her back down onto the grass and she runs ahead of us, her arms outstretched as she mimics the seagulls dipping and diving into the sea. Miro reaches for my hand and I take it, lean into his shoulder and say, 'I don't suppose you could carry me as well, could you?'

'Your wish is my command, milady.' He scoops me up in one swift movement and I feel all my troubles slide off my shoulders. My head drops back so that there's nothing between me and the sky. My eyes feast on the cool blue, broken up with slow-moving clouds.

When my feet are back on the ground again, he holds his hands either side of his mouth and calls out to Vera, 'Are you hungry yet, *cora*?'

'I'm starving!'

She comes racing back towards us, her left leg already noticeably more in line with her torso. When she's alongside us, Miro shouts, 'Last one back to the car's a hairy kipper!'

Vera sets off first and then ten seconds later I start running. Miro waits another ten seconds before he chases us both. I'm still fifty metres from the car and already flagging when I hear him behind me. I put my arm out to stop him overtaking me but he sprints past on the other side, laughing at my feeble attempt to stop him. He turns to face me, running backwards for a few steps, calling out, 'Come on, Bel! Dig in!'

I show him the finger, simultaneously laughing and trying to catch him. He dodges away from me and chases after Vera, who is squealing up ahead of us as she gets closer to the car and anticipates her win. A few more steps and she holds her arms up in the air. 'I'm the winner!'

We both come up alongside her and high-five her success.

'Did you let me win, Daddy?' she asks.

'No!' He starts back, feigning shock. 'I never let anyone win.'

We climb into the car, cheeks pink and muscles aching. Miro drives us back into town where we stop close to the best fish and chip shop on the Sussex coast.

I sit on the harbour wall and watch them join the queue outside. Miro runs his hand through his hair and I notice the narrow streak of silver grey that runs from his right temple through the black of his hair. He's growing older. We both are. One day follows another and yet somehow I only become aware of time marching on at moments like this when I am questioning myself. My own dad took off when I was two. I had the good fortune and the good sense to meet and marry Miro, who loves being part of our family and has enough energy and space in his heart for half a dozen kids. There should be another child standing next to Vera, basking in his or her dad's attention. That was what God meant for us.

They cross the road towards me, Vera carrying three wrapped portions of fish and chips, Miro carrying the drinks.

'Here, Mum.' She hands me one of the portions and sits down next to me. 'We need an even number of people in our family,' she says. 'Because it was a buy one get one free on the drinks.'

Miro is on the other side of her and he reaches across to grab my hand. 'Your mum is taking care of that.' His smile is so open, so utterly trusting that I feel my heart expand and then immediately shrink.

'Are you really, Mummy?' Vera looks at me then, her expression questioning.

'I'd love to give you a brother or sister, Vera.' I feel as if she's been reading my thoughts. 'I really would.'

She doesn't smile; she doesn't speak. Her expression changes from questioning to what I can only describe as hostile. Miro's mobile is ringing and he stands up to check the number so he doesn't see our exchange.

'Vera?' I say quietly. 'What's the matter?'

'I'm eating my chips.' She turns away from me, her back ramrod straight, so that I can no longer see her face. My heart beats faster; I can feel the pulse in my neck pound. Vera knows that the note refers to me. Somehow she's put two and two together and come up with the right answer. *How? How is that possible? Who could have told her?*

Miro sits back down again and tells Vera and me a

133

story from when he was a child. It begins with him and his friends playing football and ends with them all down the police station. It's a funny story that makes Vera laugh, and gradually her body language relaxes to include me again. Before we set off home she goes down onto the pebbly beach to collect some of the most eye-catching stones for our small rockery by the front door.

'You okay, love?' Miro puts his arm around me. 'You seem quiet.'

'Sorry, this has been so lovely.' I kiss his cheek. 'I'm just a bit tired. Going out two evenings in a row is taking its toll. And we have the quiz night tomorrow.'

'We need to defend last year's victory.'

'We do.' I take a breath. 'I'm just a bit worried about the notes.'

'Has there been another one?' he asks casually.

I realise he doesn't know about the last one but I can't be the person to tell him what it says. I feel sure that as soon as I say the words my face will give me away. 'There has.' I shrug. 'More of the same. What's bothering me is that I have a feeling it's beginning to drive a wedge between the parents.'

'How so?'

'Whispering. Gossiping. People taking sides.'

'There's always a problem with them and us in Vera's class.'

'Yeah, you're right.' I hug him tight. 'I'm sure I'm worrying for nothing.'

When we get home, Miro takes care of Vera's evening routine and I shut myself in the downstairs loo to call Nina. 'How's it going?' I ask her. 'Is Robin still being difficult?'

'He's acting like divorce was never mentioned and is

doing a number on the kids. To quote Poppy, he's the funnest, loveliest dad *ever*.' She sighs. 'What's happening with you?'

'Miro came home early and we went down to the coast. We were talking about adding to our family and Vera gave me a look, and it was . . .' I shiver. 'She knows the note was about me.'

'Are you sure you're not just projecting?'

'I'm sure,' I say forcefully. 'What will I do if he finds out, Nina?'

'He's not going to find out. You need to hold your nerve. Remember there is nothing to be gained by telling him the truth.'

There's honesty to be gained, I think later, when I'm lying in bed, Miro asleep beside me. Honesty, trust and integrity. At the moment those attributes are in short supply in my marriage – from my side, anyway. When I roll back time to that decision, I mostly see the details from the corner of my eye, or through my fingers, because it's hard to face the truth full on. But tonight I find myself drifting back, remembering how I got from Annabel Meehan, the girl who considered abortion to be a mortal sin, to the married woman who made that choice.

'My dad has cancer.' Miro stood in front of me, the phone still in his hand. 'Edina was with him at the hospital. It's not good, Bel.' His voice caught on a sob. 'I need to go over there.'

'I'm so sorry.' I held him as he cried. 'But cancer isn't always a death sentence. Not anymore. Let's get you on a plane so you can talk to the doctors.'

He travelled to Poland the next day; Vera was exactly six months old. She had spent the first few months of her life in hospital so having her home still felt new to both of us.

After Miro's first trip back to Zakopane, it quickly became clear that he was needed over there. We fell into a routine where he left for Poland every other Thursday and stayed until the following Tuesday. When he was home, he had to spend long days at work. (He'd recently started at the Foreign Office.) In between times, he did his best to be home for us but there were phone calls and emails and searching for treatments and cures that might just slow the cancer's progress. Coffee enemas, herbal drinks that were green as pond water, surgeons in other parts of Europe who would attempt to remove the secondary tumours, meditation and even oxygen therapy. Miro facilitated all of it.

In the meantime, I coped without him. Vera and I were safe and well – there were problems with her milestones and we had a scare when we thought she was deaf – but mostly she was progressing much better than the medics predicted. I was on maternity leave; I could dedicate my time to her. Miro's dad was only going to die once and I didn't want to split his focus.

My first pregnancy had been beset with problems. I vomited almost continuously. If I was awake, I was vomiting. Early on, I was diagnosed with hyperemesis gravidarum and was admitted to hospital during the first trimester, on a drip, fed intravenously. I was exhausted but happy because, joy of joys, we were having a baby.

When Vera was approaching her first birthday I discovered I was pregnant for a second time. It was a shock; I was still breastfeeding – that tends to be a contraceptive in itself. And Miro was hardly ever there! We'd taken three years to fall pregnant with Vera and here I was, against all odds, pregnant again? No way. For a couple of weeks I refused to believe it.

And then the morning sickness started. This pregnancy wasn't going to be any easier than the first.

I was immersed in caring for Vera and I found it difficult to separate myself from her, to give time and energy to the new life that was growing inside me. Vera was utterly enchanting. She was my every day, my past and my future. If my life were a map, she was where I lived, breathed and loved. Vera was my baby. Vera. Was. My. Baby. I had space for no other.

Abortion is an impossible choice for any practising Catholic. And yet, all that was impossible became possible. I could have prayed. I could have found God in our rented two-up two-down in Camden. I could have asked for help at the local church. I didn't have a network of friends yet but parishioners would have stepped up to help me, as I have helped so many before and since.

If at any point someone had said to me: 'But hang on! You're a Catholic. Maybe you should think again?' perhaps I would have. But the doctor viewed my request as perfectly reasonable, because I sold it to her just as I sold it to myself. There was no way I could cope with a new baby at that point in my life. No ifs no buts.

When we were on the spa break and I told Rachel and Nina about the abortion, Rachel, who tends towards giving people the benefit of the doubt, told me that I had the abortion for Miro, that my love for him meant that I had to make the tough decision because I could never force him to choose between being with me and being with his dad.

That's not the way I see it.

I made the choice because I was selfish. I wasn't thinking

about Miro or Vera or my unborn child. I was thinking about myself.

I put myself first, before my husband and daughter.

Before the rights of my unborn child.

Before God.

That's the truth I have to live with. And now someone else is forcing me to face that truth. What I don't know is how far they will go.

Chapter Fourteen

NINA

When we arrived home from school, the Porsche was in the drive. 'Daddy's home!' Poppy shouted as she ran inside, Lily close behind her. I took my time hanging up my jacket before joining them. As soon as I came into the room, Robin grabbed me for a kiss on the lips, his arms tight on my back. I held myself rigid, desperate to pull away from him but from the corner of my eye I saw my daughters' faces lifted towards us, their expressions open and bright.

It was only four hours since I had presented him with the divorce papers but he was acting as if that hadn't happened. I took a split second to decide between my two options: should I play along or ask him to leave me alone? Leave the house? He knew I wouldn't kick up a stink in front of the girls and I knew that he wouldn't be able to keep up this pretence for very long. I decided to say nothing, let the girls enjoy the evening. Their parents' separation would come soon enough.

I moved beyond them into the kitchen to give them some space. Poppy kicked off her shoes and started running along the back of the sofa. Lily stood next to Robin, staring up at him.

'Come here, Poppy!' Robin called out. 'I have a surprise for you both.'

'What is it? What is it?' Poppy shouted, diving onto the sofa and then skidding across the room to stand beside her sister. 'Tell us, Daddy! Tell us!'

'You need to settle down first,' he said. I could see that he was already beginning to lose patience.

'Stop jumping around, Poppy,' Lily implored, gently nudging her.

Poppy crossed her legs and took a deep breath, both hands clapped over her mouth. Being quiet is only possible if she doesn't breathe.

'Okay, good.' He smiled. 'So, I have a surprise to share, something I know is going to make you both very happy.' He paused for effect. 'I'll give you three guesses.'

'Three guesses between us or three each?' Lily asked.

'Three between you,' Robin replied.

'Okay.' Lily put an arm around her sister's back. 'We have to think carefully, Poppy.'

Poppy wasn't listening. Her hands were now clasped together at her waist, her eyes flashing around the room looking for the answer. 'Is it a puppy?' she shouted, unable to contain herself any longer.

'Yes, it is!' Robin laughed. 'How clever are you?'

'It's all I want,' she said, twirling full circle on her tiptoes. 'And it's all Lily wants too. That's why.'

'A puppy?' Lily said, glancing across at me then back to her dad. 'Did you get it with Mummy?'

He didn't answer her because, of course, I knew nothing about it. 'This is the little lad.' He took two photographs out of his wallet and passed one to each of them. 'As you can see, he's still very small so we won't be able to bring him home for a few weeks.'

Poppy's eyes lit up with awe and reverence. She began

walking towards me, balancing the photo on the palm of her hand, as if it was too precious to grasp hold of. 'Mummy, look,' she whispered. 'He's very small but I think he'll grow.'

'Isn't he sweet?' I said, looking down at the photograph of a furry, sleepy puppy with silky ears. I would have preferred it if Robin had spoken to me first but I wasn't surprised. He was laying down the gauntlet, trying to outmanoeuvre me whenever he could. It was tiresome but it didn't really matter because what he didn't know was that I had already agreed to a dog.

'He's a spaniel,' Robin said. 'From a litter of eight. He wasn't easy to find but luckily a former patient helped me out.' He promised to take the girls to visit the puppy as soon as the owner said he was ready for visitors. 'In the meantime, we have to think of a name and we need to prepare for him coming to live with us.'

With us? I put my tongue very firmly in my cheek and opened the fridge to begin preparing supper, half-listening to them talking through the logistics of caring for a dog.

'He'll need a bed.'

'And a collar and a lead.'

'And a bowl.'

'Two bowls. One for food and one for water. It's ridiculous!' Poppy shouted, her excitement hard to contain.

'We need to write it all down,' Lily said. 'In case we forget anything.'

I decided to make a fish pie and brought all of the ingredients out onto the work surface, chopping and then combining them. I was arranging the pieces of fish and prawns in the base of the dish when Lily came across with her notepad and pencil. 'We have a shortlist of three names, Mummy.' She checked what she'd written. 'We think Pickle, Bomber and Billy are all good. Do you like those names?'

I smiled at her, so pleased to see that she was her old self again, never happier than when she was having fun with her family. *Please, let there be no more notes.*

'Yes, you should also be part of the decision-making process, Nina,' Robin shouted. Mr Inclusive all of a sudden. 'Let us know if you have a favourite.'

'Mummy?' Lily stared up at me.

'I like Pickle,' I said. 'It sounds friendly and a bit naughty.'

She wrote that down on her pad.

By five-thirty the pie was bubbling in the oven and I'd had my first gin and tonic. Robin and the girls were now online going through different puppy training websites.

'This one is close by,' I heard him say. 'Mummy will be able to take you along on Mondays after school.'

Oh, will she now? Monday is one of my London days. I'm not expecting that to change even when I'm part-time.

The fish pie was well received and the meal went smoothly. I barely spoke because I was on my third G and T and was content to watch and listen, pleased that the girls were animated, keen to talk puppies and to tell Robin about what was going on at school. Poppy was on her best behaviour. She normally talks over Lily, inter-rupting and correcting her, but she didn't do that – she waited her turn, watching her sister finish her sentence before she chipped in. I was impressed by her self-control.

After slipping out to take a quick phone call from Bel, I return to see the girls have finished their ice cream. When I sit down Robin says to Poppy, 'Why don't you go off and play for a bit while Daddy and Mummy talk to Lily.'

'About Pickle?'

'No, we need to chat about the notes. Don't we, Lily?'

He's smiling at her but I can see that it doesn't fill Lily with confidence. She looks at me and says, 'Do I have to?'

'Not if you don't want to, no.' I reach across and stroke her hair.

Robin gives me a sharp look. 'Mummy and I agreed that it would be good for you to talk about what you're feeling.'

They were supposed to talk yesterday. A lot can happen in twenty-four hours.

Poppy gets down from her chair, her eyes wide and serious. She gives her sister a kiss on the cheek and says, 'Good luck, Lily.' Then she walks backwards out of the room, taking tiny, sliding steps, waving to us as she goes. My heart warms to her afresh.

Lily has stopped smiling and her worried frown is back. She's looking at her dad, waiting for the first question.

'So, Lily,' Robin says. 'Tell me about the notes.'

'They've stopped now.'

'Have they?' Robin glances at me then back to Lily. 'How do you know that?' he asks.

'Because . . .' Her cheeks flush. 'I just do.' Her eyes meet mine and I read her expression. She wants me onside, supporting her, not explaining anything, not mentioning Max. I can do that.

'Okay . . . so let's think about this. The notes might have stopped but they might not.' She goes to speak and he holds up a hand. 'You know that Mummy and Daddy love you, Lily, don't you?'

143

'Yes.'

'And we want what's best for you.' She nods. 'And we want to help you. And regardless of whether the notes have stopped or not, we think there's something to be learned from this experience.'

'You're using your doctor's voice,' she says, and I suppress a smile.

'My doctor's voice is my voice!' he says.

'Not always,' she replies quietly.

He ignores this and ploughs on. 'So, Lily, what do you think you have learned from this?'

She glances at me and I smile my encouragement. 'That people can be mean,' she says slowly. 'But what they say might not be true. It might be a little bit true but not a lot true.'

'That's right,' Robin says. 'People pick on each other. It's not nice. I wish it didn't happen, but it does. And sometimes . . .' He pauses. I can tell he's thinking about how to phrase the next bit. 'Sometimes, children pick on other children who they know they'll get a reaction from.' He makes a 'thinking' face. 'Do you know what I mean by that?'

'I get upset but Poppy wouldn't care,' she says flatly.

'And why do you think Poppy wouldn't care?'

'Because she's tougher than me.'

'Darling, that's not—'

'Wait, Nina!' Robin interrupts. He holds up a hand in my direction. 'Let Lily express what she feels.'

—*true. You are you, and Poppy is Poppy.* That's what I want to say but I remember my mum telling me when I first had Lily that one of the hardest things for her as a mother was accepting that my dad had a different style of parenting to her. And at first she didn't like it but then she realised she needed to allow him to do it his way. *Okay, Mum,* I think as I sit on my hands. *My lips are sealed. I'll let him do it his way. For now.*

'It's not just about being tough, Lily,' he says. 'It's also about how we come across. Do you talk about me and my MBE, for example?'

'I never talk about you,' she says quickly then realises it sounds harsh and adds, 'Sometimes we talk about our mums and dads but mostly we talk about other stuff.'

'So what do you think you'll take from this experience?' he asks as if he's speaking to an adult.

Lily sighs before saying, 'I need to be more like Poppy.'

'That would be a start!' He laughs, like it's all a bit of a joke. 'There's a lot that sisters can learn from each other and Poppy is more resilient than you.'

That's too much for me. It's one thing allowing him to be Lily's dad. It's another thing allowing him to knock her self-esteem. 'Lily.' I take her hand. 'You don't need to be more like your sister. You are wonderful as you are. Poppy is wonderful as she is. All Daddy is saying is that if there is anything we can do to help you feel stronger or more cared for then please tell us.'

'You do care for me, Mummy.'

Her expression is so serious when she says this that I feel an ache in my heart. I lean across and kiss her forehead.

'So.' Robin rubs his hands together. He's almost had enough now. He's spent a whole three hours with his family. It must be time for him to call M. 'Do you have any questions?' he asks her.

'For you?'

'Yes.'

She takes a big breath. 'Why didn't you go to the parents' evening with Mummy?'

Robin jerks back in surprise. 'Well, I had patients to

look after at the hospital. You understand that, don't you, Lily? Some people are very unlucky. They fall ill and have to have an operation. They need me to be there for them.'

She's very still when she replies, 'But Mummy had to go by herself.'

'Mummy had her friends with her.'

Robin looks at me and I add, 'Remember I told you that Bel sat one side of me and Rachel the other? Just like when you have Vera and Carys either side of you. It feels good to have your friends supporting you, doesn't it?'

She's staring at Robin and he is staring at her. They have identical violet blue eyes and blond hair. Robin's has faded with age but the texture is the same. She is a mini, feminine version of him. And yet, I seem to be the one who is tuning in to her feelings. I can sense that she's both angry and fed up – and I don't blame her because this could feel like an ambush and I'm so proud of the way she is holding her own.

'So the puppy is chosen,' Robin says. 'But I know that was mostly Poppy's wish. So if I could give *you* one wish what would it be?' Robin asks her. He hasn't sensed her mood; he is too wrapped up in his own idea of 'how to talk to your daughter'.

Lily thinks for a minute, her shoulders slumping back as she stares up at the ceiling. 'Can I really say?'

'Of course!' He stretches out benevolent arms, hugging the whole room and the world beyond. I expect he thinks she's going to say a trampoline or a pony but he's forgotten that our eldest daughter isn't acquisitive. Her wellbeing is dependent on feelings not things.

'I wish that you were nicer to Mummy.' She holds his eyes for another few seconds, her strength of focus impressive – it isn't easy to face Robin when he's angry – and then she looks at me and says, 'Can I go now?'

I nod and she gets down from her chair, runs out of the room to join her sister.

'Thanks for that,' Robin says, turning to me. 'You might have chipped in at the right times!' There's an irritable heat to his tone. He goes to get a lager from the fridge. 'Did you make her say that?'

'Of course not.' My tone is flat. There is nothing to be gained from me rubbing it in. Quite the reverse. I want both of us to be the best parents we can be. Especially when we will be doing it from separate homes. But there is a part of me that is glad Lily doesn't allow him to have everything his own way.

'Why would she say something like that?'

'I don't know.' I shrug. 'Perhaps because she hears us arguing, notices you're not here very much and that makes her think what she thinks.'

He drinks half the bottle in one go and says, 'I'm going out.'

'You've already had some wine. You're over the limit.'

'I'm not driving. A friend is coming to collect me.' The word 'friend' is loaded with meaning and he stares at me then, daring me to say something. He is injured by Lily's ability to see through him and I am being punished for it. 'I try to do something nice and this is the thanks I get?'

I follow him to the front door. The girls are in the living room watching TV and don't notice him leaving. He knocks back the rest of his lager and hands me the bottle. 'Don't wait up,' he says.

I wake at half past one in the morning convinced I've heard a noise. A bang? Whispering? Loud or soft, I don't know, but I have a clear sense of unease, my stomach churning, my heartbeat racing. I climb out of bed and lift the curtain to one side so that I can look through the window. The light is on in the cabin; I can see it shimmering through the leaves on the willow tree. He's back home then. His 'friend' must have dropped him off. Or maybe she's with him in the cabin?

I go downstairs and stand in my kitchen. There is the fleeting scent of a woman's perfume on the air, slight but distinct. *He brought her into the house.* My knees begin to knock together and I steady myself by holding on to the work surface. He's bringing her into the house when his wife and daughters are asleep upstairs. I'm staggered by this. First the cabin, now the kitchen. *How far will he go?* Will I find them in my bed next?

I feel a surge in anger so intense that it makes me want to rip his head off. How dare he? How fucking dare he?

I check the bifold doors and find them unlocked. I know I locked them before I went to bed. I never forget to do that; it's part of my evening routine, as predictable as cleaning my teeth. I slide the bolts in place and then go to the front door, bolt that too. Robin will not get back into the house tonight.

Chapter Fifteen

Friday morning and the Porsche is gone. I walk the girls to school, promising Lily that I'll speak to Maxine. 'I *really* want to go to Max's house. He has a big tree in his garden for us to climb.'

'Can I come too?' Poppy asks.

'No, you have your own friends.'

When the girls have run inside, I spot Maxine and ask her about a play date. 'Of course!' She's delighted. 'Sunday okay?'

We make arrangements, the words sticking in my throat – if she is having an affair with Robin I'll be tempted to smack the smirk off her face – and then I walk back home. My mind is still full of what happened last night – Robin acting as if he wasn't a cheat, as if divorce had never been mentioned, getting the girls onside by offering them a puppy, speaking to Lily as if there is something wrong with her. And then, to top it all, bringing his woman into our home.

It's too much.

Before I call my solicitor I reread her letter that accompanied the divorce petition. The tone is cautionary.

As discussed, Nina, I would prefer that we hold the line at this stage. While I appreciate you want to be generous and to go for a no-fault divorce, I am not sure this will be taken in the spirit in which you intend. As you know, in business it is important to show strength from the outset and Robin, and his solicitor, may well interpret your generosity as a sign of weakness. Based on what you have told me of Robin, I feel we should take a tougher stance now, knowing that we can give some ground as the negotiations develop. A no-fault divorce should, in theory, be straightforward but I have dealt with enough divorces to know that fairness is not necessarily at the forefront of the respondent's mind. I have, therefore, taken the liberty of dialling back on your generosity. Please see sections 3.1 to 3.5.

I scroll to the sections she highlighted. I had suggested that we give Robin half of all marital assets including the sale of my company. I also promised to continue to pay child maintenance for his two sons in Glasgow for a further four years. We would both keep our own pension pots and all personal assets. There would be shared custody of the girls.

My solicitor changed this to half of all marital assets, excluding the company sale. We would then review Robin's income and mine and I would give him, and his sons, maintenance for two years, a figure to be drawn up in accordance with our salary differentials. Shared custody of our girls would be decided dependent upon Robin's work and living arrangements but I would be considered the primary caregiver.

I hadn't wanted to go with her changes – I wanted to give him the benefit of the doubt – but now I'm glad I took her advice. If he's going to push back then I have to push harder. I know how much he loves spending; he has expensive tastes. When he does accept the fact of the divorce, he will want to get as much money as he can.

I call my solicitor and her assistant tells me she's in court but will return my call as soon as she can. In the meantime, I send her an email, summarising Robin's reaction to the divorce petition. I also mention the fact that his mistress has been in the cabin and now I'm sure she's been in the house too.

As soon as I press send, I feel like a small load has been lifted and I begin my work, checking through contracts until it's time to collect the girls. Rachel doesn't teach on Fridays so she is already waiting outside the school building when I arrive. Bel appears moments later just as the bell sounds and children start pouring out into the playground, high-energy chatter fuelling their feet. The girls say a quick hello and run off to play on the climbing frame. 'Lily! Where's your bag?' I shout after her, but she doesn't hear me.

'We had whole-school assembly today,' Rachel says. 'I came into school for it. Mrs Fleming did a really good job.'

'Here she comes,' Bel adds, and we look towards the building. The class teacher has just come out the door and is heading in our direction.

'Nina, Bel.' Mrs Fleming nods at us both. She's in a business-like mood. 'I'm sorry I haven't got back to you sooner. With one thing and another, not least Greg having a relapse—'

'Oh, I'm sorry,' I say, touching her arm. 'I thought he was better.'

'Just a blip, as it turns out. Robin fixed him again.'

Of course he did.

'Time for an update.' She looks at me. 'So, as I think you know, on Wednesday I caught Max with his hand in Lily's bag and that was when I found the last note, the one about the dead babies.'

I feel Bel tense beside me. 'Lily was very upset about it all. She's absolutely convinced it can't be him.'

'I'm inclined to agree with her,' Mrs Fleming says. 'I gave him a serious dressing-down and all the way through, he had the look of an innocent child.'

'So it's not him?' I say, relieved for Lily's sake.

'I can't say for definite but I would almost bet my life on the fact that he wasn't involved. He's been turning things round lately. He's not the boy he was in Years Three and Four. He's far less impulsive. Much more aware of the consequences of his actions.'

'And did any parents get back to you after the meeting?' Bel asks.

'No. Nobody seems to know anything,' she says.

'The trouble is, it could be anyone.' I point around the playground. 'Look at all the children's bags, left abandoned while they play.'

'I completely agree and that's why we've been keeping Lily's bag safely inside the classroom.'

'I think the assembly this morning will have helped,' Rachel adds. 'The children were really taking in the seriousness of it all.'

'I hope so,' Mrs Fleming says. She looks at her watch. 'I need to collect my granddaughter. See you all at the quiz tonight?'

We tell her we're looking forward to it.

'Well, I suppose that was pretty much what we expected,' I say when she walks off. 'And I'm pleased it's unlikely to be Max because . . .' I pause for effect. 'Guess what I'm doing on Sunday?'

'What?' They both lean in.

'I'm taking Lily to Max's house for a play date.'

'Really?' Rachel is shocked. 'But it could still be Max!

Is it fair on Lily? And if Maxine's at it with Robin, then . . .' She trails off.

'Never mind Max and Lily,' Bel says. 'Nina and Max-*ine* are getting quite chummy.'

'No, we're not!' I shake my head at her, frowning. *Do I detect a hint of jealousy?* 'But Lily really does see him as a friend.' I pause. 'And I'm being devious.'

'Devious?' Bel repeats.

'I want to rule Maxine either in or out as Robin's mistress. I think I'll be able to tell whether he's been in the house.'

'Taking the fight to her,' Bel says. 'I like it.'

'Don't forget I've been in this position before. I'm learning to be less passive. Although, I can't seem to stand up for myself when the girls are there.' I look over my shoulder to make sure no one else is in earshot. 'I'm sure Robin has taken his woman into the cabin. There's a peculiar scent down there that might also be in Maxine's house. She might even have been in my kitchen.' I tell them about yesterday evening, Robin acting as if divorce wasn't on the table, his promise of a puppy, then me waking up in the middle of the night and my gut feeling that he had brought the woman, Maxine or whoever, into the house.

'That's outrageous!' Rachel says.

'You need to get him out,' Bel says. 'He's really taking the piss.'

'I know. I've been in touch with my solicitor. I'll see what she says.' I glance across at the girls who seem to be arguing. Carys is pointing and shouting while Vera's arms are folded, her face like thunder, and Lily is staring from one to the other of them, clearly unsure of whether to interrupt or not. 'The girls are looking a bit fed up with each other,' I say.

Bel and Rachel follow my eyes. 'Just a tiff, I expect,' Rachel says. 'They'll have all evening to work it out.'

'The quiz night,' Bel says, sighing. 'I suppose it's too late for me to duck out of it?'

'Yes!' Rachel and I say in tandem.

'Drop the girls round whenever you're ready,' Rachel adds. 'Eleri has a film for them to watch. I'm sure they'll quickly forget about whatever's upsetting them.'

'What time does it start?

'Seven for seven-thirty.'

Bel still looks doubtful. 'I have a bad feeling about this evening,' she says.

Rachel gives her a hug. 'Will you stop with the gloom and doom! It'll be fine!'

'You know what?' I say. 'When this is all over we need to go for another spa day.'

'Hell yeah!' Bel says. 'That's something for me to look forward to.'

'My treat,' I add. 'We'll go somewhere impossibly decadent.'

Rachel nudges Bel. 'And we need to arrange it before there's a new baby on the scene. Did you take another pregnancy test?'

'Not yet. I have a test in my locker at work. I'll do it on Monday.'

'Promise?'

'You really are turning into my mum.'

'I just have such a good feeling about this!' Rachel says. She throws out her arms, smiling. 'I'm good at knowing when women are pregnant. It's my special skill!'

Bel's face is glum and I can't say I blame her. Chances are she isn't pregnant and I feel Rachel is being insensitive going on about it so much. The playground is beginning to clear and several mums wave goodbye and call out, 'See you tonight!' I spot Maxine and Max and we wave at one another. I remember her saying that her husband was working in Egypt and I wonder who she's teaming up with this evening.

'So, Eleri is bringing her mystery boyfriend to lunch on Sunday,' Rachel says. 'And I'm not sure what to cook.'

'That's easy. Nina will be able to help with that,' Bel says, grinning, as if she knows something we don't. 'Won't you, Nina?'

'Why Nina?'

'Why me?' I'm at a loss to know why she's suddenly grinning.

She hesitates and I sense her backtracking. 'Well . . . because Nina regularly has a sixteen-year-old boy in her house.'

'Harry?' I say. 'I don't know how representative he is, Rachel, because he's fairly limited in what he'll eat. No fish, lamb or pork. His favourites are spaghetti bolognese and a roast chicken dinner, and he's a big fan of puddings. The stickier and sweeter the better.'

'I was thinking of a roast dinner,' Rachel says. 'It's what we normally have on a Sunday.'

The three girls appear in front of us, their cheeks flushed, their hair sliding out of braids and ties. Strands of Lily's hair are tangled around the button at the top of her blouse. Carys's trousers are splattered with mud and Vera has taken off her shoes. 'Can we *not* have a sleepover tonight?' Carys says.

'Eh?' Rachel says. 'Why not? What's going on?'

'We need a break from each other,' Carys replies, using a grown-up tone that she regularly borrows from Eleri.

'We spend loads of time together,' Vera joins in. She takes Bel's hand. 'Can I be with you and Daddy tonight? We could go out again. It was so much fun yesterday.'

'Sorry, poppet, we have the quiz night,' Bel tells her. 'We can go out on Saturday, though.'

Vera drops Bel's hand. She goes across to sit on the wall and put on her shoes, her shoulders drooping down as if gravity has got the better of them. Carys gives her mum an angry look and walks off in the other direction. Lily has yet to speak. She's staring at the ground, biting her lip.

'What's going on, Lily?' I ask her, keeping my tone light.

'Nothing.'

'It doesn't look like nothing.'

'Can we go home now?' She looks up at me then and I can see that she's close to tears.

'Okay. Go get your bag.'

She goes off into the school building, walking with her head down, her arms pulled in as if she's desperate not to be noticed.

'I expect they'll be fine in an hour or so,' Rachel says.

'Failing that, Eleri might be able to get it out of them,' Bel says. 'I know Vera really trusts her.'

Lily comes back, hands me her bag and sits at the other end of the wall from Vera. I immediately search for a note, rummaging around, hopeful that I won't find anything, but when my fingers feel a folded piece of paper at the bottom, I take it out and stand completely still. Both my friends are staring at me, wide-eyed and waiting.

All the noise in the playground fades into the background as I unfold the paper. It's exactly the same as the other notes: an A4-sized, lined sheet, torn from a notepad, folded three times. I open it slowly, taking time to brace myself. Bel and Rachel lean in towards me so we all see it at the same time. Black marker pen, messy writing – just like the others.

Bel Novak is the one who killed the baby

She wont get away with it

My heart turns over; Rachel gasps.

'Oh, fuck,' Bel says, one hand clutching at her throat while the other grabs the paper from me.

I catch Lily's eye. She's white as a sheet, her mouth open.

'Is that another note?' Amira asks. I jump at the sound of her voice. She has sidled up to us out of nowhere. I look around and see several faces staring back at me.

'No.' Bel slides the note into her pocket. Then immediately takes it back out again and briefly holds it up in front of Amira. 'Look. I told you I was right.'

Amira takes Bel's arm and turns her away from us just as a couple of other mums approach.

'Was that another note?' one of them asks. 'What did it say?'

'Much the same as before.' I'm relieved they couldn't read it from where they were standing. 'I'll tell Mrs Fleming. I know she's coming this evening.'

'But what did it say?' one of them persists. Her name is Suze and she has a daughter called Rhianna who, back in Year One, told Lily Santa Claus was made up.

'As I said, I'll have a word with Mrs Fleming.'

'Why can't you tell us?' There's a quizzical, faintly aggressive look on her face. 'It affects all of us, Nina. All our children are under suspicion. Rhianna has been crying herself to sleep because Mrs Fleming has been very serious with them. It's not fair to threaten children with the police.'

'I understand how you feel,' I say. 'But I really think I'm better talking to Mrs Fleming first.'

'How can you understand how I feel?' Suze asks and then she turns away, saying something that sounds like 'right bitch'.

I hear Rachel gasp and then immediately step forward to challenge her. 'What was—'

'Don't bother, Rachel,' I say quietly, and we watch them walk away.

Rachel's face is flushed. 'This is exactly what Bel thought would happen.'

'We have to stop the whole school from finding out.'

We both glance over at Bel. She still has her back to us, Amira's arm round her waist. Amira is speaking to her in a low voice, and as far as I can tell, Bel is listening.

'Do you think this might be what the girls are upset about?' Rachel asks.

'They would have told us,' I say, glancing again at Lily, whose face is pinched as if she's about to start crying. I gesture for her to come across to me but she gives a small shake of her head. 'And Vera would have been especially upset, wouldn't she?'

'I don't know,' Rachel says, sighing. 'It's all a bit beyond me. To be honest—' her voice drops '—I don't really get it. It is only an abortion. I know it's not ideal, especially for religious people, but it's not illegal.'

'Bel and Miro are religious, though, aren't they? It's a big decision for a woman to take without telling her partner, but for Catholics it's even more serious. And whoever is doing this must know that.'

Rachel's lip is trembling. She takes a tissue out of her pocket and dabs at the corners of her eyes.

'Are you okay?' I rub the top of her shoulder.

'I'm just worried, that's all.' She looks at me then, her expression bleak. 'Believe me, Nina, what I did is ten times worse than what Bel has done. Bel had a *reason*.

158

I have no excuse.' She bites her lip and starts to walk away. 'I'm going to take Carys home. See whether she'll tell me why they've fallen out.'

As I watch her urging Carys to get up off the wood-chips, I try to imagine what she might have done. If it's something she's unable to tell Bryn then it must be something – like Bel's secret – that would affect them as a couple. Infidelity is all I can come up with, but that would be completely out of character for Rachel. Is it possible that whoever is writing the notes knows about this secret too?

I hear Poppy's high-pitched giggle and glance across at the wall. She has spent this whole time swapping football cards with one of the boys in her class, heads together, their legs swinging a few feet from the ground. Lily is sitting to her right and Vera to her left. I don't want to leave Bel without checking she's okay but her conversation with Amira doesn't look as if it will end anytime soon. 'Lily! Poppy!' I call out. 'Let's get going.'

When Poppy hears my voice, she slithers off the wall at once, her two fists bulging with cards, and runs across to me. 'I've got Arsenal's whole team now. I had to give Marcus Rashford away but that's okay.'

I wait until she's put her cards inside the pocket of her backpack and then I take her hand. 'Let's get your sister,' I say.

Lily is still sitting on the wall, her expression wide-eyed and fearful as she stares off into the distance.

Chapter Sixteen

'What's going on with the three of you?' I ask Lily when we arrive home.

She gives a shake of her head as if my question is an annoying fly that's buzzing around her. 'What did the note say?' she asks.

'We agreed you didn't have to worry about that, darling,' I say lightly.

'But I do worry. That's the whole point!' she shouts, and both Poppy and I take a step back. Tears spring into her eyes. 'I worry *all* the time because I don't like it when people get into trouble.'

I crouch down in front of her to say, 'And who do you think will get into trouble for this latest note?'

'I don't know, Mummy!' she shouts again. 'Why do you keep asking me?'

She runs upstairs and Poppy's startled eyes meet mine. 'She's upset again,' Poppy says, hoisting herself onto the banister then holding on tight as she swings underneath it so that her body is upside down. 'She's not herself.'

An adult phrase, and one my mum often uses.

'Was Rhianna's mum angry with you?' Poppy adds.

'No, not really.' I pick the coats and bags up off the

floor and hang them on hooks. 'Are you all right going to Carys's house this evening?'

'Why isn't Harry coming to look after us?' She's holding on with only her legs now, her hands dangling close to the floor, her blouse ridden up to cover her face.

'Because he's my quiz partner for tonight. Remember? He was on my team last year too.'

'And you won.' She drops back down onto the carpet and rights herself, blows her hair out of her eyes. 'Is Daddy not coming home? Because yesterday he did.'

Robin's so unreliable when it comes to arriving home on time that for years I haven't even factored him into the babysitting equation. 'I'm not sure what his work schedule is,' I tell her.

'I'm going to call him,' she says. 'I don't want him to forget that he said we could have a puppy. I've kept the photograph safe. I didn't take it to school!'

She runs off to use the house phone and I go upstairs. Lily's bedroom door is closed so I don't disturb her immediately. I give Bel a call to check she's okay but it goes to voicemail and I leave a message. Then I knock on Lily's door. 'It's me. Can I come in?'

No reply. I sneak open the door a few inches at a time until I see her lying on her bed, face down. She's not normally this dramatic – that's Poppy's domain. I sit on the edge of the bed and say, 'Lily. Is there anything you want to tell me?'

'Like what?' Her voice is muffled.

'Like why you and your friends have fallen out.'

She sits up and reaches for her teddy. 'Just because.' She stares at me, bleary-eyed and fed up. 'We'll be friends again soon.'

'Okay.' I nod. 'I understand you might not want to

162

share any details with me but you know I'm here if you need me, right?'

'I know, Mummy.' She hesitates, pulls at her teddy's ears and says, 'I'm glad you're always here for me and Poppy. But I worry that one day you won't be.'

'Where would I go?' I smile at her, nudge her shoulder with mine. 'I'm your mum. You'll never get shot of me!' She gives me a watery smile and I stand up. 'I'll make us all something to eat and then drop you and Poppy at Carys's house. Okay?' She nods. 'Change out of your uniform and I'll see you downstairs.'

When I go into the kitchen Poppy has finished her phone call and is lying on the floor singing to herself. I ask her to change her clothes while I make something to eat. 'I've fixed everything,' she says.

'What have you fixed?'

'You'll see.' She scuttles off to change and I don't give it another thought until we're halfway through leftover fish pie and peas, and the front door opens. 'It's Daddy,' Poppy says, looking up at me through her lashes.

I inwardly sigh as Robin comes into the kitchen and the girls hug him around his waist. 'I hear I'm needed,' he says to me. 'It's the charity quiz night! Prof Myers to the rescue.'

Poppy is grinning at him; Lily is watching me, alert to my every expression. 'That's kind of you, Robin,' I say. 'But Harry is looking forward to it. He was the star quizzer last year.'

'I've texted him to tell him he's not needed.'

I feel my face tighten. 'That isn't fair, Robin. It's all arranged.'

'Then we can unarrange it.' He throws me a look that tells me things will turn sour unless I give in. 'What do you think, girls? Do you think I can do better than Harry?'

163

'You're really old so you should know more stuff,' Poppy says, spearing four peas on the prongs of her fork.

'So are we making up a table with the Davies and the Novaks?' Robin asks me. 'It's a while since we've all been out together.'

I'd like to slap him. I'd *really* like to slap him. I calm myself with thoughts of divorce. Signing on the dotted line. Knowing I'm completely free. It's coming. I just have to bide my time for a little while longer. When my solicitor calls on Monday I'll ask her what she thinks is the best plan. If I need to move out with the girls while our separation is arranged, then I'll do that. What I know for sure is that I can't continue like this, with him presenting one face in front of our daughters, another face to me when we're alone and a third face when he is with his mistress.

I finish my dinner and get changed, then we drop the girls round at Rachel's. Lily drags her heels as she walks up the path, but Eleri meets them both at the door and welcomes them in. When we arrive at the school, I ask Robin to wait a second before we go inside.

He stops and smiles at me – not a real smile, a cold smile that sends a small shiver down my spine. 'Robin, please be clear that we are getting divorced.' His smile is fixed. 'I am perfectly prepared to be polite in front of the girls and in front of other people but you have to know that pretending everything is fine won't work.'

His smile widens. 'You wanted me to speak to a solicitor and I have.'

'That's good. Thank you.'

He pauses before playing his trump card. 'I told him all about your breakdown, the fact that your parents came to stay because you were incapable of caring for our girls. He says this will all play in my favour when I apply for *full* custody.' His smile is triumphant.

The small shiver becomes a chill wind that passes through me from the crown of my head to the tips of my toes. My teeth chatter as Robin moves away from me, and a group of parents call out to him, 'Great to see you!' I watch him being absorbed into their circle, shaking hands, throwing compliments, impressing them with his charm offensive.

I'm leaning against the car. My feet won't move yet. There is no feeling in them. All the feeling is centred in my heart, which is swollen and sore, an aching mass of heat and pain.

Engage your work brain.

That's what I need to do. I concentrate on slowing my breathing and then I think it through, as a solicitor would. Nina Myers isn't me. She's a woman who is petitioning for a divorce.

When Poppy was just a baby, Nina had a breakdown. She was overwhelmed with work, two small children – one who never slept – and a husband who didn't support her with childcare, shopping, cooking, anything at all. To make matters worse, he was having an affair. Mrs Myers loved him, trusted him, wanted to remain married and raise their girls together.

Can the first affair be proven? Professor Myers' solicitor asks.

Yes, it can. Mrs Myers came home to find her husband having sex in their family room with one of the parents at the girls' school. Professor Myers agreed to end the affair and the couple attended counselling. Myers admitted to the affair in front of the counsellor and agreed to terms and conditions for their marriage moving forward.

And now Professor Myers, having promised his wife that he was willing to try again, is having another affair which he is, once again, denying. Not only this, he is exhibiting signs of coercion and control. He has been bringing his mistress to their family home without the knowledge of his wife and children.

Professor Myers' solicitor will counter this by saying, 'And where is the proof?'

Having been severely traumatised by her husband's lies the first time round, Mrs Myers has gathered evidence. She has recorded him talking on the phone to his mistress, making incorrect and hurtful comments about her. She has also tracked the whereabouts of his car. The respondent has repeatedly said he is working late when in fact he is with his mistress.

Professor Myers' solicitor will say that Mrs Myers' recordings are unlawful and cannot be submitted as evidence.

Her solicitor will counter by saying that while phone hacking is a grey area for spouses, Mrs Myers has felt emotionally under threat. The tracker on the Porsche is not illegal as the car was purchased by her. And neither is the voice-activated recorder in the cabin because the family home and garden were also her purchase. What's more, she placed the recorder there to monitor her children when they were playing in that area.

If Professor Myers' solicitor does ask to hear the recordings, then after listening, he will struggle to defend his client.

A judge only gives full custody to the father if the wife is proven to be a danger to her children, either through abuse or neglect.

Neither of those things could be proven about Nina Myers.

About me.

The feeling is returning to my feet and I move away from the car, feeling better, calmer. I am Nina Myers. I am strong. I can do this.

A text comes into my mobile. It's from Bel. *Where are you??? We're at the table front right. Seats here for you and Harry xx*

The quiz is taking place in the school hall, which is normally short on atmosphere but the set-up team have done a great job this year with candles, flowers and strategically placed curtains to screen us from the gym equipment. Along one wall there is a table of finger foods and drinks – no alcohol, as the school doesn't have a licence. There are over a dozen round tables spread across the centre of the space with six chairs at each table. Amira and Aardi, her husband and tonight's quiz-master, are standing on a raised platform at the front checking off a list. On a table next to them is the winning team's prize – a basket of cheeses donated by one of the local farms.

I spot our table and walk towards it. Robin is standing in the far corner and his voice carries across the room as he tells Maxine and Suze, 'I completely agree. I think more than enough has been made of the notes and your children are being unfairly spotlighted. I'll speak to Mrs Fleming about it.'

'At last!' Bel says as I reach our table. She touches the sleeve of my blouse. 'This colour looks great on you.'

I don't answer her. I collapse back into a seat between her and Rachel and say, 'Robin cancelled Harry. He decided to come himself. He's over there.'

'Fuck no!' Bel turns round to eyeball him. 'Why does he have to be such an arse?'

I sigh. 'I'm so fed up. I could really do with a drink.'

'Here you go.' Rachel passes me a small silver flask, the sort my dad would take with him on family days out. 'Neat whisky. It'll hit the spot.'

I swallow a couple of mouthfuls, let the fire light up my throat, and manage not to wince. Miro and Bryn welcome Robin when he comes over to our table. 'Long time no see!' Miro claps him on the back. 'We'll do well on the medical questions with you on board.'

'I'll do my best!' Robin kisses my cheek before sitting down. It's all for show. The last time he kissed me in private was more than nine months ago when he was drunk after a new year party. I shrink away from him, turning my head to one side to take another swallow of whisky. When I look round again Rachel is staring at me, her expression sympathetic.

Aardi calls everyone to order. 'We have apologies from a couple of parents who are unable to make it so—' he holds up his hand '—I know you're all loyal to your teams but we'll need a couple of volunteers to move to another table to even up the numbers. We're aiming for fourteen tables of five.' He glances down at the sheet of paper he's holding. 'One person needs to move to The Influencers and another to Agatha Quiztie.'

Robin's hand shoots up at once. 'I'll move to The Influencers,' he says. 'If they'll have me.'

The Influencers are Maxine and Suze, and a couple who are parents of a boy in Year Six. 'We'd love to have you!' Suze calls out and they clap Robin across the floor towards them as if he's royalty. He does a mock bow and Maxine pats the seat between her and Suze.

'He's laying it on thick,' Rachel says.

'Sickening,' Bel adds. 'And if he is shagging her?'

They both look at me and I shrug. My emotions are

168

riding on a wave of anger and frustration. I just want this evening, this week, this month to be over.

'Tequila Mockingbird are our defending champions,' Aardi announces, pointing in our direction. 'They are the team to beat.' Miro and Bryn both stand up and flex their muscles as if they're about to go into a wrestling match. 'We'll be relying on you for the medical questions now, Bel,' Miro says.

'I'll do my best.'

Round One begins – world geography – which we're reasonably good at. We all chip in as the questions are called out although I find myself increasingly distracted. The Influencers are across from us and my eye is constantly drawn in their direction. Every time I look over Robin is smiling, his demeanour conspiratorial as he leans in towards either Maxine or Suze to discuss the answers. Both women seem to be thoroughly enjoying the attention. He even puts his arm across the back of Maxine's chair so that when she sits back it looks as if his arm is around her. He catches my eye more than once and I get the feeling he's doing this for my benefit but I'm not quick enough to look away. If he is seeing Maxine then this is him toying with me, rubbing my nose in it.

'We should follow them if they leave the room together,' Bel says into my ear. 'If they end up snogging outside I'll take a photo on my phone.'

'More evidence,' I say. 'Not that I need it. I could listen to all of the recordings from the cabin when they're both down there.' I feel the alcohol swirl through my brain, thickening my tongue. 'I've heard some of it but not her actual voice. It was all moaning and thrusting.' I start to laugh and Bel does too. 'It sounded like really bad porn. All exaggerated huffing and puffing.'

'Come on, big boy. Show me what you've got,' Bel says throatily, and that's enough for us to keep laughing.

'Do either of you know the answer?' Rachel nudges me, sounding annoyed.

We've missed the last question but we tune back in just as Aardi repeats it. 'From which country did vindaloo originate?'

'It's Portugal,' I say quietly, leaning forward so that the rest of my team can hear me.

'You're sure?' Miro asks. He is writing the answers down.

'Positive.' My dad is Spanish but his mum was Portuguese so we spent many family holidays there.

Aardi leads us through three more categories – one of which is current music, not our best without Harry on hand – and then we take a break. Miro and Bryn go straight up to the table for food and drink while I look around for Mrs Fleming. I notice her close to the exit. Robin has beaten me to it and is talking to her. Maxine is there too. When I stand up, Bel grabs my arm, fear in her eyes. 'You're not going to tell her about the latest note, are you?'

'I thought I should.' I sit back down. 'I won't tell her what it says.' I run a hand through my hair. 'How did your chat with Amira go earlier?'

'She was really kind. She even said she would help me tell Miro if I needed her support.'

'You're not telling him, though?' Rachel asks.

'I don't know.' She looks at me. 'I tore the note up, Nina. I hope that's okay?'

'Sure.' I nod. 'I would do the same.'

'What's Robin saying to her?' Rachel asks.

I tell them about the conversation I heard him having earlier with Maxine and Suze. 'It sounds as if Mrs

Fleming is being very strict with the kids and it's upsetting some of the parents,' I add.

The three of us are quiet as we watch the mums and dads in the hall, collecting food and drink, moving between tables and catching up with each other. Several of them look in our direction but nobody comes over to talk to us, which strikes me as strange.

'We seem to be personae non gratae,' Bel says, reading my thoughts.

'I don't know why,' I say.

'It's all the gossiping that's going on,' Bel says. 'They can convince themselves of anything.'

'Only one more week until half-term,' Rachel says. 'It can't come soon enough.'

'You're telling me.' Bel stands up. 'Do you want anything to drink?'

'No thanks.' I watch Bel and Rachel move off towards the table and feel a rising panic. I want to be on my own. To think. *Really* think. And to plan. Maybe I should take the girls out of school before half-term, which would also avoid more notes. But would that set Robin off? Could his solicitor use it against me?

I walk out into the corridor that runs parallel to the hall, double fire doors leading outside at either end. The toilets in this building are adult-sized and I close myself inside a cubicle, sitting for longer than I need to because it's peaceful, and I'm a little drunk and a lot tired. I have another couple of swigs of whisky, savour the heat in my throat. I hear two women come into the toilet but I don't budge. I don't want to have to make small talk. I don't want to go back out there at all. The loos are flushed, followed by the sound of running taps and the loud hand dryer.

And then I hear the conversation.

171

'Bel Novak is worse. I can't get on with her. She's so opinionated.'

'It's Lily Myers who's been getting notes in her school bag. And because Mrs Fleming is so keen to please the Myers family, she's having a go at the other kids.'

'I heard about that.'

'I would bet my life it isn't anyone in the class that's doing it. Maxine's son has been blamed and she's really upset about it.'

'Mrs Fleming isn't good with boys. She was awful with Marcus.'

'I mean, a few notes in a school bag? It's hardly the end of the world but because it's precious Lily Myers we all have to take it seriously.'

'Well, it is quite nasty, to be fair.'

'Is it, though? Or is the problem that nothing like this ever happens in Nina's perfect world? Have you seen the house they live in?'

'I know someone who worked with her in London. She had a breakdown before they moved here.'

I sit up straighter, feel heat rise into my cheeks.

'Did she? Maybe Robin wasn't letting her get her own way. He's a good addition to our team although he's really flirting with Maxine.'

'And she's enjoying it.'

'I bet Nina's high-maintenance, always controlling everything for her precious girls.'

I've heard enough. I come out of the cubicle and both their faces freeze when they see me. I step between them and slowly wash my hands, taking time to spread the liquid soap between each of my fingers and thumbs. Neither of them speaks. Suze is holding a lipstick and the mother of Marcus, a woman I've never met, is holding a hairbrush. They are both completely still, hands halfway towards lips and hair, suspended in time as if in a photograph. When I place my hands under the dryer I watch their expressions in the mirror as their eyes meet. They have the grace to look guilty.

The other mother, not Suze, follows me out of the bathroom. 'I'm sorry. That was awful of us,' she calls after me, and then she steps right in front of me so that I have to either stop or walk round her.

I choose to stop. I don't smile. I'm damned if I'm going to make this easy for her. I know gossip is rife, all part and parcel of people's insecurity, but it's still difficult to listen to.

'I'm Terri Harper.' She holds out her hand. I don't take it. 'I work for Mason and Dean Associates. I read the article about you in the March edition of the *Law Journal*. Your career is so impressive.' I frown at this. Does she think flattery will wipe out what I've just heard? 'I'd love to have the opportunity to join your team. Would I be able to send you my CV?'

'I don't know, Terri,' I say, laughing despite myself. 'Would you?'

She doesn't miss a beat. 'I realise my request might seem a bit off after what you just heard—' She waves in the direction of the loos. 'But I feel I have the right skill set to add value to your company.'

'We're not hiring at the moment,' I say, almost admiring her persistence. Her brass neck could be useful in some areas of the business.

'The thing is, Nina—'

I hold up my hand. 'Let me tell you what the thing is, Terri. None of us ever really know what's going on in someone else's life or, for that matter, their marriage.'

'No, I—'

'Thank you for your interest in working for me but, at this point in time, it's a very definite no.'

I walk away then, towards Suze and Bel who are ahead of me in the corridor. Not content with rubbishing me in the toilets, Suze looks to be having a go at Bel. As I approach, I hear Bel say to her, 'What exactly is your beef?'

I go through the open exit door beyond them and stand outside, resting my back against the brick wall. I can still hear everything that's being said inside, but instead of seeing their faces, I watch the full moon that hangs above me like a bright, polished pebble. The air is cool on my face and it helps me to breathe more easily.

'The three of you are really cliquey! And your girls are the same. And now with all of this, we have to play it your way. If there was another note then you should tell us! It isn't fair that we're left wondering. The first note said this class has secrets—'

'And you're worried your secret will be broadcast far and wide?' Bel asks.

'I don't *have* a secret,' Suze snaps.

'Well, rest assured. There was nothing about you in the note.'

'That's not good enough.'

'Well, it's all you're getting.'

'Let me break in here.' It's Robin's voice. I close my eyes and silently curse him. 'Bel, you and I have been friends for a long time.'

'I'm friends with Nina,' she replies coldly. 'Not you.'

'Would you excuse us, Suze?' he asks. I don't hear her reply but I take it she has left because Robin continues. 'I hope you don't mind me asking this but

I'm wondering whether you've noticed any changes in Nina lately?'

'You'll have to be more specific,' Bel tells him.

'I don't know whether you're aware, but just before we moved here, Nina had had a difficult time.'

'How come?' Bel asks.

'She was working too hard and her mental health suffered.'

'It wasn't because you were having an affair, then?' she fires back.

I give a quiet cheer and raise my fist into the air.

'Bel, I'm worried for the girls.' He's using his doctor's voice: professional, persuasive, knowing. 'Nina's breakdown was serious and I fear she's heading that way again.' I flinch. Bel and Rachel know very little about my breakdown but I'm almost glad Robin's doing this not-so-skilful manipulation because it will help Bel appreciate what I'm up against.

'You're not talking about the Nina I know,' Bel says.

'The trouble is that Nina doesn't always know when to ask for help.'

'Fuck off, Robin.' She's sounding fed up now. I should really go back inside and deal with Robin myself but the evening light is so calming.

'I'm worried she'll grow paranoid again, start imagining things—'

'But she's not imagining things, Robin,' Bel says. 'You. Are. Having. An affair.'

'I can see she's got you convinced—'

'Are you deluded?' she shouts.

A warning signal sounds in my brain. Bel's about to see red and then she won't censor herself. She'll say whatever comes into her head. I move away from the wall and run back inside. 'Bel, don't!' I call out.

She can't hear me. She's right in his face. 'Nina has listened to your phone calls! She's seen your texts! She knows where your car is parked!'

The words are out of her mouth in less than the time it takes me to reach her, and Robin is completely blindsided. He turns to me, his whole body shaking with pent-up rage.

Chapter Seventeen

I've never seen him this shocked and angry before, even when I caught him with his boxers round his ankles having sex with Kimberley. He continues to stare at me, his eyes wide, his expression horrified. 'You're spying on me?'

'What? I . . .' Bel is looking from him to me. 'Nina?'

'You bitch.' He comes up close to me, his spit landing on my cheek. I wipe it off with the back of my hand. 'Have you? Have you been spying on me?'

'Yes.' I take a step away from him. 'I have. And it's been really enlightening.'

'How? Why? Who made you do this?'

Like I couldn't come up with this myself? 'You made me do this, Robin. *You.*'

He stares down at the floor, taking several breaths before coming back at me. 'You will pay for this betrayal, Nina. Make no mistake.' He leaves me with a final, dark look before walking off in the direction of the hall.

Bel rushes towards me. 'Don't.' I keep her away with a look.

'I'm so sorry, Nina.' She twists her hands. 'I thought you said you'd told him about the divorce.'

'He didn't know about the spyware,' I tell her.

'But you said you were going to tell him.'

'Well, I didn't! And it was my information to tell!' I pace around in a circle, feel the stress of the whole evening gather in a tight fist in my middle. 'Some of what I'm doing is borderline illegal!'

'I'm so sorry.' She bangs her forehead with her hand. 'You know what I'm like. My mouth runs away from me. I didn't mean it.'

'For fuck's sake, Bel!' My face twists as fury erupts from my mouth like vomit. 'You never mean it, do you? You put your foot in it time and time again! And then you say you're sorry and that makes everything okay.'

'Nina, please.'

'You're a grown woman who behaves like a child. Worse than a child because you should know better!'

'But—'

'Just stay out of my life, okay?' I watch her face redden and tears spill into her eyes but I don't care. 'Sort your own fucking life out.'

I go outside and kick the wall, feel pain flood into my foot. Tears run down my face. What was I thinking? Why did I let her talk to him? Have I learned nothing about Bel?

I hobble around the car park, the pain gradually easing when a text from Eleri comes into my phone: *Lily doesn't want to stay overnight and she's wondering whether she can come home with you when you collect Poppy?*

I have no intention of going back inside for the second half of the quiz. I know how it will look when I don't return and if people didn't hear the shouting then they'll be able to draw their own conclusions for my absence – I'm upset because my husband is flirting, my daughter is being bullied, I'm being spoken about behind my back. They can take their pick. They can say what they like. I'm going to collect my daughters and take them home.

I have one last glance through the window into the main hall and see Robin talking to Rachel now. Rachel is listening intently as if his words are important. As if she believes him. Does she? Does she believe him? Aardi is watching them both, his expression unreadable. I remember that he was once on Robin's surgical team, back when we first moved south. For some reason, they didn't see eye to eye and Aardi moved to another speciality. I'd forgotten about their connection.

I can't drive because the whisky has pushed me over the limit and Rachel's house is a good mile from the school but, no matter, the evening air is mild and I'm wearing trainers. It feels blissfully simple to walk in the twilight, one foot after the other, nothing to grab my attention or set my thoughts racing. The sky is cloudless and the moon lights my way.

I turn my phone to silent after the first phone call from Bel. It vibrates in my pocket every few minutes but I ignore it. The chatter has stopped. I'm free to forget everything that's going on behind me. If only for a little while.

When I reach Rachel's house, I ring the doorbell and wait. I have to ring it a second time before Eleri answers. 'Nina! Hi! We didn't expect you quite so early.'

'I decided to cut loose.' I step inside. 'I thought I'd come for the girls now before it gets too late.'

'Your timing is good. They've just finished the movie and were about to start another.' She leans in and whispers, 'I haven't been able to get them to talk to each other. And they won't tell me why they've fallen out. It's all been a bit awkward.'

The four girls are lying on long, oblong beanbags on the floor. Normally the three friends would be squashed together on one bag but this evening Lily and Poppy are sharing a beanbag, and Vera and Carys are on separate ones. The atmosphere in the room is strained; there is a distinct lack of camaraderie.

'Evening, girls!'

Lily and Poppy jump up at once. 'Mummy! You came!'

Carys doesn't budge but Vera stands up too. 'Could you take me home Nina, please?' she asks, her eyes hopeful.

'I'm sorry, darling, your mum and dad are still at school,' I say. 'I'm sure Eleri will text them for you. They can collect you on their way home.'

She flops back down onto the beanbag, sighing with frustration.

'Vera could come with us,' Lily whispers in my ear.

I give her a doubtful look. If I hadn't just fallen out with Bel I might consider it but under the circumstances I have to shake my head. 'Not tonight, love.'

They gather together their jackets and bags and we go outside. 'Where's the car?' Poppy asks.

'I left it at school.'

'We're walking?' She lets her belongings fall onto the pavement and folds her arms. 'That's ridiculous!'

'Stop using that word, Poppy!' Lily says, her tone scolding. Then she looks at me and asks, 'Why did you leave before Daddy?'

'He ended up in a different team,' I tell her.

'Ridiculous! Ridiculous! Ridiculous!' Poppy shouts, watching her sister for a reaction.

Before Lily retaliates, I grab Poppy's stuff and run ahead of them both. 'Come on, girls! It'll be fun! The moon is lighting our way.'

They are soon running alongside me and every time they complain I encourage them on with laughs and praise. We approach the crossroads where we can either continue along the pavement or cut through the woods. 'Can we go the short cut?' Poppy asks.

'It'll be too scary,' Lily says, pulling at her sleeve.

'We have the moon to guide us,' Poppy says.

'We won't be able to see it because of the trees.'

'Let's face our fears!' I shout and give a mock salute. Poppy does the same, pulling her heels in as the side of her hand meets her forehead. 'When we're in the dense part of the forest, I'll turn on my phone torch.'

'We're having an adventure!' Poppy says.

Lily still looks doubtful. 'But what if we lose each other?'

'Put your hands in the pockets of my jeans, both of you. One either side, that's it. And then we won't get separated.'

We follow the narrow path for several metres before we plunge into the woods. I feel Lily tense beside me until the torch lights the way ahead. We walk forward, treading on broken twigs and last year's leaves, the crunch underfoot a comforting sound. Wild garlic grows either side of the path, the pungent scent filling the air around us.

'All the birds are asleep,' Poppy loud-whispers. 'Their heads will be under their wings, won't they, Mummy?'

An owl toots to our left and another to our right as if to answer her question. 'Not quite all the birds,' I say.

'When we have Pickle we'll take him out in the dark,' Poppy says. 'It'll be so much fun.'

We talk about the puppy and how much he'll love digging around in the undergrowth. I feel Lily relax as she joins in with the conversation, anticipating the good times we'll have together. A soft rain is beginning to fall as we reach the gate into our back garden.

'That was the best!' Poppy says when we're inside, breathless and flushed from the exercise. 'We should do it every night!'

They're quick to bed, and so am I, although I don't fall asleep immediately. I lie and think about what the two mums said in the toilets and about how having a breakdown is something you're never allowed to forget. Family and friends whisper behind your back. *Is she okay? She's not heading towards another crisis is she?* Mental health is meant to be seen much more sympathetically these days but, in my experience, you have to be careful not to allow people to use it against you.

I scroll back through the evening, my memory train stopping at several stations along the way. I feel as if, similar to our girls, my friendship with Rachel and Bel has taken a beating – mostly Bel, who I know would support me to the bitter end, but she would do it her way not mine. Rachel, I feel uneasy about. I can't put my finger on it but the look on her face when she was talking to Robin was troubling. Did she believe what he was telling her? Was he telling her about me or was he asking her if she knew about the spyware? And *was* it her on the footpath over the hedge who overheard Robin calling me a whore? Has she kept this to herself? Or did she tell someone what she heard?

It takes me a while to fall asleep, the tiny, furtive seeds of doubt about both my friends darkening my dreams with scenes of betrayal and isolation. When twice I wake up, it's with a strong sense of knowing what being truly alone feels like.

Chapter Eighteen

BEL

I don't normally work on Saturdays but I get a phone call at seven in the morning and say an automatic yes to covering a shift. Jeff, a fellow pharmacist, is off sick with gastric flu – or as Miro puts it – a hangover – and it's convenient for me to work today because it will keep me gainfully employed. I need to get out of the village or else I'll end up round at Nina's house banging on her windows and doors, making things even worse. I've called her umpteen times since last night and she's yet to reply to my voicemails and messages. I know I've badly let her down, and when, after the quiz ended, I told Miro what I'd said, he didn't make me feel any better.

'What! How could you? She confided in you that she was using the spyware and now you've given Robin ammunition to use against her.'

'I know. I shouldn't have. Fuck.' I grabbed his hand and started twirling his wedding ring, but the repetition that was normally so comforting did nothing to calm my spirits. 'Do you think she'll forgive me?'

'I suppose so.' He shook his head at me. 'But, honestly Bel, there's a lot going on for her. It's serious. You need to be a good friend. Not make things harder.'

I swear I couldn't feel any worse. The secret I'm keeping from Miro is a ticking time bomb and now I've messed things up for Nina. Though it's only been a matter of hours since I spoke to her, and she's entitled to feel angry with me, I can't bear the silence. I hate that I might have made things more difficult for her. And when we do speak, there will be an awkwardness between us. Maybe for weeks, months, years. Maybe forever. What if she never forgives me?

When she didn't reappear for the second half of the quiz night, I told Aardi she'd had a phone call from her parents that she needed to follow up on. I'm not sure anyone believed me, least of all Robin who eyed me with undisguised spite for the remainder of the evening.

I leave Vera and Miro together and drive to the hospital. The morning sky is the colour of shingles, washed greys and blues, and I sense that the weather could tip either way: brighten with turquoise and sunshine or darken with moody navies and slate grey. 'The weather is mirroring my life,' I say out loud, my voice falling flat in the empty car.

By the time I get to work the sky still hasn't made up its mind and when I check my mobile, neither has Nina. Not a dicky bird. I find a space in the car park and use my pass to go into the building through one of the side doors close to the pharmacy. My white coat is in my locker along with a few essentials, plus my mug with Vera and Miro's grinning faces on it, and snacks in case I have to work through lunch. I also keep a supply of pregnancy tests in my locker and I slip one of them into the pocket of my white coat. Rachel was right about it being better to use an early morning urine because the hormone levels are higher, but with everything else that's going on, I'll save the test for when I feel calmer. I want to live longer with the possibility of some good news on the horizon.

My colleague has arrived early and is making up prescriptions for patients who are attending the clinics; the medicines for the wards have already been prepared and are laid out in the large walk-in cupboard.

'I can do the ward rounds this morning,' I tell her. 'I know Jeff normally does them and I'm happy to step into his shoes. Saves rewriting the rota.'

'Are you sure?' She looks at me with surprise. 'It's not like you to get down and dirty on the general wards.'

Only because I've been promoted beyond it. I don't say that. It's true – I specialise in oncology so don't usually get involved with the day-to-day pharmacy work – but it would sound snooty and I'm not a jobsworth. What's more, I've decided to begin Operation Catch Robin Out – then I might be able to give Nina news about who he is having the affair with. I know the smart money is on Maxine but it might not be her, and if it isn't, then I want to come up with a name for Nina. It might go some of the way towards helping her to forgive me. I check the consultants' weekend rota and see that Robin is on call today. He won't come in to the hospital unless there's an emergency. Either way, it doesn't really matter. There's a particular nurse who has his ear to the ground; he's the guy I'm after.

I load the medicines onto a locked trolley, organising them sequentially according to the wards I'll reach first. Prof Myers is a respiratory consultant and, when not in surgery, can usually be found in the High Dependency Unit. Even better, I spot an insulin prescription in the fridge for him. Generally staff don't collect their prescriptions from the hospital pharmacy but Robin is an exception. He is our star surgeon and we all bend over backwards to accommodate him. I'm reminded of an occasion last year when he made a mistake with his prescription and ended up having a serious hypo. Nina has often mentioned that he is careless with his own health.

The HDU is on the top floor, at the other end of the hospital. I spend the first hour visiting the wards en route, catching up with staff I haven't seen in a while and answering any questions they have. The hospital is busy. Extra funding was given for weekend surgeries and clinics to cut waiting times so it's all systems go. The theatres are at full capacity, clinics the same, and there is a feeling of industry about the place.

Each ward has its own particular fingerprint. Some feel stuffy and hot – body odour, blood, the smell of cauterised flesh lingering in the air – while others are fresh and bright. I leave my supplies with the nurses in charge, watch it being checked and locked in the cupboard and have them electronically sign for the delivery. There are several women in labour in the maternity suite, cries echoing along the low-ceilinged corridor as their babies are delivered. Might be me, again, one day. I close my eyes and send up a silent, heartfelt prayer.

My trolley is emptying and I'm close to HDU when I spot Kevin. Just the man I want. 'And who do we have here?' he shouts when he sees me approaching. 'Touting her wares in these hallowed halls.'

He gives me a hug. A proper hug, tight and all-en-compassing. He is theatrical (am-dram in his off time), good-humoured and legendary throughout the hospital. He is one of those nurses who goes above and beyond. He's the union rep, he fundraises for the hospital and his mother-in-law has worked in the canteen since God was a boy. And we have an extra layer of affinity, me and him – we are both Scots in the land of the English.

'Looking lovely as ever,' he says. 'You're like a fairy sprite. You never age.'

We move to one side of the corridor and catch up with news about our partners and children and then I say, 'Bearing in mind you are the font of all knowledge . . .' He raises questioning eyebrows. 'By which I mean—' I bite my lip '—gossip.'

He nods. 'As long as it doesn't injure the innocent.'

'You heard any whispers about Prof Myers having an affair?'

'Well.' He grabs my arm and pulls us in closer to the wall. 'Funny you should say that. Rumour has it, he might not be quite the upstanding gentleman that we all believed him to be.'

'Meaning?'

'You're friends with Nina, aren't you?'

'Best friends.' I swallow quickly, crossing my fingers behind my back, hoping that's still true.

'We *love* Nina. Whenever she comes to functions she makes a real effort to join in, especially the auction last year.' He shakes his head at the memory, still struck by it. 'She gave more money than most of the rest of us put together.'

'She's a lovely person,' I say, knowing that, if she cuts me out of her life, I'll never find a friend like her again.

'Who deserves better.' He tilts his head. 'It's not just me. That's the general opinion.'

'So?' I fold my arms and lean in. 'Names?'

'The money's on Emily Birch.'

I think for a second. 'Hospital admin, isn't she?'

'Just been promoted to deputy. And apparently this isn't the first time the Prof's played away from home. I mean—' His lips are pursed as he looks up at the ceiling. 'It's disappointing really, isn't it? With him getting an MBE and all. I know he's not being given it for his personal life but still.'

Emily Birch – Em not M. 'Cheers, Kevin.' I look at my watch. 'You're a pal.'

We say our goodbyes and I approach the entrance to the HDU, using my pass to get inside and make a beeline for the treatment room. As luck would have it, Robin is there with two nurses who have clearly just finished setting up a trolley with several sterile clinical packs and a line of loaded syringes.

'Pharmacy delivery!' I announce, and they all look across.

'Bell!' Robin gives me a false smile. 'Twice in two days.'

'Lucky us, eh?'

'What brings you this far out of your comfort zone?' he sneers.

'Drugs,' I say. 'Drugs are always in my comfort zone.'

'Make of that what you will!' he jokes, and the more junior nurse laughs. The nurse in charge is less taken with his charms and is already unlocking the cupboard.

'And I have your insulin prescription,' I tell him.

'Great. I keep meaning to fill the script in the village but never get round to it.'

'You can do it all online now,' I tell him. 'And have it delivered to your door.'

'I didn't know that.' He smiles again. 'I'll get Nina on to it.'

'I'm sure she has nothing better to do, Robin,' I say. Our eyes meet and hold. I see the venom in his stare and I know that he'd kill me if he could. It makes my smile wider.

I trundle my trolley back along the corridors to the pharmacy, smiling at everyone I pass. Now that I have a strong lead on Robin's mistress, I have something to offer Nina to get her friendship back.

Chapter Nineteen

NINA

Saturday morning, I wake to find Poppy clambering across my bed. 'I'm going to FaceTime Grandma and Grandad,' she tells me. 'I need to show them my skipping because I'm so good now and they need to know about Pickle.'

'Okay.' I squint at my watch. Somehow I've slept until nine.

'You have lots of messages from Bel.' Poppy is bouncing on my bed now, my mobile in her hand. 'Do you want me to read them for you?'

'No, don't read them.' I sit up quickly and reach for her. 'Give me the phone, please.'

'I'll just read the first one—'

'Poppy! Now!'

She throws the phone at me, her expression startled. 'There's no need to shout, Mummy!'

'Go get Lily and set up FaceTime on the television. You know how to do it.'

She marches off, full of righteous indignation, murmuring 'ridiculous' to herself. I have a voicemail and a text from Rachel, three voicemails and ten texts from Bel and one voicemail from Robin. I don't look at or listen to any of them. I need a coffee and I need time to think.

I stand under the water in the shower, my eyes closed as it pounds the sore spots on my neck. I wonder whether Robin came back to the cabin last night but mostly I wonder what he intends to do about the revelation that I've been spying on him. We're married, so most of what I've been doing isn't illegal but it's all a bit grubby, a bit *News of the World*. I accepted that when I started out on this road. My husband is a liar and I knew that to separate the truth from the lies, I'd have to operate with a certain amount of moral compromise.

As I'm walking down the stairs, I hear my mum and dad's cheerful hellos sound out through the living room.

'Look, Grandad!' Poppy shouts, waving a rope at him. 'I'm getting really good at this!' She begins skipping across the room, the rope skimming the wooden floor with a rhythmic slap.

'Good heavens! Aren't you clever!' my dad says. 'I'm going to try that.'

I wave to them both and tell them I'll come for a chat when I've got myself a coffee. They give me a thumbs-up and ask Lily if she likes skipping. She gets up at once and Poppy holds out the rope for her to use.

Twelve years ago my mum and dad retired to the Lake District. I wish they lived closer but at the same time I'm glad they don't because they would be worried at the state of my marriage. My dad can read my every mood (not quite so easy on screen) and I know they have been quietly watching me for signs of another crisis.

The first time Robin was having an affair he denied it. I knew there was something going on because of all those subtle tells: he was vague about where he was going, what he was doing, brought me flowers and jewellery to divert my attention, booked a family holiday, only to spend most of it on his mobile, lowering his voice if ever I came close to him. Work, he would say, pointing to the handset and rolling his eyes then leaving the girls and I on the beach for hours.

Every time I brought it up, he persuaded me that I was losing my grip on reality. I was being paranoid, imagining things that weren't there. Was I stressed from work? Was it my hormones? Early menopause?

I was exhausted from caring for a small child and a baby, one who never seemed to sleep, and at the same time I was building my career. Robin was doing the same with his career and that gave him the perfect excuse to be unreliable. He would promise to be home by seven but, more often than not, turn up close to midnight.

When I caught him with Kimberley, I very quickly spiralled into depression, and was admitted to hospital. My parents came to stay at our London house to care for the girls. I was resident in a psychiatric facility for almost a month, sectioned for my own safety.

When I look back on those days it's all a bit hazy. I seemed to spend most of my time either asleep or in therapy. One thing that does stand out is that my dad visited me every day. Normally a man who could talk for Spain and England combined, he sat quietly beside me reading a book. He brought me the food I liked, small tales of the girls and various seasonal gifts from the garden – a yellow rose, a leaf veined with red, once even a tiny frog, my favourite garden creature from when I was a child, that shimmered green and gold. 'We're going to release him back into the garden later today,' he told me. 'But Lily and I thought you might like to see him first.'

Twice a week my mum and the girls came with my dad and I would hug their little bodies, try not to cry at the feel and the smell of them, so familiar and yet so strange to me. I was a pared-back version of myself. I could stand and sleep and eat. I could feel the sun on my face. I could pour a glass of water and swallow a tablet. Anything else – being a mother? What was that? How did that happen? – felt leagues beyond me.

Robin visited me twice a week after work. I hadn't wanted him to visit because I had yet to get my head around his affair but the therapist had advised that we keep 'the lines of communication open'. Despite his medical background, he didn't know how to speak to me. He would confuse me with stories of my company. My partner Jane had told me not to give work a second thought, which was just as well because I struggled with first thoughts never mind second ones, but Robin persisted in talking clients and cases. After a week of this, as soon as he started to speak, my eyes would close and I'd put my hands over my ears. Perhaps a nurse set him right because after that, he sat quietly, my hand in his.

When I came home from the hospital, still delicate in head and heart but more able to think and plan for the future, my dad was all for me leaving him. 'You can move up north with the girls. There are several properties for sale close by.' He was appalled by Robin's lies and his cheating. 'Leopards and spots, Nina. He'll never change and you could do so much better.' He couldn't get his head around Robin's betrayal. Over the course of my parents' forty-four-year marriage, they had remained true to each other. I'm sure there were low points but there was never any question of infidelity.

My mum's advice was more practical. 'Life's no fairy tale, Nina,' she said sadly. 'We all make compromises.'

'It's the lying, Mum,' I told her. 'All those weeks when he let me feel like I was going mad.'

'But what about the girls? He's their dad. You need to put them first.'

'I *am* putting them first. But I'd also quite like to have a husband I can trust.'

'I understand.' She hugged me. 'Is the couples counselling helping?'

Was it helping? Yes and no. We were listening to each other. We were being more honest with each other. At least, I know I was. I still loved Robin, I really did. But something was lost and I wasn't sure that it could be found. I hoped. But I wasn't sure.

My parents put their own lives on hold and stayed for six months. By the time they left for their home in the Lakes, Robin and I had found our way back to each other. He was once more the man I met and married: kind, thoughtful, amusing, keen to spend time with me, happy in the house, happy in bed.

'It's because of the notes.' Poppy's loud voice breaks into my train of thought. 'Someone's been writing mean things to Lily. It's ridiculous! And Mummy and Mrs Fleming are trying to fix it.'

'Bloody hell!' I say under my breath. I'd been keeping this from my parents because I know how much they worry.

I swallow a hurried mouthful of coffee and I hear my dad say, 'Well, that sounds awful. Nina!' he calls out. 'What's going on?'

'I'm here!' I sit down between the girls and they tuck in either side of me, their arms entwined with mine. 'It's really nothing to worry about. We think the notes have stopped now, don't we, Lily?'

'What did they say?' my mum asks.

'Lies about parents in the class, mostly me and Robin.'
I rub my forehead. 'We're trying not to make a big thing of it.'

'Some of the words *I* didn't even know,' Poppy says.

'And they're not to be repeated,' I warn her, not even sure how she found out exactly what the notes said. From Lily or another child at school, maybe?

'They were very rude,' she tells my parents and then giggles, her hand shooting up to cover her mouth.

My mum and dad look at each other. I can see they are concerned. 'When are you next coming to visit?' my dad asks.

'Tomorrow!' Poppy shouts out.

'It's October half-term the week after next. We could drive up.' I pull the girls in closer. 'That would be fun, girls, wouldn't it?'

'And we're getting a puppy!' Poppy says.

They move on to talking about dogs and I go into the kitchen to begin making breakfast. My parents have two dogs and my brother Dylan, who lives close to them, has a smallholding. I had one of those childhoods that seemed very normal at the time but in retrospect was special. My dad was all about fun and freedom. I expect sometimes it got on my mum's nerves – she always had to be the adult – but for Dylan and I, he was the best. He made life interesting. We would lie outside in the dark and stare up at the stars. He taught us about bugs and small animals and every year they saved for a holiday where we could experience something new: one year skiing, another canoeing, often climbing.

Before my mum retired she was an English teacher and she ensured Dylan and I got the most out of school. She is still a vocabulary pedant and as I top up my coffee, I hear her say to Poppy, 'It's not pasgetti, darling, it's spaghetti.' And then: 'Do you know how to spell that, Lily?'

The chat goes on for a while and it cheers me up no end, my dad and Poppy outdoing each other with their antics. He finds a rope in their garage and they skip together. Although miles apart, the wonder of FaceTime is something that unites us.

Just before we end the call, my dad asks after Robin. The girls have gone through to the kitchen to have breakfast and my mum is answering their door. 'He's fine,' I say, smiling. 'Working hard. You know how that goes.' I hear the false note in my voice and I check my dad's expression to see whether he has heard it too.

He has.

'Nina,' he says. He glances over his shoulder then back at the screen. 'You know we're always here for you, don't you? Don't leave it too late.' *Not like last time* is the unspoken end of his sentence.

I blow him a kiss. 'I love you, Dad.'

'I love you too, Nina.' The kiss he blows back catches in my throat and when I turn off the connection there are tears in my eyes.

Chapter Twenty

We spend the rest of Saturday together, just the three of us. Robin doesn't appear and I don't check my phone. I genuinely don't care where he is. The girls and I are a happy threesome, cocooned in our own company. We read, tidy the garden, talk, play, eat our favourite meals and in the evening we watch a film we all love. We decide that everyone sleeping in my bed is the perfect way to end the day and after I've finished reading the girls their bedtime story, I lie back and close my eyes too, let myself drift off into a sound, dreamless sleep, the restorative power of spending quality time with my girls working its magic.

Next morning, I'm awake first. I quietly slide out of bed, careful not to wake the girls, and wrap myself in my dressing gown. The Porsche isn't in the driveway and so I walk down to the bottom of the garden to check the cabin. It's empty but the sandalwood-like scent lingers again. I open all the windows and go back up to the house to make breakfast for us all. Sunday is pancake day, with maple syrup and bacon for Robin and me, chocolate spread for the girls.

Twenty-four hours' time-out from everything has

done me good and before I make the pancake batter, I finally check my texts and voicemails.

I begin with Robin's. The first voicemail arrived on Friday evening and is fifteen seconds of silence. The second, he left yesterday afternoon. 'Bel was here a moment ago,' he says, his tone terse. 'She never comes to HDU. I don't know what you're playing at, Nina, but I ask you politely to respect my workplace.'

I have no idea what this means. Surely Bel wouldn't have gone up there to speak to him about what happened at the quiz night? Has she no sense? I delete both his messages and move on to Rachel. 'I'm worried, Nina. Why did you disappear before the second half? Did Bel do something? Because she looked pretty devastated.'

I'll contact Rachel later today. I remember her listening to Robin just before I left. She looked keen to hear what he had to say but maybe I'm reading too much into it. It was an emotionally charged evening and I was barely seeing straight when I left, not because of the whisky but because of Robin's reaction when he found out about the spyware. I'm still keen to know what they were talking about, though. I need to know she's on my side, not his.

I take a deep breath before working through Bel's messages. The texts are all multiple sorrys, repeated over and over like the chorus to a song. The voicemails are similar, until I get to the final one which came yesterday around about the same time as Robin's. This one is different. She sounds upbeat, more like herself. 'I'm covering a shift at work today and I've found out something that I know you'll be interested in. Let me know when's a good time. And . . . yeah. I won't say the "S" word again but I hope you know how much I regret my behaviour last night. Lots of love.'

I keep my dressing gown wrapped around me and

take a mug of coffee outside to sit in the early morning sun and think. My life is made so much richer by having Bel and Rachel as friends and I don't want to lose them – not without very good reason. Bel's loose tongue was just that – a moment when she let rip without engaging her brain first. She wasn't betraying me; she was, in her own way, defending me. And maybe Rachel has always stuck up for Robin a bit more than she needed to but that's only because Bel goes the other way and Rachel is balancing the scales.

By the time Lily and Poppy come downstairs the pancakes are made and I've decided that I'll call both my friends this afternoon when the girls are at their play dates. I hope I'm not making a mistake in trusting Bel and Rachel again.

Max is sitting on his front doorstep when we drive into the street. As soon as he sees the car, he jumps up, grinning. I've already dropped Poppy off at her friend's in the village so I only have Lily in the car. She says a quick goodbye to me and runs off round the side of the house with Max. 'Come and see the tree!' I hear him telling her.

I've already checked the location device and know that the Porsche is within twenty metres of where I'm standing. The Mayfair house is a modern four-bed with double garage. The doors are closed to the garage but, could Robin's car be parked in there?

I ring the front doorbell, to let Maxine know that Lily is here. She throws the door wide open and says, 'Come in! You'll stay for a coffee?'

It's exactly what I hoped she would say. 'That would be great.' I smile. 'Thank you.'

Inside, the house is open plan and feels airy and

bright, all white walls and large windows, long muslin drapes framing the patio doors. In the kitchen there are piles of flattened cardboard boxes lying in one corner.

'I'm sent products to review,' Maxine tells me. 'Sometimes I have to send them back but mostly I can give them away.' She looks me up and down, her eyes narrowing. I'm beginning to realise that this is something she does. It's not a criticism so much as her eye homing in on what she likes. 'Karen Millen?'

'Sorry?'

'Your blouse.' She feels the edge of my sleeve. 'This is really good quality silk. Do you enjoy shopping?'

'No!' I laugh. 'Not at all. My business partner and I have someone who makes selections for us then brings them into the office.'

'Wow.' She gives me an admiring glance. 'What is it you do?'

'I'm a lawyer. I specialise in business law, nothing glamorous or interesting.'

'You earn a lot, though, I guess. Now listen.' She grabs my arm, her expression serious. 'Two things. Firstly, I heard that Suze and Terri were talking about you in the toilets on Friday and I want you to know that I would not have joined in with that bitchiness. Max and Lily are friends so, as far as I'm concerned, we're batting for the same team.'

'Ok-*ay*.' Is this tactical? Or does she genuinely want me for a friend?

'I hope that wasn't why you left early?'

'No, I left early because—' I'm about to tell a lie, a white one, and say that my mum was ill or Poppy needed me to collect her but instead I decide to test her: 'Robin and I aren't getting along and I'd had enough.'

'Oh.' Her blush is visible even through her make-up.

'I shouldn't have let him flirt with me. I'm so sorry! Doctors impress me and then I behave like an airhead. My husband always tells me that.'

'That wasn't my tipping point,' I say with a small smile.

'That's good.' She takes a breath. 'Suze says another note came yesterday?'

'Yes, and I need to speak to Mrs Fleming but I haven't had a chance yet.' I feel the weight of all that's out of control in my life beginning to descend on my shoulders again. I briefly close my eyes and when I open them, I stand up, suddenly sure of what I need to do next. 'Is that the door into your garage?' I ask, pointing to the corner of the kitchen.

Maxine looks surprised. 'Yeah, well there's the utility room and then another door to the garage, but . . .'

I start walking towards it. 'Do you mind if I take a look? We've been wanting to build one just like this.'

'It's a mess in there.' She follows me quickly then steps in front of me just as my fingers grip the handle. 'I mean, really a mess, not worth looking at.' She gives a nervous laugh.

'Please let me,' I say, holding her eyes. She blinks several times but that doesn't hide the fact that she's anxious. Her breathing rate has increased too, her chest heaving as if she's just come in from a run.

'Did someone send you?' she asks, a tremble in her voice.

'No,' I say, wondering what she can possibly mean. 'Nobody sent me. I'm just interested in the layout, that's all.'

She reluctantly moves to one side and I open the door. The utility room is a neat and tidy space but I don't linger here; I walk straight to the opposite wall and pull on the door to the garage. My heart is in my mouth. I expect to see the gleaming bonnet of the white Porsche but instead what I see are boxes piled high, filling the whole space. The writing on the side of the boxes is mostly what looks like an Eastern European language.

'My brother's in the import export business and he leaves his stuff here sometimes.' She's pulling at her hair. 'You won't say anything, will you?'

I think I know what she's worried about. I shake my head. 'No. Of course not. I'm sorry.' I bite my lip to stop myself from smiling. I'm so relieved that the Porsche isn't in here. I didn't want it to be Maxine. I didn't want the complication for Lily's new friendship with Max.

'I mean, it's not exactly illegal what he's doing. But since Brexit and higher taxes. And you being a lawyer. . .' She trails off.

I turn towards her and give her a hug. 'Please, don't worry, Maxine.' I start to laugh. She's staring at me expectantly, her lips twitching as if wondering whether to join in. 'I'm sorry I've made you feel uncomfortable.'

'No worries.' She still looks unsure but shrugs her shoulders and says, 'Let's have that coffee?'

'Definitely.' I feel pleasantly light-headed, as if my brain has shed a heavy weight. 'I've been hoping we'd find time to get to know each other better.'

'Me too,' she says, smiling. There are three coffee machines sitting on the large work surface and she chooses one, tilting her head to one side to see where to insert the pod, her glossy hair swishing back and forward like a curtain.

I settle myself back on a stool at her kitchen island where I can see through the window to the garden. 'Your garden is beautiful,' I say, watching Lily and Max climbing up a 'grandfather' tree as my dad always calls ancient ones like this, with a thick trunk, low-hanging branches and plenty of space for hands and feet to grip and climb.

'This whole estate was part of the old manor house's garden,' she says. 'We were really lucky that they kept the mature trees and bushes to give us a defined boundary.' She hands me a coffee. 'That's straight out of the brochure. I don't normally use words like *mature.*' She does her hand gesture again, finger pointing up and down her body. She's wearing tracksuit bottoms and an oversized hoodie that hangs off one shoulder, showing off her luminous orange bra strap. 'My husband tells me that I dress like a seventeen-year-old.'

'I think you look modern.' I smile at her. It's a real smile. Now that I know she isn't Robin's mistress I can let myself warm to her.

'He would prefer sophisticated. Your blouse would hit the spot.'

There's a shout from the garden, 'I'm at the top!' Max calls out. He is sitting on a branch several metres from the ground and Lily is close behind him.

'Will Lily be okay up there?' Maxine asks.

'Yes. She doesn't look like an outdoorsy child but she's actually really agile. She won't tackle anything she isn't comfortable with.'

'Oh! I have something that would go well with our coffee.' She opens one of the kitchen cupboards and brings out a long box, decorated in pink and gold. 'I need to review these. I don't normally do a lot of food but I promised to try these macarons.'

Delicate, sweet-coloured treats, nestle in the box like jewels. I take a lilac one, bite off half and feel it melt on my tongue. 'Delicious,' I say.

'You know . . .' She's staring at me again, her expression thoughtful. 'You have the most lush cheekbones.'

'I get them from my dad. Spanish genes.' I touch my hair. 'Hence my colouring.'

'Would you let me make you up?' She gives me the same smile that Poppy gives me when she's asking for something she's not normally allowed.

'Well . . . Now?' The last time I was made up was the fateful shopping trip before my Catwoman blunder. But that's in the past and I feel like I owe Maxine. I haven't treated her well. Not only have I been rude to her, but I've also forced my way into her garage and embarrassed her. 'Okay!' I throw up my arms. 'Go for it!'

'I've been sent this *amazing* make-up set to review and you have the perfect look to try it out on.' She disappears into the utility room and is back at once with a vanity case that she places on the breakfast bar. She begins by cleansing my face with a lotion that smells of roses, and moves on to a refreshing toner that makes my skin tingle. 'Relax and enjoy,' she tells me, and I find myself doing as I'm told. I feel as if I'm so far out of my comfort zone that I'm free to let go. This isn't my world. I don't need to strive for success or search for the clever comment. I simply need to surrender.

And my body does just that while my brain ticks on because if Robin's car isn't in her garage then either there's a problem with the software or . . . 'What are your neighbours like?' I ask casually.

She talks about the family living on her right – a couple, three teenage children and a yappy dog. 'They argue a lot,' she says. 'The mum shouts at them almost all the time. I hope I'm not like that with Max.' She dabs foundation on my forehead. 'Robin will probably know the people on the left, with the triple garage. Hubby

206

seems to work away a fair bit, two sons at university. She's an administrator at the hospital.' She pauses to choose an eye shadow. 'I'm giving you a futuristic eye.' She tilts my chin up towards her. 'This will look great on you. There's some glitter involved but don't panic.'

'Maybe I know your neighbour too, the hospital administrator,' I say, keeping up the casual. 'What's her name?'

'Emily Birch. I think they might be getting divorced.' Her voice drops to a low whisper. 'According to the elderly couple who live on the other side of them, there's a man who visits when her husband's away.' Her eyes flare. 'They're bound to be caught before too long. And then it will all kick off.'

Emily.

Em. M doesn't stand for Maxine or Margot or Maddy or Mary but for Emily.

I feel dizzy suddenly and I lurch to one side, quickly righting myself before I fall off my stool.

'Are you okay?' Maxine pauses, mascara brush in hand, her face genuinely concerned.

'I just need a minute.' I stand up and walk around the kitchen. 'Sorry.' The mystery is all but solved. I should feel better, and part of me does, while the other part of me feels gut-wrenchingly sad. I take a steadying breath and hold my hand over my stomach.

'This happened to you the other day.' Maxine is by my side, a hand under my elbow. 'You're not . . .?'

She doesn't finish the sentence – she doesn't need to. I know what she's getting at, and it's so unlikely that it makes me laugh. 'No, I'm not pregnant,' I say, shaking my head. I haven't had sex for months. 'There's no chance of that.' Bel's the one who needs that good news.

Max and Lily come running into the kitchen, breathless

207

and happy after their achievement. 'Did you see us at the top of the tree?' Max asks.

'We did!' Maxine replies. 'Are you having fun, Lily?'

'Yes, thank you.' Her cheeks are pink and her smile is wide. I sit back on the stool and she glances at me quickly then does a double take and comes over to have a closer look.

'You look like an actress,' she says, her tone awestruck. 'Wait until Poppy sees you.'

'Isn't she beautiful, your mummy?' Maxine says.

Max nudges Lily and hands her a juice. 'My mum likes doing make-up,' he tells her. 'She's really good at it.'

They disappear back outside again and Maxine gives me a motherly look. 'Are you okay with me continuing, Nina? Because I know I kind of forced you into this.'

'I'm fine really.' I reach across and squeeze her arm. 'I'm actually quite enjoying it.

'Fab!' Her face lights up and she continues brushing and smoothing away at my eyes and cheeks. 'Do you have an Instagram account?' she asks.

'Oh, I'm not on any social media,' I say. 'I'm on LinkedIn but that's all.'

'Would you mind if I took a photo of you? We don't have to see your whole face. I could just take a picture of your eyes and Instagram it. I have to do this in exchange for the PR package but you really don't have to agree.' Her eyes are wide with sincerity. 'What do you think?'

She hands me the mirror and I look at myself. Not only has she taken ten years off my age but she has highlighted my features so that I look like a model. My eyes pop with colour and glitter falls off the outer edge of my lashes to land on the curve of my cheek. 'You're a miracle worker!' I say. 'Even my mum wouldn't recognise me.'

I agree to a couple of photographs – full face, why not? – and while she is updating her Instagram, I bring my phone out to check to see where the Porsche is. The red circle is flashing on the A22. He must have driven out of Emily Birch's garage while I've been here. That's how he's been getting away with driving such a look-at-me car. It's never been parked in the street.

When Maxine puts her mobile back on the counter I stand up to go. She sees me to the door and we agree that I'll return for Lily after lunch. 'Thank you.' I hug her close. 'You've been so lovely to me and I haven't always been that nice back.'

'Oh.' She blushes. 'That's sweet of you, Nina, but I get it. I really do. I know you thought it was Max writing the notes and I don't blame you. But he's changed.' Her eyes are wide again and I realise that her innocent look isn't an act. 'He's not the boy he was last year. I promise you.'

As if on cue, I hear Lily's laugh filter over the roof of the house. 'With all that's been happening,' I say, 'Max is exactly what Lily needs.' I point towards her garage and add, 'Thank you for letting me inside and please don't worry. I have no interest in your brother's business. I won't tell a soul.'

She laughs, 'I thought he was being busted for a minute!' Then she stands on the step and waves me goodbye and I drive back home, a warm feeling in my chest. Yes, I'm still being cheated on but at least Maxine isn't part of it. And now that I know who is, I can tell my solicitor. I'm going for a no-fault divorce so don't intend to name names but we have her identity should we need it.

When I'm back inside the house, I gather some cleaning materials from the utility room and go upstairs. Two local ladies blitz the house once a month but in between times I do my best to keep things ticking over. I once read that listening to eighties music lowers blood pressure, and I need some of that right now, so I have the radio blaring as I work my way through the upstairs rooms.

Every now and then I catch sight of myself in the mirror and smile. I can't imagine going to all this effort every day but maybe I should consider being a bit more made-up every now and then? I might have to lose the glitter but it would be a real confidence boost.

Both my daughters are untidy, partly because they are overwhelmed with the amount of stuff they have. As soon as they start clearing up they are distracted by something interesting and I find them on the floor, reading a book they haven't seen in a while or colouring in with pencils that were pushed under the bed. I sort out Poppy's room first, picking everything up off the floor and arranging like with like on the shelving units. I strip her bed and leave the sheets on the landing then go into Lily's room. I scoop up the soft toys and books and dump it all on the lower shelves. She'll want to sort it herself when she gets home. When I strip the bed I see a piece of paper stuffed in the space between the mattress and the wall. I throw it into the bin and then stop. The radio is playing Cyndi Lauper and I've been singing along.

Now I'm not singing. I turn off the radio. I stare at the scrunched-up piece of paper. There are grey splodges on it that look to me like black marker pen leaked through from the other side. I take it out of the bin and press it flat.

One of you will die soon and it serves you right
I hope you rot in hell

My hands are shaking as I lay the note on the window-sill. Lily must have found this in her bag and hidden it. I know she wants to avoid upsetting anyone but this is much worse than the other notes. This is a threat, full of hate and venom.

And from a child.

But a child can't kill anyone, can they?

Chapter Twenty-one

I stare at the writing, try to digest the message, and for the first time it makes me seriously consider that whoever is writing these notes could be an adult. Because why on earth would a child write such a thing?

I walk from room to room reminding myself to breathe. Should I call the police? Is one of my friends in imminent danger? Am I in danger?

I feel hot, panicked, on the edge of tears. 'For fuck's sake!' I shout out loud. 'What's going on? Who the fuck is doing this?'

I need advice. That much I know. Robin is useless and my parents would want to drive down the motorway to be here. My dad is not the best driver. He is easily distracted by cows and kestrels and cloud formations. Bel and Rachel then. I was going to call them for coffee and a chat to patch things up, not for more of this. But needs must.

I try Bel and she answers at once. 'Oh, Nina! I'm so pleased you've called. I was so worried and—'

'Don't be pleased,' I cut her off. 'There's another note. Can you come over?'

'Sure.'

I immediately call Rachel and ask her to come too,

try to be patient as she rambles on. 'I've got Eleri's boyfriend coming for lunch but the roast is well underway and Bryn will make the pud.'

I hear Bryn in the background shouting out, 'Leave it to me!'

'I'll be there in a jiffy,' Rachel adds.

I wait at my front door. It's a beautiful early autumn day and the leaves are just beginning to change from green to a warm, rusty brown. The hedgerows either side are busy with birds hopping in and out, whistling and tweeting. This is the idyllic spot I fell in love with, my own small acre of the Ashdown Forest. I want to believe that it will continue to be idyllic and that when this is over, when no one is targeting my family, we can go back to normal. A different normal, one where I keep the house and Robin lives elsewhere, but a normal that still allows the girls to thrive.

Bel and Rachel arrive almost simultaneously. Bel's out of the car first and is walking briskly towards me until she comes to a surprised stop a few feet away. 'Are you going out?' she asks.

'You look amazing,' Rachel says, stopping next to her.

'The make-up?' I touch my face. I'd completely forgotten about it. 'Maxine did it. She had some samples to try out.' I usher them inside.

'And you agreed to it?' Bel says, surprised.

'Are you not still suspicious of her?' Rachel says, her eyes popping.

'Let's talk about that later—'

'Before you show us the note,' Rachel interrupts. 'Can we get the quiz night out the way? What happened to you?'

'It was my fault,' Bel says at once, restlessly moving from one foot to another. 'I thought Robin knew about the spyware and, Nina, I am *so* sorry. I couldn't be more sorry and I will make it up to you.'

I shrug. 'Fine,' I say, still feeling a bit annoyed. 'Let's not mention it again.'

'Okay.' She puts her hands over her face and when she drops them back to her sides, her cheeks are red and her eyes wet. 'I have something to tell you.' She holds up a finger. 'I was covering a shift for one of the pharmacy technicians yesterday so it meant I could deliver the meds to the wards and see whether I could gather any intel about Robin.'

'And did you?' I ask. I know what's coming but I let her say it. I can see that she's offering me this as an olive branch.

'I did.' She tells us about her Scottish friend Kevin and what's being whispered on the wards. 'Emily Birch is her name. I haven't met her but she's an administrator, is on the senior management team within the hospital. Married, two children away at university.'

I should tell them that I know this already, that I found it out this morning. My mouth drops open but no words come out. I don't know why I'm still so shocked. I've been secretly listening to Robin talking to Em on the phone, I've been following his movements with a tracker and I've been reading his texts, but now – it's out in the open. My friend is saying her name, and this is a concrete detail that cannot be denied or wished away. He really is cheating on me. I really will be getting divorced.

'You okay?' Rachel asks, hugging me. 'This is a shocker, hon.'

'But at least it's not Maxine,' Bel says. 'That would have been worse, I think. Wouldn't it?'

'It would.' I want to tell them about how nice Maxine

actually is but I think I'll be met with scepticism so I say nothing. 'Thanks, Bel. I appreciate you finding out for me.' I clear my throat. 'So, I found the note in Lily's room, squashed at the back of her bed.' I take a deep breath. 'Be warned. I think it's a step up from the last one.' I lay it in front of them on the kitchen island then stand back, run the palms of my hands down my jeans. 'What do you think?'

'I think it's . . . scary,' Rachel says, folding her arms and moving away from it as if it might bite her. 'What should we do?'

'I don't know.' I give an exaggerated shrug. 'I'm at a loss. I really am.'

'There's that story about Kennedy,' Bel says, a faraway look in her eye. 'It was during the Cuban missile crisis and he received a threatening fax from the Russians or maybe it was Castro.' Rachel looks at me as if to say – Now? Really? Where is this going? 'If Kennedy had answered the fax, he would have had to ramp up the war rhetoric and so he decided to ignore it.' She stares at us both. 'He simply acted as if it had never arrived. Continued with business as usual. Some historians think that decision averted a third world war.'

'But don't you think there's an implicit threat in this note?' I ask. 'And that makes it worse than the others.'

'But it's from a child,' she says.

'It might be an adult,' Rachel tells her.

'That's what I've been thinking. And it's been sent to *my* child.' I place my hand over my heart. 'One of you will die soon. Does that mean a member of Lily's family? Or one of her friends?'

'I think you should tell the youth officer,' Rachel says. 'Ask her for advice. It's like, you know how psychopaths start small? They pull the wings off bees and then kill a cat. This might be part of a progression. A known progression.'

'Or it might be similar to Twitter where the trolls love to threaten but would never do anything in real life,' Bel says. 'They hide behind anonymity.'

'I think you're right, Rachel. There can't be any harm in taking advice from the police.' I say this slowly, thinking it through. 'I'll ask Mrs Fleming for the youth officer's number, and see whether they can help put this into some sort of context.' I take a breath and move my neck from side to side to relax the muscles. I feel better now I've come to a decision. And maybe the youth officer will be able to help put our minds at rest. This might be nothing compared with the things she has to deal with.

I look at my two friends and am grateful that they're here for me. 'Time for a quick coffee?'

'I can't. I have the lovebirds for lunch,' Rachel says, heading for the door.

'Oh, so you know it's Harry?' Bel is smiling but Rachel stands stock-still, her expression alarmed.

'What do you mean it's Harry?' she says quietly.

Bel's hand is over her mouth. 'I'm sorry. I thought you meant that you knew already. I wasn't supposed to say anything. Eleri told me the other day and . . .' She trails off. 'God help me, I've just put my foot in it again.'

I'm thinking about what a lovely couple Harry and Eleri will make when I notice that Rachel has grown very pale, the colour draining from her face as if her very soul is being pulled down through her feet. I move quickly towards her but I'm too late. She falls, hitting the floor with a loud whack.

Chapter Twenty-two

RACHEL

Rachel was twenty when she met Bryn. She was working in The Hare until she decided what she 'wanted to do with her life'. She was asked that a lot. 'So what are your plans, Rachel? What are you going to do with your life? Go travelling? University?' On and on and on it went, variations on the same theme, and she would smile and say, 'I'm not sure yet. I'm weighing up my options.' As if she had fistfuls. As if she could tick off the options on her fingers and need more than two hands to do it.

England was playing Wales at Twickenham, which was nowhere close to Ashdown village, but Bryn was from Cardiff and he was a photographer so he took the opportunity to make a holiday of it. The Ashdown Forest had a lot to offer for those who liked both walking and staying still long enough to capture a moment. He came into the pub every evening for four days in a row and Rachel was on duty for all of those shifts. It wasn't love at first sight, nothing as Hollywood as that, but by the third day she was looking out for him and by the fourth, when he said he was returning to Wales the next day, her face fell. 'I'm getting used to seeing you in this seat. And hearing all about the forest, somewhere I've known all my life. It's different through your eyes. More exciting. Better.'

He stared at her then, as if for the first time, and she felt a spark jump across the space between them. It made her heart skip a beat. They swapped numbers and he said he would be in touch, gave her a kiss on the cheek. She didn't expect to hear from him but within the week he'd called her. They chatted on the phone for well over an hour.

This went on night after night for two weeks and then he invited her to stay with him in Cardiff. Her mum was dubious – who was this Welshman? And what did he want with her daughter? Bryn spoke to her mum on the phone to prove that he was legit but it wasn't enough to persuade her that he was one of the good guys so he came back to the Ashdown Forest to stay with them instead.

And the rest, as the saying goes, is history. By the time she was twenty-two she was getting married, and Bryn was moving his start-up photography business to England. He was only three years older than her but he had already done so much more. And the strange and wonderful thing was that he didn't see her as a hopeless case, the way she felt most people saw her.

He didn't see her poor A-level results as finite – she could take them again when she knew exactly what she wanted to study. He didn't think she'd 'wasted' more than two years working full-time in a pub – it was a great way to get to know people and to learn how to run a small business. She'd gleaned a lot about costs and expenditure, and she would be able to help run Davies Photography. It would be their business, Bryn said. He would take care of the creative side and she would keep track of the appointments and the finances. She was good at planning – she'd never messed a booking up at the pub – and she was good with money too.

Rachel wasn't promiscuous but she wasn't a virgin either. She'd had a boyfriend when she was nineteen. It lasted seven months and ended when he decided they should travel and she couldn't commit to that, feeling unsure about the whole backpacking thing. 'But where would we stay?' she'd asked him.

'We'll find somewhere when we land,' he'd replied. 'We'll go with the flow.'

Going with the flow was exactly what she didn't want to do, not when it came to where she would sleep. And, as it turned out, if she had gone with Joel then she would never have met Bryn and now that thought terrified her because he was her everything. He was her rock but also her river. He kept her safe but he also encouraged her to explore. It was everything people said relationships were meant to be and she knew that they would last forever.

Two days before her wedding was the hen night. She got caught up in everyone else's idea of what a hen night should be and ended up 'living it large' in a club in Brighton. 'This is your last chance to cut loose,' they told her. 'Drink and make merry!'

There was a stag party in the club too and she recognised one of the blokes. 'You're Robin Myers, aren't you? You were in my cousin's year at school. She always thought you were a right twat.' She wouldn't normally call someone a twat but drink had emboldened her. He told her he was a doctor now, in Brighton, although he was often in Ashdown village because he was engaged to Aimee who was one of her customers at the pub.

She remembered dancing with him. She remembered her hand reaching towards a line of shots on the bar. And then, the very next thing she remembered, was the shock of waking up in his bed. She had literally no memory of how she got there. Those hours were completely wiped from her mind. She was horrified, completely and utterly gobsmacked at her own stupidity. She jumped out of bed and stood in the middle of the room, completely naked, her clothes clutched to her chest. What had possessed her? *Was she completely insane?* She was about to marry the love of her life and she'd spent the night with someone she didn't even like.

He was still asleep – thank God! – so she dressed quickly and ran all the way to Brighton Station, tears streaming down her face. She couldn't remember whether they'd had sex. She felt like they might have done but she wasn't sure. She knew there was a good reason she normally didn't drink very much. Knew it. Knew it. Knew it. Why had she let the others persuade her that getting off her face was a good idea?

Fortunately, her friends thought she'd got a taxi home – apparently, she'd said she was doing that – so no one else knew where she'd spent the night. She should have gone for the morning-after pill but by the time she got home she'd convinced herself that she hadn't had sex with Robin. She would have felt different, wouldn't she? Her body would have let her know that she'd been unfaithful.

She'd come off the pill two months before their wedding date because they wanted to start a family immediately and within two weeks of being married she was pregnant. That made her think about Robin again. Had she done it with him? And even if she had – but she hadn't – then the baby still had to be Bryn's because they'd had sex every other night for months.

She put that night out of her mind, shoved it down

into a deep, dark pocket in the furthermost corner of her consciousness. And when Eleri was born, everyone agreed she was the image of her dad. 'Doesn't she look like Bryn!' they said.

When, years later, Robin came back with his family to live in the village she was jolted into remembering her mistake but he showed no signs of remembering anything about it. And she put it out of her mind again.

It was her mum's death a couple of years ago that brought it all to the fore once more. She died very suddenly of a stroke, and the transplant team at the hospital had sat Rachel down to ask her whether her mum had a donor card. Rachel was sure she did and she agreed that her mum would want to help others. They told her all about organ donation, how many body parts they could use, how many people would be helped. It set Rachel's mind off on a tangent. She remembered a real-life story that she read in a magazine about a dad who needed a kidney transplant. His son offered him one of his kidneys but when he was tested, it turned out they weren't genetically related. His mum had had a one-night stand and never told her husband.

What a time to find out that your child wasn't 'yours'. What if that happened to them? What if Bryn got kidney failure – it happened to people, out of the blue. And what if Eleri stepped up to offer her dad a kidney and Bryn, weakened and close to death, was told that Eleri wasn't his biological child?

The very thought reduced Rachel to a round-eyed, rigid panic. She took to her bed because her heart was breaking, her head so heavy with worries that she could barely lift it off the pillow. She wasn't sure whether it was grief at losing her mum or grief at what might happen in the future. She had to take a month off school. She stopped getting up in the morning, instead appearing around midday to shuffle around the kitchen in her slippers. She should have been looking after her family instead of indulging her own fears and frailty.

She loved Bryn and her girls. Her family was everything to her. And Bryn was a fantastic dad. Unlike her, he managed to be 'cool' enough to be included in their lives. When Eleri went through her TikTok phase, he practised dance routines with her, singing along to the chosen track, his baritone voice mellow and tuneful – for what's a Welshman if not a singer? Eleri uploaded the videos and they began to gather a fan club. Rachel read the comments from her bed in the evening, trying not to be jealous, trying not to worry – why on earth didn't she just join in? She thought afterwards, *What is wrong with me?*

Carys was the one who gave Rachel reassurance. 'You're going to get through this hard time, Mummy. You need to think happy thoughts. That's what Granny would want.' And Eleri, at fourteen, became her dad's right hand in the kitchen and with the housekeeping.

One evening, Rachel sat on the stairs listening to Bryn talking to the girls. 'Mum will get better. She's grieving, girls. And grief has its own time frame.'

'I think we're managing fine,' Eleri added, her tone upbeat. 'Nina and Bel are going to join a women's group with Mum. It's run by Harry's mum, Aimee. I'm sure that will help her.'

'Family hug!' Carys shouted, and Rachel heard the sounds of chairs and feet moving. She closed her eyes, imagining herself to be part of the hug, Bryn's strong arms wrapped around all three of them.

The family dynamics shifted then and stayed that way.

Now, it makes Rachel feel like the weakest link, but someone has to be and it isn't as if she doesn't appreciate her family.

She would die for any one of them.

Chapter Twenty-three

BEL

'What's happening?' I ask Nina. I'm astonished. I can't believe Rachel's reaction. One minute she's standing up talking about her Sunday roast and the next thing she's hit the deck.

Nina turns Rachel onto her side and I put a cushion under her head. 'She's breathing,' Nina says, her ear hovering over Rachel's mouth. 'I think she's just fainted.' She sits back on her heels and looks up at me. 'Why would she not want Eleri to go out with Harry?'

I shake my head. 'I've no idea. Was that what made her faint?'

Rachel's eyelids flutter and then her eyes open and she tries to sit up. 'Take it slowly,' Nina tells her. 'You really banged your shoulder as you went down.'

'Luckily not your head,' I say, sinking my fingers into the rug she's lying on. It's slate grey, thick and soft, as you would expect in Nina's house. 'It's good your head landed on the rug and not the wooden floor.'

'Shall I get you a couple of painkillers?' Nina asks.

'Yes, please,' Rachel replies. She passes her hand over her forehead and briefly closes her eyes before saying to me, 'You knew about this? You knew Eleri was going out with Harry and you didn't tell me?'

'Eleri wanted it to be a surprise,' I say, confused as to why she's making a big deal of this.

'You had the cheek to lecture me on loyalty!' Her voice grows louder. 'You had the cheek to make me feel bad, feel like a rubbish friend because I hadn't shared my secret with you.'

'I didn't mean for you to feel like a bad friend.' I'm frowning as I look to Nina, returning with the pills and a glass of water, for help. 'I'm sorry. I really am.' I'm not entirely sure what I'm apologising for but I've done so much wrong lately and like Nina, Rachel never gets angry, so this is a shocker for me.

She takes the pills and glass from Nina's outstretched hand. Her own hand is shaking, whether from the fall or because she's so angry, it's difficult to tell.

'I'm sorry, Rachel. I don't understand,' I say quietly. 'Why is it a problem?' She stares at me then. It's a look so full of malice and hurt that I back off a step. 'I would have broken Eleri's confidence and told you if I'd known it was this important,' I say. 'I promise. I thought you would like Harry!'

Nina gives me a brief, worried glance then helps Rachel up from the floor and onto the sofa. Rachel sits for a moment, staring straight ahead, her expression so sad that I want to hug her but I know that I'm better to wait and let Nina take the lead.

I slowly move towards the seat opposite, not wanting to draw attention to myself so when Rachel's head snaps up at me, I'm poised midway, sitting on air. Her eyes pin me to the spot and I feel my own eyes fill with tears. I genuinely have no idea what I've done wrong. Rachel and I have been friends for almost nine years. She was the first person I met when we moved into the area. I took Vera along to the mother and toddler group in the village hall and there were Rachel and Carys, smiling at the entrance. She'd held out a hand to me and said, 'I don't think we've met. I'm Rachel.'

Nina puts one arm round Rachel's shoulder and motions to me to sit down with the other. 'Would you like to tell us what's going on?' she asks Rachel. 'A problem shared?' She gives a small smile. 'We'll try our best to help.'

'Can I trust you both?' she asks sharply, eyeballing me in particular. 'Can I?'

'Yes,' I say, leaning forward, hoping my body language speaks of my sincerity. 'I don't tell Miro everything.' I clear my throat. 'Obviously.'

'I won't say anything either,' Nina affirms. 'Robin and I barely speak. And after tomorrow, I doubt we'll speak again unless it's through lawyers.'

Rachel nods. 'Because nobody in the whole world knows about this.' Her expression is fierce. 'You *cannot* breathe a word. I mean it.'

She tells us then about what happened on her hen night, how she woke up in Robin's bed. *Fuck, this guy gets around.* How everyone thought she'd gone home so nobody was any the wiser. How, just over two weeks later she realised she was pregnant. Nina gasps at this, covering her mouth with her hand. How she's kept it to the back of her mind all these years. How it comes to the surface every so often but she always manages to push it away again.

'So Robin is Eleri's . . . dad?' Nina says, pronouncing the last word with a halting disbelief. 'Does he know?'

She shakes her head. 'I don't think he even remembers us having sex. I'm not sure we *had* sex. I was so drunk. I literally don't remember.'

'And Aimee must have been pregnant with Harry at the time,' I say.

'She was. I worked in The Hare back then and she used to come in for lunch.'

'So.' Nina frowns as she thinks. 'Are you sure Eleri is Robin's child? You must have been having sex with Bryn then too.'

'I don't know for sure,' she admits. 'It could have been either of them.'

I bite my lip. This is very Rachel. I don't want to be unkind, but all this drama and she doesn't know for sure?

'First things first, then,' Nina says, all business-like. 'You need to know one way or the other. You can easily order a DNA test online.' She leans to one side and lifts her laptop off the coffee table. 'Let's see what we need.'

'I can't!' Rachel says. 'Don't you get it? I can't get Bryn and Eleri to agree to a cheek swab. I'd have to lie and make up some ridiculous reason, and I'm no good at lying.'

'You don't need a cheek swab,' Nina says, reading from the screen. 'You can use a hair with the follicle still attached, a toothbrush, nail clippings.' She looks up. 'Replace all the family toothbrushes, put Bryn and Eleri's into a plastic bag and send them off.'

'I could do that, I suppose . . .' She trails off. 'But what if the letter they send back to me has their address on the back?'

'You can get the result by email.'

'Bryn and I share the same email address.'

'Have it sent to me,' Nina says. She seems unfazed by all of this, as if Robin isn't her husband and all she's doing is helping a friend solve a problem.

Rachel's face is still doubtful and I'm beginning to think she doesn't want a solution when she says, 'I know it sounds sensible to get a definite answer but, what if

Bryn isn't her dad?' Her voice cracks. 'While I don't know for sure, I can live with the hope that she's his. If I find out she isn't, what do I do then?' She tenses her jaw. 'Do I tell him?'

'I would stake my life on the fact that Eleri is Bryn's child,' I say. 'Sure, she looks more like you, but she has his mannerisms.'

'That could be because she spends time with him, not because it's genetic,' Rachel says, her tone resigned. I can see that she's thought about this a lot.

'Fair enough but there is literally no sign of Robin in her. Is there, Nina?'

Nina takes a moment to think. 'I have never once even imagined she could be Robin's daughter,' Nina says. 'Honestly, Rachel, I know it's easy for Bel and me to say this, but she is so much yours and Bryn's child. Her colouring is yours and Bel's right – she does have Bryn's mannerisms. I don't believe you have anything to worry about.'

'Okay.' Rachel slowly nods her head. 'I could get the toothbrushes.'

'Do you keep your toothbrushes separately?' I ask. 'I'm thinking of cross contamination.'

'The girls use their *Frozen* toothbrush stands that they've had for ages. They have different ones, one has Anna and the other has Elsa.'

'If for some reason you can only get Eleri's, I'll give you Robin's,' Nina says. 'And I'll send them off for you.'

'You would do that?' Rachel's eyes fill up again. 'You're being so good about this, Nina. I'm so sorry.'

'It's okay.' Nina hugs her tight. 'It's not your fault my husband is a serial shagger. I know you feel guilty about what happened all those years ago but I really don't think you need to.'

'I'm glad I've finally shared it with you both,' she says reaching for our hands. 'It's been a horrible secret to keep and when you moved to the village, Nina, and I knew we would be friends, I just had to put it out of my mind.'

'It's okay,' Nina repeats.

'You've suffered enough,' I add, unsure whether Rachel appreciates that this is another load on Nina's back. 'Why don't we all meet later at my house? You can give Nina the toothbrushes and it's a good opportunity to get the girls together before school tomorrow, try to help them forget their differences.'

'Maybe we can even get them talking about the notes,' Nina says and Rachel nods. 'I feel a sense of urgency with this one. One of them surely has an idea about who's writing them.'

'I'll rope Miro in. He's is good at getting kids talking.'

Rachel's still looking anxious when she says, 'Should I stop Harry and Eleri going out until the results are through?'

'No!' Nina and I say at once.

'She's not marrying him,' I add. 'They're only going out, that's all. Is she on the pill?' I don't give voice to the worry that they might be half-siblings and that makes any sexual relationship incestuous. That's a conversation that will, fingers crossed, never need to be had.

'I don't know,' Rachel says. 'I suppose I should have spoken to her about it but you know what she's like. Always so capable. I don't think I've spoken to her about sex since my mum died.' She sighs. 'I've taken my eye off the ball. Bryn is so good with her and she seems to do nothing but study.'

'The results are returned within forty-eight hours, maybe even quicker if we express-deliver it. I'll make

232

sure to do that.' Nina is reading from the screen again. 'So you won't have long to wait.'

Rachel doesn't seem to have heard her. 'Some people meet the love of their life at sixteen,' she says. 'And what if Eleri got . . .?' She can't say the word. She looks defeated, overwhelmed by the magnitude of her thoughts, of the endless what-ifs that have been circulating in her mind for far too long.

'Okay, listen.' Nina takes both of her hands in hers. 'You have a plan now. You can go home and host the lunch and stay calm because if you get the samples to me later today, I'll send them off first thing tomorrow and you'll have the results by Wednesday.'

'The overwhelming likelihood is that Bryn is her dad,' I add.

'You're both right.' She stands up, takes a deep breath. 'I wish we'd moved back to Wales. I wanted to, you know, but Bryn loved the forest and he always got on with my mum.' She starts moving towards the front door just as her mobile rings.

'We're thinking of you,' I say. 'Try not to worry.'

Chapter Twenty-four

'I'm sorry, Nina, I know he's the girls' dad but men like Robin should have a tattoo on their chest.' I hold up my index finger to write in the air as I say, 'Use me at your peril.'

Rachel's just left and Nina and I are sitting in the garden having a coffee. We're on the swing seat, facing the bottom of the garden where the cabin is nestled in the trees. Nina is staring down at her feet, not speaking. I've been rabbiting on, so pleased to be back in her good books; she's been quiet for a wee while.

'Are you okay?' I ask her.

'I don't know.' She sighs. 'Rachel's been my friend for five years. We've all had dinner together countless times. We've even gone on holiday together. She often sticks up for Robin – have you noticed that?' I nod. 'And yet all this time she's been thinking that Eleri might be his child.' She throws up her arms. 'And she never thought to mention it to me!'

'She's kept it at the back of her mind, though, hasn't she?' I say slowly. 'I mean, it must have been awful for her, keeping a secret like that for all these years.'

'I get that,' Nina says. 'But I'm still really shocked!'

'Do you think he's a sex addict?'

'No, I think he's someone who does what he wants and bugger the consequences!' she shouts. Better that she's mad at Robin than Rachel. That's my thinking.

'I'm sure Rachel's right and he doesn't even remember.' I take a sip of my coffee and stare up at the sky, at the clouds dotted across the blue canvas like splodges of ice cream.

'What if Eleri is Robin's child?' she says, her tone hushed. 'What will Rachel do? Tell Bryn? Tell Robin?'

'If that were the case, I don't think she should tell anyone,' I say, using one foot to gently swing the seat. 'Apparently at least ten per cent of children are brought up by men who are unaware of the fact that the child isn't biologically theirs.'

'That doesn't make it right, Bel.'

'Nothing will make it right. It's a case of going with the lesser of the two evils.'

'Poppy and Lily would have a half-sister,' Nina says, with a shake of her head.

'But they wouldn't know,' I say. 'There have been a couple of cases in the hospital where DNA tests have flagged up a dishonest mother but mostly people get away with it.' I sigh. 'A bit like my abortion. The punishment is the guilt.'

'It would be hard for Rachel not to tell Bryn.'

'But harder to tell him, surely? When you think of the repercussions.'

Nina turns sideways towards me, lifting one leg up underneath her. 'You were the one who was hell-bent on telling Miro about the abortion.'

'Only when I thought another note might mention my name. And it's happened, but we've managed to keep it quiet. My fingers are crossed.'

Her face angles down towards the seat, the glitter on

236

her cheeks sparkling in the sunlight. 'Secrets make a habit of revealing themselves,' she says.

'As we're all finding out.' I sigh. I don't want to think about it anymore. 'Are you going to keep the make-up on until bedtime?' I ask her.

'I'll take it off in a minute. I don't think Poppy should see me like this. She'll either love it, and want me to keep it on forever, or hate it and tell me I'm ridiculous!'

We both laugh and then I say, 'Robin isn't going to stop at Emily Birch, is he?'

'I doubt it, but that will be her concern, not mine, unless it affects the girls.'

'Are you going for full custody?'

'It depends. Ideally, I'd like to go for shared because I want the girls to have a dad but it depends on him, whether he wants to put the girls first or keep himself front and centre.'

'There could be trouble ahead,' I say softly.

'You're telling me. Love eh?' She sighs. 'It really is blind. It all started out so well. I remember the feeling of being in love with him. The excitement, the warmth. Apart from my love for the girls, it was stronger than anything I've ever experienced. I was absolutely hooked.' Her head drops again. 'More fool me.'

'It's not all bad, Nina,' I say. 'You got two fantastic wee girls out of the marriage.'

'You're right.' She smiles, half sad, half happy. Then she draws up her right knee and leans her chin on it. 'I'm worried about this latest note,' she says, returning to that again. 'Because they have all been true so far. What if this one is true too and someone's going to die?'

I frown, trying to think back. 'Hang on. The second one said you were a whore. Which you're not, not by any standard or definition.'

'Robin called me that.' She stares down towards the cabin. 'One evening last year and there was a woman walking along the path who would have heard him. At the time, I thought it might have been Rachel.'

'Eh?' I'm genuinely shocked. 'But surely she would have said?'

'I know.' She jumps up. 'It couldn't have been her. I'll get the notes and you'll see what I mean about them being true.'

She goes back inside and I close my eyes, lean back on the seat and swing backward and forward. Light dips and brightens on my eyelids as I move in and out of the direct sunlight. Nina's garden attracts a variety of birds and they are singing all around me. I feel cocooned in this small slice of heaven until my thoughts lead me back, inevitably, to Miro.

I left him and Vera at home in the garden, laying a small brick path between the greenhouse and the shed. They work well together. He fosters her enthusiasm for growing vegetables and fruit. They're talking about getting a beehive next. If I'd gone on to have the baby, there would be another child helping their dad. A trio of gardeners. *I was wilfully complicit in the murder of my child.* I know that many people would find that statement melodramatic but for me it's completely true.

I shudder, not liking where my thoughts are going. To distract myself, I take my mobile from my pocket and check social media. I click on Maxine's latest photo, which has close to a thousand likes on Instagram. The photograph is of Nina, looking incredibly beautiful. And I'm not the only one who thinks so:

Your friend is hot!
She looks amazing!
I wish I looked like that!

238

Positive comments, one after the other, with barely a naysayer.

'You're trending on Instagram,' I tell Nina when she comes back. I hold out the phone towards her so that she can see herself.

She barely looks at the screen. 'Maxine needed a photo to prove she'd used the products.'

'Everyone is saying how fantastic you look.'

She sits back down and lays the notes out in front of us, not remotely interested in how her appearance is viewed by the world. It reminds me of how lacking in vanity she is. 'So, here they are,' she says. 'I'm going to read them aloud and you'll see what I mean.' She points to the first one. 'This class has secrets, all the parents tell lies.'

'Certainly true for us,' I acknowledge.

'Your mum is a whore.'

'Well, I don't think *that's* true but if someone heard Robin say it to you . . .' I trail off. *Why has she put up with this man for so long?* It really is beyond me. I read the next one upside down. 'Your dad is not a hero doctor; he is a cunt. A fair comment, in my opinion.'

'Your mum's best friend killed a baby,' Nina reads. 'And her husband doesn't know.'

'Again, sadly, that is true.' I sigh. 'If only I could go back in time.'

'I don't have the next note—'

'Because I tore it up,' I say.

She reaches over and squeezes my hand before saying, 'From what I remember, it said, *Bel Novak is the one who killed the baby. She won't get away with it.*'

'Yeah, that's about right.'

'It could be seen as a threat,' Nina says. 'But it's not as bad as, *One of you will die soon and it serves you right. I hope you rot in hell.*'

I immediately see what she means. This note is alluding to something that will happen in the future, not something that has already taken place. 'Fuck,' I say. 'That is a step up from the others.'

'It's sinister, isn't it?' she says. 'So who could know all these things about us?'

'Okay, let's brainstorm,' I say. 'I'll call out names and you say what your instinct tells you.'

She sits back, hands on her lap. 'Shoot.'

'Max.'

'No. He has no reason to do this. Lily was his friend before this started and his mum isn't having an affair with Robin.'

'Amira.'

She tilts her head to one side. 'Before the quiz night, I would have said an almost definite no, but then I remembered that Aardi used to be a member of Robin's team and he left much sooner than is usual.'

'Under a cloud? An axe to grind?'

'Maybe.'

'Maxine?'

She shakes her head. 'Like Max, no motive.'

'Suze or one of those other mums?'

Nina shrugs. 'Why would they?'

'Poppy?'

Nina laughs at this. 'Poppy can balance on the back of a sofa but her writing skills are poor. She can barely form the letters.'

I hesitate before saying softly, 'Rachel?'

Nina looks me fully in the eye. 'If it was Rachel on the path,' she says slowly, 'then she is the only person I'm aware of who could know about both your abortion, and Robin calling me a whore. But why? Why would she write them?' She shakes her head, her expression disbelieving. 'I feel silly even entertaining the idea! I mean really, Bel? She's our friend! I know she's been keeping a huge secret, one that impacts on my family as well as hers, but still.'

'I'm with you,' I say, holding up my hand. 'Just thought we should cover that base.' I'm about to say my own name when Nina stands up.

'I'm going to call the youth officer,' she says. I sense that talking about Rachel has made her uncomfortable. She glances at her watch. 'I need to collect the girls from their play dates. I'll call Mrs Fleming now, though, and get the youth officer's number. I know it's a Sunday but hopefully she won't mind.'

While Nina calls Mrs Fleming, I gather the notes into a pile and relax back in the seat again. She walks around in circles in front of me and I hear snippets: 'I can see why . . . I feel unsettled by this . . . Lily is my main concern.'

I think back to all those years ago and the first time I saw her, standing in the playground, smiling at me, holding out her hand. How enchanting I found her. How Miro laughed and said it sounded like I'd fallen in love. In a way it's true, and the love I feel for her is based on respect and admiration for the sort of person she is, the sort of person who puts her family first and always remains calm and collected.

When she's finished she comes back to sit beside me. 'I've got the number now.' She bites her lip. 'I can't shake the feeling that the dominoes are beginning to topple. Maybe it's not just because of the notes. Maybe I feel uneasy because of everything that's going on in my personal life. I don't know.' She stares down the garden, her expression wistful. 'I'm not sure what Robin's going to do about the spyware. He won't like me getting the edge on him. I'm expecting him to fight back.'

'I'll help you, Nina,' I say, hugging her. 'I won't let you down again.'

She smiles at me then and I feel the same uptick in my heart that I remember feeling all those years ago.

Chapter Twenty-five

Nina drives off to pick up Lily and Poppy, and I call Miro on my way back home to tell him that Carys and Lily are coming over. Miro is a dab hand at pizza dough and he agrees to make the bases with the girls and then they can add their own toppings. I stop off en route the buy the ingredients, adding some ice cream to the basket too.

Vera was really dejected when we collected her from Rachel's on Friday evening. Like Lily, she didn't sleep over as planned. I've never seen her like that before. Every now and then the girls get fed up with each other but this feels more serious than that. She won't tell me what the fight was about so I'm hoping that the long Saturday without each other has given them a chance to get over it.

When I arrive home, Miro has come inside and is scrubbing half a dozen purple beetroots at the sink. 'How did it go with Nina?' he asks me, turning to give me a kiss. 'Has she forgiven you?'

'She has.' I hug him tight. 'Problem is, there's been another note.' I tell him about Nina finding it at the back of Lily's bed and what it says, why this one differs from the others. He still doesn't know the wording of the notes that refer to me and luckily he hasn't asked. 'Nina's going to call the youth officer. Mrs Fleming has given her the contact number.'

He stops what he's doing and dries his hands. 'Should we talk to the girls about it? See whether they can tell us anything?'

'We were thinking of that.' I lean in to his chest and rest my head there. 'I don't want to make things worse between them, though. We can see what Nina says when she gets here.'

He gives me a proper kiss this time and it makes me anticipate sex, and then I remember about the pregnancy test, which is inside the pocket of my white coat. It's in the boot of my car and will stay there until tomorrow morning unless I do something about it, so I go outside and bring it indoors. I put the coat in the washing machine and hide the pregnancy test at the back of a cupboard in case Miro spots it. There's nothing wrong with him finding it but I would prefer to take the test on my own because it gives me time to manage my disappointment.

It's late afternoon when I hear Rachel's car pull up. Carys says a quick hello, then runs upstairs to find Vera. 'That's a good sign,' I say. 'How did the lunch go? No wait – don't tell me yet. Here come Nina and the girls.'

We stand side by side, waiting until Nina parks and walks towards us. 'Hello, Aunty Bel!' Poppy throws herself at me for a hug.

'It's my cherub!' I kiss the top of her head. 'Do you want to go and play with the other girls for a few minutes?'

'Yes, thank you.' She sets off at a sprint after Lily who also seems to be in a better mood. 'Wait for me, Lily!'

'So tell us about lunch,' Nina says to Rachel.

She takes a breath before saying, 'It went okay. I was a bit off my game, a bit flustered, but I blamed it on a migraine.' She touches Nina's arm. 'I'm so sorry, Nina. I feel like you're being dragged into this.'

'It's no bother,' Nina says.

Rachel brings a brown envelope out of her bag. 'Eleri's toothbrush is in here, inside a plastic bag,' she whispers as she hands it to Nina. 'I couldn't take Bryn's. I remembered when I got home that it's a special organic one he bought at the market and he would notice if I replaced it.'

'I'll get Robin's and send them both off first thing tomorrow,' Nina says, pushing it down into her bag.

'Let me know how much it costs.'

'No worries on that score.' She rolls her eyes. 'It's the least I can do bearing in mind it involves my rat of a husband.'

Rachel gives her a hug and we go inside. Miro says hello and we all chat about how his and Vera's vegetables are coming along before he says, 'I hear there's another note. Do you want to talk to the girls about it?'

We three women look at each other, gauging what the others are thinking. Rachel looks as if she's beyond computing any more information today. Her lids are heavy and her mouth is slack. Nina is firing on all cylinders as usual. It takes a lot to diminish her focus. 'I know we said we would speak to them,' she says. 'But they looked so keen to be together just now. I think we need to let them be friends again first.'

Rachel nods and I say, 'My thoughts exactly.'

'I'll call the number Mrs Fleming gave me for the youth officer,' Nina says. 'I expect they will want to come into the class this time and that might scare a child into

245

talking. Not that I want to scare a child.' She holds up a hand. 'But I think we have to up the ante now.'

'Agreed,' Miro says. 'This has gone far enough already.'

Rachel, Nina and Poppy head off home, and while the girls and Miro are making pizzas, I slip upstairs with the pregnancy test, lock the bathroom door behind me and take a few deep breaths. Okay, it's probably going to be negative – that's a given – so all I'm doing is checking whether I can have a glass of wine this evening. There's a bonus right there! Alcohol will put some distance between me and my worries. *Come on, Bel,* I say to myself. *Get on with it.*

I pee on the stick – and not for the first time. I reckon I have done upwards of twenty of these. I don't do my usual counting and staring. For once I feel both resigned and accepting. *What's for ye won't go by ye,* as my granny used to say.

I wait the two minutes then look at the stick and blink. The result reads: *pregnant, 3+ weeks.* I stare at it, I shake it, I dare it to reverse its decision in the time it takes me to wash my hands, but the result doesn't change. It stays the same, singing out its positive message to a very thankful, very grateful, utterly joyous me.

I come out of the toilet with a huge smile on my face. I want to tell Miro now, right now, before I wake up and realise I've dreamt the last five minutes. I stand at the top of the stairs and hear the oven being opened and then Vera's voice, 'Let's start the film. We can get our pizzas when they're ready.'

The girls pass the bottom of the stairs as they go through to the living room and then Miro appears. He's standing drying his hands on a towel as he watches the girls rearrange the seating in the living room, something they always do. 'Do you need a hand with the big chair?' he asks.

'We can manage!' Vera tells him, and then he looks up, sees me standing here.

'You look happy!'

I hold up the stick.

His smile meets mine, grows larger by the second. He takes the stairs two at a time and lifts me up, carries me into the bedroom and drops me on the bed, closing the door behind us.

'You're pregnant?' It's a whisper.

I nod. 'I am. We are!'

Miro is stock-still, mouth open, gawking at me.

'You're not kidding, are you?' His voice is barely there.

I stand up on the bed and step in front of him, my face a little higher than his. 'No, my love. I'm not kidding.'

He lifts me up again and hugs me hard. 'Too tight!' I squeal, and he drops me gently onto the floor.

'I love you, Annabel Novak,' he says, cupping my face with his hands.

Emotion catches in my throat. I want to say that I hope this makes up for the abortion, but he still doesn't know about that, and when I start to cry, my emotions a happy-sad tangle inside my chest, he assumes it's because I'm happy. And I am.

'I'm only three plus weeks,' I caution. 'So I think we'd better not tell Vera yet, or anyone else.' I think for a second. 'Except maybe Nina and Rachel, as I know they'll keep schtum. I'll need their help if I have the vomiting problem again.'

'Will you, do you think?' His expression flips from joy to concern.

'I'm not sure. I thought I'd book an appointment with Amira and see what she says.'

'Bel.' He sits down on the edge of the bed, shaking his head. 'I'm so happy, I can't tell you.' When he looks up at me his eyes are bright with tears. 'This is the best news ever.'

I do a five-second happy dance, twirling around on the spot as if I'm on ice and then I land on the bed beside him. We lie together for a few blissful moments before Vera calls up the stairs, 'Dad, you forgot the pizzas! They're starting to burn!'

'Oops.' He jumps up and runs down the stairs while I lie on the bed, eyes closed and hands clasped. I send up a prayer of thanks and then I ask, please God, for Miro to never know what I did.

Monday morning and I drop Vera at school. I've yet to see Nina and Rachel because Miro drove the girls home last night and I'm running late this morning, so although I keep an eye out I quickly realise I must have missed them. I'm desperate to tell them my news. I'm pregnant, and the joy is blooming inside me like a ball of warm, fuzzy cashmere. I'm about to head to work when I hear Amira's voice. 'Bel! Have you got a minute?'

'Sure.' I wait for her to catch me up.

'I thought I'd let you know about—'

'I'm pregnant!' I tell her. It's out of my mouth before I can stop myself. In truth, I want to sing it from the rooftops, to dance through the village with a sign around my neck.

'That's wonderful news!' She reaches across to give me a hug. 'I'm so pleased for you and Miro, Bel. I really am.'

'It's very early days and to be honest I'm a bit anxious

because Vera was born at twenty-six weeks and we'd prefer not to have a repeat of that.' The words pour out of me in a rush. 'Also, I developed hyperemesis gravidarum with Vera and I'm wondering about the likelihood of me getting it again?'

'Why don't you make an appointment and come to the surgery to discuss it?' Amira says, her calm expression slowing me down.

I take a breath. 'That's what I was thinking.'

'The reason I wanted to talk—' she glances over her shoulder to make sure no one is listening in '—was because I've spoken to our man in IT.'

For a second I don't remember what she's talking about – and then I do. My medical notes. I was afraid that someone in the surgery had broken confidentiality, otherwise how could 'baby killing' have been referenced on the notes?

'He gave me the times when your medical notes were viewed. He can't check the footprint beyond two years, I'm afraid, because the system was changed after that, but we can be absolutely clear that your notes were only accessed three times, and always at the time of your appointment.'

'Okay,' I acknowledge, still keen to know who's behind the notes but mostly just wanting to bask in the glow of the baby growing inside me.

'You came once last year and twice the year before. All three times your appointments were with me. I remember you had Vera with you the last time because it was when my little Amir had broken his arm and she asked after him.'

'Yes, you're right.' I was there because I'd had another IVF failure and the private consultant had wanted some blood tests done to check my hormone levels. I remember asking Amira whether there was any way the abortion could have affected my chances of conceiving. It's a question I'd always wanted to ask but had never had the courage to. I didn't say 'abortion' though, I said 'TOP' which is shorthand for one of the medical terms for abortion – termination of pregnancy. Vera was reading her book, her lips moving as her eyes crossed the page, but I know how children's ears can perk up when you least expect it; I knew she might recognise the word *abortion* but she wouldn't understand what *TOP* meant. And until this moment it's never occurred to me that she might have looked it up afterwards.

'Thank you, Amira. I really appreciate that.'

'If you want to pursue it further then please let myself or the practice manager know. And don't forget to book an appointment to see me.' She smiles again. 'I want to look after you through this pregnancy.'

She hurries off to work and I climb into my car. The children are just beginning to line up to go inside. The three girls are back to their normal selves, in a huddle and chatting ten to the dozen.

I remember the tail end of a conversation I overheard yesterday afternoon when they were in Vera's bedroom. I had just come out of my own room and was about to go downstairs.

'My mum was a bit weird with Harry,' Carys was saying. 'I'm not sure she liked him.'

'Why was that?' Vera asks her. 'He's nice, isn't he?'

'Maybe she has a secret as well,' Lily says.

'Yeah maybe,' Carys says. 'Like your mum, Vera.'

As I watch the three friends huddled together, I have a sudden flash of possibility that hits me between the eyes like a baseball. What if Carys has been sending the notes to Lily? She is well placed to access her school bag. The girls share every piece of news and sometimes friends grow jealous of each other. Lily's family is clearly the wealthiest, her dad has been in the press a lot; they have been to Buckingham Palace for the MBE. Could the notes be an attempt on Carys's part to knock her down a peg? To point out that, under the surface, the Myers family veneer is cracking?

And would she, for some reason, want to take a pop at Vera as well? Did Vera tell her that she'd gone with me to the surgery and she wondered what a TOP was?

I watch the children line up and as soon as Vera has disappeared from view, I start the car's engine. I'll have to sit on this idea for at least the next ten hours until my shift is over. I really hope I'm wrong, but at the back of my mind the phrase *like mother like daughter* has raised its hand. Rachel has kept her concern over Eleri's paternity to herself for years. Carys might be capable of the same sort of secret-keeping.

I'll have a word with Nina. See what she thinks.

Chapter Twenty-six

NINA

I'm always at the office by eight-thirty on a Monday morning. If Robin isn't around – and these days, when is he ever? – Harry spends Sunday night with us and gets the girls out the door to school the next day.

The first thing I do when I arrive at work is to print out the form for the Bryn/Robin paternity test. It was easy enough to get Robin's toothbrush from the en suite because he opened a new one that he keeps down in the cabin. I slide the form into an envelope with the toothbrushes and give it to my assistant who sends it off express delivery.

I have a busy morning of meetings, the first with all the staff where Jane and I let them know about the company sale. It's a tense gathering at times, with some people feeling as if their roles might not transition, but with reassurance, the meeting ends on a positive note. Mergers and acquisitions are the bread and butter of our business so it's unsurprising that we would ourselves become part of that trend.

Jane and I have lunch to debrief on staff requests and expectations, and I'm back at my desk for two-thirty. I close the door and call my solicitor.

'I read your message about Robin's behaviour,' she

tells me. 'My suggestion is that I send Robin an email, and a follow-up letter, asking him to move out of the family home. He is blatantly having an affair. Not allowing you to lock the door when you and the girls are sleeping inside is unacceptable, not to mention the fact that he's bringing his mistress onto the family property. You can afford to live separately and you are well within your rights to push for this.'

'We have a small cabin at the bottom of the garden and he's already been spending most of his time down there but I'd really like him off the premises altogether.'

'Absolutely. Much better if he completely vacates the family home and garden. Did he tell you the name of his solicitor?'

'No. But he has engaged someone now. He told me on Friday evening that he is going for sole custody.' She already knows about my mental health problems back when Poppy was a baby but I remind her of the details of my breakdown.

'An idle threat. Don't let him bully you. He doesn't have a hope of gaining sole custody.'

'That's a relief.' I thought as much but feel reassured by her conviction.

'Remember you're not going through this alone, Nina. I'm here to take the flak. You need not have any further conversations with him.'

'I understand.' Easier said than done.

'I'll prepare the email now and send you a copy.'

When I finish the call, I swing my chair round to face the window. The view is of rooftops and an expanse of blue-grey sky with vapour trails crisscrossing the vista like demarcation lines.

I know that her email will inflame Robin. He hates to be caught out, ordered about, asked to behave in a particular way; his ego is unable to countenance such restriction on his freedoms. He thinks he's entitled to behave however the hell he likes and he'll view my solicitor's email as a further betrayal on my part. Bizarrely, his ongoing betrayal of me will not be factored into his thinking.

Robin runs a successful department but he surrounds himself with doctors and nurses who are willing to acknowledge his genius, learn from him and be part of a cutting-edge firm. Those who consistently challenge him don't last long. As one of his colleagues put it to me once: 'He's an arrogant man, your husband. But with the skills he has, he's probably earned the right.'

My mobile rings. It's Jennie Jackson – the youth officer Mrs Fleming spoke to – returning my call. I left her a voicemail shortly after I arrived at work this morning. I give her a summary of what's happened recently. She doesn't seem unduly concerned about the notes but agrees that they are malicious and that talking to the children as a class might be enough to stop the behaviour in its tracks. As I thought, she comes across far worse in her line of work but she does agree that the last note has upped the ante. I feel reassured and tell her I'll get back to her after I've spoken to Mrs Fleming about a convenient date and time.

The phone call reminds me that I haven't had a word with Lily yet about finding the note in her bed. She didn't return from Vera's until seven in the evening and was too tired to have supper never mind talk. She was in bed by seven-fifteen, fast asleep seconds later. Poppy and I spent the rest of the evening reading together and talking about Pickle, what he might like to eat, how much fun he'll have in the garden. 'We're going to love him so much, Mummy,' she said.

★   ★   ★

After-school club finishes at five forty-five and, with the train held up before Clapham Junction, I make it to school late so the children are already milling about in the playground. I climb out of my car and spot Poppy on the wall swapping football cards again, her usual after-school preoccupation. Rachel and Bel are close to the playground and as I approach I'm surprised to hear Rachel shouting, 'This is bang out of order, Bel! How dare you accuse Carys!'

'What's happening?' I ask. Their eyes are locked and they don't notice I'm there. Lily barrels into me, wrapping her arms tightly around my waist. I put my hand on her head and say, 'What's going on, love?'

She stares up at me and whispers something I don't catch because at that moment Bel says, in a deliberately calm tone, 'I wasn't accusing Carys of anything. I was simply asking her whether she—'

'Wrote the notes!' Rachel shouts. She raises a finger and points it in Bel's face. 'How dare you? Why pick on Carys? Why not pick on someone your own size?'

The sound of their voices is attracting stares. I notice several parents glancing across, edging closer or slowing their progress back to their cars in order to listen in.

'Rachel.' I take her hand. 'Tell me what's happening?' I say quietly.

'No, Nina.' She swings round to glare at me, her mouth tight. 'Not this time. You always stick up for Bel but I won't let this go. Not when it concerns my child.'

Vera and Carys are standing close by holding hands. Vera is wide-eyed and frozen to the spot but Carys manages to step forward and pull at her mum's sleeve. 'Mum, stop now. You're embarrassing everyone.'

'We're all stressed, Rachel,' I say. 'Let's just take a breath.'

'Exactly, we're all stressed.' She's lowered her voice now. 'And *she*—' she points at Bel '—makes it ten times worse because everything is always about her.'

'That's not fair,' Bel protests. 'I actually have something important to share. And I haven't said anything.'

'She didn't mean it, Mum,' Carys says, her tone soft. 'You're overreacting.'

'I'm overreacting? Okay, right, fine.' She gives a frustrated sigh and picks up Carys's school bag. 'Come on, Carys. We're going home.'

She grabs her daughter's free hand but she's still holding on to Vera who pulls in the other direction so that for a few seconds it looks as if Carys will be torn in two. Luckily she finds this funny and starts to giggle, stamping her feet up and down as if she's trying to run forward. Rachel lets go first and walks away towards the school gate. I can tell by the heave of her shoulders that she is crying.

I immediately detach Lily's arms from around my waist – 'Give me a minute, love' – and run after her. 'Wait!' I call out. 'Talk to me, Rachel.' She stops and turns. Her face is already blotchy with tears, her eyes muddy puddles. 'I'm not going to make excuses for Bel,' I say.

She nods her thanks, starts to speak but the tremor in her lip makes her bite down instead, trapping her lip between her teeth.

'No one's quite themselves at the moment,' I add.

'She asked Carys if she'd written the notes,' Rachel says, her expression pained. 'I heard her as I was walking towards them. Carys said no and Bel said, "Are you sure, Carys, because I think it might have been you."' She shakes her head, astounded. 'What is she playing at?'

'She spoke out of turn, Rae. No doubt about it.' I give her a hug. 'But we go back a long way. We can get through this together.'

'Maybe.' She turns towards the playground where Carys and Vera are holding either end of a long skipping rope and Lily is jumping as they turn it, the motion growing ever faster until she mistimes her step and ends up with the rope tangled around her ankles. 'My turn!' Carys shouts and they swap places.

'I posted the envelope off this morning and we'll have the results emailed back to me very soon.' Her eyes fill with tears again. 'Hang on in there, Rae.'

'I don't keep things from Bryn.' She closes her eyes and the water from her lashes makes a wet trail down her cheeks. 'What if he finds out?'

'He's not going to.'

She nods her head in Bel's direction. 'She might tell him now.'

'She won't. Bel's not spiteful.'

She raises her eyebrows at this. 'Not deliberately, maybe. But you know what she's like.'

I can't deny the truth of this. I know that at some point, Robin will make me suffer for Bel telling him about the spyware.

'Would you mind dropping Carys home for me?' Rachel asks. 'I could do with walking back on my own and getting my head straight.'

'Of course.' I give her a hug. 'Pour yourself a G and T and watch something funny on Netflix.' She smiles. 'Don't let yourself dwell on anything except your own wellbeing.'

'I'll try.'

'Think about what Aimee would say,' I remind her as I walk away.

'Deep breaths!' she calls back to me and we both smile.

I walk back to where Bel is standing, her expression reflective. 'I did the wrong thing. I should have kept my mouth shut.' She tells me about the snippet of conversation she overheard the girls having when they were together yesterday, and then Amira this morning reminding her that Vera was in the room when she went for a consultation a year ago. 'I think it's possible that Vera heard the mention of a TOP and looked it up online or asked one of her friends what it was.'

'Well, maybe. I suppose. But I still don't understand what makes you think it was Carys,' I say, my voice low. 'Vera could have asked virtually any other child in the school.'

'I have a feeling.' She shivers. 'I can't explain it, Nina. There's something odd. I can almost grasp hold of it but not quite.' She stares up at the sky as she thinks. 'None of the notes mention Rachel. Could that be because Carys doesn't want to be mean about her own mum?'

I don't want to believe Bel but experience tells me that her 'feelings' usually do amount to something. She has an uncanny ability to home in on the truth and I know that she would never want to risk her friendship with Rachel unless she was sure there was something amiss. 'I'll talk to Lily this evening,' I say. 'Ask her outright whether she thinks it could be Carys.'

Bel lifts her shoulders and drops them again, simultaneously expelling a breath. 'Do you think it's too early for me to go after Rachel?'

'No. Go on. She's worried that you might tell Bryn about the paternity.'

'Never!'

'I said that.'

'I'll reassure her, and I'll apologise.' Her face brightens; she always likes to have a plan. 'Would you take Vera for me?'

'Of course.'

She goes off at a run and I watch the girls playing in harmony, leaning in to each other, sharing glances, every now and then meeting in a huddle of three, arms round each other's backs.

It can't be Carys. She wouldn't set herself apart from the others. They are a threesome.

Chapter Twenty-seven

BEL

We all have that voice in our head, don't we? The voice that says, 'Go on, eat that biscuit, have another glass of wine, you're fine to drive.' And then: 'Oh no! Why did you eat the biscuit, have another drink, drive under the influence? Now you've ruined everything! You might as well just give up.'

Even as a child I felt that opposing forces existed inside me simultaneously and the choice of how to behave was mine. I still imagine the inside of my brain like a boardroom table, where viewpoint avatars sit opposite each other: the temptress and the prude, the greedy and the generous, the brave and the cowardly, the strong and the weak. They each have their voice and it's up to me to choose which voice to run with, whether I eat that extra biscuit or don't. I generally try to go with Gandalf, the voice of reason, who sits at the head of the table. He filters out the spiteful or the weak and tends to plump for the wise and the patient.

I'm thinking about all of this, hoping to make the right choices, as I jog after Rachel. When I come out of the school grounds and onto the pavement, I see her in the distance and call out, 'Rachel, wait!' The wind lifts my voice up and away behind me so she doesn't hear me. I pick up my pace, briefly running on the road to allow a young woman pushing a buggy to take up the width of the pavement. *I'll be pushing a buggy soon.* The thought makes me smile and I automatically place the palm of my hand on my lower abdomen then glance heavenwards in a silent prayer. *Please, please let me hold on to this baby. Please, God. I promise I will strive to do better.*

I'm just a few metres behind her when I call out again, 'Rachel!'

She stops and turns around. Her expression leaves me in no doubt that she's still mad with me.

'I'm so sorry, Rachel.' I take a couple of deep breaths, my arm stretched out towards her. 'Please wait.'

She drops Carys's bag down at her feet and folds her arms. She's not going to make this easy for me. And I don't blame her. But this is my second apology in as many days and I'm determined to get it right.

'I'm so sorry, Rachel. I was out of order and I'll apologise to Carys. I get ideas in my head and act on them. It's foolish and childish and I need to be more Gandalf.'

'Gandalf?' she says, exasperated.

'Wise.'

'Yes, you do,' she says. Her lip trembles. 'You should have spoken to me first.'

'You're right, I should have.'

She picks up the bag and continues to walk. I come alongside her and put my arm through hers. 'I don't expect to be forgiven but I am hoping we'll still be friends because I'll never get through my pregnancy without you.' She stops. She turns to me, her mouth open, her eyes wide. 'You were right,' I say quietly. 'I'm pregnant.'

She bursts into tears, all her previous frustration evaporating as she hugs me. 'I knew it! I knew it!' She steps back and inhales on a smile, her eyes all dreamy as she says, 'I'm going to have a brand-new baby to cuddle.'

'You are!' I laugh.

'Does Vera know?'

I tell her we'll be keeping it quiet for a while. 'Just in case.'

'Don't say that.' Her face twists.

'I know, but we have to be sensible. Up to a third of all pregnancies miscarry, especially at my age.'

We walk back to her house together and we talk about Miro's reaction and how wonderful the news is, especially now. I promise her that I would never tell Bryn about the paternity test and by the time we reach her front door, we are friends again. She invites me in for a coffee and we stand in her kitchen chatting.

Eleri is working at the dining room table and shouts through, 'Do you have any sharpies, Mum?'

'No, but Carys's bag is by the door.'

Rachel holds the fridge door open and asks me what I think she should cook for tea. There's not much in there. 'Well . . . you have eggs and mushrooms – an omelette?'

'Carys won't eat eggs. Bryn won't eat mushrooms.'

I flick open the breadbin. 'Mushrooms on toast for Carys and—' I hold up a matchbox-size piece of cheese. 'A cheese omelette for Bryn. Do you have anything potato-ish in the freezer?'

'Look at this.' Eleri is standing at the entrance to the kitchen holding out a notepad. Her expression is serious. 'It was in Carys's bag.'

'What's wrong?' Rachel asks.

I see it at once. Words written then scored out with black marker pen. I recognise the paper and I recognise the writing.

I really didn't want to be right.

Chapter Twenty-eight

NINA

When I pull up outside Rachel's house, Carys and Vera climb out of the car and run inside to join their mums. I can see Bel through the kitchen window standing next to Rachel and am relieved that they're talking again. There's enough drama in our lives right now without them falling out.

'Can we go in, Mummy?' Poppy asks.

'No, love, it's after six. We need to get home otherwise I'll be too tired to make us anything to eat.'

As soon as we arrive back at ours, Poppy runs upstairs to sort her football cards into piles and I say to Lily, 'Could we have a word, darling?'

She stares up at me. 'What about?'

I take her hand and lead her into the kitchen. 'Have a seat. I'll just put the potatoes on.' Before I left for work this morning I put some chicken and veg in the slow cooker and the potatoes are ready to steam. I learned a long time ago that if I didn't have a meal prepared in advance, I'd come home from London with no energy to think about what to make, never mind actually make it.

'I was changing your sheets on Saturday and I found a note stuffed down the back of the bed,' I say. She immediately looks worried. 'I'm not getting at you, darling. I just wondered whether you read it?'

She gives a quick shake of her head. 'I took it out of my bag. That's all.'

'Okay.' I'm not sure I believe her and this is an uncomfortable feeling for me. 'And you've no idea how it got into your bag?'

She puts both hands over her face and then drops her head so that the backs of her hands are on the work surface. I walk across and put my arms round her. 'Lily, I know this is hard.'

'Daddy's car is here!' Poppy shouts. I hear her feet on the stairs, surprisingly thunderous for such a small child.

Lily's head comes up at once and she says, 'You're not going to talk about this in front of Daddy, are you?'

'Not if you don't want me to.' I sigh. 'But, Lily, I'm beginning to feel as if there's something you're not telling me.'

Robin arrives and gathers the girls to him. I manage to get them fed when he has to take a phone call but otherwise he gives them his undivided attention for close on two hours. I let them get on with it and tidy the kitchen, put a wash on and answer a couple of emails. All the while, I'm wondering about Bel's intuition. We've spent most of our time circling around Max and Maxine but has the answer been under our noses all this time? *Could it be Carys? And if so, what does that mean for all of our friendships?*

When Robin finishes putting the girls to bed, I have food ready for him and he sits at the kitchen island to eat it. It's the first time we've been in each other's company since Friday evening when he found out about the spyware. And I'm not sure whether my solicitor's email has arrived yet. On balance, I think not, as it surely would have inflamed him.

'I expect you think you're one step ahead of me,' he says abruptly, as if I've spent the evening actively trying to outwit him.

'That's not my intention,' I say evenly.

'Not your intention,' he repeats.

'There is no real love between us anymore, Robin. We've tried our best but our marriage has come to an end. Please let's try to get through it without upsetting ourselves or the girls too much.'

He pushes his plate away, stands up, and without pausing for breath, throws his whisky tumbler against the wall behind me. I instinctively jump and cover my head with my arms as the glass smashes into smithereens, small pieces of glass raining down behind me like jagged confetti.

'Don't fuck with me, Nina,' he says, his tone threatening, his eyes glittering with anger.

He leaves through the front door and I wait until my heartbeat settles before I move my feet, making sure not to step on any glass. I didn't expect that. He's always been manipulative but he's never been violent towards me. He wasn't aiming at me – the wall was his target – but he's crossed a line and it shocks me.

I lock all the doors behind him. I don't think he'll come home again tonight, but if he does, he can sleep in the cabin. He and Emily can fornicate down there to their hearts' content. Not for the first time I think about her husband and wonder whether he has any idea what's going on when he's away for work. Maxine told me they were getting divorced. Perhaps she thinks Robin will do the same and they can live happily ever after.

I spend the next fifteen minutes clearing up every

tiny shard of glass and when I go to bed, I notice that I have two missed calls from Bel and one from Rachel. If they're still arguing then I'm too tired to deal with it now. I turn off the light and close my eyes but it feels like hours before I fall into a restless sleep.

I wake up the next morning and notice another missed call from Bel at just after five. Has she slept at all? I get myself a coffee and call her back.

'Hi, it's me. Is everything—'

'Nina. Hold on.' I hear the closing of doors and then she says quietly, 'Carys has been writing the notes.'

'Bel, we've been over this.'

'No, really. The notepad was in her bag. Eleri found it. And when Carys came indoors after you'd dropped her off, she didn't deny it.' She pauses. 'Are you still there?'

'Yes.' I'm shocked. Although I considered the possibility, I can still barely believe it. *Carys?* Carys who's been in my house more times than I can count, who seems to have a lovely friendship with Lily and even manages to include Poppy when she's at her most annoying? 'I need time to process this,' I say. 'Are you sure someone didn't put the notepad in her bag?'

'Well, if they did she's willing to take the rap for them.'

'What does Rachel think?'

'She's horrified. She sent her upstairs, told her she was grounded, that she'd never be allowed to visit Lily again. The whole nine yards.'

'Oh God.' I can't help but feel for Carys. I'm struggling to believe she did it. Surely it's more likely that she's shouldering the blame for someone else?

'I tried to quiz Vera on the way home but she started crying and wouldn't speak for the rest of the evening.'

'What are we going to do?'

'Rachel and I thought we should get the three of them together this morning and have Carys apologise to Lily.'

'Before school?'

'We have to tell Mrs Fleming, don't we? Rachel and Bryn think the sooner the better. They both feel that Carys needs to take responsibility for what she's done. And I think Vera should be there too because I suspect she told Carys about the abortion. I want her to be truthful.'

'Okay. What time should I expect you?'

'Seven-thirty?'

'See you all then.'

I put down the phone. I don't move. I have an image of Rachel walking along the footpath over the hedge at the bottom of my garden. She's tall enough for me just to see her head. Carys, I wouldn't have seen. But she could have been there, and she could have heard Robin call me a whore. Vera could have told her about Bel and the 'TOP'. And if she knows the C word then attaching it to Robin is hardly a stretch, even for a child.

It's possible that all of the notes have come from Carys's hand.

I have a quick shower. I can hear the girls playing in Poppy's room but I'm not going to say anything yet. I can only imagine how Lily will take it. Or does she already know? Is that what their falling-out was about? She's only just renewed her friendship with Carys and we're about to break it again. This will be a body blow for sure.

The three friends sit in a row on the sofa. Both Vera and Carys look as if they haven't slept. None of them have spoken. All I've said to Lily is that Carys has something she needs to say to her. Poppy is hovering behind me, wide-eyed with interest. Rachel and Bel have mugs of coffee in their hands and are sitting on the arms of the sofa opposite the girls. I sit down between them. I'm nervous. I've barely had time to prepare for this and I don't want to get it wrong.

'So, girls,' I begin. 'I understand that a writing pad was found in your bag, Carys?' She nods. 'It's the pad that was used to write the notes.' Lily gives a sharp intake of breath and her hand goes up to her mouth. *So maybe she doesn't know?* 'I'm wondering, Carys, if you were looking after this pad for someone or if, perhaps, it found its way into your bag?'

She hesitates for a moment before saying, 'It's mine.'

Lily leans forward to stare at her. She's not upset. She's worried. That strikes me as strange. Vera is in between them both and she is as still as a stone. All that moves are the tears in her eyes, two large drops tipping from her lower lashes onto her cheeks.

'Did you write the notes, Carys?' I ask her gently.

She's staring at her hands, held together on her lap. 'Yes.'

'Why would you do that?' Rachel shouts. 'It's a very, very bad thing! You should know better!' Her voice cracks and I reach across to take her hand. 'I'm utterly appalled with you,' she finishes quietly. 'And so is Daddy.'

Carys doesn't reply so I say flatly, 'These notes have caused a lot of upset. You know that, don't you?' She nods. 'I was on the phone to the youth officer and she was planning on speaking to the class.'

'What's a youf officer?' Poppy asks, moving across to stand next to the girls.

'A special sort of police officer who comes in to schools to help sort out problems,' I say.

'So Carys could go to prison?' Poppy is panicked, her eyes wide.

'No, but—'

She drops down onto her knees in front of the three friends and cries out, 'You have to tell the truth, Lily! Please.'

I feel Rachel and Bel straighten up, all three of us pulled in by Poppy's plea. The air feels sharp and clear.

And suddenly I get it.

Chapter Twenty-nine

LILY, CARYS AND VERA

They met where they always did, at the perimeter of the school grounds, in a natural hollow at the base of an oak tree. They shared their packed lunches, laying everything out on one of their coats like a picnic. They weren't supposed to share lunches but none of them had any allergies and anyway, the teachers couldn't see them from the playground. Lily and Carys talked about the lesson they'd just had and how much homework they'd been given.

'I actually quite like homework,' Lily said. 'I like organising my books on my shelf and working things out.'

'Eleri's like that,' Carys said, throwing a grape into the air and catching it in her mouth. 'I hate homework. I pretend I'm doing it and that I need to go online a lot. Then I just do what I want.'

'What about your mum?'

'She doesn't notice.'

'Even if my mum didn't notice, Poppy would tell on me.'

'What's wrong with you, Vera?' Carys asked, throwing a grape at her head. 'Why aren't you saying anything?'

Vera had been staring at the ground, her forehead

273

creased in a frown. She ducked away from the flying grape then picked it up off the grass. 'I'm just worried.' She sighed.

'Still?' Carys said.

'You've been worried for weeks,' Lily reminded her. 'You have to tell us.'

'It's my mum.'

'What about her?' Lily asked. 'She's always really nice to us.'

'She's *my* mum, Lily!' Her eyes were overwhelmed with tears. They poured down onto her cheeks in a stream of misery. 'I know she's nice, but it's not fair on my dad.'

'Don't cry, Vera!' Carys said urgently. She held her upper arms and shook her. 'If Mrs Fleming sees that you've been crying, you'll have to have one of her chats and it's really hard not to tell her the truth.'

Vera rubbed at her face with the ends of her sleeves and gazed skywards before blurting out, 'My dad wants a baby and my mum pretends she does too but she killed her baby.'

Lily gave a shocked scream, her hand immediately covering her mouth.

'How?' Carys asked, gripped. 'Did she drown it or something?'

'No, she had a TOP.'

'What's that?'

'It's a name for an abortion. I looked it up on Google. It stands for termination of pregnancy.'

'How do you know she had one of those?' Carys asked, her voice a whisper.

'I heard her when she was with Dr Amira, because that might be stopping her getting pregnant again.'

There were a few seconds of silence while the girls

absorbed what had been said before Lily asked, 'What's an abortion?'

'It's when women have unprotected sex,' Carys said, enunciating the words with relish. 'And they're pregnant but they don't want the baby.'

'Oh.' Lily blushed, not really wanting to think about sex. It all seemed so strange and, as Poppy would say, ridiculous.

'I think it's because I made her sick so much when she was expecting me,' Vera said. 'I was born really early. And with my leg and everything . . . I think that's why.' She'd taken off her shoes and was pulling at her tights, untwisting them at her heel. 'I think she would have had an abortion with me. I heard her talking to my aunty ages ago about how hard it was when I was born.'

'It's baby killing,' Carys said. 'I saw it on Sky News. There were protesters in America with banners and pictures of dead babies. It was really disgusting. There was blood and bits of eyes and legs.'

'That's really awful,' Lily said, tears in her eyes.

'You shouldn't be sad, Lily,' Carys told her. 'Probably your mum hasn't had an abortion.'

Lily was sure that was true. Her mum didn't hurt any living creatures. When they found a frightened mouse in the cabin she gave it some rescue remedy to bring it back to life. And she especially liked frogs so they had a pond in their garden. Sometimes Lily loved her mum so much it made her panic because what if something happened to her? The thought of her dying gave her a pain so intense that she felt as if she couldn't breathe.

And she hated it when her mum was sad. Her dad was betraying them again, that's what her mum had said to him a few weeks ago, when Lily was in bed pretending to be asleep. She'd said 'betraying me' but as far as Lily was concerned he was betraying all of them. He'd told her mum he wasn't betraying her and that she was imagining it but Lily knew he was lying because at the end of the summer holidays he'd taken Poppy and her out, and they'd met a woman in the park. He pretended they'd met by accident but Lily didn't believe that. He was being all smiley and trying to make them friendly with the woman. Then they went back to her house, which was next door to Max, and played on her trampoline. And in the car on the way home Daddy had said, 'Don't tell Mummy, girls. Let this be something just for us.'

She didn't tell, and nether did Poppy, but she felt guilty about it. She still felt guilty about it.

'Maybe you should say something to your dad,' Carys said to Vera. 'He's got a right to know.'

'I can't because he'll be really upset.'

'You could tell your mum that you know,' Lily said.

'I can't. She'll shout at me.'

'We could write her an anonymous letter,' Carys said, jumping up onto her knees. 'It happened in a show Eleri watches. I don't remember what it's called but the girl gets a letter in her bag from someone, and it's the mean girl in the school who's writing it because the mean girl's mum and the nice girl's dad are having an affair.'

'What's an affair?' Lily asked.

'It means they're having sex,' Carys said loudly. 'You know what sex is?'

'Of course,' Lily said. 'I think that might be what my dad's doing. That's what Poppy said after we met the woman and then I heard him talking on the phone last week.'

'Saying what?' Carys leant in, wide-eyed.

'I want you and we should be together.' She blushed again. 'Stuff like that.' She wasn't going to say the really rude bit because she couldn't even think about the words, never mind say them.

'Gross,' Carys said, screwing up her face. 'Should we write a letter to your dad too?'

'He wouldn't read it. He's always too busy.'

'We should send notes, then,' Carys said. Her eyes were bright with inspiration. 'We could make it a game where some of the clues are false and they have to work out which are true.'

'What do you mean?' Vera asked.

Carys was pulling paper and her pencil case out of her school bag. 'We need to write down some ideas.' Vera and Lily hadn't caught up with her thoughts yet so she added, 'One of the notes can be about an affair. Max said the woman next door to him is having an affair and that his mum said they happen a lot.'

'Next door to him?' Lily asked. That made sense. The man was her dad. She felt a shake begin in her hands and she pressed them onto the grass. 'Don't write about an affair, Carys, please.'

'All right then,' Carys conceded. 'But we have to make Bel realise that she has to tell Miro about the abortion before the truth comes out,' Carys continued. 'That note could say . . .' She put the pen in her open mouth flicking it between her teeth. 'I know . . .' She started to write down ideas while Lily and Vera finished off the grapes. Lily didn't understand what Carys's plan was but she didn't want to ask. She was sure that Vera felt the same.

'I think we should start by saying that everyone has secrets like in *EastEnders*,' Carys said, writing and then scoring some of it out. 'And your dad needs to stop having an affair, Lily. We won't say the word but we'll say stuff about him and maybe your mum. It won't be true but we have to have some false clues.'

'Why?'

'Because that's the game!'

Lily and Vera looked at each other. 'I don't know,' Vera said. 'We can't make it too mean.'

'He is really famous now, your dad,' Carys said, still talking to Lily. 'And that gets people's attention.' She wrote quickly, large ugly letters sprawling across the page. 'And we could have one that says one of you will die, because that always happens on TV shows.'

'You can't do that!' Lily cried out. 'Because then it might happen!'

'It won't!' Carys laughed. 'Because it isn't true.' She thought some more. 'And we'll have to have some swearing. Cunt is the worst swear word. I heard the man who was fixing the window blinds call his friend that. Then Eleri caught me saying it and I had to stay in my room for an hour.'

'So where will we put the notes?' Vera asked.

'In someone's bag, just like in the show.'

Vera was frowning. 'Not mine because if my dad asks me about it I'd have to tell him the truth.'

'One of the boys?' Carys suggested.

'Max wouldn't care,' Lily said. 'He'd throw it away. It has to be someone who cares.'

'None of the boys would care,' Vera said.

'You, Lily,' Carys said, pointing the pen at her.

Lily's hands started to shake again. 'Everyone knows that I care,' she said, looking scared suddenly as if she'd just heard the words come out of her mouth and was shocked by them. 'The only trouble is I'm not good at lying.'

'They won't expect you to know where the notes come from. You just have to look sad.'

Lily wasn't sure she could do that. She didn't always look sad even although her dad called her Eeyore because she could be a bit of a 'sad sack'. He liked Poppy best, that was obvious, and she didn't really mind – well, she did, but she didn't because she knew her mum loved her to the moon and back. She was sure her mum's heart was big enough to love them both, but her dad's? Not so much. Lily worried about her two half-brothers, the twins who lived in Scotland. She knew their mum had remarried but still they never saw their real dad – her dad.

She wished for everyone to be happy. But wishes didn't work and even although Rhianna had told her in Year One that there was no such thing as Santa Claus or the tooth fairy, she still played along at home because Poppy believed in them – or maybe she didn't? She might be playing along too. That thought worried Lily because if everyone was playing along then how would she ever know what was real and what was pretend?

Chapter Thirty

NINA

The girls speak in halting sentences, one taking over where the other leaves off, and by the end of their confession, out of the seven of us, it's only Poppy who seems to be emotionally unscathed. Halfway through, she brings the girls some juice from the fridge. She passes them tissues and now she's squeezed herself between Lily and Vera and is holding their hands, every now and then reaching across to Carys and saying quietly, 'It's okay, Carys, you won't have to go to prison. The youf officer doesn't have to come now.'

Rachel, Bel and I have all cried and now we're quiet. 'I'm not sure where to begin,' I say, my eyes on our three girls. I'm shocked to know that Lily's involved. I'm shocked that she knows about Robin's affair. And the fact that she didn't come to speak to me makes my heart ache. 'I think that perhaps us mums and dads are going to have to sit on this for a little while before we work out what to do next. You all understand that what you did was very wrong, don't you?'

'It's mostly my fault,' Vera says, sitting up straight, tears drying on her cheeks. 'Because I was worried and they wanted to help me.'

'But I wrote the notes,' Carys says. 'And I know I got

281

carried away.' She sneaks a look at her mum. 'I know that's something I do that's wrong about me and I have to stop it. Lily and Vera didn't want me to say anything bad but I did. So that makes it my fault because then we fell out and . . .' She trails off, her lips trembling.

'But, Carys, it's not all your fault because I said I would take the notes in my bag,' Lily's voice is quiet but strong. 'We couldn't have sent the notes if I hadn't agreed.'

I feel Bel fidgeting at the end of the sofa. 'I'm Spartacus,' she says quietly into her coffee mug. 'No, I'm Spartacus.' The last ten minutes have been punishing for her. When Vera said it all began because of the abortion, she was unable to look at her mum and Bel's face was in her hands.

'Okay.' I force myself to stand up, feel the pull of gravity in each and every one of my muscles. It's as if a weight has permeated my body and wants to hold me to the floor. 'One thing I know for sure is that you must apologise to Mrs Fleming who has been extremely worried about all of this. I'm going to call her now and see whether she can meet us in the classroom before the school day begins.'

I move away to get my mobile and hear Rachel snap, 'No talking! You are all in disgrace. I'd be very surprised if Mrs Fleming will even accept you in her class today. I know that I wouldn't.'

Mrs Fleming answers at once and I explain the situation to her. There's a long silence before she says, 'Well, I'm really very, very shocked, Nina. In all my years of teaching—' Her breath catches. 'I thought . . . I mean, I *know* these girls. What on earth possessed them?'

'Getting back at their parents, I think. It's all quite disturbing. I'm at a loss to know how to deal with it.'

'Would you like me to speak to them, operate a system of sanctions?'

'Yes, please.'

'And I think it might be better for them to apologise in front of the whole class. I'm not normally one for naming and shaming, and it means everyone will find out, but it's important for them to own up to the school community. What do you think?'

'Let me ask Bel and Rachel.'

They agree that it's better to get it out into the open as that's the only way we'll be able to move on. We gather in a subdued group by the front door. Rachel is in teaching mode and has the girls lined up as if they are outside the headmaster's office.

'Do I have to come too?' Poppy asks, following me upstairs when I go to find a jumper.

'Yes.'

'But they won't go to prison, Mummy, will they?' she whispers, her brown eyes wide and vulnerable. 'Because everyone makes mistakes sometimes and they've said they're sorry now.'

Poppy's rarely worried and it makes me pull her in for a hug. 'No, darling, they definitely won't be going to prison. The youth officer won't have to come now.'

'That's a relief!' She gives a wobbly laugh. 'Because I like having a sister.'

'How long have you known that they were writing the notes?' I ask casually.

'Just a day . . .' she points her toe and turns her foot to one side to see the shine on the buckle '. . . or maybe four days or five . . . because they always sit under the big tree to eat their lunch and I went to find them because I had no one to play with and I was still hungry.'

'Oh, Poppy.' I sigh. 'Why didn't you tell me?'

283

'They asked me not to.' She frowns. 'It's not good to be a telltale.'

I take Poppy's hand and we go back downstairs. Bel is in the loo and I can hear that she's vomiting. 'Are you okay, Bel?' I tap on the door. I know she's upset but I'm surprised she's bringing up her breakfast. She normally has a strong stomach. 'Do you want us to go ahead without you?'

'I'll be out in a minute,' she says, her voice muffled.

Rachel has the girls in her car, sitting in a row in the back, downcast and miserable. 'Could I go in the front, Aunty Rachel?' Poppy asks, skipping towards her as if it's any other day.

'Yes, on you go. Sit yourself on the booster seat.' Rachel turns to me. 'I'll head off now, shall I?'

I nod. 'We'll see you there.'

I watch as Poppy climbs into the car, unable to hide her delight that she has bagged the front seat, then I wait inside for Bel. When she comes out of the loo her face is grey. 'Was it the coffee?' I ask. 'Or just the general awfulness of this whole thing?'

'I'm pregnant,' she says, a small smile bringing light to her eyes.

'That's fantastic!' I grab hold of her and we spend a few moments hugging and jumping for joy, the morning's confession very briefly forgotten.

Mrs Fleming takes charge. It's a master class on how to tell children off without shouting or threatening, just simple straightforward truth-telling and the reality of choices and consequences.

'I'm extremely disappointed in you girls. I would never have thought you could do something so damaging, so thoughtless.' She pauses. All three girls are crying now.

She passes them a box of tissues. 'You will apologise before the *whole* class this morning. You wrote the notes, Carys, so you will tell the class what the three of you planned and then each one of you will apologise. Is that clear?' The girls nod. 'I can't hear you.'

'Yes, Mrs Fleming,' they reply in unison.

'And we need to think about sanctions,' she tells them. 'We have the school play coming up. I know you enjoy art club, Vera. Lily, you were hoping to take over as library monitor. Carys, I know you excel at drama club.' She turns towards the three of us mums standing at the window. 'What do we think?'

'I think they should forgo all their extras,' Rachel says, her expression stern. 'This is a very serious matter and I'm horrified with what they've done. I'm even more horrified that they allowed other children, particularly Max Mayfair, to be blamed.'

Bel's face is grey again. 'Do you need to leave?' I whisper. She nods. 'Mrs Fleming, would it be all right if Bel and I head off?' I ask.

'Of course. We'll let you know what we decide at the end of the day.'

'I'll take Poppy to her classroom,' Rachel says. Poppy has been sitting at a desk, one eye on her drawing, the other on her sister.

Lily's eyes pull at me, both beseeching and apologetic. I give her what I hope is a suitably supportive but serious smile, kiss Poppy's head and follow Bel out of the door. She runs to the loos and brings up the rest of her coffee.

It's an up-to-London day but I call in to say I'll be working from home instead. I don't go down to the cabin; I stay put at the dining room table. Robin has claimed the cabin as his space and I'm going to leave it to my solicitor to push for him to move out. I'm done talking to him and have no intention of telling him about Lily and the notes. He's shown very little interest as it is.

I'm glad that, no matter what's going on in my life, I'm almost able to lose myself in my work. I focus on a newly completed contract with a forensic eye for the small detail, knowing that it's a misstep in the detail that so often derails an agreement. It doesn't completely stop me thinking about what's just happened. Every so often the truth of the girls' involvement leapfrogs to the front of my mind and I take a moment to think about a way forward. Half-term next week will be the break we all need and I can't wait to drive up to my parents'. It will be the perfect opportunity for me to spend time on my own with Lily, too. I feel as if, somewhere along the way, she has slipped out of my reach and I need her to come back to me.

When three-thirty arrives I finish up and walk to school. I'm hoping to have a heart-to-heart with Lily, but when I collect her from the classroom, she seems incapable of speech. Mrs Fleming tells me that they have apologised to the class, and have accepted that they will be excluded from all activities, including the end-of-term play. This is particularly hard on Carys who is a budding actress and loves to take part in all things drama.

The girls will not be allowed to stay for after-school clubs for the rest of term. Rachel suggests that she will drop the clubs she runs and take the three girls to her house on the days that Bel and I work. 'They can sit at the dining table and do schoolwork,' she says. 'And no sleepovers before Christmas.'

I take Lily's hand and find Poppy on the wall outside. I tell her we need to head home straight away and while she packs her football cards into her bag, I try not to catch anyone's eye. The air is buzzing around me, as if a swarm of locusts is coming in to land. I watch as Rhianna runs up to her mum Suze and tells her something. Suze's eyes snap up to mine and I immediately look away, see several pairs of eyes on me, and realise that I'm surrounded by a semi-malevolent interest. Rachel is still inside; Maxine, Amira and Bel, my allies, are nowhere in sight. Before Suze reaches me, I take the girls' hands and head for the exit. Not fleeing exactly. Not quite.

When we arrive home, I give Poppy the iPad to play games on and then I sit with Lily in her bedroom. I can't help but think she'll take this harder than she needs to. She is inclined to hold herself to a very high standard. 'The three of you made a mistake,' I tell her. 'But it's not the end of the world. You need to take your punishment and then move on.'

She's sitting with her back to the headboard, her knees drawn up to her chin. I place my hand on her feet and say, 'Can we agree that next time you or your friends have worries, you will talk to me about it?' She nods. 'Okay.' I stand up. 'I'm making some pasta for dinner. I'll call you downstairs in about fifteen minutes.'

'Is Lily okay?' Poppy asks me when I come back into the room.

'She will be, Poppy. But she'll be upset for a few days so we'll need to be patient with her.'

'I'll be nice,' she says. 'She can take anything she wants from my bedroom. Even my football cards.' She thinks for a second. 'Well, not Paul Pogba because he's my favourite.'

*   *   *

The rest of the evening passes quietly with Lily barely speaking and Poppy curled up beside me listening to a story tape. My main preoccupation – who was writing the notes – is now gone but I can't rest easy because there's still so much of my life that's bent out of shape.

It's almost eleven o'clock, and I'm doing the rounds, locking doors and turning off lights, when the front door opens and Robin comes inside. I immediately wish I'd pulled the bolts across earlier to stop him using his key. I'm sticking to my decision not to tell him that the girls were writing the notes, but I intend to let him know that Lily and Poppy are aware of his affair. I'm about to open my mouth but he's whistling so loudly that I wouldn't be heard. I literally haven't seen him this upbeat for years.

'Good evening.' He smiles at me and I follow him into the kitchen, baffled by his good mood. He strides across to the bifold doors and that's when I notice he's carrying a hammer. He aims it at the bolt that locks the door and uses all his strength to strike.

'What are you doing?' I grab his arm. 'You're going to damage it!'

He takes another swipe and the bolt separates from the fixings. 'I received the email from your solicitor earlier.' His smile is even wider now. 'And let's be clear, I will not be locked out of my own house.'

'Now I won't be able to lock the door!' I tell him. I should have anticipated this but I forgot to check my emails after I collected the girls. 'Our children sleep here!'

'And so do I!' He jabs a finger at his chest. 'And don't you forget it.' He walks towards me, raising the hammer up into the air and I instinctively duck out of his reach. He laughs then, and goes down to the cabin, the hammer swinging at his side. He's whistling Sinatra's 'My Way'.

If he's trying to scare me, it's worked. My heart is

racing; my mouth is dry. I swallow some water and listen from the bottom of the stairs in case the girls have been woken by the noise. I can't hear anything so I sit down at my laptop and then read the email my solicitor sent to him. Her tone is firm but there is nothing in what she's said that isn't true. I reply to her, describing what's just taken place. I knew that divorcing Robin wasn't going to be easy but I didn't expect him to resort to violence quite so quickly.

Although, I didn't for one moment believe he was going to hit me with the hammer because he's not that sort of man, is he? And then I remember the glass smashed above my head.

It makes me wonder what the third thing will be.

Chapter Thirty-one

BEL

I spend the whole day at work thinking about how I'll talk to Vera. I blame myself – how could I not? I took her into the doctor's surgery with me. I chose that appointment to ask about the abortion. I know that Vera is bright, but still I spoke in front of her.

The identity of the note-writer was staring us in the face the whole time. And yet we didn't see it. What's worse is that none of the girls were able to be honest with us. Most especially Vera, who kicked the whole thing off. I'm gutted that she was wrestling with the knowledge of the abortion for so long, torn between protecting me and telling her dad the truth.

I collect her from school and take her straight home. She doesn't say a word. Her face is turned away from me in the car and when we reach the house, she goes straight up to her room. I make her favourite dinner: pasta, carrot sticks, grated cheese and a pile of sweetcorn. As soon as it's ready, I call her to the table and she comes, obediently. I sit down opposite her with a herbal tea. I'm managing to last about an hour between vomiting so I'm not going to eat anything now. Amira called me this morning to say she'd read my notes and has referred me to an obstetrician as a matter of urgency. I'm hoping they will be able to help me get through the first few months, otherwise I fear I'll end up hospitalised like last time.

Vera upends the ketchup bottle and squirts a small amount on the edge of her plate.

'Is it okay for us to talk?' I ask her.

'Yes.'

'How was school today?'

'Okay.'

The smell of her food wafts towards me and I feel the urge to retch. I pull my head back and concentrate very hard on not being sick.

'What's wrong with you?' she asks, her expression sombre. 'I heard you being sick at Nina's and then you had to leave the classroom this morning.'

'Just a tummy upset.' I manage a smile. I need to wait so that Miro and I can tell her about the pregnancy together. He's staying with his sister's family in London tonight. He goes there for dinner once a month and won't be home until tomorrow after work. 'I'm sorry that you were upset when you came with me to the doctor's.'

'I wasn't upset about going with you. I just wanted to know what a TOP was.'

'So you looked it up?'

'Yes.' She chews slowly on a carrot stick. 'And then when I saw it was . . .' She stops. She has yet to look me in the eye and now she lowers her head further. 'I felt sorry for Daddy because he wants a baby and . . .' She stops again, and then dares to half-look at me, one eye completely covered by her hair. 'Does he know about it now?'

I swallow down my fear at the thought of breaking the news to him. 'No, he doesn't,' I say.

She nods like this was expected.

'But it was a long time ago and I have been wanting to have another baby with Daddy for several years now.' My hand drops reflexively to my lower abdomen. 'I'm going to tell him about the abortion.' Just voicing the intention is enough to make my heart squeeze. 'He's at Aunty Sophia's tonight but when he comes home tomorrow I'll tell him.'

She pierces a piece of pasta with her fork and brings it up to her mouth. 'Will he be upset?'

'He will.'

My lip trembles and seeing this, she says quickly, 'You don't have to tell him.' She flicks her hair out of her eye and stares at me, her expression sincere. 'I won't say, so you don't have to either.'

'Thank you, love, but he needs to know.' I smile sadly. 'I should have told him a long time ago.' The whole idea of telling Miro terrifies me but I'm going to have to do it. If I don't, then the secret will hang between us like a sword that could drop tomorrow, in three years' time or in ten. My secret is out and there's no way I would expect my daughter to be complicit in hiding something this incendiary from her dad.

'Would you be able to tell me why you didn't talk to me about all this?' I ask her.

She eats a carrot stick before saying quietly, 'Sometimes you might not listen. You're busy and—' she shrugs '—I don't want to make you mad.'

I gasp at this, ashamed of myself. I'm the first to admit that I'm not always approachable but even to Vera? What have I missed? How has my love for her not been trans-lated into always being available?

Since I was a child, trouble has always felt like heat and I can feel my temperature rise. It makes me want

293

to wriggle out of my skin, to go back in time, to go up to London right now and tell Miro. To take my daughter's hand and somehow make her see how much I love her.

Chapter Thirty-two

NINA

Next day, I wake up and find Lily in my bed. She's obviously had another one of her sleepwalking episodes because she's as surprised as I am to find herself there. She's still quiet and won't meet my eye but she is answering 'yes' and 'no' to questions, which is more than was the case last night, and Poppy even manages to get a smile out of her.

After I drop them at school I meet Bel and Rachel for coffee. We go to our favourite café in the village where the coffee is strong and the cake is sweet and we can sit in the corner for hours having regular top-ups without the owner expecting us to move on.

'I had two phone calls from parents in the class last night,' Rachel says. 'Jeremy what's-his-face and Amira. She was concerned about the girls and wants to know whether she can help. He was trying to resist gloating but not doing a very good job of it.'

'I had a couple of missed calls,' I say. 'One from Maxine and another from a mum of one of Poppy's friends.'

'We'll have to put up with stares and whispers behind our backs for a while.'

'Let them whisper,' Bel says. Her hands circle a mug

of peppermint tea. 'I'm going to tell Miro about the abortion tonight.' She looks dejected. 'There's no getting away from it.'

'Because you're pregnant, telling him might not be as bad as you think,' Rachel says. 'I mean the pregnancy kind of cancels out the abortion, doesn't it?'

Rachel still doesn't really get it and I'm surprised that Bel doesn't say that to her but she just gives a fatalistic smile and says, 'It's about trust, isn't it? Keeping a secret like that for all this time. And not just any secret, one that violates our core values and beliefs.' She pauses to think. 'I spoke to Vera when we came home from school, and afterwards I wondered why she didn't ask me why I had the abortion.'

'She's young,' I say. 'That will be a conversation for when she's older.'

Bel wriggles her shoulders as if trying to shrug it all off and asks me, 'How was Lily last night?'

'She was in bed by seven. I think she's ashamed more than anything.' I take a bite of my coconut cake, which would surely earn a place in heaven. 'They're all good girls really, aren't they? They did something that was very silly—'

'I think it's worse than silly!' Rachel is still angry. 'It was malicious and potentially dangerous.'

'I know. But they were trying to hurt *us*.'

'Well, me and Robin,' Bel says.

'I think it would be worse if they were picking on another child,' I say. 'We have broad shoulders. And the intention was to help sort their parents' lives out. That's what started it! They did the wrong thing for the right reason. And they're being well punished for it.'

'You think we're being too hard on them?' Rachel asks.

'Maybe. I don't know. To be honest, I feel like I've got bigger fish to fry.' I tell them about Robin and the incident with the hammer last night. 'I've emailed my solicitor again. She thinks Robin should move out but I'm willing to take the line of least resistance. Next week is half-term and we'll drive up to my parents' for a week. And when we come back, we'll move into rented accommodation. I've seen a couple of houses online that would work for us.'

'You can't let him have the house!' Bel exclaims. 'He's never there!'

'I know but moving myself and the girls out would take some of the heat out of the situation. I don't want to add fuel to his fire.'

'You presented him with divorce papers, Nina,' Rachel says. 'That was pretty fiery.' She looks as if she wants to say more but she quickly takes a sip of her coffee.

'You think that was aggressive?' I ask.

'No, but, normally people separate and then they talk about divorce and then the lawyers get involved.'

A thought occurs to me. 'Is that what he said to you at the quiz night?'

'What do you mean?' She blushes.

'I saw him talking to you when I was leaving and you were really listening.' I'm staring at her; she looks caught out. 'I get it, Rachel. I know how persuasive he can be.'

'All he said was that you weren't being fair.' I see Bel raise her eyebrows at this. 'And it's not that I believed him! But people like Robin are hard to disbelieve.'

'He's a liar.' I lean forward. 'Let me explain. After I caught him cheating on me the first time, we had months of couples counselling, and we drew up an agreement that said one or other of us could file for divorce if there was another episode of infidelity. We both signed the document.' I pause to breathe, annoyed that Rachel fell for his bullshit. 'He had to know this was on the cards. He just doesn't want to accept it.'

'I'm sorry,' Rachel says. 'I really am. I promise I'm not on his side.'

'Robin likes sleeping around,' I say, flatly. 'He likes the buzz and the thrill, but he also wants to come home to a wife and children. He's exactly like his father was.'

'In all seriousness,' Bel says, resting her hand on the back of mine, 'if there is any danger of him hitting you or the girls, moving out might not be a bad idea. You can still fight for the house.'

'You know how you've got your spyware?' Rachel says. 'Maybe you should record all of your conversations with him too otherwise he might say the lock was already broken and you were making it up.'

'I've been thinking that too,' I say. 'I could use the recorder on my phone. That's easy enough to switch on when he's in the room.'

We go on to talk about Bel's pregnancy, her frequent vomiting and the help she's going to need. Rachel mentions the DNA test, her eyes anxious, and I promise that I'll let her know as soon as I get the email.

I leave them at eleven to go back home and catch up with work. My solicitor has replied saying she will be speaking to the family court judge and that Robin will be issued with a final warning with regards to his violent behaviour. If he doesn't agree to leave the family home then he will be evicted. In the meantime, I should get a locksmith in to replace the broken bolt. I give her a call to say that I am willing to move out.

'In the short term, only,' she says. 'And only for the safety of yourself and your children.'

Before I get back to work, I glance outside to see

whether Robin's car is in the driveway. It isn't, and I'm keeping my fingers crossed that he'll stay away all day.

When I walk along to collect the girls in the afternoon they're both standing by the pick-up point waiting for me. 'No playing today?'

'Why did you walk?' Poppy asks, her expression serious.

'You know we always walk unless I'm coming from the station.' They each take one of my hands and Poppy starts to drag me towards the school exit. 'Has someone been giving you a hard time?' I ask. Neither of them reply and I glance at the faces around me, most mums looking away as if to meet my eye will somehow contaminate them. 'Have people been saying mean things to you because of the notes?' Still neither of them is willing to speak. It isn't just Lily who is subdued. Poppy also seems to have caught the bug.

When we get home, they both sit down on the sofa, backs up straight, as if they're waiting for someone to collect them. I place flapjacks and juice and a mug of tea for me on the side table and sit down next to them. 'What's going on?' I ask.

Poppy glances at her sister.

'Really, girls, please.' I reach out and touch both their knees. 'Tell me what's up. Is it because of what was written in the notes?'

Poppy glances at Lily again and sighs. 'You're divorcing.'

I feel a long drop in my stomach. 'Who told you that?' I ask. No answer. 'Girls.' My eyes fill with tears. I go down on the floor in front of them and say, 'You *have* to tell me. It's very important that we're honest with each other.'

'Daddy came to school today and he took us out of the class.' It's Poppy speaking. 'And it was my favourite lesson and he said that now we have to live with him and Emily.' Lily puts her forearm over her face and begins to cry. 'I don't like Emily very much but she has a dog,' Poppy adds.

I sit up on the sofa between them and pull Lily into my chest, feel her tears soak into my blouse and her sorrow pass through me in a wave. I grit my teeth against the pain and say, 'When did you meet Emily?'

'This morning, but we met her before when Daddy took us out. Lily was there too.' Poppy touches her sister's back, gently, as if it might burn her fingers. 'We went on the trampoline. She lives next door to Max so you could play with him, Lily,' she says a bit louder. 'It would be easy because you could climb over the fence. And if the fence is too high you could go on the trampoline and bounce over.'

'I don't want to live with her!' Lily shouts. 'I don't like her!'

'Okay, listen,' I say firmly. 'Both of you, look at me.' Poppy wriggles on the seat, turning round towards me and sitting up on her knees so that our faces are level. Lily pulls back and wipes her face on a tissue.

When they're both looking at me I say, 'Are you listening?'

'Yes, Mummy,' Poppy says.

'Lily?'

'Yes, Mummy.'

'You are not moving in with Emily and Daddy,' I say fiercely. 'You are *my* girls and you will always live with me. *Always*. I am going nowhere. Do you understand?'

They both nod.

'Daddy and I are getting divorced and I am very sad

about that.' I take a moment to try to breathe but my lungs will barely inflate. 'Daddy and I are leaving each other because we don't love each other anymore. He is *not* leaving his girls. You two will always be his girls.'

'Because he has three boys,' Poppy says.

'Sometimes you might have to stay with Daddy for a night or two,' I add, not wanting to say this, not wanting them ever to leave my side but the reality is they will want to spend time with him, whoever he is living with. 'But we will ask you first and if you're not comfortable then you don't have to go.'

'The twins never see him because they live in Glasgow and he never visits them,' Lily says, tears beginning to flow again. 'And that makes me worry.'

'They have a new dad,' Poppy says. 'So they don't miss our daddy.'

'It was very wrong of Daddy to take you out of school,' I say, keeping my tone level. 'I'm going to speak to your teachers so that it doesn't happen again.'

He's pressing my buttons. He knows that if the girls are upset, I'm upset. I want to slap him hard. I want to rant and scream and call him names. I never, ever want to see him again.

I make the rest of the evening as normal and happy as I can. We play Jenga together and Poppy ends up laughing so much that she almost wets herself and goes off to the toilet, hand between her legs, waddling like a penguin so that Lily laughs too. At seven-thirty we climb the stairs and I read to them. When I've responded to 'just one more page, Mummy, please!' three times, they settle down for the night in their own beds and I go back downstairs.

The Porsche is back in the drive. Robin must have gone round the side of the house and down to the cabin that way. I wait for another half an hour until the girls are fully asleep then slide my feet into my shoes and open the bifold doors. I intend to confront him but when I'm halfway down the garden it occurs to me that she might be in there with him. I'd rather not come face to face with her. She will be more power to Robin's elbow and he is already intimidating enough.

I come back inside and open the app for the voice-activated device in the cabin.

Emily Birch is there. This is what I hear:

'Nina has a borderline personality disorder,' Robin says. 'She's always been very difficult.'

'It must be so hard for you.' Her voice is syrupy with sympathy.

'It's been tricky.' He sighs. 'And I worry about her influence on the girls.'

'You need to fight her all the way, Robin. Through the courts if necessary.' Thirty seconds of kissing noises and then: 'I'll help you,' she says. 'The girls can come and live with us.'

I've heard enough. I shut off the recording and lean my forehead against the wall. Could this get any worse? I wish I was able to cry but my eyes are completely dry. I feel like I'm running on empty, anxiety and adrenaline the only reason I haven't conked out in the corner.

Chapter Thirty-three

The next day, I drop the girls at school and ask their teachers to please not let them go anywhere with Robin. 'If he insists then I would appreciate you calling me,' I say. 'We are in the process of getting a divorce.' They both look as if they'd like to know more but I don't elaborate.

Mrs Fleming, in particular, is deeply shocked. 'No!' Her hand goes up to her mouth. 'I'm so sorry to hear that.'

I give her a sad smile then walk away, already sure that whatever line he feeds her, she will believe him over me.

It's one of my days for working from home and I'm back at the dining table. Robin's car is still in the driveway. I'm not sure whether they've had an extended night of sex or whether she's gone. I don't want to listen in. I'm going to leave them to it and get on with my arrangements.

Before I get down to work, I call Bel. 'How's it going? Have you told Miro yet about the . . . ?'

'I couldn't do it,' she says. 'He's so happy I'm pregnant but he's worried about Vera. He doesn't understand why she was involved in the notes because he never found out about the wording on the dead baby one or the one that named me.' She sighs. 'I have to tell him before he has a heart-to-heart with her because it puts her in an impossible position. I don't want her to have to lie to her dad.'

'Of course not,' I say. Poor Vera, stuck in the middle. Not unlike my own girls, being pulled in either direction. 'What are you doing over half-term?'

'We're flying to Poland to stay with his aunt. I don't want to spoil the holiday.' She sighs again. 'I'll have to go, Nina. I feel another vomit coming on.'

I get stuck into more case files and three-thirty comes round again. I'm back at the school gates where the fallout from the girls' behaviour continues. Suze comes up and says to me, in a pleased-with-herself tone, 'You must be feeling embarrassed.'

'Why? Was I talking behind your back in the toilets?'

She smirks at me. 'Ashamed. Of your daughter.' She walks off again and is immediately absorbed into the warmth of her friendship huddle.

Maxine is watching this, frowning. I noticed yesterday that she has detached herself from this friendship group. 'I'm really sorry, Nina,' she says. 'Don't pay any attention to her. Kids do stuff. I said to Max last night – did you know the girls were sending the notes? And he went all sheepish, the little bugger!'

'It's been such a shock,' I say, blinking against the sudden welling up in my eyes. 'It never even occurred to me that the three of them could be responsible.'

'I think the punishment is a bit steep,' she says. 'Not being in the class play is harsh.' Her face lights up and she touches my shoulder. 'By the way, the photo of you has been my third most liked post on Instagram *ever*. I've got another sponsorship deal off the back of it so if you're ever looking for a second career.'

I laugh. 'I'll know where to come.' She goes off to speak to Mrs Fleming and I see Rachel in the distance. I know she is on tenterhooks about the DNA results. 'Nothing yet,' I tell her. 'I promise you I'm checking my emails every half an hour.'

'It's torture,' she says. 'The longer it takes, the more likely it is to be bad news. I know that doesn't make any sense but the feeling of impending doom increases.' She presses a hand against her chest. 'I'm a wreck. Eleri keeps going on about Harry and how much she loves him.' Her voice drops to a whisper. 'What if I have to break her heart?'

I try to reassure her but my words sound empty even to me. The girls and I head off home and after I've fed them, they sit in front of a film and I lock and bolt the front door. Unfortunately, Robin can still come into the house through the bifolds. I've booked a locksmith but he can't fix the broken lock until the day after tomorrow.

'I'm going for a bath, girls,' I say. 'Come up and tell me immediately if Daddy comes home. Okay?'

'Okay, Mummy,' Lily says.

The water smells of honey and almonds. I close my eyes and relax back, try to forget what's behind me and what might be up ahead. I concentrate on the good stuff. At the weekend we'll drive up to my parents' and relax in the peace of the Cumbrian countryside, so different from here, the landscape rugged and rocky, rising hills and rivers that flood into lakes. I lose myself in that image, at the same time practising the breathing exercises that Aimee taught us at the women's group. I'm just finding a rhythm when there is a knock on the door.

'Mummy?' It's Lily. 'Daddy's home and Poppy has given him the password to your laptop. Daddy said it was okay but I wasn't sure. Is it okay?'

My eyes snap open and I'm out of the bath in seconds. I grab my robe and tie it round my middle then open the door. 'Where is he?'

'In the loo.'

I run downstairs. I'm not thinking about the spyware or my solicitor's emails, or anything to do with work. He can check my bank accounts, read whatever he wants, in any folder he chooses. But what I don't want him to see is the result of the DNA test, just in case Rachel's fears are justified. I pray that the email hasn't arrived yet and knock on the door. 'I'd like you to give me my laptop back, please, Robin.' No answer. 'Robin?'

Poppy appears beside me. 'I thought you'd want me to,' she says. 'Because he's your husband and this is a good way to be friends.'

'But Daddy has his own laptop,' Lily says.

'But if they *share* things more then they might not be divorcing and then we can stay as a *family*.'

A rising panic courses through me. I knock one more time. 'Robin? I'd like my laptop, please.'

Still no reply so I run back upstairs and find my phone. When I open my emails, I see at once that the message from the test centre arrived ten minutes ago and has been read. I collapse back onto the bed, my blood running cold when I read the message and see that the DNA test is a match. Eleri's DNA matches with the DNA on Robin's toothbrush.

Bryn is not Eleri's father.

Robin is her father.

'Fuck! Fuck! Fuck!' I say under my breath. Robin's name is not written on the page but Eleri Davies is. And the sample is a paternity test. Unless he's completely blanked out his night with Rachel, it won't take him long to put two and two together. Could I get away with saying the samples were Bryn and Eleri's and that Rachel was simply looking to prove an avoidance of doubt?

I pull on some underwear and a tracksuit and go back downstairs again. 'Girls, I'd like you to go to your rooms for a little while, please, because I need to have a conversation with Daddy.'

'But I want to have something else to eat,' Poppy says.

'You've only just had something.'

'I'm still hungry.'

'Poppy, will you stop!' My jaw is tight as I say this, and at the same time, I grab her by the arm and shake her. I don't shake her hard, but as it's not something I ever do we are both shocked. 'Poppy, I'm sorry.' I reach for her but she bursts into tears. Lily gives me a scolding look and hustles her little sister up the stairs.

I'm upset to have frightened her but right now I have something more urgent to worry about. I wait several minutes until Robin comes out of the loo. He looks triumphant, gloating and self-satisfied. I follow him into the kitchen. He places my laptop on the kitchen island and stands in front of me, arms folded. 'Eleri is my daughter,' he says.

'What on earth?' I am fully prepared to defend Rachel's position. 'That's absurd!'

'I saw the results of the paternity test, Nina.'

'So what? The test sample is Bryn's.'

'So why would it be sent to you?'

'Because Rachel was here when we were talking about it and my laptop was handy.'

'It's been sent to you because she can't risk Bryn seeing it.'

I pull my neck back and laugh. 'That's some conclusion you're jumping to!'

He leans in towards me. 'As I'm sure you now know,

seventeen years ago I had sex with Rachel. Just the once. And nine months later she had a child.' I'm about to speak and he stops me with a loud, 'Don't bother, Nina! Really. It's not difficult maths. Yes, of course, Eleri could have been Bryn's child but she has the look of my mother, don't you think?'

'No, I don't,' I say, wondering how long he's been thinking this. 'Not in the slightest.'

'Well, I tell you what, how about we go and have a chat with Bryn and Rachel? Let's see what they think.'

He'd do it. He'd walk into their house and blow their whole family apart just to force me into submission. A feeling of dread settles in my chest, takes root, wraps sticky fingers around my heart. 'Robin.' He goes to walk past me and I stop him with my foot. 'Rachel and Bryn are good people. Your fight is with me, not them.'

'That's right.'

'Please don't say anything. It would be cruel.'

'Ah.' He opens his eyes wide with mock surprise. 'This is something you want from me?'

'You're not a bad person. And I think that if you consider the bigger picture, you'll know that dragging Bryn and Rachel into our quarrel is not the right thing to do.'

'The right thing to do?' He smiles again. 'Okay. I'll do the right thing. I won't say a word. I'll even sacrifice a relationship with *my* daughter. But.' He holds up a finger. 'You also need to do the right thing. You need to contact your solicitor and dismiss the divorce petition. Tell her you've changed your mind.'

'Robin—'

'It's my first and final offer, Nina. Eleri seems like a nice girl and if she's my child then I should be allowed to acknowledge her—'

'Unless I do what you want,' I say coldly.

'That's right.' His smile is reptilian. 'It's your choice, Nina. You save your friend from being revealed as a cheat and a liar and, at the same time you save your marriage. It's a win-win.' He walks away from me then. 'I'll give you twenty-four hours to think about it.'

My whole body is shaking, my chest heaving with an all-consuming panic. He has me trapped. Both options are equally hard to stomach. I promised Rachel privacy and I've let her down. I can't allow Robin to ruin their lives. I can't do that. But the reality of staying married to Robin stretches before me as a bleak wasteland of lies and loneliness.

I'll have to tell Rachel the result of the test; telling Bryn the truth is her decision. I'm not sure whether I have to tell her that Robin knows about it. I pace up and down the kitchen, biting my nails, trying to think through possible scenarios where both families are together and he drops a hint or mentions it outright. But if I promise to stay married to him then he won't do that, will he? And if he finds out that Harry and Eleri are going out together? What then? They are half-brother and -sister. They can't continue to be in a relationship. It might not be sexual but that could only be a matter of time. Again, that is for Rachel to deal with. My cross to bear is that Robin will continue to be my husband, in name only, for as long as he can hold this threat over my head.

I start to cry, overwhelmed by the crushing weight of opposing choices. I curl myself into a ball on the sofa and try to silence the voice in my head that tells me: *This is your own fault, Nina. And it's up to you to fix it.*

309

Chapter Thirty-four

I barely sleep. I lie in the dark, staring up at the ceiling where shadows deepen until a navy blue darkness surrounds me. The couple of times I drift off, I dream of people hiding in the bushes, a ghostly draught blowing through my kitchen and a dog that won't stop barking. This goes on until morning when I dress quickly and text Rachel: *We need to meet today. Are you working?*

She texts back: *No, I'm not working. It's bad news, isn't it?*

We meet after we drop off the girls. She's standing away from the parent huddles, and as soon as she sees my face, she begins to shake. I link my arm through hers and walk her down onto the path that leads to my house. I don't want to take her back to mine. The Porsche wasn't there this morning but Robin could just appear, as he has a tendency to do these days.

We sit on a wooden bench on the ridge that overlooks the reservoir. She is completely silent. She isn't crying, which is unusual for Rachel. Her face is pale and drawn, her eyes hopeful until I say softly, 'I'm so sorry, Rachel, but Robin is Eleri's biological parent.' At once the hope is extinguished and she gives a small cry, like the sound of a trapped animal. I take her hands and wait until she's ready to speak.

'It's what I've always feared,' she says, her voice little more than a whisper. 'It was when I had Carys that I really knew Eleri wasn't Bryn's child because she had a completely different quality to her sister. And I know two babies are never the same but . . .' Her head drops towards her chest. 'I knew.'

'Rachel.' I stroke the backs of her hands. 'I'm so very sorry.'

'What should I do, Nina?' she pleads. 'Should I tell them both?'

I shake my head and whisper back, 'I don't know.'

'Did you tell Bel?' she asks.

'No,' I say.

'So nobody knows apart from you and me?'

I want to say *that's right* but my face won't let me lie. She starts back, her eyes aflame. 'Who knows, Nina? Who? Lily? Poppy?'

'Robin took my laptop.' I hear the words come out of my mouth and want to bow my head with shame.

She gives a loud gasp and stands up as if stung. A dog walker several metres away hears her and turns to look our way. I hold my hand up to reassure him it's okay, pull her back down beside me and say, 'Robin won't tell anyone. I *promise* you.'

'He can't be trusted! You of all people know he can't!'

'He will *not* say anything, Rachel.'

'You don't know that!' she hisses at me.

'I do.' My voice is strong. 'I've agreed to stay married to him. That's what he wants. That's what he'll get.'

'What? But you can't do that.' She is incredulous now. 'He's horrible to you.'

'It is what it is,' I say, and manage a careless shrug.

312

'It will be more of the same. And every now and then when he's between women he'll probably take an interest in me.'

'Nina.' She recoils. 'That's so sad. You can't do that for me! You can't live like that.'

'I can and I will. I have my girls. It's more than lots of people have.'

She stares off across the reservoir, her forehead creased in thought. 'But if I tell Bryn and Eleri then you'll be able to get divorced, won't you? Because Robin won't have anything to hold over you.'

'I don't expect you to tell them. I really don't.' I tighten my hold on her hands. 'You do what you feel is right for your family.'

'We're both between the devil and the deep blue sea,' she says. And then she leans her head on my shoulder and closes her eyes. 'I wish we could just fall asleep here and never wake up.'

I spend the rest of the day on autopilot. I work from home, checking contracts and signing off on proposals. My mind is able to focus while my heart is absent, trapped in a box, where it can neither be seen nor heard.

I collect the girls from school and find Lily silent and Poppy grumpy, still carrying the grudge from yesterday evening when I shook her. I let them eat whatever they want, watch as much television as they want and they slowly thaw towards me, not because I'm giving in to them but because they can tell I'm not really present and it worries them.

'What's wrong, Mummy?' Lily asks me.

'I'm really tired, love,' I say, not even trying for a smile. 'I didn't sleep so well last night.'

'I'm sorry about the notes,' she says.

313

'And I'm sorry I gave Daddy your password,' Poppy pipes up, her dark eyes locked on to mine. 'I thought it was the right thing to do.'

I reassure them that I'm just tired, I'm not angry or disappointed, and that it's almost half-term so we can drive up to the lakes, go hillwalking, bake with Grandma and go cycling with Grandpa. They're both shouldering the burden of their parents' failed marriage and I want that to stop. From now on I'm going to shift my focus and pretend to be that happy family. Other people do it. I can do it too.

Robin gave me twenty-four hours to make a decision and I wait for him to appear, but he doesn't. I listen to the device in the cabin and hear them having sex. I'm not even bothered. It means I can go to bed. When the girls are settled, it's still only half past eight, but I go into my room and climb under the covers. I'm so exhausted that I fall into a deep, uninterrupted sleep.

The next morning I'm up around six as usual and when I check my phone, I see that Bel rang after nine last night when I was already in bed. I wonder whether she's told Miro and what his reaction has been. I know he'll be hurt but hopefully he'll see the bigger picture. Their marriage should be strong enough to survive this, especially with a baby on the way.

As well as the missed call, I notice that the alarm for Robin's glucose monitor is flashing red. I always have my phone on silent so I didn't hear the first warning bell, which according to the app, sounded about one in the morning. His blood sugars reading is 1.2. That's so perilously low that it doesn't seem possible. Normal blood sugar levels are between 4 and 8, depending on when food was last consumed. There must be something wrong with the sensor. He wears it on his upper arm. Perhaps he knocked it off when they were having a particularly energetic session? I know Emily was with him so I feel it really isn't my concern anymore. I'm his wife in name only.

At breakfast Poppy tells me that Bel came to the door last night. 'You weren't here,' she says. 'I answered the door because the knocking woke me up and you'd gone out.'

'Of course I was here! I was already asleep!'

'I told her you might be in the cabin so she went down there.' She takes a huge spoonful of Coco Pops. 'I think she was crying.'

'Poppy you're spitting on the table!' Lily cries out.

Really? Could I have missed the sound of the doorbell? It's possible. I was so exhausted it would have taken a bomb to wake me up.

When they've finished breakfast we get through the rigmarole of teeth and shoes and making sure they have everything they need. Lily is in a particularly tetchy mood and that winds Poppy up. By the time they're ready to leave the house, it's too late to walk.

Before we climb into the car, I notice that the wooden gatepost has been scraped by something blue, paint from the metal digging into the grooves in the wood. Another thing to add to the list of jobs.

The queue from the other direction onto the school driveway is lengthy so I pull up just outside. 'Half-term tomorrow,' I tell them as I kiss them goodbye. 'Enjoy your day!'

'See you later, Mummy!' Poppy skips into the school grounds, her feet light, smile wide. Lily doesn't look back but sidles off, hugging the rhododendrons down the side of the walkway as if she wants to disappear.

I drive back home and am just settling down when the doorbell goes. It's the locksmith. 'For your bifolds,' he tells me.

'Brilliant.' I show him into the kitchen. 'You can see where the bolt has come away.'

'That doesn't happen by itself,' he says, assessing the damage. He whistles through his teeth. 'Someone's done this deliberately.'

My husband took a hammer to it. 'Cup of coffee?' I say brightly, and I make us both a cup then go to work at the dining table.

It takes him less than an hour to fix another lock in place, this time with keys so that I can lock the door at night. Robin will still be able to get in if he uses his set of keys. Because, whether I like it or not, I have to let him have access to the house, and I really don't like it. But I think of Rachel and what would happen to her marriage if Robin turned up at their door and claimed Eleri as his child.

I see the locksmith away just as my mobile rings – it's Andy Parker, Robin's registrar. He says a rushed hello before: 'I don't want to alarm you, Nina, but we're looking for Robin. He should have come in for a surgery this morning and it's not like him to be late.'

'I think . . . sorry, Andy.' I remember Robin's blood sugar readings this morning and experience a flash of panic so intense that I feel it in my scalp. 'Let me check down in the cabin. He might be having a sauna.' Robin never misses a surgery. If his levels are as low as the reading suggested then, wherever he is, he is in serious trouble.

I run down to the bottom of the garden and open the door into the cabin. There is a plate of cheese, bread and fruit laid out on the side. Robin's clothes and mobile are on the sofa. No sign of Emily and no sign of him. I stand still but can hear nothing except birdsong. As I'm about to leave, I pull on the door handle to the sauna just in case he's in there. The door is locked. And that's unusual because we never lock the sauna. The key is always in the keyhole on the outside of the door but we don't use it.

I feel a deep sense of foreboding as I unlock the door and open it, not expecting to see Robin, not really imagining for one moment—

But he's there. Robin is lying on the floor.

Chapter Thirty-five

I blink and blink again, not believing what I'm seeing, expecting that the scene will change and Robin won't be lying there; he'll be lounging on a chair reading a magazine or grabbing his keys to go out for a drive.

The sauna is still warm so he must have fired it up last night. And then somehow been locked inside with no way to cool himself down. I can see that he has sweated profusely and that will have played havoc with his blood sugars. I get down on my knees and feel for a pulse. It's faint, barely palpable. His skin is pavement grey.

I scramble back into the living area of the cabin and grab hold of his mobile to call an ambulance. 'Please come quickly – my husband is in a diabetic coma.' They stay on the line as I run up to the house to get the glucose gel from the fridge. Seconds later, I'm running down to the cabin again where I quickly rub some gel on the inside of his cheek. He's unconscious and unable to swallow sugar but he'll absorb the glucose through the inside of his mouth. I know this from the last time he had a hypo.

This is more serious, though. Last time he was drowsy; now he is deeply unconscious.

When the paramedics arrive they start a drip to give him glucose intravenously. I stand and watch, my bare feet cold on the ground. Much as I hate him, despise him, have wished him dead, my overriding sense is that I don't want anything to happen to him. Not like this. Not at home where he should be safe. *Please God, don't let him die. I don't want my daughters to lose their father. Please, please, please.*

They move Robin onto a stretcher and then into the ambulance. I pull on my trainers and follow in my car. My hands are shaking and twice I have to brake sharply because my eyes are on the back of the ambulance and my timing is off. He's taken to the hospital where he works, and I know that the staff will do their absolute best to save him but I feel a crushing sensation across my chest, like pressure building before a storm.

Somebody locked Robin inside the sauna. That's the stark, unarguable truth. And it's written in gigantic, luminous letters at the forefront of my mind.

I begin to add up the sequence of events. I heard Emily and Robin in the cabin at about eight-thirty before I went to bed. Bel came to the house last night when I was fast asleep. Poppy told her I was down in the cabin. The door to the sauna was locked from the outside. From what I've heard of their time together, Emily was crazy for Robin. She wouldn't have locked him in. Unless he'd told her we were no longer getting divorced and she lost her temper, locked him in? This seems unlikely because the Robin I know would have been more inclined to string her along, create his own narrative.

Bel, on the other hand, by her own admission is impulsive. She says and does things she later regrets. She has never liked Robin and has always been unconditionally on my side. After telling him about the spyware, she promised me she would 'make it up to me'.

They take Robin into one of the resuscitation rooms in the Accident and Emergency department and I sit outside on a hardback chair. The news of Robin's admission spreads quickly through the hospital and various staff members come to find out how he is. I was hoping Bel would be at work but one of the pharmacy assistants tells me that she's called in sick. Every so often a doctor comes out to tell me what's happening. 'We are trying to stabilise Robin's blood sugars but at the moment he is not responding.'

'What does that mean?' I ask, fighting against a dizziness in my head that wants me to lie down. 'That it will take more time, or . . . ?'

'We would expect a response at this stage.'

'So that's not good news?'

'No. I'm sorry, Mrs Myers.' His expression is regretful. 'We will keep trying.'

I don't know what to do. I should call someone. I try Bel but she's not answering. I expect her sickness is particularly bad and she's unable to get to her phone. I try Rachel but she must be in a lesson. I try my mum and she answers at once. 'It's me,' I say, my tone flat. 'Robin's in a diabetic coma and it doesn't look good. Could you and Dad come down, please?'

'Of course. We'll pack now.' My mum is ever practical. No details required. I've made a request and she responds. I could cry with relief. 'Manny! Come here!' She's shouting for my dad. 'Take the phone. It's Nina.'

My dad has a thousand questions and to almost every one I say, 'I don't know, Dad.' Until finally, I say, 'Please help Mum pack and let her do the driving. I'll stay in touch.'

There's a woman coming along the corridor, walking with purpose, her heels clipping the floor with a click-clack sound. She's medium height, slim, red hair and has a sharp nose, freckles across her cheeks. 'I'm looking for Prof Myers,' she says to one of the nurses. 'Which room is he in? Quickly!'

The nurse immediately leads her to the door. She's about to go inside when her gaze meets mine. Her lips tighten. She follows the nurse inside. She's in there for about five minutes and when she comes back out again, she's holding a tissue up to her eyes. She stares at me again and then comes right up to me. 'How could this have happened?' she spits at me. '*How?*'

It's the question I've been asking myself too but I don't tell her that. I pull back from her venom and she walks off, her steps unsteady.

It's just after one and I'm still waiting, when Rachel calls me. 'Sorry I didn't answer earlier,' she says. 'I had the Year Sixes for science.' She sighs. 'Are you okay?'

'No.' I tell her what's happened and she gasps.

'*What?*'

'Listen.' I know what I'm about to tell her and it makes me shudder inside. 'Robin might not make it. So . . .' I leave the rest unsaid and I hear her gasp again. 'Did you see Bel this morning?'

'No, and Vera's not in school today,' she says immediately. 'But, Nina—' Her voice drops to a whisper. 'Are you saying that Robin might pass away?'

'Yes.' It feels pre-emptive saying this out loud but I feel that Rachel deserves to know that this is a possibility because it might influence whether she tells Bryn and Eleri about the DNA test or not.

'Jesus!' She takes a loud breath. 'That's terrible news.

I . . . I don't know what to say. I mean . . .' She's unable to finish the sentence.

'So Bel hasn't been in touch with you?' I ask again.

'No.' Her voice sounds high-pitched. 'Why, does this have something to do with her?'

'No, no,' I lie. 'Only that she came round last night but I was fast asleep. And they told me here that she called in sick, and if Vera is off too, then I'm just a bit worried that she's told Miro and her world has imploded.' I take a breath. That's not all I think. I'm wondering what happened when she went down to the cabin, whether Emily was still there or she found Robin on his own.

A young woman close by has just been given bad news and she begins to cry, the sound echoing in the corridor. I catch the anguish in her eyes before I move away, cupping my ear with my hand. 'Anyway, my parents are on their way but they won't get here before this evening so would you be able to collect the girls from school?'

'Of course. What shall I tell them?'

'That Daddy's unwell, and I'm at the hospital with him.' The door to Robin's room opens and two doctors come out. 'I'll call you later, Rachel.' I move a little closer and strain my ears to tune in to their conversation. I catch odd words but nothing that makes any sense. Then one of the doctors looks up and spots me staring. He comes across and gently leads me towards a private room.

We sit opposite each other on padded chairs, a box of tissues on the table between us. 'We haven't met before, Nina. My name is Druv and I specialise in endocrinology.'

'Hello.'

'Are you aware that your husband is extremely ill?'

'Yes.' Druv has kind brown eyes and a calm voice that

makes me feel Robin is in safe hands. 'I'm not sure how long he was unconscious before I found him.'

'I see.' He nods. 'What do you know of Robin's diabetes?'

'Well . . . I know his insulin prescription was changed recently. I also know that he went through periods where he couldn't get the levels of insulin quite right and so his blood sugars would fluctuate.'

'And that is not ideal.'

'No.'

'Recently some of his test results showed that his condition was becoming unstable.' He goes on to explain that this happens in some people and that it can lead to irreversible organ damage. Robin didn't tell me any of this. So much for being his wife. 'We are working very hard to save Robin but I need to let you know that the prognosis is not good.' I try to nod but my neck won't bend. I'm becoming increasingly rigid, my spine fusing into one long steel rod. 'Is there another family member who can come to be with you at this time?'

'I've called my parents and they're on their way. Our daughters are both under ten but I have friends who will help.'

'That's good.' He stands up. 'We have your phone number so do allow yourself to have some fresh air. You'll be able to see him very soon.'

'Thank you.'

At three o'clock in the afternoon, Robin is moved to the High Dependency Unit. He is on a ventilator, attached to a range of machines that bleep and flash almost constantly. I stand beside his bed and look down at him while the nurse moves efficiently, straightening sheets, writing down observations and injecting medicines into various lines that are attached to his body.

Druv speaks to me again, this time to say that the outlook has moved from 'not good' to 'bleak'. Time is of the essence and he suggests that I bring the girls in to say goodbye. There is a specialist nurse to help with this and she comes to speak to me. She explains how children view the machines and the best ways to alleviate their fears. She takes down the girls' names and ages, asks for details of their personalities, how much they know about death, what our family beliefs are, how scared I think they'll be.

I answer all of her questions as best I can. The whole experience feels surreal as if at any moment I'll wake from the nightmare and find myself in bed at home, Robin asleep beside me, wondering where such a dream could come from.

I call Robin's ex-partner in Glasgow so that she can tell the twins that their dad is not expected to live through the night. She sounds both shocked and saddened, and I promise to keep her updated. The harder phone call is to Aimee. She too is deeply shocked – 'He's only forty-five! How could this happen?' I know that Harry is visiting Birmingham University and it takes some time before Aimee is able to get hold of him. As soon as she does she texts me to say that she will bring him straight from the train station to the hospital.

I call Rachel again and she brings Lily and Poppy straight to the HDU. They have eaten dinner at Rachel's but are still in their school uniforms. They look wide-eyed and worried and they run towards me, hugging me tight. Rachel leaves the girls with me and goes to my house to wait for my parents who have been frequently texting me and are now about an hour away from the village.

Telling the girls about their daddy's illness is the most

difficult thing I've ever done. I sit in the family room and explain to them that something went wrong with his blood sugars and that he is really not very well at all.

'He needs more of his injections,' Poppy pipes up.

'I'm afraid that's not working this time, darling,' I say. 'A special nurse called Louise will help you understand what will happen next.'

Neither of them cry as I take them onto the unit and Louise comes across to introduce herself. My legs won't hold me up so I sit down on a chair a few feet from Robin's bed as Louise explains to my little girls that their daddy is going to go to heaven. Lily asks about all the machines and Poppy says, 'Will he visit us from heaven? Because he promised to bring us a dog called Pickle.'

Harry and Aimee arrive just as the girls have said their goodbyes to their daddy. Aimee holds me in a hug and the girls cuddle Harry round the waist. 'It's very sad,' Poppy tells him. 'Because Daddy has to go now.' Harry gives a sob and covers his face with his hand. 'But it's okay, Harry, because you still have us,' Poppy tells him, stroking his free hand.

The three of us leave the unit at ten in the evening and I drive us home. Poppy falls asleep at once. When I look in my rear-view mirror to check on Lily, she is wide awake, staring into the back of the passenger seat, her eyes unblinking.

The girls are comforted to see my mum and dad and I leave them together to go down to the cabin and stand in the space. My body runs hot and then cold as if there are taps inside me that are being turned on and off. I'm hot with fear and dread. And then I'm cold and numb. Robin is dying and I don't know how or why. I didn't love him anymore but I didn't want him to die. Not like this.

I step inside the sauna and examine the back of the door. The handle is loose where it has been pulled and pulled. I feel sick and ashamed. I don't want to think about how panicked he must have been because as soon as I do, my body responds with a racing heartbeat and a sense of dread so all-encompassing that I feel as if I myself am dying.

I take the voice-activated recorder from the socket in the wall and slip it into my pocket. At intervals throughout the day, I've thought about listening to what happened last night, but the more I mull it over, the more certain I am that I'm not ready to hear it because if Bel locked Robin in the sauna – and who else could it have been? – then I'd rather not know about it. I won't be the person to give the evidence to the police. I can't do that to her. Robin is dying. There's nothing to be gained from hearing it happen, or punishing Bel.

I return to the house and find my mum upstairs with the girls, settling them into bed. 'Hot chocolate?' my dad says, handing me a mug.

'Thank you, Dad.' I sit beside him on the sofa, my head resting on his shoulder. He knows when to stay silent, my dad, and he asks me nothing, just lets me be.

When I've finished the drink I kiss his cheek and stand up. 'We'll get through this together, Nina,' he says quietly, and I nod, knowing that it's true. I climb the stairs and slide into bed. Sleep, when it comes, is fitful and I dream of Robin banging on the door, growing hotter and hotter, burning more and more calories while his sugar levels dropped dangerously low.

I wake several times with a recurring thought – *Robin must have known that he was going to die.* What did he feel? Did he think about the girls and me, or about his sons, or Emily? About his patients? Or about how he would be remembered?

Or did he think of absolutely nothing because the fear was all-consuming?

Chapter Thirty-six

Robin passes away during the night, with Aimee and Harry by his bedside. I'm pleased they were with him because I wouldn't have wanted him to die without at least one of his children beside him.

The next few days go by in a haze of arrangements and phone calls, tears and what-ifs. My mum and dad are relentlessly upbeat throughout the girls' waking hours, only collapsing on the sofa when the girls are asleep. My dad goes on the internet and reads some of the news reports aloud to me. All of the local and national press describes Robin's death as 'an unfortunate accident', say that he was 'a brilliant surgeon taken far too soon', and mention the 'underlying medical condition that led to his death'. On the Facebook community page, there is a 'conversation starter'.

So sad to see the death of such an amazing surgeon. Born and bred in this village. RIP Professor Myers.

There follows more than one hundred comments, most of them supportive until about halfway through when Emily Birch has written: *I don't believe that Robin's death was accidental and I have alerted the police re my suspicions. If anyone has any information they can share, please DM me.*

Most of the remaining messages are along the lines of 'let the family grieve in peace' and 'you should be very careful before making statements like that'. But several people have joined in and one woman, calling herself well-wisher, has written: *This family are not squeaky clean. There was a huge incident in the daughter's class recently when she was receiving bullying notes. Turns out she was writing them herself!*

'Of all the cheek!' my dad says, laying aside the iPad in exasperation. I told my parents about the three girls writing the notes, and although they were shocked, they have been unfailingly supportive. 'Why are they allowed to put stuff like this up on the interweb?'

I have no answer to that.

After the half-term week the girls go back to school and the playground is also alive with rumour. I feel the other parents' curiosity and judgement circle me like a drone. There are whispers that Robin was murdered. That the girls are witches. Several parents stop me to offer their condolences and then they hesitate, wanting to ask more.

I don't comment. *I just need to get through the funeral.* That's what I think every morning until the day finally dawns, bright and beautiful, a gentle breeze lifting the air into a cloudless blue sky above us. There are over two hundred mourners and the girls are overwhelmed. They cling to my side like limpets, only letting go to move into the arms of their grandparents or Harry. Harry has been sad but strong, and while the loss of his dad is heartfelt, I know that he will recover. And I will do my level best to keep him as part of our family.

Emily Birch attends the funeral. My solicitor told me I was perfectly within my rights to keep her away but I decide it's better not to create a scene. She is openly talking about her affair with Robin and has been actively trying to gather other members of staff onside with regards to her 'suspicions'. Twice she has called me on the phone and before I've had the chance to end the call, she's said, 'Robin was moving in with me. That's why you killed him, isn't it?' And at the wake, she comes up to my ear, whisky on her breath and hisses, 'It was you. I know it was.'

Rachel found out through the school secretary that the Novaks are staying in Zakopane for a bit longer so neither Bel nor Miro attend the funeral. I send her several texts and finally she replied with:

I'm so sorry, Nina. I'm overwhelmed here with Miro being so upset about the abortion, Vera worried and me being sick all the time. Please be patient. I think of you every day and will be back as soon as I can. Lots of love xxxxx

Rachel supports me throughout the day. And at the end, when the speeches are over, the funny stories told and tearful eyes wiped, we stand outside together and talk about what she's going to do about the DNA result.

'I'm not going to tell either Bryn or Eleri,' Rachel says, reading the doubt on my face. 'I've thought about it long and hard, Nina, I really have, and if the day comes when one of them needs a kidney and they do genetic testing then I'll have some explaining to do.'

'I understand,' I say. I'm not sure I agree with her but telling them doesn't feel right either especially with Robin gone. 'What about Eleri and Harry?'

'They've already broken up,' she says, relief in her voice. 'Eleri told me this morning. She wants to go to university and he's not sure. And with his dad dying, he's told her he wants to travel. You know Eleri, always focussed on her academics.'

'Good news.' I attempt a smile. Harry and Eleri are

half-brother and -sister. And they don't know it. That feels uncomfortable to me. And for my own girls who'll never know that they have an older sister.

We walk back to her car together and she tells me that Bel has been in touch with the school. 'They're staying in Poland for another few weeks. They've enrolled Vera in the school and everything. Apparently there's a really good clinic in Zakopane that's helping Bel with her morning sickness.'

'Great.' I say the word without any feeling. I try to feel happy for Bel but am hurt that she didn't tell me this. Is she afraid to come home because of what she's done? She might be thinking that I listened to the recording and found something incriminating on there. Or is she simply worried that I'll tell the police she was at my house that night?

It's as Rachel's driving away that I notice a scrape down the side of her car. A gash in the electric blue. I frown, try to remember why this rings a bell. And then it comes to me. That morning, just before I found Robin in the sauna, I noticed that the gatepost at the entrance to my driveway had paint scratches on it, as if a car had turned into the driveway and the driver had misjudged the space. Blue paint. It hadn't been there the day before. I'm sure of that.

Did Rachel come round that evening too?

If so, why has she never mentioned it?

Three days after Robin's funeral, there is a knock on the door and I'm really hoping it's Bel, having changed her mind and come back home at last. I run to answer but it's not her. A man with neat, gelled hair and a woman with startling grey eyes hold out their police IDs. 'Mrs Nina Myers?'

'Yes.'

'My name is DC Quinn and this is DC Pontin. We're sorry to disturb you. We know this must be a very difficult time for you all but we wondered whether we could ask you a couple of questions about your husband's death?' It's the woman who's talking, her tone level.

I open the door wide. 'Please come in.'

My parents have taken the girls out to Brighton so I'm on my own. I point the officers in the direction of the sofas. I haven't had much to do with the police, not in my personal life anyway. My first year out of law school, I spent time questioning suspects in custody suites but I very quickly moved away from criminal law. It was too unstable for me, too dependent on truth and lies, who could be believed and what could be proven. I preferred the more cut and dried environment of commercial law.

But that doesn't mean I don't know my rights.

'Mrs Myers?'

'Yes.' I smile. 'Please sit down.' I wave my arm expansively. 'What can I help you with?'

'We are following up on a complaint from a Mrs Emily Birch. Do you know her?'

'Yes.' She is still talking to whoever will listen, spreading rumours, determined to prove that Robin's death is suspicious.

Maxine called me to tell that she'd knocked at her door, informed her about the affair, claimed that they were in love. She told Maxine that Robin must have been deliberately harmed because when she left him, he was fine. 'I told her to sling her hook,' Maxine said to me. 'I have no time for women like her.'

'I'm glad you've called, actually,' I say to the police. 'Because she's becoming a nuisance and I'm worried that her behaviour will begin to affect my children.' I sit down opposite them. In order to be interviewed, the police have to suspect that an offence has been committed. 'Are you here to interview me?' I ask them.

'No, we're not here to interview you, Mrs Myers. Cause of death has been established by the post-mortem. We simply wanted to have an informal chat.'

'I see.' Emily Birch is kicking up a fuss and they have come here simply to report back that they have done their due diligence.

'Are you satisfied that his death was accidental?' DC Quinn asks.

'Yes, I am. I found him collapsed in the sauna at the bottom of the garden. He suffered from Type 1 diabetes, which had recently become unstable.'

'I see. And you have no reason to suspect that anyone was involved in keeping him down there?'

I frown. 'How would that be possible?'

'I understand there is a lock on the door into the sauna?'

Emily must have told them about the key. I give a short laugh. 'I think Emily was down there with him,' I say. 'Have you asked her about the lock?'

'She told us that Robin hadn't yet gone into the sauna when she left, but that the key was in the door.'

'Yes, the key is always in the lock but we never use it.' I stand up. 'You can come to look if you want?' I say this knowing that they won't. They don't have a warrant. They don't even have a crime, and if in the future they did suspect that a crime had been committed, the fact that they went to the sauna today could compromise a legal case.

'No, that won't be necessary.' They stand up too. 'Thank you for your help, Mrs Myers. And again, please accept our condolences.'

I close the door behind them and collapse against the back of it, sliding down until I'm sitting on the floor. I've been thinking about the paint on the gatepost. Could Poppy have got it wrong? She was woken from sleep that night, went down the stairs with her eyes half-closed, her brain half-engaged. Was it Rachel, not Bel, who came to the house to speak to me but ended up going down to the cabin instead?

I'm not sure how important the right answers are, how much difference it makes because the end result is always the same – Robin is dead.

The truth won't bring him back.

Epilogue

One year later

'Is Vera really coming today?' Lily asks me.

'Yes, with her new baby brother, Jan.'

We live in the Lake District now so I haven't seen Bel since before Robin died. A month after his death I realised that it would be so much better for all of us if we moved close to my parents, my brother Dylan and his family. Within weeks the house adjacent to my mum and dad came on the market and by Christmas we'd moved in. Harry has been to visit us five or six times and twice Maxine and Max came to stay. Maxine and I ended up having another make-up session while Max and the girls ran wild with my dad.

I still miss Rachel and Bel, and I know the girls miss their friends too, but we very soon made a new life for ourselves. Lily has put on weight, her cheeks are pink and she smiles all the time. And she hasn't sleepwalked since Robin's funeral. Poppy has her own dog because, before we left the village, we got in touch with the breeder and took Pickle with us. The fact that the puppy was chosen by Robin has helped the girls stay connected to him. 'He left Pickle on earth to look after us, Mummy,' Poppy told me.

My company is sold and part-time work is perfect for me. I go down to London every other week for a night or two but mostly I work from home. And Jane logs in from Thailand to check up on me, palm trees her tropical backdrop.

Miro has a work commitment so can't some to visit this time but Bel, Vera and the baby arrive just before lunch and we have a busy couple of hours of hugs and catching up, eating and drinking before my mum and dad take the girls outside to see the menagerie of animals in their backyard.

Bel is softer, not so brittle, not so inclined to sarcasm. We talk about the village and school and what happened after she told Miro about the abortion. 'He was really upset. In a bitter, un-Miro-like way. It was awful. He spent a lot of time hillwalking with Vera while I was either vomiting or praying in the church.' She gives me a sad smile. 'We got there in the end. And he's so in love with Jan.' She touches her small son's head as he sleeps beside her in the bassinet. 'He's made our family complete.'

'You look so happy,' I say, smiling.

'I am.' She stares at her baby again, maternal love honey-sweet.

'And Rachel and Bryn moved back to Wales.'

'I know. I still feel abandoned by you both.' She reaches across to take a swipe at my knee. 'I'm trying to get Miro to agree to live back in Scotland.'

'It's not always easy moving children. Whenever I speak to Rachel on the phone, she says that Carys still really misses the girls. And she's been having nightmares about that last note.'

'The somebody will die one?'

I nod. 'She thinks it's her fault Robin died.'

'That's harsh,' Bel says, her eyes lifting to mine. 'I hope she manages to put it behind her.'

'Me too.'

We sit in silence for a few minutes before Bel asks lightly, 'So what was the result of the paternity test? When I asked Rachel she quickly changed the subject.'

'I don't know.' I feign innocence. 'I must have filled the form in wrong because the result was never returned to me and then Robin died.' I can see she doesn't believe me but I won't break Rachel's confidence. It's old news, best left alone.

We talk about Robin's death and the funeral. We've done this before over the phone but never in person. And then I seize my moment, and take the conversation to a place it's never been. 'You know the night before he died, when you came to the house?'

Bel's expression clouds. 'I've always wanted to explain about that.' She sits forward and says slowly, 'The things I said to Robin and Bitch Birch, and I realised afterwards that you would be able to listen to it all.' She screws up her face. 'It wasn't my finest hour but I was so shocked to see her there, and I'd just told Miro about the abortion so everything was blowing up at home.'

I still haven't listened to the recording from that night. For months I couldn't face it, didn't want to know if it was one of my friends who had locked Robin in the sauna. I kept myself busy settling the girls into school, making the house a home and getting used to my new role at work. But these last few weeks, it's preyed on my mind. For me to really move on with my life it feels important that I close the Robin chapter as fully as possible. When Lily and Poppy are older there will be the question: 'So what exactly happened to Dad, Mum?' and I'll need to have an answer ready for them. It won't be the truth – I'll never tell them that their father was locked in – but it's vital that I come to terms with his death myself. And the only way I can do that is by listening to what happened.

'Emily Birch was convinced that Robin was murdered,' I say quietly, watching Bel's reaction, alert for any minute, telltale signs.

'Really?' Jan begins to stir and she lifts him out of the bassinet to give him a feed, wincing as he latches on. 'How?'

'She thought the door to the sauna could have been locked with him inside.'

Bel's eyes widen. 'And was it locked?'

'No.' I lie. 'No, of course not. But she really had me spooked for a while. You know what it's like when you're awake at night and your mind begins to overthink things, and then I thought maybe you could have tampered with his insulin.'

'Me?' She's startled. 'How could I have done that?'

'You're a pharmacist,' I say.

'You thought I killed Robin?' She is astounded. 'Nina, you know I love you. We're great friends. And you heard how awful I was on the tape but—' She stares down at her baby, shifting his position slightly and says, 'I wouldn't kill for you.'

I don't say that I haven't listened to the recording yet because she will pressure me to do it, and when I do listen, I have to be alone. I know it will be harrowing and I need to be able to switch it off when it becomes too much to bear.

Bel stands up and props Jan on her shoulder to wind him. 'So, I know you're going to try to get away with not talking about this,' she says, moving the conversation on. 'But the girls mentioned a farmer who's been coming around a lot.'

'Did they now?' I feel myself blush. 'He's called William and he has a rare-breeds farm about fifteen miles from here.'

Her cheeks dimple. 'Tell me more.'

'There isn't a lot more.' I feel both pleased and embarrassed to be talking about it. 'He's a widower, two grown-up children.' I smile to myself. 'He's slow off the mark and so am I, so our courtship may drag on for some time.'

'But it is a courtship?' Bel pushes.

'I think so.' My smile is wide. 'He's kind and caring and easy to be with. And the girls get on with him. He's teaching them about different breeds of sheep and ponies.'

She goes off into the realms of fantasy then, has me married to William with a baby on the way. When we part to go to bed, Bel and Jan in the spare room, Vera in beside the girls, I feel happy to have spent time with her again but also newly troubled.

Bel would have admitted to locking Robin in, and if she hadn't actually said the words, I think I would have read it on her face. And if it wasn't Bel, then who was it? Before I left the village, I asked Rachel about the scrape on her car. She was very apologetic about damaging my gatepost, said she'd done it the day she drove the girls to school, after their confession about the notes. She was harassed, she said, and over-steered. I thought at the time that she was telling the truth and it had just taken me a couple of days to notice the damage. Now I'm back to thinking I shouldn't have believed her. Did she come to the house to reason with Robin and things got out of hand?

Was it Rachel all along?

* * *

Bel and the children leave the next day in a flurry of promises to visit again, and we make arrangements for the girls and I to drive down at Christmas. After we've waved them away, Lily and Poppy go into the field to help my dad feed the two donkeys and I watch from my bedroom window. Unless I have work to do, I would normally join them. But not today. I can no longer avoid the inevitable. The time has come for me to listen to the recording. After my talk with Bel last night, I know I can't put it off any longer. I need to know how Robin died, and I can turn myself inside out for years trying to work out how it happened, or I can be brave enough to listen.

To listen to him dying.

Just listen, I tell myself. *You can switch it off whenever you choose.*

I log onto my computer and open the folder containing the audio files from the cabin. I click on the file of the final recording, the one from that night. I briefly listen to Robin telling Emily that, 'Nina's been begging me to stay. She's showing signs of depression again.' A pause before he adds, 'I'm sorry, my love, but this isn't the right time for me to leave her.'

I shake my head against his lies and fast-forward to the part where Robin and Emily are interrupted by Bel opening the door. 'What the fuck?' she shouts. 'You have to be kidding me?'

I hear Robin protesting but she persists in calling them both names until it sounds like he pushes her out. 'Get your filthy hands off me!' she shouts. And the door slams behind her.

Emily and Robin then discuss how awful she is. 'Common as muck!' Emily says.

I fast-forward again to the point, around 11 p.m., when Emily says she has to go. 'Remember to eat something,' she tells him. 'I've prepared this plate for you.' There's the sound of kissing and a prolonged goodbye and then she leaves.

My heart starts to race. I fast-forward in short bursts, expecting, at any moment, to hear Rachel's voice, to hear her try to reason with him. Was he cruel and thoughtless? Did he threaten to tell Bryn about Eleri? Did she wait until he left the living area inside the cabin to go into the sauna, and was it at that point that she came back and quietly turned the key?

Ten minutes pass, with Robin whistling as he fires up the sauna. I hear the dull thud of logs as he picks them up from the log store in the corner behind the door. More minutes . . . then the distinctive squeak of the outside door, and Robin says, 'Lily. What are you doing here? It's well past your bedtime.'

I feel a rush of shock and dread. I stop the recording and sit stock-still unable to move or breathe. Unbidden, a memory from only yesterday catapults to the front of my mind. I overheard the girls chatting to each other before they fell asleep. Vera was asking my girls if they were okay without a dad.

'It's not *too* bad having a dead dad,' I heard Poppy saying. 'Because we have Uncle Dylan and Grandpa and Mummy's new friend William who's teaching us about ponies.'

'And Mummy doesn't cry anymore,' Lily added. I heard the satisfaction in her tone. 'She's really happy now.'

I lean in closer to my laptop, my hand shaking as I reach for the keyboard and press play. 'Sleepwalking again,' I hear Robin say, under his breath. 'I expect you'll find your own way back. I'm going for a sauna.'

There's the sound of a door opening and closing. And then . . . seconds later . . . the scrape of a key turning in a lock. The door into the sauna? *Is it? Could it be?* And then, the squeak and slam of the outside door.

Fifteen minutes pass and I hear a door handle being repeatedly shaken and Robin's voice, faint but distinct. 'Lily! Lily! Open this door!' The handle is rattled and rattled. 'This is not a game, Lily!' Robin continues to shout. 'Open this door, *now!*' There's fear and desperation in his voice. I want to be sick, feel bile rise up into my mouth. I switch off the recording and sit back, wide-eyed and terrified, my jaw clamped shut.

It was Lily.

I think back, remember that the locksmith came to fix the broken lock on the bifolds on the morning that Robin was lying unconscious in the cabin. So the doors would have been unlocked when Lily came downstairs the night before. The doors aren't heavy. She could have opened them in her sleep.

It was Lily.

I stand up, my knees knocking together so that I have to lean against the wall for support. I look through the window again and watch the girls outside, brushing the donkeys' coats. My two happy girls, running and laughing with their grandpa.

It was Lily.

I don't know what I do now. I don't know whether I say something to her. Do I ask her whether she remembers anything about that night? She was sleepwalking, though, wasn't she? She wouldn't be aware of her actions.

She glances up at me then, and waves. Our eyes meet and she gives me a wide smile, a smile that tells me she has everything she wants. She is happy.

Life is perfect.

I pull back from the window and press my knuckles

to my teeth, biting down on my hand until I feel the skin begin to split across my fingers.

Once during therapy Robin accused me of being risk averse, of avoiding the hard choices. I told him that having children meant I couldn't possibly be risk averse. Because suddenly my heart existed outside of my body, in two places at once, in the bodies of two little girls who would run and play, grow into three- and five-year-olds, then ten-year-olds who have sleepovers and go on holidays with friends, teenagers who walk home after midnight, drunk and reckless. My own heart, my own life depended on their wellbeing, on their choices.

If having children isn't taking a risk then I don't know what is.

And, while my girls are children, I'm responsible for their choices.

And for their actions.

I go to my computer and let my finger hover over the delete button before I press down and watch the file disappear.

This is a secret that can never be told. One I'll carry to my grave.

I walk downstairs, my steps slow but steady, and join my family outside.

'All okay?' my dad asks, his eyes searching as he stares across at me.

'All's well, Dad.' I smile at him. 'There's nothing wrong here.'

Acknowledgements

I'd never get there on my own.

Thank you to Georgina Aboud, Neil McIntosh and Mel Parks for their scrutiny of my early chapters as I found my way into the novel.

Thank you to my son Sean who gave me advice on police procedure and spyware – any mistakes are mine!

Thank you to my agent, Euan Thorneycroft, who's always onside.

I'm lucky to have two editors: Jo Dickinson and Beth Wickington. Sincere thanks to you both for your early interest in my idea and your enthusiasm to get me there, most especially Beth who has held my hand throughout and whose thoughtful comments helped shape the characters. I look forward to working with you on the next one!